THE GRAND TOUR

VOYAGE OUT, BOOK TWO

MIREILLE PAVANE

ISBN: 9781393584643

To my friends, for the trip we never took to Europe—and Vicki, for the one we did. (I'm sorry I revisited Paris without you.)

To Ramya, Egypt was a blast—encore sometime (with afternoon tea at the Old Winter Palace)?

To the Bombells and everyone at Burwood Exercise Prescription and Physiotherapy. (Thanks for the cocktail recipes.)

To my long-suffering family, as always.

And to the little wild wine-dark rose that somehow flew into our back garden, and stayed.

Beware the fury of a patient man.
—John Dryden

Après nous, le déluge. ("After us, the flood.")
—Madame de Pompadour

PART TWO

THE GRAND TOUR

A London Season

July 1929, London

11

LUCIA:

If I had been asked to give a report to my mother or Aunt Merry, Celeste, Frankie, Belle, or any number of our acquaintance back in New York, I could have drawn them a glowing picture of England in the blossoming summer, of a procession towards a bucolic fairy-tale wedding in Oxfordshire, of a London that was not a chaotic snarl of noise and wares and foul mechanical smells and uniform gray weather but a lively theater of people and leisure and fashion coming into the height of the Season.

It would have been truthful, entirely believable, and a deliberate misrepresentation.

"Tessa's wedding and a London Season to start our Grand Tour and foraging for a suitable husband in the undergrowth. Plenty to occupy our time." Charley gave a smile of limpid innocence to Ginny, looking as if her mind was fixed on nothing but gowns and parties and picturesque ruins and outings and dances with eligible gentlemen and she was not plotting anything.

Ginny narrowed her eyes. "What are you up to? If anyone were to believe Matthias... Lucia?"

I gazed innocently back at Ginny. "Exactly as Charley says. Tessa's wedding and a London Season before we start our Grand Tour."

Ginny's face broke into a broad grin and beamed its brightness upon us. "I knew you wouldn't disappoint, Trouble. I can't wait!"

Ginny Marchmont delivered us to London, filling us with news and gossip and complaining of Matthias's high-handedness in insisting on sharing cicerone duties after he had lost the coin toss over who was to meet us and bring us to the English capital.

We had taken a suite at the Savoy Hotel on the Strand rather than one in

5

Oxford. It was more conveniently situated for the London shops and modistes that were lined up in our schedule and we had also thought it best not to be underfoot during the assorted wedding preparations bedlam taking place at the Hartleys' Belgravian townhouse notwithstanding the Hartleys' repeated invitations. More important, our fellow passengers from the RMS Mauretania had chosen for their London stay to bestow themselves upon Claridge's, Brown's, the Goring, the Langham, the Ritz, the Carlton, and any number of other grand old hotels around St. James and Mayfair. This was a stroke of luck given that the reservations had been made without our consultation by Aunt Merry, who had simply booked the usual hotel favored by the Elyots when they had been in London. The prospect of not accidentally running into Mrs. Stuyvesant at breakfast brought great relief. Charley and Tilly were also rather excited about the art scene and the grand parties at the Savoy: the artists and musicians we might run into in the corridors or American Bar (Noel Coward or Cecil Beaton perhaps, but it was unlikely George Gershwin would return four years later for another rendition of Rhapsody in Blue—wasn't he in Hollywood?) as well as the Savoy Bands, comprising the best musicians imported from America, performing jazz on a stage and dance-floor permanently installed in the Savoy's Thames Foyer.

"Oh, there will be no shortage of parties," Ginny assured us. "Or of chaperons."

"What are we to do with those?" Charley asked.

Ginny gave her an arch quizzical look.

"We've already got Tilly!" Charley protested.

Matthias, Ginny warned us, was to be taking us about town when the Hartleys were not. We could depend on being under the constant protection of the Hartleys' or Matthias to ward off the idle, feckless, unsavory types and other undesirables which my mother and Aunt Merry would undoubtedly want as far away from us as—

"But how disappointing, Ginny," Charley said. "I'm as idle and feckless and easily distracted as Toad of Toad Hall. Why can't we meet these unsavory types? They would be absolutely my cup of tea. You can save the upstanding ones for Lucia."

Ginny was of the view that Matthias had his work cut out for him, but since he had volunteered for the part, she spared him no sympathy.

Matthias would be meeting us at the Hartleys', so that we could "settle in before the hordes descend," Ginny said.

London was to be our pursuit, where the cream of London Society and the Season's parties were to be found. London was also, apparently, full of private clubs where Charley's secret correspondents were to be found.

After Ginny dropped us off at the premises of our hotel—"I'll see you later, Trouble, don't be late to the fitting!"—the first thing Charley did was to hail one of the porters to inquire if it were possible for some letters to be delivered to certain clubs around London. The answer in the affirmative led her to ask the porter to wait a moment (which included trailing us all the way to the suite with our luggage, looking for paper and stationery and waiting for all the necessary items to be brought to the room for madam) while Charley penned a number of brief notes, adding folded pages of letters that showed Diego's penmanship, and inserting them into envelopes that she addressed to the Reform Club, Brook's, the Travellers' Club, Pratt's, White's, the Athenæum Club, the Turf Club, the Gresham Club,.. Envelopes which bore names I recognized, corresponding to a number of those on Charley's destroyed list.

"Charley?" I ventured.

Charley pointedly did not reply.

"Might these be delivered at the earliest convenience today?" Charley asked sweetly, holding out the letters and a munificent tip to the porter.

The porter (another captive to Charley's charms and bribery) left our suite only a few minutes before a knock announced a visitor. Tilly opened the door.

"Mr. Vandermeer!" cried Tilly in unsuppressed delight.

"Hello, Tilly," said Matthias. "Welcome to London. I hope the trip wasn't too tiring and that you are keeping well?" His sturdy, robust and powerful form were as familiar as his gentle voice and courtesy. Matthias stepped into the suite and presented Tilly with a bouquet of vermilion colored roses. An attendant in the Savoy's black and green livery followed Matthias with a covered trolley and began decanting its contents, a gorgeous array of cakes and tea and silver and china, into our suite. A second attendant came in, asked for Miss Masterson, and presented her with a wire.

"What are you doing here? Ginny said you'd be at the Hartleys'," said Charley. She had read the wire, swiftly crumpled it up and tossed it into the trash, and gave the attendant a generous tip in addition to the one Matthias had handed him.

If one did not look too closely, if one allowed oneself to be distracted by her unmannerly bluntness, one might easily have missed the guilty, angry flush that crept up Charley's cheeks. I was not going to give Charley away, but Matthias was observant. He did not mention the discarded telegram and Charley's unforthcoming silence, he was warm and cheerful in greeting, asking after us and everyone back in New York, but his eyes roamed over us, studying, absorbing, assessing, as he smiled at us and helped Tilly fuss and bustle around to find a vessel for the roses.

"Ginny told me Trouble would be rolling into town today. I thought you'd need some fortifying refreshments before being attacked by the Hartley mob," Matthias replied. "Miss Masterson. Miss Bernhardt. Miss Fairchild." According to his custom, he gave us a jar each of candy: pretty

English crystallized violets and violet mints. "Did you have a good crossing? I hope your charges were not too taxing on you, Tilly? Have you need of anything? Is there anything I can call for? I can have a table reserved for the River Restaurant or Grill Room downstairs if you'd prefer it to having tea served up here in your suite—"

I burst out laughing. Charley relaxed and smiled.

"You haven't changed one bit, Mr. Vandermeer," I told Matthias. "It's nice to see you, too, after all this time."

Tilly nodded and patted his arm fondly in agreement.

"Oh, this is quite grand enough a spread to appease a voracious appetite. The Hartleys will be feeding us again anyway, so we should probably exercise some restraint," said Charley, inspecting a scone thickly bedaubed with jam and clotted cream. "So long as there are no society ghouls downstairs to bother us and spoil the view of the Thames, you may certainly book us a table in the River Restaurant for another day to take afternoon tea. The cake selection is bound to be even bigger, won't it? Lucia must try the fraises à la Sarah Bernhardt especially created by Escoffier for—"

"We aren't related." I rolled my eyes for the hundredth time at Charley. "I don't particularly like strawberries with pineapple and Curaçao either."

"When have you even tried Curaçao during Prohibition?" retorted Charley, grinning. "After you try the fraises à la Sarah Bernhardt, we must go sample the cocktails in the American Bar."

"Which society ghouls are you expecting?" asked Matthias.

"Mrs. Stuyvesant," muttered Tilly, remembering the forced indignities of scrambling to disembark away from Mrs. Stuyvesant's hungry predatory gaze.

"She was a fellow passenger on the ship. We missed breakfast because she wants Charley's mounted head on her wall."

"The forlorn designers and decorators to the Vanderbilts and Rockefellers and all the overreaching society mamas have to settle for me because the lovely Miss Lucia Bernhardt is too unattainable up there on her pedestal," said Charley.

"I see," said Matthias, a faint line creasing his brow. "Perhaps—"

"Don't even think about it, Matthias. We have everything in hand," said Charley.

The line on Matthias's brow deepened. Matthias had a long memory of when Charley had taken things in hand and dragged me along as deputy.

"These are delicious," said Charley, popping the violet sweets into her mouth as she changed out of her coat and removed the lusciously sleek hat from her head. (Charley seemed to own more stylish hats than she did dresses despite her professed lack of interest in shopping for the Grand Tour.) "But we need something more substantial by way of victuals.

Absolutely famished."

Matthias kindly obliged. "Let's feed you cake then," said Matthias, gesturing to the waiter to begin serving.

Tea and cake restored order to our world: Tilly could not be restrained from chattering and bustling about, catching Matthias up on all the news and happenings at Montrose and about Aunt Merry and New York in general (although Charley did her best to lead Tilly away from mentioning any of her capers); Matthias was attentive and only mildly interrogative; Charley (when not otherwise engaged in elaborate misdirections) was amiably vague and evasive; and I drank my tea with a firm neutrality. If we had been at Wimbledon, I think Charley would have been awarded the match.

As tea was being cleared away, Matthias reminded us of our appointment to meet Ginny and Tessa Hartley at the dressmakers. Or rather, he reminded us that he could provide a means of escape from our ties.

"You still have some time to spare. The weather is fine. Would you like to go for a drive about town?" Matthias said.

"Are you and the Hartleys engaged in a competition to see who can lead us the furtherest astray? By all means, please lead the way, Mr. Vandermeer," said Charley. "Come on, Tilly, London awaits!"

"But the unpacking!" protested Tilly.

"How can you act as our lady's companion and chaperon, Tilly, if you aren't accompanying and chaperoning us? There is no point in unpacking, it will just make an extra bother to pack it all up again when we travel on to the next stop."

"But," Tilly repeated, a bit more tersely.

We had told Matthias over tea of our lucky deliverance from the attempted jewelry theft on board the RMS Mauretania, and he reiterated his offer of the use of his bank's safe if we felt uneasy about leaving our valuables in the hotel.

"Oh, it will be fine. We have everything in hand," said Charley, picking up her beautiful hat and coat.

That faint line appeared again on Matthias's brow.

"Are you certain?" Matthias asked in concern.

Tilly gave a subdued nod.

"Truly," I said in support. "Give us a few minutes."

"I'll be waiting outside at the elevators," Matthias replied after a brief pause.

It was to be the first of many dances to maintain neutral ground over the coming weeks.

We shared a somewhat rambunctious elevator ride down with another family (rather like a lively gaggle of ducklings waddling after their paterfamilias) who spilled into the Art Deco foyer and out onto the bustling Strand. When we came out of the Savoy Court entrance off the Strand, a shiny olive green Bentley drew up alongside us and Matthias got out. We all exclaimed at its beauty.

"A Bentley Speed Six! Is it yours? Are you one of the Bentley Boys now? Have you taken it to Le Mans! What is it now—four years in a row? How fast does it go? May I try it?" asked Charley, eyes sparkling. Considering the notorious hard-driving, hard-partying playboy reputation of the Bentley Boys, this might have seemed a bit forward, but Charley's attentions were all on the motor-car.

"When did you learn to drive?" Tilly and Matthias cried almost in unison.

"I've known for a while," Charley answered obliquely and not at all smug.

"But you've never driven in London," Matthias pointed out.

Charley gave him a look that told him exactly how much he was grasping at straws, but then her face broke into a smile. "You're right, Matthias, if I owned such a beauty, I wouldn't let anyone else drive it either. You go ahead and drive. I shall observe and, by observation, learn and become familiar with how you drive on the wrong side of the road here," she said. "And I shall patiently wait till we get to French shores before I jump behind the wheel."

Matthias handed us into the motor-car in his courtly manner and then stepped into the driver's seat. He knew from long practice when to concede, but the ensuing familiar bickering was inescapable as the Bentley drew us into the English sunshine.

Matthias showed an easy familiarity with the city that had been his home for the last three years, pointing out the city's sights and quirks and delighting, and alternately horrifying, Tilly with the history of the quaint street names (Pudding Lane being Thomas Farriner's bakery where the Great Fire of London started in 1666 and named after the "puddings", a medieval word for offal, which would fall from the carts coming down the lane from the butchers in Eastcheap as they headed for the waste barges on the River Thames). It was Tilly's first time in the city and to her gaze, it was wondrous. Charley and I had been here briefly before with Charley's father and her Aunt Merry, but the London Matthias showed us was a changed and different place to the remembered city fogged over by the mists of childhood. Charley, it seemed, had put childhood firmly behind her and saw the drive as if we were taking a cab through downtown Manhattan instead of flitting about Tower Hill, over Tower Bridge, around Pall Mall, Trafalgar Square, Green Park and St. James, Kensington, Hyde Park Corner, Oxford and Regent Streets, Piccadilly, Haymarket, Charing Cross, Temple Bar, Fleet Street, St. Paul's, Cornhill, Threadneedle Street ("Do they keep gold bricks there in the Bank of England's vault?"), the Royal Exchange ("Where are your offices located, Matthias? Can we go visit them? Are they near the Rothschild headquarters at New Court? Isn't that where they fix the global price of gold at 11 o'clock every day?"—a daughter of Old New York, reared in the ways of her genteel class, asking about the grubby, distasteful cogs and gears of money and commerce and wanting to visit the City—the horror!), Gray's Inn, the Royal Courts of Justice, Blackfriars, Pimlico, Westminster, Lambeth, Vauxhall, Greenwich, and weaving around the tree-lined Embankment on both sides, keeping close to the river so that we would not be too far away from our pending appointment at Norman Hartnell's Bruton Street salon for the final bridal dress fitting. Between Tilly's exclamations of wonder and curiosity and Matthias's responses, Charley's indifference was an oddity—was this not a piece of the rowdy, expanding, exhilarating world outside the windows of the Colony Club that had once so thrilled her? The landscape of the city, punctuated with people scurrying about like urban rats and the ubiquitous red double-decker omnibuses, drifted past her unseeing eyes and rote murmurings. Charley's attention seemed to have seized upon something else entirely, taking note of Matthias's ease in London—no doubt compounded by Tilly's remarking: "London suits you, Mr. Vandermeer, but we do miss you in New York"—and asking about Matthias's life and habits and work in the metropolis, peppering him with such questions of inconsequential minutiae as to seem wandering and trivial, bored and trying to while away time, but were, I was certain, building towards an understanding of how well Matthias had settled into life abroad, how happy he was, and whether he really would uproot himself again from such a pleasant situation to return home—was it home anymore?—to New York.

As interrogations went, Charley's was a greater success than Matthias's candid and direct forays. I marveled at how casual, how subtle, were her feints. I wondered where Charley had learnt and practiced such powers of subtlety, and why she had felt it necessary to employ them.

When the Houses of Parliament and Big Ben on the opposite bank swung into view, Matthias spoke of Guy Fawkes and Bonfire Night, reciting the nursery rhyme:

> Remember, remember,
> The Fifth of November,
> Gunpowder treason and plot;
> For I see no reason
> Why Gunpowder Treason
> Should ever be forgot.
> Guy Fawkes, Guy Fawkes,
> 'Twas his intent.

To blow up the King and the Parliament.
Three score barrels of powder below.
Poor old England to overthrow.

I could not help repeating to myself my prayers of gunpowder, treason, and plot. I saw a fleeting expression pass over Charley's face and knew she had been thinking the same thought.

Never mind that the Gunpowder Plot had failed.

When Matthias finally dropped us off at the appointed Mayfair address, Charley looked up at the establishment of the young Englishman who was said to represent the spirit of the Bright Young Things—the darling of the English royals and favored wedding designer to the socially prominent, capturing the hearts of the younger stars of stage and screen in England and France—and sighed inaudibly. Matthias caught her look, saw her dragging her feet, and asked if she was all right, assuring us that we had only to holler if we needed a quick getaway.

"My hero," Charley said in her coolly ironic tones, but there was real gratitude in her eyes.

"You're not even the one getting married or fitted for a dress," I reminded Charley. "We're just here to coo encouragement and approval and bolster the numbers in the chorus soothing Tessa's nerves."

Tilly reminded Charley of her spoken intentions of buying a new Grand Tour wardrobe in London or Paris since she had not had sufficient time to prepare in New York.

Matthias began to tell us to holler if we needed additional credit for any unplanned purchases that we wished to make, but Charley cut him off immediately with a withering glare.

"Paris," Charley said to Tilly. Then she turned to Matthias: "You are not paying for anything. You'll lose a hand and all your fingers if you try it. Go away and kill time wandering around Henry Poole or Huntsman or some other Savile Row outfit if you cannot sit still and behave. And I'm holding you to your word."

"Yessum." Matthias grinned. "I'll keep the motor running."

"What's so dreadful and frightening about a modiste?" I whispered to Charley as we entered the salon.

"Untimely regrets for spending too much money. Bumping into Mrs. Stuyvesant and her ilk. Fatal boredom," was Charley's reply but her mind seemed distant, her words more playfully deceptive than sincere.

The ghost of Charley's destroyed list of names, her allusions to a need to find a matrimonial prize, and the mysterious telegram, resurfaced and silenced me. These solemn thoughts were set aside when Ginny and Tessa came and met us with boisterous Hartley warmth.

Tessa's Hartnell wedding dress was an ivory silk, crystal and seed pearl embroidered gown. She looked ethereal in it. Tessa had apparently been so swept away by the gown that she had asked Mr. Hartnell to clothe the entire bridal retinue, the bridesmaids, the mother and father of the bride, the honeymoon wardrobe and trousseau, as well as the groom's family, that is, the one younger sibling who might or might not show depending on whether he was caught sneaking away from his boarding school again.

"Papa and Kit will be working off the debt in the salt mines later," Ginny said, and received a dig in the ribs from Tessa for her pains.

Completely dispelling her strange mood with a return to lively mischief, Charley was rucking up trouble of her own. "I think Tilly needs a new Grand Tour wardrobe as befits her role as our esteemed lady's companion and chaperon," she pronounced when she saw Tilly admiring the daywear designs in the salon. Charley then proceeded to trample over Tilly's mortified protests in accomplishing just that.

"You're kind of a tyrant," I told Charley as we stood admiring the end result of Tilly Companion-Chaperon Resplendent.

"Would you like a new Hartnell Grand Tour wardrobe too, Lucia?" Charley asked, unperturbed.

"I think Tilly looks dazzling enough to catch the Prince of Wales's eye," Ginny said, and Matthias and Tessa and Charley and I all agreed with enthusiasm.

"You've all lost your marbles," huffed Tilly.

We headed from the dressmaker's to the Hartleys', where we were greeted like returned lost daughters and plied with much food and warmth and noisy familial attention and inspection, and from there, we drifted back towards the Strand via Covent Garden. Charley said there might be a chance of seeing Fred Astaire in a show in the West End (and insisted that Tilly wear one of her new Norman Hartnell outfits), but I think she was driven more by a horror of running into Mrs. Stuyvesant the moment we stepped out onto the pavement.

Fred Astaire was not in the West End that evening. However, Matthias spotted a poster for the Covent Garden Opera Syndicate performance of "La traviata" at the Royal Opera House, Covent Garden, which our party agreed to be a reasonable compromise, and while he went off to hunt down some tickets, the rest of us went for a stroll around the open central Covent Garden piazza crowded with colorful street performers amongst the human traffic and the fresh produce and flower market and craft shops.

Charley was leading us on a haphazard goose chase around the square—scampering about hither and thither in search of a phantom flower seller whose roses exactly corresponded to the tiny carmine rosebud that she had found lying on the flagstones which had exhaled an enchanting scent—while talking about finding the place where Eliza Doolittle met Professor Henry Higgins when I felt a bulwark weight slam against my back, pushing me into Tessa who was walking beside me. We stumbled and tottered to the ground as a sudden wind rushing past reached out and made a powerful wrenching tug at my wrist. An outraged cry from Tilly confirmed that it had not been the wind but a thing of flesh and blood that had stripped me of my purse and was disappearing ahead into the press of the Covent Garden crowds. "Stop! Thief!" Charley and Ginny helped us back to our feet, then took up the chase after the thief. Tilly remained behind, gathering Tessa and me to her side, checking us for injury and fussingly ascertained our well-being. Passersby stopped and surrounded us with concerned inquiries and kind offers of assistance.

A short time later, perhaps only minutes, Ginny trooped back with an entourage: the paterfamilias of the curious family of ducklings with whom we had shared the Savoy elevator, and a gentleman with startling green eyes whom I recognized as our fellow passenger, Mr. James Dorsey, from the RMS Mauretania. The paterfamilias greeted me with heartfelt commiserations about the state of the world and evil bag-snatchers. Mr. Dorsey came up to me and handed to me my stolen purse: "I believe this belongs to you?"

I thanked them, confused.

These were our heroes, Ginny said, good eggs.

The paterfamilias—a Dr. Gregory Bommel—had been out strolling with his family, enjoying the festive activities in the square, when they heard cries of "Stop! Thief! Stop!". A bearded man emerged with great urgency from the crowd, holding a lady's purse, running towards Dr. Bommel's direction. The thief deftly evaded bystanders and loiterers in his path but when he turned his head to look over his shoulder to check that his pursuers were losing ground, he ran straight into Dr. Bommel's outstretched arm, which Dr. Bommel—tall, broad, solid as an oak—had stuck out like a turnpike, and down went the surprised thief, blinking in shock.

"Brain the size of a pea," was Dr. Bommel's opinion of the thief.

Ginny, Tessa, Tilly and I thanked Dr. Bommel again. He brushed off our gratitude in his expansive way, relaying how he and the members of his large family party recognized Charley—who had caught up to the scene by that time—from the Savoy elevator. But where was the big handsome fellow who had been with us earlier?

It was lucky that Charley was not present—Charley would have had some choice remarks to make. Mrs. Bommel (who, we found out later, was also a physician but only answered to Dr. Robyn Bommel in their shared clinic because it was too confusing socially as there were many more practicing doctors in the Bommel family) and the rest of the young Bommels had apparently decided to stay behind and keep Charley company, chatting as animatedly as ever, standing guard over the thief. Ginny, who was present and seemed inured to Dr. Bommel's forthright manner and frequent outlandish comments, explained very reasonably that Matthias was obtaining us tickets to an evening show else he would have dealt with the thief quick smart.

Mr. Dorsey happened to have been one of the bystanders who witnessed the affair and helpfully picked up the purse that the felled thief had dropped on his way down.

"It seems to be my fate to return things to my fellow passengers," he said with a wry smile.

His green eyes, flecked with gold, were beautiful and changeable and mesmerizing, like the flames of firelight, but for all their brilliance, I thought, they held no warmth. When his smiling gaze passed over me, I held myself from shivering. Wasn't that how he had looked at Charley that evening on the RMS Mauretania when his gaze had followed her about so assiduously—appraising, puzzled, intent? His dapper handsomeness certainly seemed to melt away the cold scrutiny, but... It was wrong, I reminded myself, to judge Mr. Dorsey based on so brief an acquaintance. He did not deserve so much groundless speculation aspiring to discernment. He had, after all, been nothing but distantly courteous and helpful on the RMS Mauretania and he had interrupted his evening to return a stranger's purse.

"Thank you," I told him.

Mr. Dorsey graciously denied the need for thanks. He was all that was courteous and proper in wishing us all a good evening and then his handsome presence evaporated into the evening, returning, I supposed, to his prior engagement.

It took nearly an eternity to find the rest of our acquaintance in the crush. Dr. Bommel accompanied Ginny, Tessa, Tilly and me in locating Charley and the rest of the Bommels, engaged in spirited "jaw exercises" (according to Dr. Bommel, they were champion athletes), and we joined their circle of concerned onlookers, standing watch around the fallen thief, awaiting the arrival of the authorities.

"The manner of company you attract, Lucia! How persistent is your Mr. Dorsey," Charley said when she met us, her eyes surveying us with the depth of concern that belied her light words. She glanced down with a frown at the prone figure of the thief lying on the flagstones. "I wonder if we can go back to order some armor from Mr. Hartnell's collection. We may be needing more than a few fashionable gowns for this Grand Tour."

Matthias, when he returned with the sought-after tickets, immediately stepped into the role of knight-protector that Ginny had cast him in her exchanges with Dr. Bommel. He was quick to take stock of the situation and pragmatic in showing his solicitous concern, ensuring we were all unhurt, conveying generous thanks to our saviors, and efficiently dealt with those representatives of the Metropolitan Police when they did arrive, all in his kind, unassuming way. Dr. Bommel gave his approval, deeming Matthias an admirable man of action, and wondered aloud if Matthias was amenable to taking one of Dr. Bommel's daughters off his hands. I did not catch Matthias's response—he had turned to attend to some other unfinished business—but I heard the by now familiar sounds of the Bommels' chorus of chortling laughter, and Tessa said that she had seen Matthias blushing.

Everybody made a fuss over me but I felt more unlucky than unsafe or deeply shaken, surrounded by such walls of the most sedulous care and protection and concern. I was rather more embarrassed than anything else to have been the cause of the fuss. What a great to-do over what turned out to be little more than a compact mirror, handkerchief, postcards and candy lozenges that I had bought earlier at a street stand, and a few pound notes.

"But such a pretty purse," said Tessa.

"That's probably why," Ginny said. "Pretty things do so attract magpies and thieves."

"Well, that's no reason not to have pretty things," said Tessa.

"Of course not, dearest," Ginny smiled. "The wedding will be perfect."

It had been, everyone agreed, a full day, and we all fell in readily with the suggestion of ditching the show and going back to the hotel for supper instead. (Charley had, by this time, sadly resigned herself to giving up the quest to reunite her orphaned rosebud with its elusive family.) Of course we invited our new friends, the Bommels, to join us. The Bommels had been on their way back to the Savoy anyway and accepted our invitation. They had come up from Kent for the birth of the first Bommel grandchild and they shared with us an endless well of stories of their first day's errant sightseeing adventures in the capital, marauding about Greenwich, trying to lock their fellow siblings up in the Tower of London with the ravens, uncivilized games of hide-and-seek in the British Museum, disturbing the peace at Westminster Abbey, giggling at the Yeomen of the Guard, trying to provoke an expression from the Queen's Guard at Buckingham Palace, running riot in the National Gallery and the National Portrait Gallery, winning the distinction of being barred from Madame Tussaud's, convening with Lord Nelson and his leonine and pigeon guards and fountains in Trafalgar Square, and a greatly anticipated planned excursion to the Roman spa town of Bath ("tea at Sally Lunn's and Bath buns—absolutely topping!"), Stonehenge, and the ancient chalk carvings of the Salisbury Plain before heading home to prepare for a family wedding...

It was a lively evening in the River Restaurant, gaudy with vibrant chatter and laughter and music and color, where the live Savoy band played and champagne flowed like fountains and everyone kicked up their heels and danced. It was an even livelier time in the American Bar afterwards. Mellowed from the gin and liquor and seemingly endless rounds of cocktails, our fellow diners reminisced about the famous idols and society women and royalty seen in full regalia in the Savoy dining and supper rooms and the legendary parties of yore such as the gondola party hosted by the American millionaire Mr. George A. Kessler who had the Savoy's central courtyard flooded to a depth of four feet and scenery erected around the walls in a recreation of Venice, where his two dozen costumed guests dined in an enormous gondola, after which, Enrico Caruso sang, and a baby elephant was brought in in an enormous birthday cake. Our evening was considerably more humble but it did have the merit of one of the guests being recognized by giddy fans and his genial agreement to stand up and croon a few tunes, accompanied by the Savoy band. The younger Hartley cousins hastened over at the news in answer to Ginny's summons, as did Lord Ruthven dutifully hasten from his club to his wife's side, bringing with him a fellow member with whom he had been sharing the club's port and cigars—a Lord Trevise-Fitzgerald who was drawn, apparently, by the name of Miss Charlotte Masterson rather than by the celebrity of Ivor Novello. Tessa was taken out to dance as often as Tilly and the Bommels during the course of the night's revelry, but she still managed to find a telephone to ring up Kit in his Oxford digs to tell her fiancé how much she missed him but how wonderful a time she was having and how Ivor Novello had answered a special request to serenade her, Tilly, me, and all the female Bommels and Hartleys in turn. (Was it the handiwork of Ginny, Charley, or Matthias?) Charley's good intentions of dissolving into the background to avoid further teasing and scrutiny at the hands of Ginny and Matthias came to an abrupt halt with the arrival of Lord Ruthven. Charley cordially greeted the earl's friend, Lord Trevise-Fitzgerald, when they were introduced. Lord Trevise-Fitzgerald's eagerness to meet Charley (according to Lord Ruthven) when he had heard that she was part of Lady Ruthven's party dining at the Savoy that evening transformed into a meek, pale shadow of itself upon their meeting in the River Restaurant. Their polite, temperate conversation and conduct, which would not have offended the sensibilities of any society matron, only served to raise Ginny's and Matthias's suspicions. After making Charley's acquaintance, and very shortly after one obligatory dance, Lord Trevise-Fitzgerald left. It was widely suspected that a subsequent assignation had been arranged. Charley, naturally, declined to say anything on the matter. Though I was burning with curiosity myself, I refrained from adding kindling to the fire by asking whether Lord Trevise-Fitzgerald had been one of the recipients of Charley's letters. Tilly, conveniently, was kept so busy dancing that she was spared the chore of having to deny any knowledge or understanding of Charley's comings and goings.

The gaiety of the evening was in full swing and Charley floated about its bower with a light step and a blithe, determined ease. She succeeded in vanishing, briefly, from the merriment several times. Her absences were noted, by the Bommels, for whom she had become a favorite object of their teasing; by Ginny and Tessa, who wondered which of the gentlemen had had the genius to entice her away; and by Matthias, whose brow had developed a permanent line through it that I could have christened with her name. Charley laughed it off. She had been replying to cables from home, she said, and left it at that. Everyone accepted her explanation, wrapped up in all her carefree effervescence and wit and vivacious charm—it was undeniable that the concierge had indeed presented Charley with a batch of calling cards and telegrams earlier upon our arrival back at the Savoy— everyone except Matthias, who had the benefit of knowing Charley for a lot longer than the others had (except perhaps Ginny and Tessa but they had not known about as many of Charley's scrapes as Matthias did), and was therefore naturally suspicious where Charley's charm offensives were concerned. It was, after all, also undeniable that Charley had quickly spirited away the cards and telegrams—but not before Matthias and Ginny had caught sight of a few names.

"Major Enderby? Colonel McGillivray? Lord Hastings?" Ginny asked.

Charley, I was sure, pretended not to have heard, so deeply engrossed was she in conversation with Mrs. Bommel and several of the Misses Bommels about Howard Carter and his archaeological discoveries in Egypt, which compelled Ginny to turn her interrogations on me.

"Old friends of Charley's father's from the Royal Yacht Squadron," I said, hoping Charley appreciated the blackening of my soul for her sake.

"Pish and tosh," Ginny replied. "How many more gentlemen do you have squirreled up your sleeve? So awash in them that it wasn't even worth your time to bother to ask that handsome Mr. Dorsey to stop by and renew your acquaintance from the voyage here?"

Ginny's gentle taunts wrought a new line to Matthias's brow.

"He was also a passenger on the RMS Mauretania?" Matthias asked. "How closely acquainted were—"

"Evidently not nearly as close as he would have liked, although nothing like this horror of a Mrs. Stuyvesant who seems to scare the living daylights out of Charley. Poor Charley had to feign that she remembered him. Is that why she called him your Mr. Dorsey, Lucia? Tell me, how many hearts did you and Charley break over the course of the ocean crossing?" Ginny laughed.

Matthias's expression clearly indicated the extent of his skepticism and concern, although it was unclear why he was unhappy.

"It's merely a coincidence," I insisted. "You know how Charley jokes. We barely ran into him during the crossing."

My assurances had absolutely no impact on Ginny's or Matthias's views of the matter. Ginny continued to grumble and tease, and Matthias continued to silently brood.

"Are you sure you are all right, Lucia?" Matthias repeatedly asked throughout the evening.

He asked, too, if something was up with Charley. Who were all these men—and what was their relation to Charley? He was distrustful of Mr. James Dorsey, to whom he seemed to have taken a dislike after finding out how we had become acquainted with Mr. Dorsey on board the RMS Mauretania. It seemed illogical of Matthias—who was reasonable, good-natured and trusting, without a mean bone in his body—to form such a swift aversion when he bore no ill feelings, in fact, quite the reverse, towards the unruly and heartily energetic Bommels. Ginny and Tessa would have resurrected as a possible explanation those fanciful stories floating around from time to time about Matthias and Charley (for which the Calvert boys had been in some way responsible) which completely discounted their tendency to bicker violently every time they met and made it into some furtive affaire. It could not possibly be something as unimaginatively pedestrian as that, could it?

"Lucia, irrespective of what Charley tells you to do or not do, you will tell me if she is in trouble, won't you?" Matthias asked. "In trouble and too stubborn to ask for help?"

"What makes you think Charley is in any trouble?"

"She's hiding something. I think she's somehow gotten Diego involved—and that cannot be good. If she is in over her head..." Matthias sighed. "I want make sure she is all right but I don't know for certain what is wrong."

I chose my words carefully. "I trust Charley," I said.

"I'm sure Charley herself will tell you that that is so often a foolish sentiment." A ghost of a smile passed over Matthias's features. "Very well, I'll leave it for tonight, but you will come and let me know if circumstances change?"

"What are you so worried about, Matthias?"

Matthias relapsed into his brooding.

The party was still going strong at midnight but it was pumpkin hour for us. We bid good night to the Bommels, thanked them again, and exchanged adieus. As we were shuffling our way out through the milling crowds to the Thames Foyer, I saw Matthias and Charley alone by the Restaurant doors, talking in low voices, engaged in some sort of unspoken tug-of-war from which Charley pulled away, her impenetrable jauntiness untouched, leaving Matthias with a dissatisfied, perplexed frown which was swiftly becoming a permanent fixture on his countenance.

"There's trouble brewing," Ginny said.

The following morning, Matthias presented himself at breakfast at the Savoy with roses (a very close match to the rosebud Charley had found in Covent Garden but, alas, not quite identical in appearance or scent), more candy, and the disappointing news that the apprehended thief had escaped from police custody. He was being escorted by officers to police headquarters to be charged and locked up when the officers were attacked and knocked unconscious, presumably by the thief's accomplices, and the thief was set free.

Matthias also bore the expressions of thanks from the Bommels for the great Fortnum and Mason hampers and baby gifts and flowers delivered to the Bommels' suites—apparently from all of us—which the Bommels had shown him when Matthias himself had gone to deliver his own thanks to the Bommels in the form of season box tickets to Covent Garden.

Matthias was about half an hour too late to convey the news in person to Charley—for undoubtedly Charley was the culprit responsible. Charley had been up since daybreak (unlike others, Charley had had the foresight on the previous evening to observe a clear-headed temperance worthy of Prohibition), scribbling industriously away at cable forms (which she entrusted to no one but herself to take to the telegraph office to dispatch) and sprightly reports back home to Aunt Merry and replies to the other calling cards and invitations which she delegated to Tilly to execute on her behalf as she saw fit (that is, to evade and on no account accept or promise anything) prior to answering a call from the concierge announcing the arrival of Lord Hastings for Miss Masterson downstairs. Charley had, before swanning away, promised that she would be back for tea with the Hartleys.

"She's gone already?" Matthias asked, frowning. "Where?"

Charley was considerate enough to have also left behind a program of outings and activities for Tilly and me during her absence, to take up if we so chose, if it did not clash with anything the Hartleys or Matthias had planned for us. In addition to her duties as Charley's secretary, Tilly was instructed to take advantage of her new Hartnell wardrobe and make use of anything else required—a man at Maison Chaumet would be happy to provide assistance, another at Boucheron if Chaumet was not to taste, names and numbers squeezed into the margin of Charley's note—to attend any of the Season's offerings and events which struck Tilly's fancy, in Miss Charlotte Masterson's stead if necessary, accompanied by Matthias if he would be so kind and Tilly did not object—the temerity!—with only the necessity of discharging companion and chaperon duties when unsuitable gentlemen came to call on me.

Tilly, still smarting in incredulous mortification from the episode at the Norman Hartnell salon, only partially assuaged by the gaiety and attentions of the previous evening, vowed disobedience—until Colonel McGillivray and Sir Eustace Maynard arrived to take us to Royal Ascot. It took soothing persuasions from Matthias and Ginny and me to bring Tilly out of her horrified swoon to agree to go along with the arranged amusement. Our hosts were affable and warmly hospitable and made it such a pleasant and enjoyable outing that it was impossible to harbor regrets or resentment. (Colonel McGillivray was a distant Elyot relation, it seemed, so I had not been too far off the mark.)

"What is Charley up to?" Ginny wondered.

Matthias kept silent.

That morning was to be a taste of the coming weeks.

"The Lords Calthorpe, Delamare, Vane, and Warwick stopped by this afternoon while you were both out and left their cards, asking when it would be possible to call upon Miss Charlotte Masterson," Ginny read, riffling through the daily replenished silver salver of cards. "How do the Lords Calthorpe, Delamare, Vane and Warwick know to come a-courting here? And where has Charley scuttled away to now? Oh, blast it, and here's another one from Lord Dalyrymple! What is Charley up to?"

"What is Charley up to?" became a refrain that Ginny would come to repeat in many variations and often.

"Is Charley setting up an auction for her hand?" Ginny grumbled, throwing down the social pages of the newspapers, featuring fresh reports of Charley and her plague of admirers. The latest one was of her and an upcoming young M.P. and entrepreneur, a Mr. Evans-Pritchard, at Kensington Gardens. "I feel positively redundant. What on earth were your mother and Aunt Merry thinking asking me to line up an array of suitable young gentlemen, Burke's and Debrett's finest, for you two? They've been popping out like fungi after the rains! I've never seen such fierce competition. We'd heard rumors of Sir Nigel Anstruthers coming back from New York and lecturing his recently betrothed heir on his rash choice of American bride-to-be, but until Norland came to call on Charley, I never thought that... How many more suitors are going to pop out of the woodwork? Can you seriously see Charley as the wife of a country squire? She'd be bored within weeks—or have set the place on fire. But if she landed someone loftier, she might be persuaded to shave off some of the cream from atop the Montrose fortune and channel it into reforming the— no, no, that would never do, Charley would have her own ideas. What is Charley up to?"

Matthias's frown deepened with each repetition.

Charley's letters, it appeared, were bearing plentiful fruit. Even the tenacious Mrs. Stuyvesant would have forgiven Charley for not giving her a look-in.

"Isn't there a rose arbor at Kensington Gardens?" I said in Charley's defense. "Aunt Merry likes roses."

Charley was everywhere and nowhere all at once. People spoke of her as one speaks of sightings of a unicorn or chimera. She was the American heiress who seemed to snub the Season's official calendar of society events and yet was admired by the Prince of Wales set for her dash and blamed for upsetting the debutante balls and teas and dances and country house weekends and dinner parties and drawing room maneuverings and social arrangements of London's society hostesses by luring away the most eligible bachelors and choicest of the aristocratic partis. She stirred up memories of Jennie Jerome and Consuelo Vanderbilt, of the irresistible allure to the male British aristocrat of the American Buccaneers with their minauderies and their massive American fortunes. This latest shining bright specimen of Miss Charlotte Masterson from New York appeared even more dangerous than her predecessors, the hapless blue-blooded prizes snared within days of her arrival on English shores.

Charley was not wholly elusive. She may have thumbed her nose at the social obligations of paying and receiving calls and being seen at London's most sought-after drawing rooms and house parties and everything else that the Season entailed, but she turned up punctually to all of the Hartley luncheons and suppers and pre-wedding engagements for Tessa as she had promised, always bright, never bruised by fatigue, and although she was evasive in divulging any useful details of what she had been up to, we saw and heard a great deal about her in the Tatler and the Sketch and the daily gossip rounds and social pages: Miss M. of New York spotted about town with Viscount so-and-so at the Royal Academy of Arts Summer Exhibition, Miss M. dancing with Baron such-and-such at Ciro's and dining in exclusive establishments in Mayfair and Knightsbridge and with James and Dorothy de Rothschild at their London house in St James's Square (I was sure that I had seen other Rothschild invitations arrive for Charley to Waddesdon Manor, one of the Rothschild family piles in Buckinghamshire, and another from Baroness Emma Louise Rothschild and her son, Walter, to Tring Park whose private natural history museum was of note, and more besides to Mentmore Towers, Ascott House, and the Exbury estate, home to a woodland garden of an ambitious scale on the southeast of the very beautiful New Forest), Miss M. emerging with Lord so-and-so from the London Underground onto Bond Street, Miss M. wandering around the Wallace Collection and the Natural History Museum (impressed by the replica plaster cast donated by Andrew Carnegie of Diplodocus carnegii in the Hintze Hall whose original fossil, discovered near Medicine Bow, Wyoming in December 1898, resided at the Carnegie Museum of Natural History, Pittsburgh) and the Victoria and Albert with the eldest son and heir of the Duke of such-and-such, Miss M. chauffeured about Mayfair (the south east corner of Grosvenor Square was also known as "Bentley Corner" for the Bentley Boys who owned flats in that block and the number of Bentley motor-cars parked outside), Belgravia, Kensington, St. James Square and Park Lane in fur tippets and spangled silk evening frocks in sapphire and ruby and turquoise and so mouthwateringly cut they must have come straight from Paris, Miss M. strolling with Sir so-and-so through Hyde Park and Lincoln's Inn Fields, Miss M. popping into Foyles bookstore and Paxton & Whitfield cheesemongers (the pungent, heavy wheels of Stilton and washed rind double brie were vastly enjoyed by the Hartleys and Lord Ruthven with oatcakes, quince confit, and generous glasses of port) and bespoke tailors H. Huntsman & Sons and Selfridge's department store on a whim with the Hon. Mr. such-and-such before heading to the Rivoli Bar or afternoon tea in the Palm Court at the Ritz, Miss M. showered with invitations (confirmed in the sheaves of cards delivered to our Savoy suite every day) to enjoy the lavish hospitality of Mr. Harry Gordon Selfridge at his home in Lansdowne House at 9 Fitzmaurice Place, Mayfair, just off Berkeley Square, and on his private yacht, the SY Conqueror, to cruise the Mediterranean alongside such illustrious guests as Mr. Rudyard Kipling...

It was strange. Charley and I had been brought up to avoid straying into public view. It was unbecoming to be the subject of idle gossip amongst one's social class, so much more so was it to find one's name in print, splayed across yellow press no less, and bandied about by the general masses. We were not like the Astors or the Vanderbilts or the Rockefellers or the other society darlings. Speculation was one thing, that was beyond anyone's control, but the St. Clairs and Elyots had always eschewed courting attention, jealously guarding their privacy. Charley was no stranger to keeping her business to herself, she had kept her comings and goings completely hidden for over a year, hadn't she? So was this flickering in and out of the British eye carelessness or flirtation? After the inactivity on board the RMS Mauretania, it seemed as if Charley had had a sudden burst of energy and was now diligently in pursuit of a matrimonial prize. A last hurrah, Charley had said.

And yet...

Ginny asked, on one of the rare occasions when Charley's gentlemen callers had arrived at the Hartleys' door and had accepted the Hartleys' invitation to join them for cocktails before whisking Charley off for the evening: "Whatever wiles that has the Lords Hastings, Mallory and Trevise-Fitzgerald so in thrall to our Miss Charley, I am impressed. Rivals so civilized and well-behaved! They do seem to be the front-runners in this race, don't you agree?"

"You could just ask the Lords Hastings, Mallory and Trevise-Fitzgerald themselves."

"Now why would I do that when you were close by and must have caught their conversation."

"No, I really wasn't—"

"Lucia," Ginny berated me with a stern look.

"All I heard was the Lords Hastings, Mallory and Trevise-Fitzgerald complaining about the Smoot-Hawley Tariff Bill passing the House of Representatives in May, and Charley saying that many economists and businessmen strongly opposed the bill, including Mr. Henry Ford and J.P. Morgan's chief executive, Mr. Thomas W. Lamont, even President Hoover himself—"

Ginny shook her head in disappointment. "Charley's certainly got you trained up well."

"But it's true!"

"I'm sure it is, Lucia, and that is all that they discussed within your hearing."

"Well, they probably also talked about the America's Cup Challenge, but —"

"Does Charley realize," Ginny lowered her voice to avoid catching the ear of Matthias who drifted past, watching the three lords and Charley like a hawk (or, as Tessa noted mischievously, like a sunflower turning its head to follow the sun), "that people are starting to whisper about her afternoon delights?"

The social columns and gossip circles had been documenting the rising trajectory of Miss Charlotte Masterson's notoriety with almost as keen and salacious an interest as the news of the seizure by Scotland Yard of thirteen paintings of male and female nudes by D. H. Lawrence from a Mayfair gallery on grounds of indecency under the Vagrancy Act of 1838.

"Charley is a delight at all times of the day," I replied.

"Oh, the pair of you!" Ginny's low laugh sounded more like a groan. "So innocent and yet no end of trouble. I hope we don't get to the point of Matthias calling the whole of London out to defend Charley's honor. By all accounts, you seem to be picking up Charley's dreadful heartbreaker habits."

"Ginny—"

"At the current rate, London will run out of men by this time next week. What are we going to do about you two?"

It was easy to be blinded by the dazzle of Charley's fluttering butterfly wings, her golden comet's tail. It was easy to accept the impression of a beautiful, languid and purposeless life. Perhaps that had been her aim, to hide in plain view.

Did Charley know what she was doing, where she was drifting? I sometimes wondered if her answer might have echoed Henry James's heroine, another American in Europe: "No, I haven't the least idea, and I find it very pleasant not to know. A swift carriage, of a dark night, rattling with four horses over roads that one can't see—that's my idea of happiness." Yes, that was the friend I knew: audacious, fearless, eager to meet adventure head-on.

I have vague memories of Charley crawling back into the Savoy suite in pre-dawn darkness—Tilly and I had tried and failed miserably to stay up to that ungodly hour waiting for her. Each morning, the sun rose upon an empty Savoy Bed of faintly disarranged sheets. Each morning, a Savoy attendant brought in a silver salver refreshed with new calling cards, messages, telegrams and the morning papers, folded and beautifully ironed. Each morning, the table in the sitting room of our suite would silently greet us, covered with the cards and invitations delivered on the previous day, read, sorted and neatly cataloged, to be answered or declined as per Charley's dashed off instructions, alongside a brief message from Charley, attaching directions, tickets, and other details regarding where she had gone and her suggestions for the day's amusement and the callers we could expect to escort us to those amusements. Each morning, we would find the trash bin, emptied from the previous day by the Savoy housekeeping staff, refilled with torn up telegrams and discarded cable forms (thoroughly shredded and useless to snooping) and closely-perused sheaves of the previous day's newspapers (the Times as well as, by special order, the New York Times and the Wall Street Journal), the evidence of Charley's dawn toils. Each morning, Matthias would arrive with roses and candy and a smile of greeting which would only slightly darken (so punctilious was he not to rattle Tilly further) when met with Charley's renewed absence. Only a few scattered items of clothing, delicate chemises and tennis dresses and drop waist frocks and bias cut silk evening gowns by Vionnet and Lanvin and Worth, and Charley's beautiful hats and scarves lying on the couches, and the jars of candy from Matthias lined up in a row on the sideboard, gave any sign that the suite was occupied by Charley. Such order and tightly-regulated discipline did not speak of a feckless mind or indeed of a lady of leisure living amongst the strawberry leaves. What had happened to the girl staving off restless ennui and an unnamed dread and the constricts of Old New York with playing cards? What was Charley up to?

As exasperating as it was to be left in the dark by Charley's high-handedness, Tilly and I succumbed to the delirium and became marionettes to Charley's perverse whims and machinations. Each day, Tilly punctiliously followed Charley's instructions and endured the wonders of the Season's delights with grumbling and disapproving mutterings and the guilty, reluctant enjoyment of one who has been coerced against her better judgment into a pact to sell her soul but cannot deny the pleasures it has brought. Each day, when I was not with Ginny or Matthias, I allowed Charley's nominated callers—invariably a titled lord, chosen with impeccable precision to impress the likes of the society matrons of Old New York and my father, if and when such news spread back home—to escort me about London, accompanied by Tilly, to picture galleries or concerts or Wimbledon tournaments or some other sport or recreation or amusement, even an invitation to dinner at Clarence House, which got my name in the social pages, too, and had the Hartleys crowing with delighted awe and admiration. Neither Tilly nor I could find it in our hearts to complain about Charley's intolerably presumptuous interventions or her absences. We were, in our hearts, secretly grateful; Tilly for the vistas she had never imagined she would ever see, and I for the reprieve from the race to find a suitable husband (notwithstanding the disapproval which would meet the vulgarity of appearing in the tabloid rags, it was a perfectly efficient means to achieving its end). Charley seemed as much present with us each day as she was physically absent from them.

We were not the only ones haunted by a benign, maddening ghost who was everywhere and nowhere. As regular as clockwork, beautifully wrapped parcels from Liberty's and Asprey's and Puiforcat and Royal Brierley and Baccarat and Lalique and Limoges and John Lobb and Alfred Dunhill and Hatchards and Jermyn and Bond Street boutiques arrived at the Hartleys' for Kit and Tessa. Ginny and her husband, wanting to arrange a surprise gift to help defray the cost of the wedding, were advised by a clerk at the Norman Hartnell salon that the bill for the Hartley-Tremaine wedding had already been settled in full. When Matthias asked to confirm the honeymoon plans of the soon-to-be-wedded couple, thinking to surprise them—Kit and Tessa, trying to be prudent and save for their future together, had previously discussed the idea of a modest weekend at the Swanage Hotel and the beautiful historic Dorset coast—the Hartleys showed him a leather folder of travel documents, confirming the luxurious parador reservations for the honeymooning couple in Seville, Granada, Madrid, Córdoba and Ronda and Toledo, which had been delivered to their door and sent Tessa into a swoon over realizing her dreams of seeing the streets lined with blossoming orange trees, and the treasures of the Prado, and the Alhambra and Sierra Nevada, and the steep gorges of Ronda, and the Visigothic-Moorish heritage of Córdoba and the imperial city of Toledo elevated above the rapids of the Tagus, and all the wondrous art to be found therein. It left Matthias with little choice but to arrange for a side trip to Paris and the French Riviera and Florence (all those museums and galleries and palazzos nestling around the Arno!) to be annexed to the Spanish honeymoon. Kit Tremaine rang up from Oxford that same evening to tell of the contribution that their parish priest had received for the church upkeep funds and for masses of flowers and other decorations for the church on their upcoming wedding day, and to ask when would Charley be coming down next to Oxford, he could organize for someone from the colleges of Somerville, Lady Margaret Hall, St. Hugh's or St. Hilda's to speak to her friend, Lord Mallory, about scholarships and bursary endowments for women at Oxford. Tessa relayed the message to Charley when she arrived at the Hartleys' townhouse, shaking off raindrops from her hair. Charley had supposedly been out to Kew with Lord Mallory that day to enjoy the roses and sunshine. Poor Charley—everyone else in London had enjoyed sunny and clear skies all day—and poor Kit, complaining of the sudden shower which caught him unawares as he was cycling home to his Merton Street digs from the Bodleian Library. Matthias had been present when the message was relayed. His watchful gaze showed that he had absorbed everything—Charley's damp Marcelled bob and shoulders and her blank face blooming into an expression as surprised as everyone else's over the gifts from the benefactor (who wished to remain anonymous, a humble admirer of Tessa's paintings and sculptures and her bright young Oxford don's promising career, sending felicitations to the couple upon their coming nuptials) and Charley's innocently asking as she daubed and blotted herself dry: "Oh, are there any items left on the wedding gift registry for the other guests?" but he said nothing, only looked thoughtful.

I wondered if Matthias would have behaved differently if he had known that on a previous afternoon, Charley and her elderly gentleman caller had insisted on taking Tilly and me along with them to the Proms in South Kensington. It was a pleasant but strange outing during the course of which he seemed to put me through a conversational sort of examination, grilling me on the state of the London financial markets (of which I knew little) and the American markets (of which I knew a little bit more). Mr. Grenfell took us to supper afterwards at Simpson's-in-the-Strand and then dropped us back at the Savoy, bidding us a very fine evening. And then he paused to say that it had been a surprise but a great pleasure to meet me and asked if he or his American partners might call upon me again when they were next in New York, or, if I was staying longer in London, to please look him up, upon which he gave me his card, tipped his hat and left. Charley was beaming from ear to ear. It was only later when I examined his card that I found out that the gentleman was a senior partner of Morgan, Grenfell & Co. in Great Winchester Street, the largest American merchant bank in London, started by the late American financier George Peabody, and one of the oldest and once most influential merchant banks in Britain. When I tried to question Charley further about it, she said that she thought he might be a director of the Bank of England: "Do look him up, Lucia. He was impressed. Another one bites the dust. Sorry, Lucia, I must be off. Sir Peregrine is taking me out dancing. Don't want to keep his motor-car idling on the kerb."

Perhaps not. After all, Matthias was the one that the Hartleys commissioned to go snooping around to find the name of the wily benefactor to whom they should give thanks. Matthias came back with C. Hoare & Co., Robert Fleming & Co., and Morgan, Grenfell & Co., bankers, he told me privately, who handled the interests and family holdings of Montrose in the British Isles and other territories.

A sense of déjà vu descended upon me: the passing weeks in London before Tessa's wedding felt very much like the three day prelude to our transatlantic crossing when Charley had also disappeared for stretches of time—very much like Charley's unexplained year of absence from New York. The markets followed a similarly baffling pattern. Disregarding the troubling economic signals and the market slides in March and May, disregarding the Federal Reserve's February 2 attempt to prevent the reloaning of Reserve funds by the banks to brokers without raising the rediscount rate (already raised to 5 per cent in July with only a momentary impact on the violent speculation) and its March 25 warning of excessive speculation which had prompted the National City Bank's announcement that it would provide $25 million in credit (effectively pegging the call money rate at 15 per cent—and described by Senator Carter Glass as a slap in the face of the Reserve Board) to stop the market's slide, the Exchange bounced back, stocks resuming their advance, gains continuing almost unabated, up and up and up, basking in the glory of high summer.

Sometimes I thought I caught glimpses of a grand design in the salvers of calling cards and the telegrams and disappearances and the neatly ordered notes laid out like temple offerings on the sitting room table every morning, more illuminating clues surely than any of the economic barometers. But then everything settled back like dust motes in the sunshine and I was left hovering in the background like Matthias in an agony of unease and perplexity and worry.

12

CHARLOTTE:

"MONTROSE GROUP ACCOUNTS FROZEN BANKERS REFUSE JOINT SIGNATORY ACCESS PENDING YOUR AUTHORIZATION PLEASE SEND WITHOUT DELAY NICHOLAS MASTERSON"

"URGENT AWAITING REPLY SEND AUTHORIZATION POST HASTE NICHOLAS MASTERSON"

"CHARLOTTE YOUR TARDINESS IRRESPONSIBILITY PUTTING MONTROSE BUSINESS IN JEOPARDY SEND AUTHORIZATION AT ONCE NICHOLAS MASTERSON"

It was less easy to ignore or hide from Matthias.

The busy London social whirl did not keep me safe. I thought I had been careful to shake off his watchful eye since the night he cornered me at the Savoy and quizzed me about James Dorsey, Trevise-Fitzgerald, Hastings, and all his other imagined perils. Perhaps I had grown complacent. Matthias ambushed me one evening at the Hartleys'. After supper, the radio was turned on and everyone listened in—tuned into the BBC Radio Times, Children's Hour, news bulletins, running commentaries on sporting events, plays, the Promenade concerts, dance music, Duke Ellington and Louis Armstrong crooning "West End Blues"—gathered about the drawing room, on the couches or armchairs or lazing about on the carpet before the fireplace with the family terriers, helping the Hartleys to draft speeches and assemble pouches of bonbons to hand out at the wedding to the children of the attending congregation, or playing charades. Coffee was being served around the room by the maid along with biscotti and sweets. I needed to stretch my cramped legs after squatting on the hearth rug and decided to fetch a cup from the side table set up in the corner. One moment, I was waiting in the cosy, pleasant warmth of the room for the water to boil, the next moment, I found myself roused by a "Wake up, sleepyhead" in my ear and suddenly being lifted up and carried across to another corner and deposited into an armchair. Thank God the others were occupied elsewhere or my humiliation would have been complete.

"You dozed off while still upright." Matthias smirked.

"I did not!"

"You did. Another second and you would have planted into the tea cups," he insisted, plumping and rearranging the velvet cushions around me and querying whether placing them in this or that position was more comfortable. He looked ridiculous, his big hands and bulk moving about, trying to organize the pieces and tuck me in.

"Stop fussing. You're worse than Tilly!"

Matthias's gaze roved over my face, examining me with concern. "You've been burning the candle at both ends for too long."

"I am—"

Matthias stuck a cup of aromatic coffee under my nose. "Do you want more biscuits?"

Matthias came and sat by me on the scroll of the armchair and talked amicably for a while, feeding me biscotti and catching me up on the gory tales that the Hartleys had been telling while I had—allegedly—briefly shut my eyes. It would have felt like the intimate comradery of our past if I had not been on guard, wary of his purpose. One must always be wary of Matthias's niceness. It did not take long for him to launch into a barrage of questions.

"Is London Society living up to your expectations, Charley?" said Matthias. "Wasn't a year's worth of excitement and parties along the East Coast enough for you? Aunt Merry seems to think you wore out more shoes than the twelve dancing princesses."

"It's hard to resist a good party. Or the new dances. A socialite's itch for frivolity requires endless scratching."

"The burglary at the Holyoke Masquerade Ball must've been exciting, in a different way," Matthias said.

"I don't think I attended that one. I think I was in New Orleans."

"Are you sure?" Matthias probed. "I recall someone mentioning seeing you there."

"Are you going to make me swear an oath, Matthias, and describe what gown each female guest was wearing? There were too many parties to remember."

"Of course... Is Aunt Merry aware that you are intending to move to England, Charley?" Matthias asked. "Is Diego helping you to make arrangements?"

"I don't know what you mean."

"This carousel of men coming to call, all the hearts apparently laid to waste. They are all English. If you marry, say, Trevise-Fitzgerald, he'd expect you to leave New York and take up residence here," said Matthias.

It was unfair that Matthias could parry and dodge our curiosity regarding his intentions of returning to New York but felt no compunction about trying to pin me down.

"I have no intentions of marrying Lord Trevise-Fitzgerald. I don't think he—"

"Good," said Matthias. "You deserve better. He's hard-up, the family fortune is not what it was in his grandfather's day and continues to dwindle impressively."

"Are you accusing me of being mercenary?"

"I'm saying I'm glad he isn't in your sights. If you need help, Charley, come to me first."

"Matthias, I am not—"

"In any case, I believe Trevise-Fitzgerald is already engaged to a girl from Yorkshire. Her family is from trade so he has had to keep it quiet."

"Yes, Hubert introduced me to her. I hope you are not suggesting that that is a match of convenience. She's lovely. We picnicked on the lawn of his family estate, just-picked strawberries and freshly churned cream and Pimm's lemonade and no Wimbledon crowds. Yum."

"He introduced— Then why—"

"I think I might have some time tomorrow afternoon, perhaps, for your cross-examinations, Mr. Vandermeer."

Matthias harrumphed. "So you know exactly when to run away again?"

"You're being obnoxious and ridiculous. I do not—"

"You haven't said yet whether you're intending to settle here with an Englishman."

"Haven't I? Fancy that."

"Holding out to see what awaits on the Continent?"

"I'll keep you apprised of any developments on that front, shall I?"

"I don't think any of them will be suitable, frankly," said Matthias.

It took a supreme effort not to sputter. "More secret fiancées in the offing?"

"Ginny seems to think this Grand Tour is meant to find you and Lucia each a husband. Surely you don't mean to go along with that? You've seen the precedents. When have you ever bowed to social dictates? I don't believe Aunt Merry would—Charley?"

"Why not a last hurrah? We all have to turn in our dancing slippers sometime. I'm looking forward to studying the Almanach de Gotha. It's meant to be an even more thrilling read than Debrett's and Burke's."

"There isn't a dire need or urgency for you, or indeed Lucia, to wed," Matthias continued, "is there?"

"It must be Tessa's wedding. The flurry of excitement and romance and all. How can a girl resist?"

Matthias looked me directly in the eye. "Charley," he said gravely.

"Every girl dreams of the fairy tale."

"We've been friends for a long time, Charley," Matthias said. "You will tell me if you are in need of help, won't you?"

I thought ruefully of Rhys Hadden and then banished him from my mind. "I'm grateful for your concern," I told Matthias. "I'm not in need of help."

Matthias sighed. "I thought as much." He pulled out a scrap of paper from his pocket and gave it to me.

"What is this?"

"You were asking Kit about scholarships and bursaries for women at Oxford. This man will be able to give you all the information you need. I can help you set it up when you are ready to give Cecil Rhodes some competition." Matthias pinned me again with his gaze. "Is Lucia—are her parents—aware of what you are scheming? Or is this inquiry on your own behalf?"

"And what exactly do you think I am scheming?"

"Leading Lucia to freedoms denied by her father. Others, too. What do you intend to call it? The Masterson?—the Elyot?—perhaps the Montrose Scholarship?"

"You make some wild leaps of imagination, Matthias Vandermeer. Sloppy ones, too. It was Lord Mallory who was interested, not I."

"I apologize. Would Lord Mallory also be interested in obtaining the details of the Cambridge counterpart at Girton and Newham Colleges?"

"It wouldn't be any trouble for me to pass the information on to Lord Mallory. I'm sure he would be appreciative of your kindness."

"Don't hesitate to let me know if I can be of any further use to his lordship," Matthias said unconcerned by my sarcasm. "Do you want more biscuits or chocolate?"

I ground my teeth into a smile and asked for the chocolate. When people are not kind, one is incommoded, but it is often much worse when they are.

At a Savoy private party, to which we were invited by the Bommels, I met another fugitive who was apparently also running from the rounds of being watched and hunted.

I was briefly free of shadows. Matthias, Tilly and Lucia were lost to the corps of Foxtrotters. I sauntered alone through the suite of the Dowager Countess Sidonie Honorine de Clermont de Montmorency-Beaumont. It was a freedom of sorts, being physically carefree. I hardly noticed. My mind was occupied with other matters and drifted in and out to take in my surroundings. There was a game of baccarat being played at one table and another group at the next table getting their fortunes told. "You will meet three men: a dark stranger who is bad for you, a handsome man who is selfish and indifferent, an ugly man who secretly loves you..." The Bommel girls waved to me from the piano where they stood near the jazz band, one of the boys was speaking to the trombonist and saxophonist, probably trying to negotiate a turn on the instruments. Earlier in the evening, the Bommels had been treating their father's patients at the card table, a patrician gathering of Ancien Regime aristocrats with great dignity of carriage and droll, razor-sharp repartee, as guinea pigs ("...No different really from being treated by Gregory, but far less painful...") by feeding them experimental cocktails to wean them off their favored staid tipple and to try something new and different. One of those new cocktails—cognac, brandy, and sweet vermouth, or alternatively gin, lemon juice, triple sec, Lillet, and absinthe—named the Corpse Reviver—"It's medicinal!"—was scorned by Dr. Bommel as being too fussy and newfangled. Dr. Bommel himself swore by straight gin on the rocks with a dash—the tiniest spoonful —of fruity marmalade as the cure for all ills. I suggested the Bentley, whose recipe the bartender was familiar with, presumably shared by the hard-partying Bentley Boys and then belatedly felt sorry for the guinea pigs who may or may not have been fond of Calvados or Dubonnet but were doubtlessly going to be subjected to it anyway. In appreciation of my suggestion, the Bommels gave me a sample of one of their recherché concoctions, a very simple recipe comprising gin and tonic water on the rocks enlivened with cucumber and black pepper. It had been quite refreshing. I realized I was thirsty and went to look for the butler to make another Bommel cocktail. The lights flickered on and off, dipping the place into a cavern of darkness, sparking off a lightning bug chorus of excitable feminine squeals, crashing glass, and the screeching off-key wails from the band, a wobble that uprighted itself into zozzled hilarity as soon as the lights flickered back on and the party continued as if it had never paused.

As I was making my way through the suite, I heard a deep male voice behind me declare: "Darling, there you are!" A moment later, my hand was seized by a fast grip and an arm wound around my waist, swinging me into the fray of the dancing. When I tried to extricate myself, the proprietorial grip only tightened.

"Look, mister," I began.

"Please," came the same deep voice, low and close against my ear. I looked up into a pair of brilliant changeable green eyes in the face of a man who seemed familiar. The man steered me through the swaying crowd, loosely mimicking the motions of the dance but not letting go. He was clean-shaven, he carried himself with debonair confidence, his bone structure would have been considered good, regular, even handsome, but his eyes, up close, under sharply defined brows, were his most arresting feature: they lent his countenance mobility of expression, humor, intelligence, alertness, intensity, fascination. There were rings around the irises of a different shade, a flickering golden-brown around the sea-green. Heteroglaucos, according to Aristotle. Not entirely the same condition that Alexander the Great and the Byzantine emperor Anastasius I Dicorus were said to have had but more closely resembling that of Rózsika Rothschild, the widow of English banker Charles Rothschild. The young man's chatoyant irises flared with urgency as they darted from side to side as though searching for lurking danger before they came back to settle on my face. His lips hitched into a wide smile as he stared down into my eyes but his next whispered words were at odds with these expressions of fawning adoration: "Please, bear with me. I'm running from some very tenacious prospective society mothers-in-law."

It took several moments for it to sink in. My brain could find no great mischief in playing along with this charade and so I smiled back at him to indicate my cooperation. He seemed to relax a little in response although he did not loosen his hold. And then realization dawned. "Oh, I know you! You're...the man who rescued my friend's purse in Covent Garden."

"James Dorsey," he said. "My apologies for the liberties I've taken, I was—am—a desperate man. You're Miss Charlotte Masterson, I seem to recall."

"How do you do?" Old habits were hard to shake.

We made clear of the jostle and press of dancing bodies. His eyes still flickered about occasionally as he propelled me around the suite. I tried to follow the direction of his gaze but saw nothing that indicated danger, only a handful of girls we passed who stopped and gawked at him with open admiration. It was odd. Hadn't Lucia said he was not a matrimonial prize, that he was the pursuer of heiresses rather than the quarry of ambitious mamas? Perhaps Lucia had merely been misinformed, perhaps even intentionally misinformed, by jealous mamas? I was tempted to question him but this seemed to be a step beyond the bounds of courtesy and propriety.

"Are they still hot in pursuit?" I asked instead.

"Who?"

"The prospective mothers-in-law."

"You're doing a good job of scaring them off," said James Dorsey, and appreciation lit up his bright green orbs. "You've saved my hide. Thank you."

Laughter bubbled out of me at the ridiculous nature of our conversation. "It's my special talent, scaring away mothers-in-law."

"I should think the opposite is true. Aren't you the American trophy that all the bachelors in town are hoping to carry off to their castle in the clouds?"

"You mustn't believe everything you read in the papers, Mr. Dorsey."

"I'm not simply repeating what I've seen in the papers, I've the evidence of it before my eyes. If anything, I would say the interest has only intensified since the ocean voyage, with just cause. May I impose upon your company for a little longer?"

"Well, only if you wouldn't mind tamping down your theatrically extravagant flattery. And I'd like to get a drink, too."

A tray of cocktails floated seemingly towards us but then disappeared into the undulating sea of people. I mourned its passing.

"I'm wounded that you doubt my sincerity," said my brazen captor.

"Oh, Mr. Dorsey, is this why the mamas are chasing after you?"

"But of course, my charming compliments, my knack for retrieving ladies' personal items—and my irresistible face. These are highly-prized commodities." James Dorsey clinched his argument with a cocky megawatt Hollywood matinee idol grin underscored by a dancing mischief that reached deep into his eyes. It was hard to avoid a chuckle or refuse to play along.

"Modesty and beauty, what a heady combination. You are indeed a catch."

"I meant it, you know," he said after our shared laughter had died away, leaving us in charity with each other, solidifying the civility between strangers, especially those who meet under such unorthodox circumstances, into the warmth of feeling that opens the approach to friendship.

"About the irresistible face?"

"About my sincerity."

And that was how I spent a frivolous quarter of an hour or so with a Bommel cocktail in my hand and in the company of a fugitive more desperate than myself before we all got caught up in the business with the missing diamonds. He was amusing company and his attentions were certainly flatteringly potent, I was not surprised that his easy charm caught Mrs. Stuyvesant's daughter and niece and the Fabens heiress. "The world is changed because you are made of ivory and gold. The curves of your lips rewrite history." Overdone nonsense until it passed through his laughing lips and became something exquisite and breathing of life and not some passed off line of Wilde. Those poor girls would not have stood a chance against his powers of enthrallment. He seemed curiously rootless though, but then so did so many of the pleasant, inoffensive and rather forgettable young men I had met. A great contrast to the earnest and annoying thorn that was Matthias Vandermeer. I wondered if Aunt Merry's former fiancé— he of the glittering enchantments of falsehood—had been of a similar mold. Like Sir Lancelot, designed to lure women to their doom. If Mr. James Dorsey kept crossing paths with us... It did not matter whether I was immune to those charms or not, I could not afford not to be, but I hoped that Lucia was sensible enough to stay immune to them.

Of course, the diverting respite did not last.

13

LUCIA:

Two days before we were due to head down to Oxford for the wedding, Dr. Bommel invited us along to a party held in the Savoy suite of a former patient of his.

The Hartleys had already headed down to Oxford to make the final arrangements for the big day so it was left to Matthias, Charley, Tilly and me to represent—well, I was not entirely sure what we represented exactly —to make up the expatriate New York contingent.

We could hear the strains of the party, sporadically overlaid with Dr. Bommel's distinctive bellows of "Rob! Amy! Hannah! Daniel! Disni! Ashley! Jayden! Take a look at this! Jared! Deborah! Sharon! What happened to—" to his clan of ducklings, from down the corridor as we approached the suite of the Dowager Countess de Clermont de Montmorency-Beaumont. The party was lavishly supplied with refreshments and entertainments and guests: a crowded buffet of shiny, exotic hors-d'oeuvre, a stacked bar attended by a butler serving champagne cocktails, liquor and lemonade (the marble en suite bathtub was filled to the brim with ice), card tables, a singer with a voice like dark molasses and a band playing hot jazz, scatting and riffing and tooting with convivial abandon, lapped up with blissful enthusiasm by a medley of people and accents and new arrivals drifting in from the corridor, drawn by the same breadcrumb trail of jazz notes and laughter.

The party also included a smattering of continental aristocracy looking upon the activity with indulgence. They were invariably the patients, former or current, of the Bommels. The Ladies Micheletta and Guineveta di Saluzzo, Lady Elizabeth Urquhart, Baroness Lesley von Fürstenberg-Montbéliard, Margravine Anne-Louise von Baden-Pforzheim and her consort Sir Kazpary Przychocki, the Lady Bridie Penrose, Lady Theresa Ambrose de Lannoy, Lady Audrey Honfleur, Lady Louisa de Villiers, Lady Maria St. Aubyn, Lady Patsy Holbrook, Lady Sue Claymore, Lady Pinja Ghislaine, Lady Hazmah Deladon, Lady Elsie Darrow, Lady Marian Thorndike-Middleton, and the sundry Sirs Siva, John, Michael, Warren, Bob, George, and Brian (whose full names, dignities and honorifics had escaped me), were the most vocal in showing their exasperated and fond regard for their physician and their delight over the photographs of his new grandchild (Lady Mira Cardogan retorted: "Congratulations, Gregory! You'll have to buckle down now and set a good example to your first grandson. The beard at least is a start—did I not advise you that it would lend you the distinction befitting a grandfather by covering up more of your face?") when he made the introductions appendaged to such provocative remarks as "...who is lucky to have been treated by me and is still breathing..." and "...you'd never guess it, she looks like a flapper, but she is really two hundred years old..." and "...fits right into this madhouse, doesn't she?" The introductions led to the dreaded round of questioning to place who we were and where we stood on the social hierarchy, except that when our identities and pursuits, and that of generations of our forbears, were established (if it had been Mrs. Stuyvesant, Charley would have been ready to bolt), they promptly dismissed it all with a kindly pat, as if to say, "Never mind, you cannot help the family or station to which you were born, clearly meant by the good Lord to compensate for the personal qualities with which you were, unluckily, not endowed, poor dear, but we shall befriend you regardless" Imagine what the grande dames of Old New York would have made of that! Charley and Matthias and I were relieved and delighted. They went on to ply us with the sort of irreverent conversation that characterized the Bommels' welcoming and easy chatter. These friends of the Bommels monopolized the card tables with barbed witticisms and high stakes bridge and baccarat (ruled over by the margravine's domesticated pet otter who poked his head out from time to time), a little distance away from the racket of the young things' scene of wild dancing and libations, to which Tilly's furtive glance (and Charley's amused one) flitted back and forth with fascination until the mischievous twitch to Charley's mouth caught Matthias's attention.

"Isn't this fun?" said Charley.

I had learnt over the London Season that these were Charley's danger words. "Isn't this fun, Lucia?" usually preceded me being gently pushed towards conversation or dancing with an approved gentleman caller and Charley vanishing into thin air. This time, however, Charley appeared to be on good behavior. A moment's whispered conspiracy was all it took to have Matthias drag Tilly out to learn the Lindy hop.

The eddies of voices and breathless laughter and music swelled higher in pitch as the evening aged. The tables broke up into the serious card players and the slaves to fashion who wanted to have their palms read or fortunes told in tarot or to hold a seance. The amateur seance caused the lights to flicker several times before plunging into a few moments of complete darkness, during which someone tripped and smashed some crystal and silverware, and then the lights came back on and the eager, lurching conviviality resumed its prior rhythms.

The party came to a sudden jarring hush when the band abruptly stopped playing and the soft electric lighting was turned up to a pearlescent glare. I saw several uniformed Savoy staff arrive at the door and confer with the hostess. Dr. Bommel went to stand reassuringly by her side, looking uncharacteristically serious.

At this juncture, Charley appeared out of the party crowd, her whispery soft gown glimmering like a will-o'-the-wisp. Mr. James Dorsey was beside her. They spoke intimately. He took her hand, deposited a gallant kiss on her knuckles—a gesture hinting at somewhere between amusement and mockery, which amused a smile out of Charley at least—and then departed. Charley wandered over to join me.

"What's happened?" Charley asked.

"I don't know. Who were you just talking to?"

"Maybe the Bommels know more... Oh, you remember James Dorsey, don't you, Lucia? I was just helping him hide from a prospective mother-in-law. Isn't it funny—he has his own Mrs. Stuyvesant. Are Tilly and Matthias still out dancing?"

So the informality that had never been established on board the RMS Mauretania was cemented in the grand Savoy suite of the Dowager Countess de Clermont de Montmorency-Beaumont. How strange it was that we kept running across James Dorsey, as if it were preordained.

"Small world," I said.

"It is, isn't it?" said Charley.

Tilly found us. She was equally clueless. Matthias had been taken aside for a word by a Savoy attendant, Tilly said, and had not yet returned. We asked those around us, but no one knew anything.

One of the uniformed Savoy staff stepped forward to call everyone to attention. He apologized for the interruption and explained that some items had gone missing and, unfortunately, a search of the suite and everyone present was necessary. He apologized again and asked for our patience and cooperation so that this matter could be resolved as swiftly as possible.

The announcement was met with cries of protest and dismay and confusion but the Savoy manager stood firm. It was unpleasant for his team to conduct a search, he insisted, but preferable to being forced to hand the matter over to the police. That got some more grumbles but ensured a sulky compliance.

We all submitted to the search of our persons and watched other Savoy staff comb every inch of the Dowager Countess's suite. Time ticked by. Tilly fretted and wondered and speculated wild possibilities (courtesy, I supposed, of all those crime potboilers and the Agatha Christies she had recently discovered). Charley peered thoughtfully around the suite and we pondered what "items" had gone missing to prompt a need for such measures.

Matthias finally appeared. "Are you all right?" he asked.

"Do you know what is going on, Matthias?"

"Some diamonds have gone missing," Matthias answered.

His words were met with a clamor of reactions ranging from shock to excitement. Diamonds!

"Be prepared for another round of searches—and a long night. No one is to leave the suite. Nothing is allowed to be touched or moved. The first round search that the Savoy staff conducted came up with nothing, They are doing another sweep but are not optimistic about the outcome. They have called in the police," Matthias explained. "It has been rather upsetting for the dowager countess, of course, and for the Bommels."

"Are they under suspicion?" I asked.

"The son of an old friend, a M. Francis Meilland, was the last person to handle the diamonds before the lights went out," said Matthias.

"A French cat burglar?" cried Tilly.

"M. Meilland grows roses," said Matthias. "His father is well-known in the rose breeding world and his son, despite his youth, looks destined to follow in his father's footsteps. Our hostess had invited him over from France to discuss the rose gardens of a family estate near Paris which she had intended to give to her god-daughter, along with the diamonds made into a parure set to be designed by the talented M. Mellerio of Mellerio dits Meller, for her god-daughter's engagement. The dowager countess was introducing M. Meilland and showing off the diamonds to the group at the card table when the darkness descended. Everyone who had touched the diamonds—the Bommels, the dowager countess's friends at the card table —were all considered above reproach on account of their reputation or aristocratic standing, which left M. Meilland, a stranger, a commoner, a foreigner and a Frenchman."

"But he's just a youth! He was so polite, so gravely formal—so very, very young—how horrible to be the one to tell his parents of such suspicions," I said. "He was searched, too, wasn't he, and no diamonds were found on his person?"

"No, none were found," said Matthias. "The dowager countess and her friends were understandably vocal in their outrage but with the diamonds still missing—"

"'Made into'?" Charley echoed. "Loose diamonds?"

"Yes," said Matthias. "Clear, uncut, fresh from the Kimberley."

"But why M. Meilland?" Charley asked. "Stealing from a patroness who has handed him an important commission hardly seems the best way to recommend himself to her good graces. Was there some other suspected motive? What about the other guests who have been drifting in and out of the suite? Whoever took the diamonds may have left already."

"There was a great deal of confusion during the darkness. Somebody tripped, the card tables were thrown into disarray, drinks were spilled, a tray and glasses smashed. A lot of chaos. The diamonds were noticed to be missing very soon after the lights came back on, when the mess was being cleaned up. The Bommels and their friends did a search of the area and came up with nothing. The Savoy management were alerted and they have detained, searched and questioned all the guests who were on or had access to this floor. I'm sure the police will do the same. There is not a lot to go on. Unfortunately, M. Meilland is the man unlucky enough to be the only suspect at the moment."

We all had many questions for Matthias which he tried to answer as best as he could. Charley had the most by far. When it came to inquisitions, Charley was no novice. She ended with a series of sharp left hooks.

"Why did the Savoy staff call you aside? Why are you so au fait with this matter?"

For the first time all evening, I saw Matthias hesitate before carefully answering: "They were advised to speak to me. I work for the company who insured the diamonds."

"Do you believe M. Meilland is guilty?" Charley asked.

"You know it would be inappropriate of me to answer that," Matthias replied.

"Of course," said Charley. "Were we absolved of suspicion because you vouched for us?"

"Charley," I said.

"I did not intervene with bias on anyone's behalf," said Matthias.

"So in your official capacity—"

"I will do everything I can to have this matter cleared up," said Matthias. Charley gave a brilliant smile. "I'm glad we've clarified that," she said.

Along with everyone else who had attended the party, we were detained for questioning when the police detectives arrived. It was a very tedious way to pass time. There was not a great deal we could do, however. As soon as we were free of the questioning and given leave to go—we were only two floors down and, as Charley impishly pointed out, well known to their insurance man who could easily get hold of us if we should abscond—we went to take our leave of the hostess and the Bommels and their friends, lending our ears and sympathy and support for this lamentable incident. Matthias said he would come find us if anything new turned up.

We were unhurried in leaving the dowager countess's suite. Charley and I walked leisurely through the limited confines of the grand suite to which access had not been cordoned off or blocked from view, surveying as inconspicuously as we could the card tables, the scene of the crime. We discussed the progression of the evening's events which led to the diamonds going missing. I could see Charley pondering the matter deeply, turning it around this way and that in her mind.

If the diamonds had not been found on any of the persons at the party, could it be that they were still somewhere in the suite? The fifth floor suite faced the Thames. It would have been quite difficult and impractical as an escape route in so short a time without risking being noticed, or falling to one's death. Tossing the diamonds out the windows to an accomplice waiting below? Fortunately, the suite's windows had been closed and locked all evening (Matthias had confirmed this), so that left the suite itself filled with bored, anxious, increasingly annoyed guests still awaiting their turn at being questioned by the police.

"And hotel staff," Charley pointed out.

"And unknown drifters in and out who have not been caught," offered Tilly.

The Savoy attendants and butler who had been on duty had all been questioned by the hotel's management and again by the police.

The brief blackout had been identified, Matthias had told us, as coinciding with the time the diamonds went missing. Nobody could remember who exactly suggested the seance that necessitated the flicking off of the lights. Had it been an intentional diversion or simply someone seizing hold of an opportunity amid the chaos of the darkness?

We returned to our suite very much unsatisfied.

As the night wore on, and no news came, we had nothing to do but wait and watch the lights play over the darkened view of the Thames that Monet had painted obsessively from his hotel room.

Nobody could sleep. Our minds were too awake, too busy puzzling over the missing diamonds and poor M. Meilland and the unanswered question of cui bono? Finally, Charley jumped off the couch and announced that she was heading back to the dowager countess's suite.

"They would never let you back in," said Tilly.

Charley slipped the antique pearl-drop girandole out from her ear lobe. "But I think I lost an earring at the dowager countess's party doing the Shimmy," she said. "And I was more than a little ossified to boot."

Tilly and I followed Charley back to the dowager countess's suite with trepidation. We were not going to let Charley loose on her own. At worst, Tilly and I decided, we would call upon Matthias to bail us all out.

We were amazed that Charley, without batting a demure eyelash, managed to bamboozle the policemen at the door to let us in. One of them remained at his sentry guard position. Calling for a backup to replace him, the other policeman escorted us around the suite to help us search for Charley's missing earring.

Charley wandered about, attempting wherever possible to edge closer to the cordoned off areas of the marble bathtub filled with ice, the ice buckets and glassware at the bar, and the bins standing near the card tables and about the rooms, but was dissuaded away each time by a severe, glaring, burly sentry and she dared not let a reckless gesture destroy her guileless charade before our gallant police officer escort.

Another door of the suite opened from within and Matthias strode in. He drew up short, his bearing tensing briefly, but continued towards us.

"What are you all doing back here?" Matthias asked. A frown line had emerged between his brows.

The police officer informed Matthias of our quest for the Charley's missing earring. Matthias, to his credit, maintained his composure, assuring the police officer that we were known to him, had been searched, questioned and cleared, and that he would take over accompanying us.

When the police officer left us to return back to his position at the door (with many expressions of thanks from Charley for his kind assistance), Matthias turned to Charley and said: "You were wearing both earrings when you took your leave earlier. I'm willing to bet that if we looked, we'd find that earring back in your suite. What are you really looking for?"

"Colorless pebbles," Charley said.

"You believe the diamonds are still here?" asked Matthias.

"So it occurred to you too?"

"Yes," said Matthias.

"I remember the first time I was shown uncut diamonds," said Charley. "I mistook them for rough pebbles and colorless glass. I thought, possibly..."

"The shattered glass during the blackout," I supplied.

"Had the trash already been taken out before the police did a search, before the Savoy management's searches?" Charley asked.

"No," said Matthias, "I've been informed that nothing was touched or moved."

"You'd lose the bet," said Charley. "You're wrong about my earring."

Matthias smiled faintly. "How so?"

"You would not find it back in our suite," said Charley, "because Lucia has it, here, inside her jeweled tote."

"Charley, I do not—"

Charley snapped open the jeweled jaws of my tote evening pouch and sure enough, there was her pearl-drop girandole earring.

"When did you—how—"

"Have you seen a magician perform sleight of hand or a card trick? It's

43

very clever. All it takes is a second's lapse in attention, a distraction," said Charley. "Even with the multiple searches, I just wondered... Would it have been possible for a thief to tuck the diamonds somewhere already searched —beneath the couch cushions, in a pot plant, for instance—or on another's person who had already undergone a search, and for the thief to then submit to being searched themselves, then to come back and retrieve the stones? The sleight could be repeated endless times, whether with an accomplice or borrowing the pockets of an unsuspecting fellow guest— most likely a male guest, female attire has so few conveniently accessible pockets... But then, if everyone leaving the suite faces another final search at the door, as we did when we left, perhaps an alternative plan would have been to hide the diamonds somewhere to be retrieved later when the investigations and suspicions have died down, Somewhere where there is a low chance of being searched again or a high chance of being overlooked such as the trash being taken out or of the bathtub being drained by someone in a Savoy uniform. It's possible that the diamonds could be hidden inside an ice bucket, or the bathtub of ice. The stones would be camouflaged well enough. Someone dressed in the Savoy uniform could be mistaken for a true member of the hotel staff... But it would be risky because there is no telling how long one would have to wait before it would be safe to retrieve the diamonds without detection—by then, the ice might have melted, revealing the stones... And if the hotel management are certain that all its staff are accounted for... I wondered if letting the diamonds go down the drain might have been considered, but the retrieval would involve a more complicated plumbing effort, with a higher risk of being noticed and identified and the risk of losing the diamonds altogether to the sewers... Perhaps the glass or crystal shards from the crash during the moments of darkness? I presume they were swept away into the trash bins? A bed of broken glass and crystal in the trash as a means of hiding the uncut diamonds does not hold the risk of melting that ice does. And it would only have taken the work of a moment. Perhaps the smashing of the glass during the temporary blackout had not been an accident but a deliberate attempt to create a diversion? Or perhaps, after all, the unknown thief or accomplice has already escaped..."

Matthias looked at Charley for a long interval, a curious gamut of expressions chasing each other across his face. "I was on my way," he said slowly, solemnly, "to let you know that the investigations are likely to take a little longer. The police have yet to finish questioning all the party guests and they will require more time to undertake the additional searches that I have in mind to suggest. As you've pointed out, it would be worthwhile for the detectives to go through the contents of the trash again, carefully, as well as the ice. Not many laymen would recognize uncut diamonds. I shall also ask them to make sure that they separate the searched persons and monitor the searches, before and after, thoroughly, to catch any sleights of hand, and to pay attention to the door searches."

"Oh, well, you seem to have everything in hand. It's been swell chewing the rag with you. I've found my earring now, so I guess we'll be off," Charley chirruped. "Good luck."

Matthias escorted us to the door and then went away to speak to the investigating detectives.

Tilly blew out a breath, her cheeks deflating like a balloon. "Miss Charley," she breathed in dazed awe.

"What an diversely edifying education you've had during your year of absence, Charley," I mused. "Motor-cars, gambling, sleight of hand, diamonds—"

"I hope they find the diamonds and clear M. Meilland," said Charley.

When the Bommels paid us a visit the following morning, they were disappointed to find that they had missed Charley (gone at her usual uncivilized hour) and had been beaten by only a few minutes by Matthias to be the first in relaying the wonderful news that the detectives had located the uncut diamonds at the bottom of a trash bin amongst the sparkling pieces of glass. Rumor had it (according to Dr. Bommel, not to be outdone) that the police had followed up on an idea suggested by a young female guest at the party which had led them to uncover the location of the missing diamonds. The thief or thieves could not be identified but there was nothing that could be pinned on M. Meilland and he was therefore spared a detention at Her Majesty's pleasure. The dowager countess was immensely grateful.

Tilly repeated her awed utterances and relief into her tea.

If he were a thief, Dr. Bommel opined, he would be careful to steer clear of sweet, innocent-looking young American ladies in the future.

The Bommels had brought with them another visitor to our suite: the slender, dark-haired young gentleman whom we had met at the dowager countess's party. He had been stiff and formal at first, as he had been on the previous evening, but this quickly melted into eager, animated smiles and English inflected with the ready wit and Gallic lilt of his mother tongue (Lyonnais accent, I was told) as M. Meilland greeted us with an outpouring of heartfelt gratitude for snatching him away from the claws of a calamity which would have destroyed his poor Papa and Maman. He regretted that he had missed Mlle Masterson, that he could not stay longer, it was his last day in England, he would be departing for his home on the afternoon tide, however, he had been advised that we were due soon to travel to the South of France, and also that Mlle Masterson was fond of roses, and he wished very much to extend a warm invitation to us to visit his family's nurseries in Tassin, near Lyon, and at Cap d'Antibes if we should find ourselves in either of those locations in the future...

We spent the majority of the day with the Bommels on an outing to Hampstead Heath, viewing Kenwood House and enjoying a picnic luncheon and the view of London and St. Paul's Cathedral from Parliament Hill, coming back to the wander the shops around Piccadilly and Oxford and Bond Streets to stock up in readiness for the upcoming family wedding (including fur tippets and sturdy umbrellas and other weather guards as the forecast had mentioned the chance of rain and possibly even hail). We were easing into the rumbling and tooting Praed Street traffic, headed on our way to Selfridges, when one of the Bommels poked a nose against the glass pane of the automobile window and cried, "Is that Charley coming out of Paddington Station?" which caused a rush to the window and many opinions espoused as to whether it was or wasn't and whether Charley had hailed a cab or stepped into a waiting motor-car or had run for an omnibus or... Upon two points were the Bommels all agreed: Charley had been alone (not, as Charley had written that morning, off on a jaunt with Lord Cholmondeley) and she had vanished.

Matthias sat rigidly behind the wheel of his Bentley without comment.

Matthias had been more subdued in manner when he arrived in the morning. Charley's absence had not been a surprise but it did nothing to soften that line between his brows. Matthias's brooding had taken on a stern new edge overnight, keener in alertness and a conflicted, almost pained uncertainty, as if torn between his natural inclinations and his duty. Charley had wrought that look when she had questioned the execution of his official capacity, challenging his actions and his loyalties, stomping all over his impartiality to fear or favor, and testing the soundness of his mettle for the sake of finding the missing diamonds and saving the innocent young friend of the Bommels. Matthias had borne it with equanimity the previous night, discharging this duty in an irreproachable fashion, but it had begun to take a noticeable toll. I was right to dread that Charley—bold, irreverent, valiant Charley—had roused a slumbering dragon.

After we had bid farewell to the Bommels, I saw the storm clouds gathering fast and thick. How would the inquisition that I feared— something Charley was far more familiar with receiving than Tilly or I, and far better equipped to meet head-on—come about? Would the ground rumble and quake before it began to spew forth a downpour of molten lava? Would the wick to the eruption come in the guise of an invitation from one of Charley's gentlemen callers? Or flowers sent from one of her suitors? Or a note from Charley stating that she had been delayed and might be late to tea and for us to go on ahead and not to wait for her?

The polite, oblivious attendant handed over the brief note addressed to me in Charley's hand. I relayed its contents to Matthias, there was no way to sugar-coat the pill. Matthias quizzed the messenger as to when and from whom and where it had been delivered. A bank clerk from Barings at

Bishopsgate, he was told. The note was crushed between Matthias's fingers. I braced myself...

...but the inquisition never came.

At least, it seemed a much tamer storm than the one I had dreaded so deeply, more of an irruption. Matthias looked like a warrior ready to charge into battle, brisk, powerful, impenetrable. He wasted no time launching into his questions.

"Lucia, can you tell me where Charley has really been today? Can you tell me where she has been and what she has been up to these last few weeks? Can you tell me what she has been up to this last year?"

Matthias would have asked the same of Tilly if she had not ducked out (coward) to see to packing for the trip down to Oxford.

I spoke for Tilly and myself, truthfully, when I told him: "Your guess is as good as mine."

Well, maybe not entirely truthfully. But that was all speculation really. It would have been slanderous to... Charley was such a terrible influence.

With my promises to Charley repeating clearly in my mind, I readied to defend another strike.

"But I've told you before," I reminded Matthias, "I trust Charley."

And just like that, Matthias's formidable conquistador's stance crumbled to dust.

A lengthy, heavy silence fell between us.

"The substance of things hoped for, the evidence of things not seen," Matthias said, his voice suddenly immeasurably weary. "I know that she was not in Saratoga Springs, New Hampshire, Philadelphia, Charleston or any of the places she said she was—not, at least, when she said she was."

This was news to me, or rather, it was confirmation of my suspicions but I had never thought that Matthias knew, or might have proof.

"Charley was present at a number of the balls when she wrote in her letters that she was elsewhere and," Matthias continued, "notwithstanding the assertions of Olivia Routledge, Junius and Francine Cutler, Freeman Byrd, Hamilton Lichfield, Winnifred Létourneau, Edward and Louise Delano-Grenville, Emmeline Sloane, or Hetty Adams, who have all vouched for her, Charley was absent at other events that she said she had attended. Everything happened exactly as Charley says it happened. Nobody says otherwise, not tight-lipped Diego, not her eternally accommodating Aunt Merry, not Titus, not Mrs. Stone, not Tilly, not you."

I trembled for Charley. It was far, far worse than I had dreaded.

"How do you know? How can you be certain?" I asked.

From the ashes of the fallen conquistador, a glimmer of our old friend Matthias Vandermeer arose and smiled wanly. "Ginny was right to remark that Charley has you well trained. Don't mistake me, Lucia," he said when I made to protest, "Charley should be surrounded by friends. Guard her well."

It seemed such a strange, defeated thing to say.

"Are you—do you not count yourself amongst that number, Matthias?"

Matthias's expression became hooded. His voice rang somewhat hollow without his usual smiling gentleness and firm conviction when he said, "Of course. But the more the better, right, Lucia?"

Matthias then directed my attention to the evening's entertainment available at the West End for our last evening in London before Tessa and Kit's wedding. The squall seemed to have pass quickly. Although I had passed through it, I could not find traces of its existence. We did not revisit the subject of Charley's whereabouts. Everything seemed returned to its former place, no rancor, no ill-humor lingered but there was a false note somewhere in the great orchestral chorus. How strange it felt! Something gnawed at Matthias like a ravenous wolf at his belly but he fiercely resisted coming to the point on what it was.

When afternoon came and Charley finally arrived (a little late but not so much that she missed us), we appeared perfectly in accord. Charley was very pleased about the news of the diamonds and M. Meilland though sorry she had not had the chance to wish him and the Bommels farewell in person. Matthias and Charley did not poke or bicker at each other once. We dined early in the Savoy Grill, everyone well at ease and bursting with garrulity about the dowager countess's party of the previous night and the coming wedding day, and then we went on to see Bitter Sweet, an operetta by Noel Coward starring Peggy Wood and George Metaxa which had recently premiered to good reviews at His Majesty's Theater, before turning in for the night.

It was all so confused. None of it made sense. These friends who had been as steady and familiar as my own reflection had suddenly turned as vaporous and shimmery and elusive as morning mist. The outline of some strange, pale djinn emerged from their cast as if an earthquake had passed through the land and its tremors had shaken the spirit loose, releasing something long imprisoned, something forged in hidden subterranean fires.

I went to bed telling myself: this was why people warned you to be careful what you wished for, this was what happened when you were granted your heart's desire. Gunpowder, treason and plot.

AN OXFORD LOVE STORY

Late July 1929, Oxford

14

LUCIA:

On the day we were due to depart for Oxford, the morning salver brought its usual batch of invitations and telegrams but, unusually, one of the telegrams was for me.

"LUCIA TELL CHARLOTTE RESPOND MY CABLES IMMEDIATELY NICHOLAS MASTERSON"

I showed the cable to Charley who was for once sitting in our suite with the pale early morning sun shining on her crown as she munched her way through a full hot English breakfast. Charley took it and tore it up into confetti to line the slops bowl.

"If you receive any more of these, just ignore them," she said, then turned and accepted from Tilly another slice of hot buttered toast onto which she liberally smeared honey.

"We will not speak of this then? I shouldn't ask about it?"

Charley smiled. "Best not to," she agreed.

"Is there any way that I—what can I do, Charley?"

"Don't give another thought to it. Thank you." Charley gave me another little cryptic smile. She behaved as if it had been nothing of consequence but ire burned bright in her eyes.

Charley quenched that fire, hiding it behind the steam rising from her coffee cup, when a knock on the door admitted Matthias into our suite. He was attired in a formal dove gray morning suit and instead of roses and jars of candy—impractical to carry on our trip to Oxford—he brought a paper bag of boiled sweets for the journey (as if Charley and I did not still have full jars of candy packed away by Tilly in the trunks).

Another gentleman followed Matthias into the suite with a discreet knock and good morning, carrying a briefcase. After some formalities, wherein Charley surrendered her signature to the paperwork, affixing it to the bottom of each page, he opened the briefcase and handed her a large black velvet case stamped with a faded crest, bowed slightly and left.

"Aren't you going to open it?" Tilly's eyes sparkled inquisitively.

"I'm sure he checked for missing pieces." Charley smiled.

The case contained an opal and diamond parure set comprising necklace, earrings, bracelet and a diadem of stupendous marquise-cut stones.

"That's very fancy to wear to the wedding breakfast," I said. "I'm not sure it will go with your current frock." The fire opals were exquisite in their bed of frantically winking diamonds, the smallest one the size of a plump gooseberry, spraying shimmering splinters of light everywhere. As for the diadem... It was unassuming in its refined simplicity, as delicate and finely wrought as the other pieces, a close cousin to the jewel collections of imperial Europe and Russia. "And you're already wearing your pearls."

"It's much more sparkly than when it was taken out of the bank vault," Charley remarked. "The pieces do clean up nicely, don't you think? M. Boucheron did a fine job. I hope Tessa likes them. If not, she can always pawn them for a second honeymoon or improvements to the art studio or when a baby comes."

Matthias's eyes spoke eloquently what did not pass his lips.

Charley's wedding gift of the opal and diamond parure set (as opposed to the other gifts over which she had never claimed responsibility) was added to the pile building up on the wedding morning including the joint Elyot-Bernhardt gift of the keys and deeds to a freehold (which I had been entrusted to deliver), a sweetly rustic cottage on the outskirts of the university town, with a pretty garden and fixtures and furnishings lovingly provided by Tessa's large extended family, along with a post office savings account to start off their married life, and a brand new Hispano-Suiza from Lord and Lady Ruthven, and the many other gifts and wishes and blessings of the colleagues, students and friends of Kit's and Tessa's and the Hartleys', invited to the celebrate the amalgamation of the Hartley and Tremaine lines. The pile of amassed gifts and the billows of warm regard sent Tessa into a greater fit of weeping than she had already expended earlier, although the tears this time were of a less distressing nature as Ginny reminded her that she and Kit were as much loved by a great many people as they were reviled by the Tremaines (excepting Kit's younger brother, who had been kept away from contacting Kit by their parents).

There had been, Ginny told us, something of a crisis before we arrived. Kit's father, the 3rd Viscount Venables, had shown up to repeat one final time his arguments as to why his son should not be polluting his lineage and throwing away his position and inheritance and the chance to wed a gently-reared blue-blooded bride by aligning himself instead with, pah, the common Hartley girl in this shabby corner affair, no matter how pretty or how many other noble lords had also been entrapped into marriage by her siblings or cousins or how much royal or aristocratic or nouveau riche patronage she was rumored to enjoy. Was his son so foolhardy and selfish and unfeeling as to turn away from his own family for the sake of this nobody? Did Kit not regret the suffering he caused his mother, his sisters whose marriage prospects would be forever tainted by this unholy union; did he not feel remorse for poisoning the mind of his younger brother with the same distorted lies which sang the praises of this Miss Hartley?

Lord Venables, according to Ginny, had apparently almost had an apoplectic fit and swallowed his teeth when Lord Mallory—who had come by to deliver his own felicitations to Kit and Tessa when Lord Venables showed up—interrupted the mighty sermon, sheepishly apologized and stuck beneath the viscount's nose, well, all right, politely handed over a private word of congratulations to Kit and Tessa from St. James's Palace.

"Served the blighter right," Ginny growled. "Tessa just about stopped crying long enough to take off her dress and leave a note behind to call off the wedding. Didn't want to ruin Kit's life."

Kit, Ginny said, ran after Tessa and called her an idiot and dragged her back.

"Do you know how much time it took to put her to rights again?" Ginny said. "Anyway, Lord Venables stormed off in high dudgeon after that and no trace of him has been seen since. Good riddance. Poor Kit, he and Rupert must've been changelings, or else they got the recessive kindness gene. They are ever so much alike—like Russian nesting dolls, standing next to each other, one the—"

"Whatever do you mean, Ginny? Wasn't Rupert forbidden from attending?"

"Oh, you haven't seen Rupert yet? The junior Hartleys are probably still hiding him from Lord Venables. A driver arrived this morning with the little stowaway in his Daimler limousine. Rupert says the driver had turned up and handed some letters to his headmaster which placated the headmaster enough to allow Rupert to have the day and leave with the driver. Of course he was roundly scolded for accepting rides from strangers but he claimed the driver had informed him that Kit had arranged everything, though Kit was as surprised as anyone. It's quite a mystery. Certainly the permission had to have had legitimate authority—had to have come from a guardian—but... Do you know anything about this patronage business, royal and otherwise? Tessa hadn't a clue, thought it was just some gibberish that Lord Venables was ranting about. I'm a bit unsure, I know they say that Charley is greatly admired by the Prince of Wales set but... Could she have arranged a private message of congratulations from the Prince of Wales himself? She's the only one I can think of. None of us move in those circles to warrant that sort of consideration. And Rupert being snuck—legally—out of school for the day to attend the wedding. It all smells a bit suspect to me, like all the other business to date."

I privately agreed with Ginny. The patronage of Tessa's art might have seemed like gibberish but I had no doubt that it would not be so in the very near future when Charley's machinations would bear fruit. I was certain Matthias shared this view.

After the early storm clouds cleared, the wedding proceeded in showers of cloudless sunshine sent down by St. Frideswide, the patroness of Oxford. Tessa and Kit came out of the 12th century Norman church, with a 20th century stained-glass window and set back from the river to safeguard it from flood, wreathed in smiles and surrounded by a halo of well-wishers and peals of joyous laughter amidst the over-excited tolling of the church bell rung by the children of the parish under the indulgent supervision of the curate.

Ginny cried (as did all the Hartleys) copiously. "An unholy union indeed," she muttered. Rupert Tremaine, beside Ginny, gently patted her arm and gave her his handkerchief, and had his neatly combed brown locks rumpled by Ginny for his trouble.

"Do you think your parents will ever come around, Rupert?" Charley asked.

Rupert shrugged. He looked back towards his brother with Tessa, decked out in happiness and love and all of Norman Hartnell's enchantment of finery. "Not Kit's loss," he said.

"No," Matthias agreed, also watching our newly-wed friends, "she is the bane and light of his existence."

The green behind the church had been profusely decorated with gorgeous flowers (as riotous as the floral explosion which had decked the church interior) and two long tables had been set up on the manicured lawn, covered in crisp linen and loaded with food and drink and wedding cake. After the completion of the ceremony, the congregation poured out of the church doors and converged between the tables and five-piece band playing old favorites and the latest popular tunes, leisurely milling about, enjoying the festive air, eating and drinking and gossiping and chatting with the vicar and curate and newly-weds and bridal party and laughing, while small children, shrieking and giggling, ran in and out and crawled and tumbled across the soft grass and clover.

As I wandered through the crowd with Ginny and Charley, stopping here and there for greetings and introductions, we returned to discuss the excitement of the morning.

"'I will permit no man to narrow and degrade my soul by making me hate him'," Charley quoted. "Although it does seem unfair to allow only one man to corner the market on being despicable... 'No race can prosper till it learns that there is as much dignity in tilling a field as in writing a poem.'"

"That could only have come from an American," Ginny said, smiling to her husband who was with Tessa and Kit, talking to the Reverend Norgate. "A proper English aristocrat looks down upon a man who earns his living by labor or trade."

"A good few American aristocrats would concur," said Charley.

"But it's acceptable to marry for it," I pointed out.

"Both sides of the Atlantic agree on that one," said Ginny. "A snob is a snob is a snob whichever way you cut it, God bless them."

"I'm not sure the ritual sacrifice agrees," I said.

"Chattels aren't usually accorded rights or feelings," said Charley.

"Has it really come to that?" asked Ginny. "Surely... Is someone forcing you to walk the plank?"

"Oh, I was speaking in a general sense of the andeluvian niceties of Society," said Charley.

"And what about you, Lucia, were you only speaking in a general sense?" asked Ginny.

"The world is my oyster," I said.

"God forbid." Ginny swore. "Why didn't you say so sooner? I thought you were fine, what with Charley sending all of London into an uproar and you with the never-ending line of gentlemen taking you out—"

"That was Charley's doing," I said. "And they did not suit."

"Everything is fine. Don't fuss, Ginny, it gives you wrinkles."

"You're a holy terror, Charley Masterson," said Ginny. "You could do worse than confiding in Matthias. He worries about you two."

"Well, you aren't to encourage him. Men get wrinkles, too, you know, Ginny."

"You ought to know. You're the cause of most of them. I understand you have been rather busy with your social whirl about London but do you realize how much of a catch our Mr. Vandermeer is?"

"Oh, Ginny, now you're just scraping the barrel for laughs!"

"Before you start laughing your fool heads off, look over there." Ginny waved our gazes to where Matthias was standing with Tilly and Rupert within a circle of Hartleys and the curate and other guests, an audience held captive by Tilly who was retelling the highlights of the recent matches she had witnessed at Wimbledon. "You remember how friendly and admiring those parish girls were earlier when I introduced them to you and Lucia? They weren't just awed by your reputations from the social pages. You two and Tilly are the only ones to whom Matthias has shown any special marks of attention. (Well, obviously the Hartleys don't count, we overrun everything and everyone and we're safely off the market.) They were gobsmacked and not a little envious that you've known him for so long that your familiarity enables you to bandy about with Matthias as though he's the village oaf without incurring his offense."

Charley's response was a typical snort of laughter.

"It isn't just the parish girls," said Ginny. "Didn't you receive the same envious reception when you were being squired around London by Matthias? Matthias doesn't advertise it but he's as much of a draw on the marriage mart as any other aristocrat of the Season. He's not a detrimental either: he isn't a boor or a brute and he has been formally announced as his grandfather's heir."

Our ears finally perked up at this.

"Who's his grandfather?"

"Albrecht Matthias Godeffroy," said Ginny, "who, up till now, has been known to have one son and heir: Volker Godeffroy."

"The Wall Street banker," murmured Charley. Her eyes were bright and swimming with cogitations that would have been dizzying to watch if my own mind had not been spinning on the same axis.

"Yes," said Ginny, "Matthias has been named heir to the Godeffroy financial empire and banking fortune. Volker Godeffroy has been cut out altogether from the will apart from modest settlements on his daughters. The news has probably reached New York financial circles by now. I give it a day or so before it becomes general knowledge."

"No reasons were given for the change?"

"Matthias has done well in the European operations in the years he has been here. I think he was groomed from the outset to take over the business. The announcement is only a formality."

"Then it isn't just about business, is it? It goes deeper. Is Volker Godeffroy Matthias's father? Because if he is, this is an even bigger slap in the face than Godeffroy's inviting Matthias to its London headquarters after the Godeffroy's New York branch rejected him."

"Well, unless Matthias's grandfather had other children we don't know about... There is no doubting the family connection between Albrecht Matthias Godeffroy and Matthias. Matthias looks like his grandfather."

"I met him," Charley whispered.

"What?"

"Matthias's grandfather," said Charley. "Only I didn't know he was—I didn't recog—I was—" She lapsed into deep thought, then resurfaced. "Has this to do with Matthias's intention to return to New York?"

"Perhaps you should ask him yourself. He's very guarded about the matter," said Ginny.

"If Volker Godeffroy is Matthias's father, who is... Matthias's mother can't be Gwynne Godeffroy, can she?" I asked. I remembered that beautiful, cold, disdainful woman, one of the Gilberts, and her stern husband, and the three Godeffroy girls made in their image. Did they really share the same blood as Matthias?

"Nobody knows who Matthias's mother was. Do you?"

"No, he's never spoken of his parents. We've always assumed that they had passed away. He was brought up by servants, family retainers we'd assumed, alone at Sutton Place."

So many things began to fall into place. Matthias's childhood, the ghost which had stalked him through New York with such unkind intent, his guardedness about discussing the invitation to work in Europe when all other doors in New York had remained stubbornly closed to him... And so many others remained in shadow.

"This does not change anything," Charley said. "Unless you are suggesting that it does? Tilly said that Matthias might be bringing home a sweetheart, remember, Lucia?"

"Does Tilly know something that no one else does?"

"It was speculation. But since you say that Matthias is such a catch, it isn't outside the realm of possibility... But why New York?"

We looked contemplatively towards Matthias again who, perhaps suddenly feeling conscious of our gazes upon him, turned his head, saw us and smiled back, unawares, and then began to disengage himself from his conversational circle to come over to join us.

"What do you two mean to do?" Ginny asked, bringing our talk to safer ground. We followed her lead and steadied our expressions into an assumption of nonchalance.

"Tour the Continent as planned, perhaps lose our way on the Nile and not find our way home. Don't wrinkle your nose, Ginny. You might read all about us next in Cairo. I'm sure the Egyptian press will love us as much as the London ones."

"My dear Trouble, I've no doubt of it," said Ginny.

As to the question of whether Matthias preferred his new home and whether he was making a mistake in choosing to return to New York, Charley, after speculating back and forth since our day of arrival in London, finally decided to take the direct route and asked him:

"Are you happy here in Europe, Matthias?"

"It is a pleasant place. But there are things back in New York— What are you asking, Charley?" Matthias replied warily.

"Very simply whether you are happy with the life you've built here."

"It isn't the same as New York," said Matthias.

No one knew what to say to that.

"There's Lord Mallory," said Charley. "I should go to keep him company. He looks a bit lonely and he was awfully brave this morning to poke the ogre."

And so off Charley flounced, leaving Matthias to stare after her with a bewildered frown. Ginny shook her head. Squeezing blood from a stone,

Ginny's eyes seemed to convey, that was what their conversations had been like recently. Trouble brewing.

"Come on," Ginny said, herding Matthias and me with her back to the crowd at the refreshments tables. "It's about time they cut the wedding cake."

Charley—when I sought her out later—was near the walled border of the rectory vegetable patch, conferring closely and solemnly with Lord Mallory. I slowed down in my approach, not wishing to intrude on them. They looked very different together, a far cry from their earlier incarnation in the midst of the crowd, talking and laughing animatedly about whether those high grim busts on Broad Street of the Roman emperors were the same ones that Mr. Beerbohm had looked upon and written about in his witty Oxford novel; where one found the prettiest of the multi-colored shades of ivy, the pretty russet hues of the tendril vines covering the walls of Kit's Merton Street digs or in the botanic garden; and would one dare to roast and eat the fallen fruit of the sturdy chestnut trees lining the walks and cobbled lanes beneath the dreaming spires; and what fun it was chasing after the adorable squirrels running across Dead Man's Walk and the Broad Walk from Merton Fields to Christ Church meadow in between bouts of cheering on the Rowing Blues (or "Rowed Scholars", as Charley liked to call them) training on the Isis and poking about all the quaint little shops, all of which Charley had done on past visits. Lord Mallory departed after their conference leaving Charley standing, rather forlorn, amongst the cabbages and vegetable marrows and bulbs peeking out of the darkly turned furrows of earth.

I called out and waved to Charley. She looked up, her face brightened when she recognized me, and she climbed over the neat herbaceous borders and came to join me for a turn out of the churchyard and along the green.

"Weren't you keeping Lord Mallory company?" I asked.

"He's gone to take his leave of Tessa and Kit. Has to return back to London soon. Important man, busy, engagements and whatnot."

We made our way beneath the shade of a stone arch that led out of the vegetable garden into the churchyard and through its neatly-tended floral borders to walk in the scent of roses.

"Did you send him off a disappointed man?"

"What?" Charley startled.

"Did you refuse his proposal? Isn't that why Lord Mallory left so soon?"

Charley looked at me as if I had turned into a Coney Island chorus girl. "Lord Mallory did not propose."

"He came down here expressly to bring the congratulations personally from St. James's Palace?"

"That and to wish Kit and Tessa well."

"It was very kind of Lord Mallory."

"Yes."

"He really didn't—"

"No."

We headed towards the edge of the river bank, away from the churchyard endowed with open blooms and rose bushes laden with red-tipped buds and tender green shoots of new growth. Nature was free and wilder here, the numerous dips and depressions of the green scattered with tall grasses and copses. The music and chatter and laughter from the wedding reception faded into a distant bell-like tinkling behind us.

When I taxed Charley about the mysteries Ginny was still puzzling over, Charley, as one would expect, denied everything. I thought she had merely been acting coy. After pressuring her for several rounds, she relented and though she still denied any knowledge of Rupert's delivery to his brother's wedding—Charley said she suspected Matthias—she started chuckling about poor Lord Mallory being forced to step in and behave like an equerry in order to stem the flow of Lord Venables' wrathful tirades. It wanted for imagination and finesse but, as Lord Mallory himself argued in his defense, he had been hard pressed and it had nevertheless done the trick.

"So it was you! However did you manage it? Are you acquainted with his Royal Highness?"

"I met him once," Charley admitted.

Charley had attended a private party at the Ritz with Lord Mallory. "To get our names in the social pages again," she said, an odd and telling thing to say considering the effort she had expended to be invisible. After the obligatory rounds and paying their respects to their hosts, Sir Donald and Lady Joycelyn Erskine, they had made a discreet early getaway. They had been headed for their motor-car and were about to get in when another formally dressed couple came out of the rear entrance and hailed them. The couple had seen Charley and Lord Mallory earlier in the hotel and wondered if they might trouble them in sharing the ride? The couple, it appeared, had also been eager to steal away to more congenial destinations. The couple had turned out to be His Royal Highness The Prince of Wales and the prince's current favorite companion, Mrs. Freda Dudley Ward. His Royal Highness and Mrs. Dudley Ward had chatted quite engagingly with Charley and Lord Mallory. (They had seemed to know all about Charley, the elusive American heiress, and were very taken with Charley's driving skills —yes, she had been driving on the wrong side of the road, it really wasn't too bad, and the Bentley that Babe Barnato had lent her was a dream—no, don't tell Matthias!) The following day, Charley had received a note from the prince's private secretary as well as one from Mrs. Dudley Ward thanking her and Lord Mallory for their kindness and discretion of the preceding evening and inviting them to St. James's Palace.

"Wait, 'Barnato'?—as in Woolf Barnato?—related to the Joels?—heir to the late South African diamond and gold-mining magnate, Barney Barnato? —the Bentley Boy who is the owner and chairman of Bentley Motors?—he lent you a motor-car?"

"Had to pay perfunctory visits to old family friends and associates while in town... Besides, his Bentley was blocking up Grosvenor Square—and my way. He doesn't really have much to do with the Joels after the legal dispute, or even his own Baromans investments business, spends more time breeding horses and throwing lavish motor-racing parties at Ardenrun— yes, the de-facto home for the Bentley Boys, that terrible den of iniquity— and playing first-class cricket with the Surrey County Cricket Club and racing these days. He and W. O.—that is, the great engineer and founder of Bentley Motors, W. O. Bentley—were trying to dissuade me away from a rather distracting Lagonda."

"It's no wonder the Prince of Wales set know all about you! Given the exploits of the Bentley Boys, I'm surprised you haven't featured in the gossip columns more often or had your—but then Aunt Merry doesn't really rain down scalded moral outrage or descend upon rakes with torches and pitchforks to tear nice girls away from their dreadful disreputable clutches, does she? Perhaps Tilly might step into the breach...? But the invitation—what happened?"

Charley shrugged.

"You mean... Tilly didn't mention anything about declining a royal invitation on your behalf."

"I had to write it myself. Discretion and all that."

"Tilly will feel rather cheated if she finds out," I told Charley. "So that was all? Was the note of congratulations a fake then?"

"Oh no, that was real enough. I mentioned Tessa's wedding during the course of the drive from the Ritz. Mrs. Dudley Ward was very kind when I wrote to her and asked if she wouldn't mind... It was a bit presumptuous but I am an American after all, what do I know of British protocol and convention?"

"She's Anglo-American, Charley, she's not a fool."

"Well, she seemed to have taken a liking to me. Or my wild driving, I'm not sure which. Maybe she just wanted to find out the name of my modiste. She admired and complimented me on my raspberry silk tea gown which apparently matched the color of the cocktails they'd been drinking. And I had nothing to lose by trying it on. At any rate, I'm sure it was amongst the most innocuous and boring correspondence that ever passed Sir Alan Lascelles's—that is, the prince's private secretary's—inspection."

"You never had any contact with them after the Ritz? Were they not offended by your declining the invitation? I don't think it's the done thing."

"No, only by a brief correspondence. Where would I find the time for hobnobbing with royalty? I thanked them and apologized. I had pre-existing engagements which, however humble, were I to give them up in favor of seeking a more elevated royal one, would cast my character in a very poor light. In addition, Society and Publicity gave me hives which was what had driven me to run from anything that might throw me in its path. If they were miffed, they must've forgiven me. The congratulatory note is proof of it. I rather think they were sympathetic though. They haven't spoken ill of me or given me the cut direct yet, have they?"

I laughed. "Was all that an euphemism for you finding them dull company?"

"Not at all. Mrs. Dudley Ward was lovely, charming, very amusing, easy to like."

"Only Mrs. Dudley Ward? What about the Prince of Wales?"

Charley paused. "I'm not sure that he's a nice man," she said.

"Charley! What was he like?"

"A bit... I don't know... Frivolous and adolescent. Harmless enough, I suppose."

For Charley, it was an extraordinary assessment to make. I was sure she was aware of the irony that those appellations had been applied to her by Old New York, less deservingly perhaps than the playboy Prince of Wales.

We walked further along the green, edging closer to the sleepy river bank.

"What was Matthias's grandfather like?" I asked Charley.

"Old," said Charley, then laughed. "Distinguished as you would expect of an elderly gentlemen, big and tall like Matthias, softly-spoken but whip-sharp, alert. Now that Ginny has pointed it out, I can see the resemblance, but... I wonder how much he knew..."

"He never made it known? He never hinted at his relation to Matthias?" I asked.

"He hinted that he knew of me. But so many people say that, it really has lost its meaning. I don't know if he knew of me from the papers or if Matthias mentioned his friends to him."

"Was it so bad that he had the advantage over you of knowing who you were?"

"It wasn't... It didn't come up in conversation much. We... It wasn't a social call. It happened quite by chance—at least, I thought it did. I'm not so sure now... If he knew who I was... Mr. Grenfell introduced me to him almost in passing and we had a brief conversation. Looking back, perhaps he had been assessing me. I'm not sure I came up to scratch, not in the way you impressed Mr. Grenfell. Matthias's grandfather has bushy silvery eyebrows, you see, which are quite intimidating. It may be just as well that I didn't know who he was or else I would've been scared witless."

"What were you... Is this one of those things I'm not to pry into yet?"

Charley nodded apologetically.

"Do you think he is influencing Matthias to stay or go? The disinheritance of Matthias's father is quite... There's a great deal we don't know about Matthias's family history, isn't there? Do you think Matthias wants to go back to New York to confront his father?"

"I don't know. That would be an enormous temptation. If Volker and Gwynne Godeffroy are Matthias's parents, well, they are as heartless as they come. They could've made his life in New York so different but they didn't lift a finger to help Matthias, didn't acknowledge him at all. Quite the reverse, in fact. The thing is," Charley said, "there's no reason why they should both have refused to acknowledge Matthias as their own. They stopped trying for a male heir after the third daughter if you believe the gossip, which means, if Volker is Albrecht Matthias Godeffroy's only child, it'll be a great scandal when New York hears—and Volker Godeffroy will deserve every single sordid second of the infamy and disgrace."

"I was thinking about that too. It never occurred to me to wonder before who looked after Matthias when he was growing up—financially, I mean. He didn't seem to want for anything in that respect."

"Yes, exactly. Follow the money. I suppose it was his grandfather."

"Do you think the Godeffroy girls knew about Matthias—that they had a—well, a half-brother?"

"If it was the scandal we suspect, I don't think Volker and Gwynne Godeffroy would've told anyone, including their children. A lesser guilt hasn't made the Godeffroy girls more pleasant than their parents—in general and to Matthias in particular. You would've witnessed this for yourself. The sisters weren't wanting for opportunity or time to extend the olive branch. Look at Rupert Tremaine, a boy still in school, expressly forbidden and prevented from seeing his brother, but he still... Well, each to their own, I suppose. It's not my place to express reproach or otherwise about the Godeffroys when Matthias has never said a word about it."

"I wonder if Vandermeer is Matthias's mother's name."

"I've been going through all of Old New York in my head and can't find anyone who might answer to the requirements."

"I feel bad for speculating like this. I feel worse for Matthias. Can you imagine the talk in New York?"

"I'm not sure that it matters very much to Matthias. Not anymore at least. I mean, he's lived with worse for years. They could hardly treat him worse than before, can they? Or maybe insincere sycophancy would be worse?"

"A victory of sorts."

"It would be a hollow victory. Or a hollow revenge. They can't give back to him all the years they treated him so horribly. Knowing his father will be swallowing the bitter pill might be enough... I don't know." She blinked several times, looking rather bleakly at the trees and grasses and verdure surrounding us.

The river murmured softly as it glided by as if chattering to Debussy's Deux arabesques. I almost expected Rat and Mole and Badger to come ambling through the wistful curtains of the weeping willows beside us and then for the tranquility to be suddenly broken by the brazen tooting of "Poop-poop-poop!" to herald the glittering vision of plate-glass and rich morocco—and, of course, Charley would step into the magnificent motor-car and drive off, singing:

"The world has held great Heroes,
        As history-books have showed;
    But never a name to go down to fame
        Compared with that of Toad!
    'The clever men at Oxford
        Know all that there is to be knowed.
    But they none of them know one half as much
        As intelligent Mr.—"

"Did you bring it up with Matthias?"

"Did I...?"

"After Tessa and Kit cut the wedding cake, I saw Matthias with you." Ginny and I had both noticed the shift in Charley from her earlier exuberant warmth to cool, friendly civility. This bout of moodiness could not have escaped Matthias.

Charley's cheeks pinkened. "I never mentioned anything to him about that. If he doesn't wish to volunteer the information, I'm not going to pry. It doesn't change anything."

"He would have brought it up himself if he wanted us to know," I agreed. "I wonder when Matthias found out."

"Trying to answer that only makes Volker and Gwynne Godeffroy appear more hateful."

"If you didn't ask Matthias about his grandfather and parents, what were you both talking about so intently?"

"His intentions."

"To return to New York?"

A hardness came into Charley's eyes. "I think he should stay here. There's nothing waiting for him in New York."

"Please, Charley, no lies."

Charley looked away towards the susurrant reeds and bulrushes swaying in accord with the drowsy willows. "He's happy here. Liked, respected, welcomed. He's made a life here. What is there in New York besides the old resentments and tormentors and the opportunity for revenge in rubbing his father's and everyone else's nose in it? We want to keep Matthias from being dragged down to their level, don't we? We don't want his soul to be tainted with any more of what he has already endured? Isn't being happy the best revenge?"

"This is what Matthias wishes?—you've consulted him and managed to change his mind to stay?"

"And leave him with the burden of choosing what he thinks he ought to do—what he thinks best serves others—serves justice or us or whatever else he thinks is a higher consideration—rather than himself? Not this time, not in this. Staying is the better choice. He can sail over to New York anytime to visit and say hello to his friends, or vice versa. But he's better served in staying here."

"Matthias wouldn't like it—he would be very angry with you, Charley—for deciding without him."

"Let him be angry with me, so long as he is happy."

We stood together on the level ground, above the gently undulating carpet of green dipping towards the church, observing the lively wedding reception in the distance. The trees whispered around us, stirred by a faint breeze, as though conspiring.

Presently, Charley turned to me and said: "The wedding cake was delicious, wasn't it? I'm going to get another slice. Do you want one?"

I watched Charley leave. I dallied alone for another long stretch in the quiescent greenery. After a time, a figure emerged from the wedding reception throng and came up the mild slope towards me. It was Matthias.

"What are you doing here on your own, Lucia?"

"Communing with nature." A solitude of space/

A solitude of sea, I remembered Charley had once told Tilly.

Matthias laughed. "Ginny is asking after you," he said. "Have you seen Charley?"

"Charley has gone to steal some more wedding cake," I told Matthias.

I descended the green with Matthias towards the wedding crowd. Matthias looked about the refreshments tables for her person but could not see her. Of course he would not have. When Charley left, she had gone in the opposite direction to the crowd gathered at those tables, climbing the path away from the walled churchyard towards the lychgate and the road.

O, what a tangled web we weave when first we practice to deceive!

There was another round of toasts being made at the refreshments table (we had all lost count after the official toasts accompanying the cutting of the wedding cake). Tilly still held Rupert and the curate transfixed with her Wimbledon tales. Some of the children had begun a game of cricket on the lawn. Things had settled down a bit, Ginny said, and Tessa and Kit were finally being afforded some peace to eat their own wedding cake.

Tessa beamed and said it was delicious. Kit agreed, adding that it did not matter what the cake actually tasted of, it was his wedding cake, of course it was damned well going to be delicious.

One of the younger Hartleys ran up and said another guest had come. Ginny rolled her eyes as the new arrival appeared, coming down the gravel path. Tessa and Kit put down their forks and plates and went to welcome him. The man congratulated the newly-weds, apologizing for his unfortunate late arrival owing to a bad transport connection on his journey down. He exchanged warm and familiar greetings with Ginny and Matthias. Lord Ruthven shook his hand and said: "Faneuil, good to see you. I hope your fiancée, Lady Georgiana, is well?"

"She is very well, thank you."

"Lucia, you remember Mr. Vincent Faneuil? He was at Ginny's wedding last year," Tessa said.

"Pleased to meet you again on this happy day, Mr. Faneuil," I said.

"The pleasure is all mine," he said. He took my hand as he had done with the others in turn. His grip and his gaze were warm.

He was offered wedding cake and told of all the dramas and wonderful gifts which had attended the wedding.

As he was plied with cake and attention and everyone was engaged in the freely flowing conversation, I excused myself quietly to Ginny, and went to find Charley, hoping she had not left.

As it happened, I found Charley sooner and more easily than I thought I would. She was close by. I recognized her dark, sleek bob and the swish of her ruthlessly stylish tubular fluted silk frock, shimmering with beaded frivolity and loveliness, and her nimble steps. She was coming down the trellis-covered way woven with flowering vines and jasmine, switching from time to time at windblown cascades of stray blossoms and floating petals and foliage with her delicate meringue of a cloche hat in a humor that was less lackadaisical and more like that of a fractious child attacking inanimate things with an aimless pique. Charley paused mid-step when she saw me.

"What's the matter, Charley?"

"Nothing. Why?"

"Are you sure?"

"Yes. Should something be the matter?"

"Charley, is there anything, or anyone, that would keep you here, in the immediate future? Is there any chance—"

Charley's eyes had grown round like saucers, however she replied with perfectly droll lightness and composure: "Bored of England already, Lucia? I'm ready to flee right now if you wish it."

"I'm eager to start our Grand Tour sooner than planned if that wouldn't put—"

Charley put a stop to my reservations. "We're on our way."

What a wonderful conspirator Charley proved to be! She was as good as her word, a swift whirlwind in commandeering every means and arrangement and discretion necessary for our premature flight. I did not know what she told Ginny, much less anyone else, but we were shepherded out around the back of the churchyard to an awaiting cab at the postern gate as soon as Tessa and Kit had passed through the ebullient showers of cheers and rice to the waiting Rolls-Royce Phantom II Continental, which was to take them on to their honeymoon, and tossed the bride's bouquet into the squealing crowd in their wake.

"My dear, lovely chums, my sweet partners in crime, it has been too, too brief a visit for it to already be time to say farewell! May the gods bless you and keep you naughty and bring you back again soon!" Ginny embraced and kissed us both and waved us off.

I remember our flight from Oxford to the French coast as a blur. Perhaps it had been merely an extension of Charley's impressive whirlwind, spreading charm and money and chutzpah around like, well, the archetypal overbearing American (except, I imagined, Charley used more charm and money to camouflage and sweeten the chutzpah). We motored back to London at great speed. Charley wrangled three first-class tickets on the Golden Arrow, the recently introduced Southern Railways all-first-class service between London Victoria and Dover; two of these we used to board the mustard and maroon British Pullman carriage at London Victoria, the third Charley had delivered to the Savoy for Tilly to follow us to Paris in due course.

The Golden Arrow took us through rolling English fields to the Dover Marine docks where we caught an afternoon ferry across the English Channel to Calais Maritime and from Calais Ville proceeded on the Flèche d'Or passing through northern France via Lille and directly on to Paris Gare du Nord.

I had no idea who was displaced or bribed handsomely to give up those seats on the Golden Arrow. Wood-paneled interiors inlaid with decorated marquetry and gilt fittings, thickly carpeted floors, plush curtains at each window, a parlor car furnished with upholstered, free standing armchairs, each one facing another across a table for two, a cocktail bar, a public address system in both English and French, electric lighting, steam heating and air-conditioning, the bocage landscape of northern France flying by past our windows—such luxuries and novelties were ours, blurred into a muted background, measuring out the passing of time and distance against Charley's amiable pleasantries and speculation over the speed of the locomotive compared to the speed of an automobile (she was confident that she could coax a Bentley to beat that train and Babe Barnato could bite her dust!) and her determination not to press me to talk and her insistence that I do justice to the fine afternoon tea on board. Between dozing and waking, the melancholic wail of Louis Armstrong singing "St. James

Infirmary Blues" followed me, attending the rattling of the train carriages and the call of the gulls and the churning of the waves. I must have heard it somewhere—had the band played it at the wedding reception?—Charley was a fan of Louis Armstrong as were the Hartleys—but I have no impression of it from that journey apart from its lyrics and plaintive melody swimming about between my ears.

"I went down to St. James Infirmary,
Saw my baby there,
Stretched out on a long white table,
So cold, so sweet, so fair.
Let her go, let her go, God bless her,
Wherever she may be,
She can look this wide world over,
But she'll never find a sweet man like me..."

Charley and I reached Paris as the moon rose.

15

CHARLOTTE:

It was not in Lucia's nature to be histrionic. She had a horror of the unnecessary and gratuitous emotional excesses in which many girls indulged —that is, when we were not laughing at their silliness.

True distress in many respects was not easy to recognize in Lucia for she preferred to hide her sadness and woes, but if there was ever any hint or suspicion of distress about her person or particular circumstances, only a fool would have thought it a trifle, Lucia was not a girl who cried wolf.

A year ago, when Virginia May Amaryllis Hartley wed Rex Edgar Marchmont, 15th Earl Ruthven, Tessa had pointed out one of the groom's friends to us. His name was Vincent Faneuil. He was in banking and also knew Matthias. That was what had recommended him to us: he was Matthias's friend.

"Isn't he dreamy?" exclaimed Tessa.

"Oh, he's a magnificent specimen of a man," had been my contribution to the conversation.

Oh, wasn't he, Tessa had gushed in admiration, he was beautifully made, on the grand scale, and perfectly proportioned. Lucia had reminded Tessa that Tessa and Kit were walking out together. Tessa had giggled in response and invoked the artist's prerogative to appreciate beauty in all forms.

Except it had been Lucia that Vincent Faneuil had approached to ask for a dance. When Lucia and I returned to New York, that, I thought, had been the end of it. A brief summer affair was the most it could have been, if there had been anything at all. There had been no mention of him since. Lucia, after the Nate Knowle affair, did not readily or rashly form lasting attachments.

Twelve months on, at another Hartley nuptials, I saw the man alight from his motor-car as I was returning back from my walk. Vincent Faneuil was as tall and fair and dashing as he had been a year ago. He was dressed immaculately in a morning suit, shoes, hat, gloves and buttonhole in perfect order, and he walked confidently and without haste despite the hour. He snagged a passing Hartley to ask for directions and was soon led to the wedding reception tables and the newly-wed couple. He exchanged greetings with Tessa and Kit, Matthias, Ginny, Lord Ruthven, and Lucia. I was not near enough to hear what they were saying. The pleasantries had all appeared very agreeably commonplace, the renewal of acquaintance very friendly and welcoming. Cake was pressed upon him which he accepted good-humoredly.

When I saw Lucia frozen in place next to Ginny amongst this happy circle, so still and small, like a trapped animal that curls in upon itself in the hope that a predator will not notice its presence and pass on by, I knew that the hour had come.

Lucia gradually drew her eyes away from Lord Ruthven upon whom her gaze had been fixed, avoiding the glances of consternation darting her way from Matthias. She waited for an opportune moment and then quietly excused herself, and walked at a swift but unhurried pace back towards the church porch.

I was underneath the covered walk, standing around in the mottled shade, still dithering about whether I should run away to hide and give her privacy or not, when Lucia approached. She seemed relieved to find me.

Lucia said: "Charley, have you concluded your business? Is there anything that needs keep you in London or England?"

"Not a thing."

"Are you sure? You're not simply humoring me?"

I repeated my assurances.

Still hesitant, haltering in awkwardness and embarrassment and wordless pain, Lucia said: "Then may I ask a favor? We were not due for Paris right away but I have a sudden hankering for—"

"We'll be in France by nightfall, I promise. I'll go fetch—"

"Charley, we don't have to go right this minute! We'll miss seeing off Tessa and Kit!"

"Everything will be taken care of, Lucia. Don't worry. We'll be ready to go the moment the newly-wed Tremaines ride off into the sunset."

"Oh, well, all right, if you think it won't cause too much fuss... Oh, Charley, if you wouldn't also mind—please, don't tell Matthias just yet?"

"Your feet will touch Calais before anyone hears about it."

I had already put plans of departure in motion before I returned from my walk. There were only a few things left to arrange before we could dash away. Ginny was understanding and did not ask many questions, promising to relay our apologies and regards, and to give Tilly my directions (Lucia and I did not want to spoil Tilly's enjoyment prematurely, she would have fled with us out of loyalty and concern).

When the time came, neither of us looked back.

ET IN ARCADIA EGO

August 1929, Paris–Blois–French Riviera

16

LUCIA:

In Paris, we seemed always to be in motion.

On the flimsy pretext that we had brought no luggage and needed clothes to tide us over until Tilly arrived, Charley dragged me to Parisian modistes with a zest she had never exhibited in London. She drew me along to the Vionnet boutique on Avenue Montaigne, where she was welcomed with great warmth. (Mademoiselle, according to the vendeuse, was a dear client of its Fifth Avenue boutique in New York City.) She dragged me to the Babani boutique on Boulevard Haussmann for Fortuny's hand-pleated silk Delphos gowns whose artistry Marcel Proust had expounded in his magnum opus. (Wouldn't Tilly love these—and Aunt Merry too?) To Jean Patou for tennis dresses. To the ateliers of Louise Chéruit (Proust mentioned her too), Georges Doeuillet, Jacques Doucet, Paul Poiret (what a pity the Galerie Barbazanges and Poiret's Salon d'Antin exhibitions, readings and performances of Picasso, Modigliani, Gauguin, Matisse, Chagall, Dufy, Max Jacob, Guillaume Apollinaire, Satie, Darius Milhaud, Stravinsky, Georges Auric et al were no more!), Jeanne Paquin (did I remember that reference in Mrs. Wharton's The House of Mirth?), Redfern & Sons, Callot Soeurs (the silver dress worn by American socialite Rita de Acosta Lydig in her Giovanni Boldini portrait was a Callot Soeurs creation), and Charles Worth—on the rue de la Paix and Place Vendôme and rue de Rivoli and Avenue Matignon—many of whose designs had been featured between the pages of Vogue and the fashion journal La Gazette du Bon Ton—Parisian couturiers who lived in the present age but whose hearts dreamed of the Belle Époque. Charley led us to the Augusta Bernard and Lanvin boutiques on the rue du Faubourg Saint-Honoré (as if Charley did not own enough beautiful Lanvin frocks). And then suggested we step, for just a moment, just out of curiosity, inside the fashion house of Edward Molyneux, who regularly dressed European royalty and Hollywood's trendsetting actresses with his impeccably refined simplicity, at 5 rue Royale. We were distracted for another mere moment when Charley ordered a few items in the garconne style from the Coco Chanel boutique at the rue de Cambon (not surprisingly, a more interesting selection than that available at Henry Bendel's on Fifth Avenue). And then proceeded to order a great many more from Maison Premet, a favorite of the French nobility, renowned for its perfectionism and creation of the original La Garconne black dress (named after Victor Marguerite's sensational novel) not the Haas Brothers copies, discussing each gown intently in halting French and gestures with the chief modelist, Mme. Revyl, and her assistant, Mlle Alix Krebs.

"Tilly will be relieved to know you have recovered a serious interest in fashion," I told Charley as she stood frozen in position while Mlle Krebs carefully draped folds of silk jersey about her form, making Charley resemble a Greco-Roman statue.

"Don't most women consider fashion to be armor?" Charley shrugged. "Or disguise?"

During the day, we also visited Napolean's apartments and viewed exquisite sculptures and paintings and tapestries and antiquities at the Louvre and Musée du Luxembourg and Jeu de Paume and Musée de l'Orangerie and Musée de Cluny, whose Lady and the Unicorn medieval tapestry cycle reminded me of the six Hunt of the Unicorn tapestries, purchased by John D. Rockefeller, Jr. in 1922, which hung in his New York home (the remaining fragments apparently retained by the La Rochefoucauld family). We strolled through the Jardin des Tuileries. We wandered amongst the collection of drawings, photographs, objets d'art, paintings by Van Gogh, Monet, Renoir, and Rodin sculptures in the gardens—with the view of the golden dome of the Invalides in the background—of Hôtel Biron in the rue de Varenne, where Auguste Rodin had once rented some ground floor rooms to use as a workshop, and which had been turned since his death into the Musée Rodin. (Charley drew me to the room full of works even more vehemently turbulent than the ones we had seen elsewhere in the museum—the cast of The Waltz and the marble Sakuntala mesmerized the eye, like a Michelangelo or an Artemisia Gentileschi, as The Kiss had not—these were the works of Camille Claudel, Charley said, who had been Rodin's muse, lover, and co-sculptor sans credit on such pieces as The Gates of Hell, much admired by Debussy with whom she may or may not have had an affair, a genius like Berthe Morisot, the only well-known female painter of the 19th century, Claudel had died in loneliness, poverty, and obscurity.) We squinted up at the 13th century façade and flying buttresses of Notre-Dame and, inspired by the magnificence and gravity and serenity of its exterior and interior, gazed up in wonder at the soaring vaulted ceiling and the echoing stonework and steles and pietas and frescoes and chapels and organ and the sunlight streaming through the rows and rows of beautiful stained glass windows, and climbed up the tower stairs to share the unrivaled city views from the roof with the stone gargoyles watching over Paris. We made our way through the crush of the pavements and browsed through the grand magasins of Galeries Lafayette and Printemps with ordinary Parisians where we ordered a good quantity of gifts to be dispatched to the Bommels for the approaching wedding and then, notwithstanding the couture she had ordered for us both, Charley went on to purchase two very plain outfits which rendered her quite nondescript—I knew by now not to ask why, it was clear enough that this was a uniform of incognito. We loitered in the bookshop Shakespeare and Company at 12 rue de l'Odéon run by the American Sylvia Beach who had published James Joyce's Ulysses which was banned and burned in New York. (Charley, of course, bought a copy—was Montrose's vast library not already home to many such works, a repository of dangerous ideas, the great and beautiful and seditious, a sanctuary to flammable, ruinous, magnificent knowledge?—along with a volume of poètes maudits and Colette and Paul Valéry.) We climbed to the summit of the Sacré Coeur for the panoramic view of the rooftops across the famous, but now passé, artist's quarter of Montmartre.

As the sun set, we sought out the city's joie de vivre, roaming the cobbled streets to an indeterminate destination. We dined at cafes and brasseries and bars in the newly fashionable artist's quarter of Montparnasse on the Rive Gauche. We visited the cabarets and dance halls and nightclubs on the Rive Droit where we saw Josephine Baker and Mistinguett perform at the Folies Bergère (the façade of the building redone in Art Deco style by Maurice Pico in 1926) and Broadway star Adelaide Hall at the Moulin Rouge. We watched Serge Lifar and the Ballet Russes dance Prokofiev's Le Fils prodigue at the Opéra de Paris. (It had been superlative, but Charley was a little disappointed that it had not been the premiere of Maurice Ravel's Boléro.) We sat through ten minutes of a play by French dramatist Jean Giraudoux at the Comédie des Champs-Élysées (it was a sign of our distraction that it had not occurred to either of us until the curtains rose up that our rusty French might not be up to scratch to follow the performance) before repairing to Harry's New York Bar at 5 rue Daunou which seemed to be frequented by an American expatriate crowd going to town on the varied cocktails. (We preferred the French 75 to the absinthe-tinted Monkey Gland.) George Gershwin, we were told, had composed An American in Paris there—Charley said its Carnegie Hall premiere was marvelous—but didn't that mean that she had actually been in New York on December 13, 1928 and not in Bar Harbor? There seemed, in fact, to be a lot of Americans in Paris partaking of the bohemian charm and exuberance and gaiety of spirits everywhere in the city. We floated through this atmosphere in the same spirit, shielded by a sense of submerging, unremarkable and unremarked, into the multitudinous crowds, keeping our anonymity. This was easy to do in one respect. No more grand social whirl or glamorous parties or introductions to members of the cercle de l'Union interalliée or invitations to cocktails at the American consulate for us in Paris under a trained eye. We were straying from the original intent of our Grand Tour. We were interlopers in the artistic crowd. If it had not been for a wire from Charley's friends at Yaddo (in place of the letters of introduction which Tilly brought with her a few days later), we should not have been given entry into the Saturday evening salon at 27 rue de Fleurus held by Gertrude Stein ("Don't mention Hemingway, they've quarreled and fallen out," Charley warned) and her companion Alice Tokias. We did not actually end up having to mingle all evening with the daunting talents of modern literature and art brought together by Miss Stein, no, we were entertained in another room comprising a gathering, hosted by Miss Tokias with delicious cake and tea and fragrant colorless liqueurs which tasted of the fruits from which they were distilled, of the wives and lady friends of the talents, an arrangement which allowed us a smaller window within which to disgrace ourselves by revealing our gauche ignorance and lack of literary or artistic talent and our execrably faltering French. "Did you ever think you would travel to Paris to be segregated like in Old New York? Would it have been fatal, so disgracefully heinous, for genius to be exposed to a bit of village idiocy?" Charley giggled afterwards. We did see a lot of marvelous art though: paintings by Henri Manguin, Pierre Bonnard, Pablo Picasso—whom we briefly met that evening—Paul Cézanne, Pierre-Auguste Renoir, Honoré Daumier, Henri Matisse (what a pity he was not here but invited to America to sit on the jury of the 29th Carnegie International exhibition), Henri de Toulouse-Lautrec...

In later years, when we came across a book or painting or composition, or someone mentioned a familiar-sounding name, I felt an odd jolt in connecting the creation to the man to whom we had been introduced in the Stein salon. When in a mischievous or perverse mood, Charley would remark that she preferred the work to the man—excepting Paul Valéry, who was married to a niece of Berthe Morisot, and Colette whom Charley regretted never having met though both had been resident in Paris at the time and moved in the circles of the Comtesse Anna de Noailles, a friend of the Margravine Anne-Louise von Baden-Pforzheim—but Charley did refrain from making up stories about them as she had done with Mr. Cole Porter.

The experience with the Stein salon led us to shy away from the other salons as much as the homes of sociable hostesses around the city, many of which were maintained by American expatriates, such as Natalie Clifford Barney's salon in Neuilly, where the entertainment included new paintings by Marie Laurencin and poetry readings and theatricals in which Mata Hari and Colette had once performed and Peggy Guggenheim (of the wealthy New York City Guggenheims, bohemian daughter of Benjamin Guggenheim who went down with the RMS Titanic) was a regular. Showing up there, possibly accidentally running into someone who knew us or those connected to those we knew in New York amongst all the interesting people at the salons, would have ended that precious anonymity and announced ourselves to the world.

"It is not given to every man to take a bath of multitude: to play upon crowds is an art; and he alone can plunge, at the expense of humankind, into a debauch of vitality, to whom a fairy has bequeathed in his cradle the love of masks and disguises, the hate of home and the passion for roaming.

Multitude, solitude: two equal and interchangeable terms for the active and creative poet. He who does not know how to populate his solitude, will not know how to be alone in the bustling crowd."

Everywhere we roamed in the French capital, even from the windows of our hotel suite, we glimpsed the Eiffel Tower on the horizon, a sturdy gray metronome piercing an overcast sky or a taciturn sentinel in the darkness like the glowering Notre-Dame gargoyles, the needle at the center of our compass.

I was not sure why Charley felt she had to fill every moment with activity. Her stamina was as boundless as ever, but, as it had been in London, her enthusiasm seemed to taper off sporadically, at times mechanical and distracted. Did she feel that she consulted my needs in trying to plug every waking hour with new sights and experiences to escape facing the landscape within, or was she also considering her own, replacing those endless card games on board the RMS Mauretania with this new game of perpetual motion? Perhaps it had something to do with the telegram that had arrived on the second evening in Paris. Poor Charley, forever being hounded by telegrams. We checked out of the glamorous Ritz Hotel that night and moved into the comparably decadent Louis XVI style dowager duchess of Le Meurice on the rue de Rivoli under the name of Elyot. "More private and closer to the Jardin des Tuileries anyway," Charley said, "and we'll also have a pretty view of the gardens from our suite." (The upstarts had looked promising but... George V on avenue George V was continuously filled with Americans descended from transatlantic steamers, God forbid we should run into someone who knew us... Hôtel Le Bristol at

112 rue du Faubourg Saint Honoré was too close to the tempting boutiques... Hotel Plaza Athénée at 25 avenue Montaigne was nice but, well, did it have a grand salon Pompadour with white trimmings or a restaurant with marble pilasters and gilded bronzes in tribute to the Treaty of Versailles or a wrought iron canopy over the lobby or an elevator that was a replica of the sedan chair used by Marie Antoinette? No, Le Meurice it had to be, serving us with as much refined discretion as it had served high society and dignitaries and royalty since the 19th century.)

Charley turned up one morning in a Chanel day dress, leather helmet, gloves, and a gray scarf, at the wheel of a beautiful green Bugatti—lovely, cool, independent, untouchable—and beckoned to me to get in.

"We're going to Blois," she said.

Charley had spoken of so many schemes and peregrinations as we criss-crossed the city on foot or emerged from the bowels of the underground into the sunshine through the distinctive green cast iron Art Nouveau "lily-of-the-valley" Metro station entrances designed by Hector Guimard. Charley painted such beautiful dreams. There were innumerable possibilities before us, so many worlds to discover and explore whilst touring abroad: we might head to Rome first and then, taking the classical route to Greece, divide our time between German spas or Swiss resorts... Or loiter awhile in France, going to the races at Longchamp on the way to Bois de Boulogne... Or travel through the Pyrenees, perhaps trek to Spain and see the 16th century El Escorial and its legendary library... Or wander even further, following the trail of scallop shells, along the Camino de Santiago pilgrimage to Cape Finisterre to stand at the edge of the world and gaze upon the wild Mare Tenebrosum, the Sea of Darkness... Or drop in to Biarritz to see what the fuss was about—stay at the Hôtel du Palais, built originally as a summer villa for the Empress Eugénie... Or pay a visit to the seaside resorts of Le Touquet or Deauville—Margravine Anne-Louise von Baden-Pforzheim had spoken of an haras there owned by an uncle of hers who was of a like mind to Louis Henri I, Duke of Bourbon, Prince of Condé, who believed he would be reincarnated as a horse... Or take a cab to Gare de l'Est and jump on the Orient Express to Vienna or take the Simplon Orient Express to Venice—float about in gondolas, tour Italy, see Florence and Rome and mess about with funiculars and views in the lake district heading up to Switzerland, take in Lucerne, Interlaken, journey over the Wengern Alp and up the great Jungfrau, see Berne—or head all the way to Constantinople to search for attar of roses and drink lots of mint tea and eat lots of Turkish Delight in the Grand Bazaar... Charley had been so unfailingly eager, so like a giddy child, face pressed to the window of a French pâtisserie, ogling the wonders of couverture and crème Chantilly and marrons glacés within, that I did not think she would actually go through with the drive to Blois.

"What's in Blois?" I asked, holding fast onto my hat while the countryside flew past to the purr of the Bugatti's engine under her reins.

"A royal château and bloody history and pretty views and luncheon," Charley replied, engaging the forward gear to plunge us into a tunnel of dappled sunlight beneath the linden trees, "away from the Parisian-American crowds."

Charley meant well, but she was wrong.

17

CHARLOTTE:

In 1889, George Washington Vanderbilt II, the youngest child of William Henry Vanderbilt and Maria Louisa (née Kissam) Vanderbilt, began the construction of a 250-room mansion in Asheville, North Carolina, for a summer estate which he named Biltmore. Vanderbilt and his architect, Richard Morris Hunt, took for their model the Château de Blois and other châteaux of the Loire Valley, and then finished it with the icing of American baronial opulence.

"How do you think it compares to Biltmore?" Lucia asked when we arrived at the Château de Blois.

The château appeared spare from a distance and grew steadily and undeniably more grandiose on approach (564 rooms and 75 staircases, filled with ornately decorated floors and ceilings, tapestries, sculptures, paintings and ornaments, only 23 of which were used frequently). It was regally situated above a hilltop with views of the city skyline and famous cathedral and the Loire river. The legacy of Blois' history and intrigues and political prominence as a royal court and favored stronghold seeped deep into the very earth and air. Biltmore was impressive but it strove for its magnificence. Blois was the least visually imposing of the Loire Valley châteaux, more like a grand country mansion, and yet its understated majesty had an arrogance of its own, an acknowledgment of power, like a monarch who need only walk into a room for it to hush. A mounted Louis XII and his emblem, a crowned porcupine, stood above the entrance to the château with the motto: qui s'y frotte s'y pique. Cross swords with me at your peril. There was no contest when we wound beneath the shadow of the château on the peak of the steep cliff-face, up a road wrapped around a tremendous Atlas cedar and reached the stately red brick and gray stone façade of the Château de Blois—an illustration of the evolution of French architecture from the Middle Ages to the 17th century, from flamboyant Gothic in the profiles of moldings, the lobed arches and the pinnacles, to elements of the classical and the Renaissance, reflecting its character as royal residence and fortress—and stepped over the same echoing flagstones of the central courtyard that the French kings and queens had walked across, breathed the air in the rooms and wings where they had lived (and died, of natural and unnatural causes) and from which they had ruled the kingdom, and touched the bricks and stones that had heard Joan of Arc in 1429 being blessed by the Archbishop of Reims before departing with her army to drive the English from Orléans.

"I will say this," I told Lucia, "Biltmore is more comfortable, with all the modern amenities installed, and probably less drafty. It has a good library and collection of artwork and, as far as I know, no one was assassinated by the king's Forty-five guardsmen there. Aunt Merry always did prefer the gardens though."

Lucia smiled indulgently upon my impertinence as she wandered away from the terrace battlements and shaded garden surrounding the remnants of the 13th century Tour de Foix and the sweeping views across the Loire and the church of Saint Nicholas and the old town on the opposite bank, and back across the courtyard to climb the steps of the grand polygonal open ceremonial staircase, covered with fine bas-relief sculptures and motifs of fire-breathing salamanders, its white loggias spanning the full height of the mansard roof and protruding from the façade of the François I wing, which looked out onto the château's central court.

I lingered in the shade of the trees. It was open and breezy and quiet and pleasant there: next to a sturdy feudal watchtower, a former royal residence behind me, the sky and a city and the flow of the river ahead. The waters above, the firmament below... Next to me stood the Saint Calais chapel, which had once been the private place of worship for Louis XII and Anne of Brittany, tucked behind the Louis XII wing of the château. It, too, was deserted and peaceful, filled with an unostentatious splendor, the beauty of its gilded vaulted ceilings and stained glass windows in harmony with the rest of the château and its environs. In this simple, quiet place, I felt a helpless and inexplicable urge to weep.

I came out from the Saint Calais Chapel. The loggias of the circular staircase stood before me across the central court. A man's retreating back was disappearing up into the winding staircase, his rapid footfalls on the stone echoing dully over the courtyard. Something about his build and Savile Row London cut suit... Was that—

"Charley."

I turned my head away from the base of the staircase to find Matthias's eyes upon me.

For a long moment, we stared at each other.

Then Matthias said: "You told me that Lucia wasn't feeling well and that you were taking her away from the wedding crowd to some peace and quiet, not that you were spiriting her away to Paris."

That shook me out of my stunned daze. I found my voice: "What exactly is your accusation? Do you go about feeling affronted and accusing every lady of untruthfulness when they say they need to go powder their noses?"

"That is not—"

"Lucia never asks for favors, Matthias. Never. But she asked me if we might not leave for our Grand Tour a bit earlier. I may not have heard what was said but I was there. I recognized Vincent Faneuil. I saw her face. Be thankful we only crossed the Channel and not an ocean."

"I'm at fault," Matthias said. "I should have—"

"Why exactly do you think you are at fault?"

"It was through me that he knew Lucia was to be present at the wedding. He took me into his confidence and asked for my help."

"That was a gross miscalculation on your part. What could possibly have misled you to help someone who would drive Lucia to flee?"

Matthias winced and apologized. "It was a misunderstanding."

"A mis— That is a dismal excuse! Did he come with you? Was that Vincent Faneuil that I saw vanishing up the staircase?"

"Yes, we came—Charley, wait!—stop!—hold on a minute!"

"Let me go, Matthias! What is the matter with you? Is his friendship worth more to you than Lucia's? If you won't help, fine, but don't stand in my way. He upset Lucia once. I'm not letting that happen again. Wasn't Nate Knowle enough punishment for a lifetime?"

"Charley—stop—listen! Vincent answered Ruthven in the way he did so that his engagement to Lucia would remain a secret."

"What?"

"Lucia didn't tell you?"

"I told you, I was too far away to hear a word, and I've given Lucia her privacy. All I know is that Lucia is hurt and your friend Vincent Faneuil is responsible."

"I'm sorry—Charley!—please!—listen—just for a moment—let me explain. It shouldn't have happened like that. Vincent was held up talking to Kit and Tessa and then Lucia slipped away before I could speak to her, and then you came and said Lucia wasn't feeling well, so I waited, and then you and Lucia were gone. Out of the country! Mallory didn't even know where you were."

"What has Lord Mallory to do with this?"

"He brought the prince's message at your behest, didn't he? The only reason he was at the wedding was you. And he left early. And then you and

Lucia were gone—"

"Why would I bother Lord Mallory about this business with Lucia?"

"Isn't he..." Matthias flushed.

"You are an idiot, Matthias Vandermeer!"

"I am," he grumbled, "but it wasn't an unreasonable conclusion—"

"If you or Vincent Faneuil are looking for an apology, you aren't going to find one."

"That's not what I meant, Charley. I'm just—" Matthias shook his head like a clumsy, sore-headed bear. "I'm sorry. I wish it had happened differently. Will you stay a moment now so that I may explain the situation to you?"

"You're asking me to leave Lucia alone up there, at that man's mercy? This is the extent of your friendship now?" I glared at Matthias. "Easier to ask for forgiveness than to ask for permission?"

Matthias sighed. "You're right. I'm sorry. Let's go."

As soon as he let go, I charged beneath the royal salamanders on the mantel at the base of the staircase. Matthias made an unhappy second, but I had little sympathy to spare for him. The chastened apology in Matthias's pained brown eyes and his swift assumption of another's guilt irked me. "Lucia isn't blaming you. She knows you're his friend, if she thought anything, she would imagine that you were trying to do something kind." We ascended the smooth stone steps at far too slow a pace for my taste: I had not Matthias's long-legged stride but he was still a step or two below me. "I'm not so forgiving."

Matthias again proffered his regrets and—

"Not at you. You were just being an idiot, I assume, thinking kindly of everyone instead of questioning their motives. What kind of man, who has convinced Lucia to a secret engagement, goes off and leaves her in limbo for a year? At least I presume it's been a year and not longer. It happened at Ginny's wedding, didn't it?"

Vincent Faneuil had been engaged to Lady Georgiana Charteris, Matthias explained, when he met Lucia at Ginny's wedding—no, Charley, wait!—it was an arranged marriage that neither of them wanted—which necessitated keeping his attachment to Lucia a secret. He had been working steadily to make arrangements to move to New York. Vincent was no longer engaged to Lady Georgiana but that news had yet to be made public.

It seemed a very careless, mismanaged business, giving wisdom to the old adage of being off with the old before getting on with the new. Matthias acknowledged this, which again infuriated me and I quickened my feet up another curving flight of steps. Where was Vincent Faneuil's remorse? I wanted to have at him and box his ears so he would think twice about doing something like that again. Perhaps push him down the staircase, or tip him over the balustrade into the courtyard, once we had found him.

"That's very restrained of you, Charley," Matthias said. "I was afraid you were planning to run him over with the Bugatti."

"I never said I wouldn't do that too," I said. "How do you know about the Bugatti?"

"Same way we tracked you and Lucia here."

"I know Tilly didn't give us away, nor Ginny."

"No. But I knew you wouldn't leave Tilly behind. So we followed Tilly. The delay in London, sorting out the ransacking of your Savoy suite, nearly killed us. Vincent hoped at the time that it would draw you out, that you would be anxious enough to come back to deal with it."

"Did you think that too?"

"No. But it didn't make the wait for Tilly's departure any easier." Matthias peered at me. "He doesn't know you or Lucia as well as I do. And he was frantic about not being to find Lucia. Don't judge him too harshly for it."

"Am I?"

"You're burning him in hellfire and brimstone."

"He doesn't seem to understand the relative value of things, does he? What is important, what is not."

"Charley—"

"Is this the kind of man one would wish to be entrusted with Lucia's future happiness?"

"Charley—"

"Vincent Faneuil didn't press Ginny or Tilly for where we'd gone?"

"He wasn't aware that they knew."

"But you did and yet you didn't tell him."

Matthias paused on the wide step. He stood against the salamanders and decorative relief of the loggia. Behind him was a framed view of the courtyard and the Saint Calais Chapel and the trees of the Tour de Foix terrace garden and the gargoyles and mansard rooftops of the Louis XII wing and the cobalt blue sky. The waters above, the firmament below. I turned my eyes back to the steps before me. "He's my friend but so is Lucia," Matthias said from behind me. "I tried to help as much as I could without infringing on her interests but I seem to have failed both of them."

"I'm tired of your redundant apologies, Matthias. They serve only to remind me of the absence of his."

"I'm sure that, at this very moment, he is—"

I tripped, caught myself, and hastily spun around and nearly plowed straight into Matthias who, lurching to an abrupt stop, had bumped up behind me and reached out to steady us both. I nudged him forcefully to turn about-face. "All right. You were right. Let's go back down." Matthias did not need a second glance to be persuaded; he immediately joined me in bounding back down the spiraling steps.

Yes, we had found Lucia and Vincent Faneuil.

Matthias and I hastened down the circular staircase as noiselessly as we could and almost ran across the cobbled courtyard, as far away as we could reach, to the battlements of the shaded garden terrace around the Tour de Foix.

The view of the Loire distracted only a little from the awkwardness. Neither of us spoke for a long time. I was still shaken by what I had seen on the staircase.

"Have you been enjoying driving around Paris?" Matthias ventured eventually.

"Only got the Bugatti this morning."

I heard a low exhalation of relief gust out from him.

"Don't be rude. I'm a decent, respectable driver. I drive at a very sedate pace. You can ask—well, you can ask Lucia when she gets back."

We lapsed into silence again.

"Doesn't your office miss you, Matthias? Or are you on holiday?"

"I'm... My employer is accommodating."

"Oh. You wouldn't find that easily in New York."

"Charley—"

"May I ask you something, Matthias?"

"Of course." But his countenance molded itself into an anticipation of something bad.

"Can I trust you to stand by your friendship in the future insofar as a choice of whose interests to subordinate when you come across a conflict? Can I rely on you not to help another to interfere with or hurt Lucia?"

"Charley, has something truly damaged our friendship that you feel the need to reassure yourself by asking me this?" Matthias looked hurt but he added steadily: "You can always rely on me."

"I will hold you to this, Matthias."

"I expect nothing less from you, Charley."

I nodded, satisfied, and extended my hand out to him. "Then we are in accord."

Matthias paused for an infinitesimal second before enveloping my hand in his.

18

LUCIA:

Luncheon in Blois was a subdued, awkward affair.

There was no mention of the scene at the château, no reference to poor Charley's horrified expression before she high-tailed it down the staircase, Matthias following behind, no allusion to engagements or fiancées. We all met and shook hands civilly upon introduction and made polite conversation as if we had run into each other by chance in the town square. It almost farcically resembled a meeting of rival Park and Fifth Avenue socialites lunching at the Colony. Oh so civilized.

"Oh yes, I remember you, you're Matthias's friend from Ginny's wedding," Charley had said with a bright smile towards Vincent.

Matthias and I had to stop ourselves from cringing in pain.

Charley was exceedingly courteous and charming, smiling when she and Vincent were reacquainted, showing only well-mannered inquisitiveness, chattering about our touring plans, nodding and making agreeable noises when Vincent made friendly suggestions about touring the treasures of the Loire Valley that we had yet to see, to be met by an effusion of historical gossip that burst forth from Charley. Oh, the monumental unity of Château de Chambord!—didn't Henry James allude to "a touch of madness in its conception"?—and hadn't Francis I's sister, Marguerite de Navarre, complained of always getting lost? The picturesque loveliness of Château de Chenonceau!—wasn't that where Henri III was assassinated?—oh, wait, no, Henri III was stabbed at Château de Saint-Cloud, what a pity Saint-Cloud was destroyed during the Franco-Prussian War!—wasn't it Henri III's widow, Louise de Lorraine-Vaudémont, who turned into a house of mourning Chenonceau from what had been for three decades a pleasure palace since the widowed Catherine de Medici turned Diane de Poitiers, her husband Henri II's chief mistress, out of it in 1559?—poor Henri II, what dreadful bad luck, fatally poked in the eye at a jousting tournament, leaving his estates to be fought over by vengeful women! The idyllic Château de Villandry and its beautiful gardens! The elegance of Azay-le-Rideau on an island in the middle of the Indre river! The graceful Château de Cheverny! —was the history of the château not a deplorable moral lesson?—its master, M. Henri Hurault, a cuckolded courtier of Henri IV's court discovering his wife's betrayal and rushing home to kill his wife's lover, who jumped out the window, then considerately offering his unfaithful wife the choice of a bullet or poison—his wife chose the poison—but being insufficient revenge for the humiliation, monsieur's rage still not assuaged, the house accepted the price of the master's rage, being razed to the ground, and Fate decided to take pity on M. Hurault, rewarding him with a blameless second wife, Marguerite, and daughter, who oversaw the construction of the new home—what was one to infer from this unhappy tale? The storybook Château d'Ussé, used by Charles Perrault as the model for Sleeping Beauty! The dramatic Chaumont and Saumur! The regal Amboise haunted by the ghosts of Leonardo da Vinci and the French kings! —poor Charles VIII, accidentally striking his head on a door lintel and dying at the tender age of 27. The infamous Château le Vaux-le-Vicomte built by Nicolas Fouquet!—whose magnificent splendor outshone a king, precipitating the fall and imprisonment of Fouquet—"On August 17, at six in the evening Fouquet was the King of France: at two in the morning he was nobody"—superintendent of finances to Louis XIV who, in a jealous fury, confiscated and plundered Vaux-le-Vicomte's contents and artisans to endow the royal palace and gardens at Versailles...

And finally Charley sighed, exclaiming that we had gotten so caught up in the history of Château de Blois that we had quite forgotten about the rest.

I thought that we had come to the end of the recital but my relief was premature. I began to worry anew when Charley took a breath, a sip of verveine tea, smiled, suggested it might be pleasant to order a bottle of the sparkling Vouvray to accompany our meal, and picked up the thread without hesitation, continuing on to descant on the fascinating intrigues and mayhem of the French court played out at Blois, the War of the Three Henrys, Catherine de Medici's "chamber of secrets" and infamous "Flying Squadron" of female spies, the St. Bartholomew's Day Massacre, the assassination of Henri I, Duke de Guise, and his brother, Louis II, Cardinal de Guise at the Château de Blois, the assassination of Henri IV by a fanatic monk in Paris on May 14, 1610 while riding in his coach when it was stopped in the rue de la Ferronnerie by traffic congestion related to his wife Marie de Medici's coronation ceremony...

Vincent could not understand why Matthias and I were all atremble over

Charley's gurglings of delight. He thought our nervousness unwarranted. He did not see the cannons pointed at him inscribed (as Louis XIV had had all his cannons inscribed) with "Ultima Ratio Regum". The Last Argument of Kings. Charley's patter, Vincent said, was like a vivid stroll through history, she did not behave at all like the angry one that he was led to expect, not a hint of frigid disdain either, why, she was perfectly amiable.

Oh, if he only knew how warily I watched his glass from the corner of my eye, how my heart nearly stopped every time the waiter came around to our table. I would not have put it past Charley to succumb to the temptation of bribing the waiters in exacting what she believed was a just retribution... But no one except Tallis Lloyd-Chase—who had stood in bemusement when Charley had returned to him the bottle of Ex-Lax purgatives after his house party, puzzling and puzzling and puzzling until, finally, the penny dropped—would have understood my fear.

Matthias might not have known the exact nature of my anxieties but he sympathized. He saw clearly the veiled blood-thirstiness in Charley's every beguiling word and smile. He watched the proceedings too with a tense and rueful concern and tried diplomatically to curb Charley's murderous desires as she finished a recitation of the royal deaths from 1498 to 1612—such were the tragic ends of kings!—but oh, never mind, a few broken eggs to be tolerated for all the marvelous châteaux those kings had built and gifted to posterity!

I wondered how much grief Charley had given Matthias. Charley had always been a hair-trigger for charging into battle on another's behalf. It made me wish once again that I had managed things better. I wished I had told Charley earlier. How strange that such a dense fog of unhappiness could dissipate and clear so quickly. A misunderstanding. How idiotically I had behaved. It had been a year since I had seen Vincent and the pleasure of being in his presence again returned with an overwhelming force. I had, I supposed, lost my head. A misunderstanding would not be as easily explained to Charley, the righteous, avenging knight, as it had been to me. It was, nevertheless, comforting to be witness to Charley's veiled bad humor, so diametrically opposite to my father's shows of displeasure when he felt his wishes had not been executed to his liking, I felt bathed in the depth of Charley's protective concern for my well-being. I had missed her in the year that she had been absent from New York, her and Matthias's letters had sustained me, admittedly, more than Vincent's irregular missives, whose openings had always been so fraught with wild imaginings and dread, but they were, after all, my oldest friends.

After a leisurely wander around Blois' old quarter, we returned to Paris, Matthias and Vincent following in their own motor-car, Matthias's Bentley, alongside the Bugatti. On the drive back, Charley did not press for any explanations or demand any apology, she did not express anything other than warm and friendly concern as she quietly listened to my confession of what had taken place at Ginny's wedding to all that had led up to the encounter at Tessa's.

"He...dazzled you?" she asked when I finished my account.

"He didn't know who I was. He knew me as Lucia, a friend of Ginny's —he came and spoke to me and asked me to dance and was so attentive— he courted me, he proposed to me—Lucia—instead of the daughter of the Bernhardts of New York."

Charley nodded. "But even if you were not the daughter of the Bernhardts, it is still very rushed. To take his measure... How can you know..." Charley's features grew taut with remembered pain. "How can you be sure that he loves you?"

"You're not very romantic, Charley."

"I leave all the romance, the billing and cooing business, to you lovebirds," Charley said, looking a bit green, probably still in shock at the kiss she had disturbed. "If this were a mere fling, I would not dream of wasting your time or mine in weighing up every word or act, I would happily wash my hands of it. But he upset you. And an engagement was mentioned. And therefore my concern is to ensure the longevity of your happiness, and that demands solid assurances, certainty."

I drew no offense from Charley's uncertainty. Charley was recalling Nate Knowle. The great outpouring of words that she had expelled in roasting Nate's black soul for his treatment of me had been the least of the consequences of that affair; Charley's anguish that she had not done enough led to a fierce protectiveness in turfing out all the wrong men who dared to set their sights on my heart. Charley did not care for romance, so often the window-dressing of nasty, brutish things. Nate had killed off the last vestiges of any belief we might have had in the notion of romance, which, having grown up with the customs of Old New York, was not a lot —plentiful examples of calculating ambition and cold self-regard, but selfless love and kindness?—that was a rare beast indeed. Even knowing this, the easily tickled disdain of our sensible friends, Celeste and Frankie, for all things ridiculous could still occasionally be eclipsed by the thrills of a good romantic tale. But not Charley. The scallywag Miss Masterson invariably became as sober as a judge at the mention of a suitor's affections or attentions. For one so intrepid and fearless, she was quite in awe of a breakable heart. The question that occupied Charley—and, inevitably, me— was expressed in the same words that girls in New York and all the world used, but they carried a great solemnity and import and a far stricter litmus test. "Does he love you?" was only successfully answered by a man whose virtues equaled those of Hector of Troy—an impossible standard, I had frequently argued, but Charley disagreed. "I ask nothing of beauty, wit, wealth, pedigree, nothing except a kind, true, loyal and loving heart—

someone who will make you shimmer with happiness and light—is that too much to expect for you? You offer that when you offer your heart, Lucia, when you give of yourself so unreservedly, why should you not receive the same in return? Why must it be so hard to find? Why do the wild transports of love have to be rudely interrupted and weighed down with having to worry about boring fundamental details such as morality and consequences because a man cannot be trusted to do right by you? Hasn't everyone been taught ad nauseum the definition from Corinthians?" Charley had railed. "If a man cared, if he truly loved, he wouldn't need Corinthians to prompt him to treat you as the most precious thing in this life, to bend the world to bring you happiness rather than allow you to settle for contentment—not true contentment but the sort that is really only an euphemism to spare one's feelings." How could anyone be cross at Charley when she argued thus, for caring so deeply? It wasn't her fault, Charley pointed out, that the men were so frequently gutless and did not come up to scratch. As for Vincent... Was it a love strong and steadfast enough to withstand and thrive in sunlight or was it one of those furtive creatures that only come out in darkness and twilight?

"Can anyone be absolutely sure?"

"Well, yes. By his deeds. Do you know him well enough to be confident you wish to spend the rest of your life with him?"

"I shall be. We've exchanged letters—"

"That is hardly sufficient to know that he puts you and your interests and welfare ahead of his own."

"I know, Charley. I've tried to guard against falling into that trap. I may not know him as well as I might, but I think Vincent will pass the test. It was his kindness to a stranger at Ginny's wedding which drew my attention to him."

"You are a soft touch, Lucia. What opportunities are there in a social setting for distinguishing whether someone is honorable? It's all pageantry."

Charley was wrong. She had done it for me when she stood between me and an angry, resentful Nate Knowle, bucking spitefully against his fall from grace. She had done it on multiple other occasions when she could not stomach the subtle, vicious maneuverings of the New York cliques in shunning and excising their victims. Charley rode in on her white steed and showered her attentions and support and favor on the ostracized victim with all the aplomb that a Masterson heiress could muster. Vincent had done no less at Ginny's wedding for Miss Latimer, conversing and dancing and sitting with her when her escort, having proposed only a fortnight earlier, had humiliatingly abandoned her to indulge his roving eye, including chasing after a Hartley bridesmaid, who had turned out to have been the Hartley matron of honor, which brought him to the less than pleased attention of her husband and the new bride.

"Miss Latimer?" Charley echoed, her face clouding over.

"Ginny mentioned her, remember? It was her wedding day and she had so much going on but she was worried about another."

"Yes," said Charley, frowning, "I remember." Her throat worked but then she paused. "Ginny has a kind heart like all the Hartleys."

"As has Vincent."

Charley looked like she was about to speak but stopped again. "It was a kind deed," she conceded.

"Since we are judging on deeds: Vincent is giving up a lot to move to New York to be where I am."

"That still isn't quite... Well, I suppose it will have to do for now. I can barely believe this is Lucia, my sensible, rational, level-headed friend who speaks."

"It's all your terrible corrupting influences over the years, Charley!"

"The dam has broken at last."

"Still sensible enough to insist on his being free of ties first before making any plans."

"What?" Charley nearly swerved off the road, earning piercing glowers of questioning concern from Matthias in the adjoining Bentley which she ignored. "But—I thought—you were so—"

"I thought I had mislaid my trust—again—I'm glad I was wrong. Vincent isn't Nate, Charley. It was my fault for letting my memories and emotions get the better of my reason. It felt so—I thought I was facing the horror again of being failed in faith by the one who was meant to be my whole world."

Charley sat blinking blindly in confusion. "He's moving to New York even though there isn't an—an understanding?—between the two of you?"

"We agreed to become engaged—if neither of us had changed our minds—when he was no longer fiancé to Lady Georgiana Charteris. He was being discreet, staying away from London while we've been there during the Season. I think he accepted a temporary assignment to Brussels. Godeffroy's has a branch there."

"Oh, Lucia!"

"Was that not sensible and level-headed enough? I didn't want to intrude on others' unfinished business, to build something on shaky foundations—perhaps on someone else's confusion and hurt—to cause pain to someone else who'd done me no wrong. I should probably not have agreed to the secret correspondence, but I was weak. Such a long time, and so much distance—"

"I take it all back! You're still my good and kind and sensible and rational and level-headed friend. I should in all likelihood have eloped and lived to rue the day. He's a fool though to leave you unattached—across an ocean—swimming in New York's shark-infested waters—for so long alone.

A fool, and more, to ask it of you. You say it's a great sacrifice on his part to move to new York. I hope he realizes how much you've sacrificed in keeping this secret, in keeping to this—understanding—the chances you've given up?"

"You mean those irresistible proposals arranged by my father?"

"I mean that you put your life on hold for him. You didn't even spare a glance at anyone else—didn't spare a thought to the notion that there might've been someone more deserving of you, who wouldn't have left you unprotected and uncherished and waiting for a year—and you did all this and stood your ground against the parental pressure bearing down on you —because you keep your promises."

"Charley, that isn't fair, it isn't how—"

"Judging by deeds, Lucia."

What a great height to plunge from a chaos of overwhelmed and reawakened senses, touch and nearness and urgency and smells and murmurs overturning thoughts and emotions in a whirlpool, to a cold dissection of a barely-formed love affair. No, Charley was not a romantic. "Things like this are complicated. They take time. There are other people's feelings and welfare to consider."

"This is precisely what I mean. You considered others whereas he should've been considering you above others. You are too good for him. He might be just as much of a fool as those other suitors who pursue you for your pedigree."

"Charley!"

"Oh, I'm not going to slap him into clarity, if that's what you're worried about, Lucia. If you want me to be civil, I will be, er, as civil as an orange."

"You're such a hopeless clown, Charley!" Charley grimaced back at me. "You won't tell anyone? You'll keep it a secret until things are more settled?"

"Of course. I wish you happy, Lucia. And I shall send my Forty-five after him if he ever fails to come up to scratch."

"Charley!"

"What? You'd prefer to offer him a choice of bullet or poison? When is Lady Georgiana's new engagement being announced?"

"In tomorrow's London papers I think."

"We'll ask for copies to be sent to our suite with breakfast. Would it be tempting Fate to go out tonight and celebrate?"

We did end up going out and celebrating. Vincent suggested going to La Tour d'Argent or Prunier's or Fouquet's but we headed instead to the colorful Montparnasse quarter and dined at Café du Dôme, another intellectual gathering place referred to as the "Anglo-American Cafe" (we had drawn lots between Le Dôme, La Rotonde, La Closerie des Lilas, Le Coupole, and Le Select in Montparnasse, and the Café de Flore and Deux

Magots in Saint-Germain-des-Prés which she and I had already frequented) and ended up later at Henry's and then finishing the evening at the Chatham, old Parisian bars that were also frequented by Americans but whose genteel businessmen patrons were not as loud as those of Harry's New York Bar.

Tilly had checked in and had a nap and room service in the hotel suite when we returned to Le Meurice. Charley suppressed an urge to check out and move to another hotel and instead kindly suggested that Mr. Faneuil might like to go out and see the sights of Paris with me tomorrow. Tilly, not yet knowing about Vincent, assumed that he was another in the long line of gentlemen callers and that she would be playing chaperon again. We were all too embarrassed to correct this assumption and so we agreed to meet in the lobby for the outing on the following morning. Matthias and Vincent bid us good evening to return to the Hôtel de Crillon. Matthias hesitated several times, looking like he wanted to say something and changing his mind; I wondered how many times he suppressed an urge to ditch the Crillon and ask at reception to book a suite here, I was sure he suspected Charley of planning to bolt.

There was a good deal to catch up on with Tilly. I found out that evening that Charley had kept from me the news of an attempted robbery in our Savoy suite, the reason Tilly was delayed in joining us. Tilly assured me that the authorities were still investigating, that nothing had been taken —that my mother's necklace was absolutely safe—and that all the disordered clothes had been put to rights—and that she was sure that everything would be sorted out and all right in the end.

"Charley!"

"You had other more pressing matters on your mind."

"But we left Tilly to—"

Tilly again assured me everything was fine and taken care of, that Mr. Vandermeer had been most kind and helpful, and that the trip from London Charing Cross to Paris Gare du Nord to Le Meurice had been quite an adventure. These hotels just got grander and grander, didn't they? The elevator was like a museum piece, Miss Lucia!

"See?" Charley grinned. "Tilly has a natural eye and innate taste for opulence. I told you the Marie Antoinette elevator would turn heads. Wait till you see Versailles, Tilly. The gardens!"

I taxed Charley and Tilly for more details but there was not much insightful detail to be derived from the exercise. It had all been more of an untidy inconvenience. The thieves had wasted a good deal of effort for little gain, tossing up the contents of the Savoy's hotel suites to find that the occupiers of the suites had entrusted their valuables to the hotel's safe, leaving behind only cash and some minor possessions—as had been the case on the Mauretania, ours had not been the only one violated but it had been the one that suffered no losses—and the Savoy management had been terribly embarrassed and apologetic that we should have encountered two such dreadful incidents during the course of our stay, which they were taking additional measures to ensure would never recur. The Queen of Sheba, Charley said, would expect no less excitement were she to travel as I did with such tempting jewels.

"I suppose we are lucky that the thieves had been inept bunglers?" I asked.

"Yes, that too," said Charley. "If I were a jewel thief, I'd do my homework better. Now, what would you like to add to tomorrow's itinerary?"

We visited Versailles the following day as well as the Jardin du Luxembourg, at Charley's (and later, independently, Matthias's) suggestion, to admire the magnificence of its gardens and fountains and palaces. It was unimaginably lovely to be strolling through the royal splendor and mirrored halls and immaculate parterre paths with Vincent at my side. Had that no been what I had once dreamed of? Paris, the City of Lights, the city of lovers. Paris, where Tessa and Kit would be spending part of their honeymoon. Vincent and I had a lot to discuss, a lot of time to make up. He was attentive and good company. If ever it fell short of my expectations or imaginings, I reminded myself that we were becoming reacquainted again as if we had met for the first time and starting the courtship anew.

Poor Tilly and Matthias! Charley had stopped short of revealing the secret "engagement", informing Tilly that there had been a tiff at Tessa's wedding, that Vincent had suffered in unrequited silence for a year, and then rushed to Paris to find me and declare his undying devotion etc., resulting in Tilly and Matthias trying to trail at a long, tactful distance behind us all day and averting their gazes whenever Vincent, with a glint in his eye that made my pulse quicken, curled his hand around my wrist and pulled me into a secluded alcove or behind a column or tree or royal hedge. There were times when I almost wished that Tilly and Matthias had been less considerate. Between the breathless exhilaration of the stolen kisses and fugitive touches and unspoken promises in the most fleeting of glances, time did not acquire a greater rose-tinted hue. My happiness at Vincent's being here made me more aware of the things that did not seem to be imbued with his wonderful glow and there seemed to be a multitude of them; time did not wait upon us, it simply passed in its indifferent colorless fashion, as if flowing around us, around our moments of joyfulness, as a current flows around smooth riverstones. It was odd, but I began to notice it more and more as the day passed. Rapt passion, it seemed, was sometimes not enough against the familiar surety of lifelong knowing and being known. There was something missing without Matthias's familiar, easy-going company, and Tilly's inexhaustible enthusiasm and good-humor and scolding and periodic eruptions into excited chatter—those relaxed days in London when Matthias had escorted us about town—and Ginny and Tessa's joking and teasing, and Charley.

When morning had dawned at Le Meurice, Charley had already been up and dressed (in one of the plain outfits she had purchased at Printemps), fast broken, telegrams (forwarded on Charley's instructions from the Ritz) and newspapers read, the London papers dog-eared to the society notices page.

"Lady Georgiana's engagement is official," Charley said.

"What are you doing up so early?" Tilly fretted frantically. "You're not —Where are you going?"

"I have to run out to the American Express office," Charley said. "I'm afraid I have to fly, if I don't get there and back to the Gare de l'Est in time, I shall miss my train. I'm sorry I'm going to miss your outing today, but you all enjoy yourselves!"

"But Charley—"

We gaped after the empty doorway.

Matthias, bearing bunches of fragrant roses for each of us almost as large as the bouquet Vincent handed me, could not believe it either when we met in the lobby later.

"Did something happen? Was it another telegram?" Matthias cursed, gritting his teeth. "Today, of all days."

"What is special about today?" Vincent asked.

"A telegram from Diego." There had been a single telegram left on the salver, the only one addressed directly to Le Meurice instead of being redirected from the Ritz. (The pile of telegrams forwarded from the Ritz had been quite voluminous, even depleted as it had been by the ones that Charley had torn up.) It had come from Diego de Almadén relaying love and wishes from the De Almadéns and Aunt Merry and everyone at Montrose and, of course, all those wishes pouring into Montrose for Charley. "Charley's gone to Château-Thierry."

"Charley likes her châteaux, doesn't she?" Vincent laughed.

I could not help my thoughts drifting throughout the day, wondering about Charley, unfair as it seemed to Vincent and his efforts to please. Without Charley's irreverent chatter and mischievous lunacy and exasperating intrigues and kindness, the city—the passing of time itself—seemed more ordinary, losing some indefinable quality of vibrancy and eccentricity and undiscovered fun, the sense of unfettered boundaries, an unconquerable spaciousness. But it was not just Charley's company that I missed, I wondered about the implications of that telegram, the one that had survived and the ones that had perished at Charley's hand. It had found its way to us at Le Meurice through the great clamorous silence from all of Charley's ardent suitors—not a single peep, as far as I was aware, had been heard from them since our arrival in Paris. What was Charley up to? The fact that Charley had seemed bright and calm when she had flown out the door this morning was not a reliable indicator of how things really stood with Charley. Not on this day.

There was no need for me to make excuses to Vincent for my growing distraction or to beg off for the evening to chase down Charley and make sure she was all right. Now that he was officially a free man, Vincent was headed back to London on the afternoon train, he was eager to start making arrangements for us. We rode together to Gare du Nord and made our bittersweet, lingering farewell, agreeing to correspond further regarding our plans. "Next time we meet, Lucia..." his voice trailed off and I met the fullness of his gaze with my own. His words and the promise in his eyes would have to sustain me until then.

The taxi brought me back to Le Meurice where I ran impatiently up to the suite to collect Charley's gifts—a parcel (one volume from a crate of books by the Bloomsbury set, currently on its way to New York to await Charley's return to Montrose, with handwritten inscriptions by the authors, including Virginia Woolf and E. M. Forster) from Ginny on behalf of all the Hartleys that had been entrusted to Tilly to bring with her to Paris which Tilly successfully managed to smuggle past Charley into our Savoy suite, and a first edition of Middlemarch that Matthias and Tilly and I had tracked down in London for Charley, to add to the vast beloved library at Montrose. It seemed odd to rush down to the lobby again, carefully carrying Charley's gifts, so shortly after I had left Vincent, more anxious and thrilled than I had been all day, awaiting Matthias and Tilly's return. After we had parted at the Jardin du Luxembourg, Tilly and Matthias had gone to Gare de l'Est, hoping to meet Charley when her train pulled in. Charley had been surprised to find them waiting for her but had not otherwise made any sign of annoyance or distress or betrayed any emotion stirred up by her trip. She was pleased by her gifts, a little embarrassed as she usually was when she was on the receiving end, and entirely too placid to be believed.

We had a grand dinner planned but Charley begged to go somewhere low-key, such a terrible fuss to make over another misspent year of youth etc. (Tilly, who had discovered the hoard of Parisian couture treasure in our suite, managed to bully Charley into changing out of her plain canton frock at least.) Matthias frowned and reluctantly acceded to Charley's wish, adding his promises of future retribution to ours. Then he gave her a set of car keys and pointed to a green Bugatti waiting patiently out the front of the hotel, beyond the stone arcade of the rue di Rivoli, attended by one of the Meurice staff. Tilly admired the beautiful steed.

"That's Charley's." I recognized the motor-car that had taken us to Blois and back to Paris.

"No, it isn't," Charley said. "It was only hired for the day and I've returned it."

"Yes, it is," said Matthias. "When you're done driving it around France, it will be shipped to wait for you back at Montrose."

Charley blinked and looked down at the keys in her hand, speechless. "I can't accept this, Matthias."

"Well, I guess that is just too bad, Charley, now we'll have to walk all the way to dinner."

"Don't be an idiot, you know I can't possibly—"

Tilly, quite inured to their squabbling, and hungry, and impatient to give Charley our gift too, interrupted them and asked if she should go ask the nice doorman to flag down a cab?

Many minutes later, Charley was hustled into the Bugatti.

Charley finally said, "Babe Barnato is not going to be happy." And then, softly, "Thank you. I'll try not to dent it too much."

We took Charley out that night to celebrate her birthday at La Rotunde. (Again, we drew lots: "I don't care how grand or poky it is, I care about the company not the place," Charley insisted.) The cafe was crammed full with its eclectic bohemian crowd whose merry-making tipped at times on the verge of punch-throwing. Tilly was unimpressed by the clientele at the smoky cafe, even less with the artworks littering the walls of La Rotunde, even when we told her we had met one of the artists, M. Pablo Picasso, only the other day, and that in 1917, there had been an exhibition of his paintings at the Cosmopolitan Club in New York—they did not meet Tilly's standard of Art, she knew her Old Masters, and we paddled against an implacable current to persuade her otherwise. Tilly had welcomed the detour to the more salubrious Ritz Bar and its respectable, regular crowd where Matthias ordered champagne and the bartender brought out several magnums of Louis Roederer. "Tilly," Charley chided, "don't be such a snob. M. Libion is so hospitable! La Rotunde has fed and nurtured a generation of the greatest artists and intellectuals of this century. The artworks on the walls will one day be hanging in the Metropolitan Museum of Art—if they haven't been snapped up first by Peggy Guggenheim! That gentleman who was paying you such flirtatious attentions at La Rotunde? That was M. Constantin Brancusi. His work is very popular, well, notorious —avant-garde. It was his sculpture, Birds in Space, an abstract representation of flight, which caused that fuss at Customs when Edward Steichen—you've seen his photos for Vogue and Vanity Fair—shipped it to the US. Why, if you hadn't turned M. Brancusi down, he might've asked you to model for him. You would've made Mrs. Stone quite green with envy."

Matthias roared with laughter, and then had to explain to Tilly what was so amusing. (Which, Charley deemed, was punishment enough—the notorious scandal of Princess X—épater les bourgeois, ha!) It would be a while before Tilly would be reconciled to the harsh fact that the greater the artistic and intellectual legend, the greater the chance that they would be rather disappointingly ordinary in person with the usual human foibles, fears and vices.

While Charley was out of earshot, preoccupied chatting to the bartender about the Dîner des trois empereurs for which Louis Roederer had created his prestige cuvée Cristal and the special clear lead glass bottle in which the champagne was served amongst seven other wines over eight hours and sixteen courses to Tsar Alexander II, Kaiser Wilhelm I and Otto von Bismarck for the Exposition Universelle in 1867, Matthias had quietly confirmed that she had gone to the town of Château-Thierry to visit the memorial that commemorated the sacrifices and achievements of American and French troops in the region during the First World War and the United States servicemen, including Charles Redmond Masterson, who fell in the Battle of Château-Thierry, during the Second Battle of the Marne under the German Spring Offensive on the Western Front, and were interred in nearby cemeteries. This much Charley must have herself volunteered as an innocuous piece of information. I could not see how it was connected to Diego's telegram. How did Diego know to find us at Le Meurice instead of the Ritz which had our original reservations and still received and redirected our mail as instructed (I had told no one, not even my mother that we had moved from the Ritz) unless Charley had told Diego herself? Had he and Charley been in continuous close correspondence—closer than anyone else to the extent that even Aunt Merry had cabled her birthday wishes to the Ritz for Charley? Had Diego sent those other telegrams that Charley had torn up? Diego had fought in the Battle of Château-Thierry too. He had dictated the letter to Aunt Merry and Charley to a nurse because he had been too heavily wounded to write it himself... His promise to his friend... The loyal, stalwart steward at the helm of the Montrose empire... Diego, the keeper of mysteries, the only one who had known where Charley was in her year of absence from New York, the only one who had the slightest clue about Lottie Fairchild and a life submerged in secrets...

Matthias was concerned about Charley and more solicitous and protective and careful in his attentions than usual, but far from being saddened, grieving or subdued, Charley had returned to Paris with a jaunty determined step. What Matthias had overlooked in his chivalry was that this was the birthday that Charley had spoken of in the past with alternating flippancy and dread: this day marked Charley's endowment with legal and financial independence, when the control of the Montrose inheritance passed fully and exclusively into her hands. By this reckoning, Charley did not down the champagne and those potent Rainbow cocktails served by the nice bartender, M. Meier, in carefree conviviality, she was drowning herself in libationary good cheer because she was very likely absolutely terrified.

I did not know whether Charley would want me to share my deductions. They seemed to hover in the realm of all those things to which she had sworn me to secrecy. But if Charley was scared, would she not have wanted the support of her friends? My words to Matthias mocked me. I trusted Charley, didn't I?

We were in the midst of an increasingly busy and crowded bar, the music and chatter becoming almost too loud to talk against. Tilly had been plucked from our table by a line of admirers—reluctantly, given a little encouraging nudge and push by us—and was being tugged between these gentlemen seeking to monopolize her attention. Matthias was kept busy drifting between Tilly's circle of courtiers and us, gallantly bringing drinks over and keeping a weather eye on everyone. When Charley had urged him to give up his duties—"Let Tilly be. How is she ever to reach her full potential for misbehavior with you hovering? I might add that we are eminently capable of telling someone to go, shoo, Matthias, and also quite adept at summoning a bartender. Shall I teach you how?"—Matthias's response had been an unimpressed grunt before he went off to collect another round of drinks, ordering, I was sure, watered down cocktails, disguised in luridly attractive colors to avoid Charley's immediate scorn, rather than the rainbow ones that Charley had been imbibing like nectar.

"Charley," I whispered so that no one else could hear. "I know that you will trounce whatever it is that is troubling you."

"I haven't a clue what you are talking about."

"'Out of the night that covers me,/ Black as the pit from pole to pole,/ I thank whatever gods may be/ For my unconquerable soul.'"

Charley snorted. "I don't know if I'm too corked to understand, or you have reached the stage of maudlin drunkenness, Lucia, but I'll happily raise another toast to—whatever you like." She waved to M. Meier. "Is it because you are missing Vincent? Why isn't he here tonight? Didn't you have a good day?"

How like Charley to divert attention away from herself. I took it as confirmation that she had far more weighing on her mind than she would ever say.

"Can I offer you a Mimosa, madam?"

"Yes, why not?" said Charley. "And also a Sidecar. And a Kir Royale for my friend, Lucia, here. (Forget whatever insipid order our friend, Matthias, has given you. Or just top it up with more gin.) And a Rose too, please. Tilly would enjoy that, don't you think?"

"You're utterly mad," I told Charley. "But I have complete faith that anything in your capable hands will—"

"And that is a very foolish thing to hold to," Charley said in admonition.

"Oh, I think not. Let's toast to Charley Masterson—the one-eyed king."

Charley's eyes widened. "This is disturbing, Lucia," Charley said. "I rely on you to stop me from doing outrageous things, things beyond the pale, to tie me to the mast and disregard whatever I argue or plea, to steer me away from stupendous foolishness and ruinati—"

"Isn't that precisely the point, Charley? Nothing you've done has required intervention. You must trust that your judgment is sound."

"But—"

Charley was interrupted by the enthusiastic exclamation of a male voice from across the bar. Following the shout, Matthias came back followed by a soigné gentleman whose eyes were fairly snapping with delight.

"Charley, Baron Andre d'Erlanger claims an acquaintance with you," Matthias said with a hint of disapproving curtness.

"Acquaintance! Bah!" said the man. "Charley Masterson. I knew it was she the moment I walked in here."

"Baron."

Baron d'Erlanger took Charley's hand graciously and kissed her knuckles according to the Gallic custom and his instinctive savoir faire. He did the same to me when Charley introduced us. The baron was apparently one of the Bentley Boys who came in third at Le Mans this year. His effusiveness at seeing Charley rather begged the question of why and how, and I suspected that the answer was the reason for Matthias's less than wholehearted welcome.

"Barnato didn't say anything about you being in Paris. Are you here for a race or testing one of the new prototype models?"

"Oh, Matthias is the one who drives a fast lorry—he owns a Bentley Super Six." Charley laughed. "I'm afraid I must fly traitor's flags. It seems that in France, I drive Bugattis."

Baron d'Erlanger's splutterings of disbelief and dismay drew the attention of others at the Ritz Bar and we soon found ourselves in the midst of a spirited debate between the baron and a party of bar patrons who had drifted over to us, waxing quite lyrical upon discovering that Charley was the owner of the beautiful green Bugatti Type 43 Grand Sport parked out the front that they had been admiring. Among them were the Bugatti racing drivers M. Jean-Pierre Wimille, M. Philippe Étancelin and his wife Suzanne who served as his crew chief, and Mr. William Grover-Williams. It made for a lively evening of passionate debate and cocktail lubricated insults flung back and forth regarding the comparative merits of Bentleys and Bugattis; of the recent win—the third successive win—by Bentley at Le Mans (Babe Barnato and Tim Birkin taking first place in a Bentley Speed Six); of the superiority of the supercharged Blower Bentley models ("Isn't it rather fuel hungry? W. O. did contend that increasing displacement is preferable to forced induction... Yes, the engineering that Tim is developing with Amherst Villiers is impressive, I'd be happy to try them out... I know that Mercedes-Benz have been using superchargers for years, but... Sorry," Charley told the baron, "W. O. won me over to the Speed Six. You know why I have a soft spot for it. And it did win at Le Mans, didn't it?"); of British racing driver Violette Cordery, again driving an Invicta to earn her second Dewar Trophy after being the first woman to be awarded the Dewar Trophy at Autodrome de Linas-Montlhéry by the Royal Automobile Club two years ago; of French model-dancer-racing driver Hellé Nice who had entered the third Women's Motoring Day at Montlhéry, driving an Omega 623, taking out the Women's Championship, the Women's Grand Prix, and the Concours d'élégance, becoming the toast of the town, and rumored to be soon joining the Bugatti ranks. There was even talk of the last Vanderbilt Cup held in San Francisco in 1915 (the motor race was canceled in 1917 after the United States joined the Allies in the First World War) and whether the race would ever be held again. We found ourselves enjoying a good time and inundated with invitations. Baron d'Erlanger said he was headed down to the Cote d'Azur to meet his friends, staying at the Carlton Hotel in Cannes, and adjured us to join the party. Somehow that invitation turned into a motor race and somehow, despite repeated refusals, Charley managed to be conscripted into agreeing to take part—on one condition.

"What does Baron d'Erlanger mean he wants a rematch?" Tilly demanded, quite forgetting her admirers in her anxiety. "What did Miss Charley mean by 'I will if the prize is the same one that Ba—Mr. Barnato agreed to when I won last time'?"

"Oh, it's just a silly gamble, Tilly," Charley said.

"Charley," Matthias ground out, truly hovering like a black storm cloud now.

"It is," Charley insisted. ("Is she often disobedient and intractable?" my father had once demanded of Aunt Merry.)

"Lucia." Matthias looked to me for support.

I looked at Charley, who gazed steadily back at me, exquisitely sober. "I'm told that the Bugatti Type 43 can hit 110 mph when most fast cars can only reach 70 mph. I wasn't really paying attention when Charley was telling me about how fast the Calais-Méditerranée Express traveled. Was it no more than an average of 40 mph, Charley, taking into account all its stops and detours? Simple arithmetic suggests that there would be a fair experiment to undertake. And I think it would be rather exciting to find out just how fast a motor-car can fly beside a train while we race the baron to the Cote d'Azur. Would you let me be your navigator, Charley?"

Well, we had already wandered off the original Grand Tour path set by our parents and guardians, what harm would come of taking another step?

Charley and Matthias and Tilly stared at me in shock. Baron d'Erlanger grinned triumphantly, undeterred by the mention of Bugatti, and ran off to ring up Woolf Barnato, promising to be back as soon as he had gotten Barnato's agreement.

Much later, hiding from Matthias and Tilly, Charley asked me: "Did you mean it?"

"Didn't you think I was serious?"

"I'm grateful, Lucia, but I'm certainly not going to hold you to it and no one else shall either, I'll make sure of it. I release you from your rash announcement. You're far more mad than I am."

"On board the Mauretania, you spoke of circumstances and opportunities, the chance to strike out on one's own, at one's own risk, to only be answerable to oneself, to be elevated, or to fall, by one's own hand. This probably wasn't what you meant but... I did tell you that I had developed a taste for gambling."

"You haven't. You're still my sensible, reasonable friend."

"Well, this is me stopping you from doing something outrageous."

Charley laughed.

"It's true. If I wasn't in the motor-car, you wouldn't care so much about being reckless or not, would you?"

Charley stopped laughing. "I don't give you enough credit for cunning," she said. "But I wouldn't have been reckless."

"This isn't a silly gamble?"

"No," Charley said.

"That's what I suspected."

"Suspected?"

"It just occurred to me. I remember Woolf Barnato's name being on your list of supposed matrimonial prizes, Charley. You've not been chasing him for a ring, have you?"

"Haven't I?" Charley asked, with a pulse of alarm.

"No, no matter what racy tales they weave. The Bentley Boys might've earned their reputations but not you. And Woolf Barnato is already married —to the daughter of a Wall Street stockbroker no less—with two young daughters of his own. This is about...well, about something else. Am I right?"

Charley was silent. Then, slowly, she nodded.

"What did the baron mean by rematch, Charley?"

"Oh, just a race at a party at Ardenrun, Babe Barnato's house in Surrey. D'Erlanger and a few of the other boys were a little complacent, but the nice Speed Six that W. O. offered me was a reliable beauty."

"It wasn't a silly gamble either, was it?"

Charley shook her head.

"And the prize?"

Charley sighed. "Babe Barnato had heard that I had connections to a horse that he and Dorothy Paget—of the American Whitneys, the racehorse owner—both coveted for their stables and stud farms. He offered a handsome price for Bronte. I made him a counter-offer. A race, to make it interesting, Babe Barnato likes a gamble. If I lost, the horse would be given to Babe to add to his bloodstock, if I won, he would buy the horse for the price he'd offered. Babe thought I was joking when I proposed it. None of the boys apart from Babe knew about the wager, they thought it was just another of their many races. None of them thought I had a hope of winning. I wasn't expecting to win either, at most, I hoped to lose with my respectability intact. W. O. took pity on me and was so kind in giving me advice, gave me every advantage he could to help me, including the best Bentley."

"I don't see... Why did you propose that wager? You don't seem to gain much out of it, in fact, you had a greater risk of loss, whereas of course Woolf Barnato took it. It placed him in the same position as what he was offering you to buy the horse in the first place, and one better, the chance to get the horse for free. What did you gain from it?"

"Discretion," said Charley. "And an intangible advantage. I might go with my cap in hand, but I don't go a-begging."

Pride and dignity were not words usually associated with Charley, but she proved at that moment that nothing and no one could touch her, that dignity belonged as much to a magisterial potentate or haughty duchess as it did to the most abject, defeated, and friendless. I tucked Charley's utterances away to turn over later, they hinted at more which, it seemed, Charley was not yet ready to reveal.

"I didn't know you owned a racehorse."

"Nor did I until fairly recently. At least, I don't own Bronte. Montrose does. Bronte has illustrious bloodlines tracing back to Matchem—whose offspring, I'm told, are noted for their good temperaments—Herod, Eclipse (although I understand that most thoroughbred racehorses have Eclipse in their pedigree), Bend Or, and Selima, one of the foundation mares of the American thoroughbred, which means Bronte is also related to George Washington's stallion, Magnolia."

"But the prize for this rematch—how can it be the same as the prize agreed for the first race if you and Woolf Barnato have already agreed that Bronte is to be sold to him?"

"Because Bronte has a sibling, Astrape. Thunder and lightning, after the twin goddesses who were given the task of carrying Zeus's thunderbolts. Dorothy Paget was not the only racehorse owner who wanted the pair of them."

"I see." But I did not see, not really, not the things I most wanted to understand. "Then what do the Bentley Boys think the prize was?"

"A new Bentley—the one Lord Mallory and I were driving around in London," said Charley.

"I thought that was lent to you."

"It was. Babe and W. O. wanted to give it to me, but I declined. What was I going to do with it upon leaving London? Where would I garage it?"

"Matthias—"

Charley gave me a look of reproval which made me giggle.

"If you win this race, do you think he'll give you another new Bentley?"

"Now your drunkenness is showing, Lucia." Charley shook her head. "We shall see if Babe agrees. Otherwise we shall just have ourselves a pleasant drive through the French countryside. You didn't really mean that speech about racing the Calais-Méditerranée Express, did you?"

"Isn't that what you were talking to me about on our way to Paris?"

"No, not specifically, more about trains in general, speculating about the Flèche d'Or. I hadn't thought so far as the Riviera."

"Oh. The Bugatti drivers were so keen, they made it sound like their motor-cars could fly, and when I thought about the speeds that they'd claimed and the flotsam and jetsam you had told me on the train to Paris... I'm sorry. I've made a muddle of this, haven't I? This is why Matthias is looking so thunderous and we are hiding."

"I think you might've overlooked the fact that the Calais-Méditerranée Express is a night express which departs Paris in the early evening, stopping at Dijon, Chalon, and Lyon, before reaching Marseilles early in the morning and then making stops at all the major resort towns of the French Riviera from St. Raphael, Juan-les-Pins, Antibes, Cannes, Nice, Monaco, to its final destination, Menton, near the Italian border. Everyone calls it the le train bleu or the Blue Train for its dark blue sleeping cars. If we were to race it, we would have to navigate the roads by night. I may be prone to silly gambles but I'm not going to be that reckless. Besides, I'd like to win. But, as it happens, I like the idea. If I were a more seasoned driver and knew the roads better... It does sound thrilling."

"I'm not sure a lifetime in hiding from Matthias sounds thrilling. Not to mention Tilly."

"Poor Tilly. We should—"

"Well, if it isn't the gallant rescuer of harassed men!"

Charley turned her head and her eyes lit up in laughter when they landed on a young man in elegant dinner dress, the familiar face of Mr. James Dorsey.

"Why, if it isn't the despair of prospective mothers-in-law," Charley returned. "It's quite a coincidence running into you again. Are you following us?"

"I was wondering the same of you," James Dorsey replied jovially. "I'm with that rather rowdy party in the corner. You?"

"Just here for a quiet drink."

"Of course, you and your friend—Miss Bernhardt, it is a pleasure to see you again—are very welcome to come and join us."

"Oh, well, that is very kind. We appreciate the invitation but we are here for a quiet evening with several other friends and—"

And that was when Matthias's falcon eye caught sight of us from across the crowd and he swooped in.

Charley said to James Dorsey: "On second thought..." and then we all scattered.

Matthias caught up with me before I could camouflage myself in the Bugatti camp. He was scowling fiercely, his entire being threaded with strain and apprehension and concern.

"Andre d'Erlanger is looking for Charley because Barnato has agreed to this damned race. Lucia, it's madness. You must see that. You must see that we need to talk Charley out of it? It isn't safe."

"Charley has everything in hand, Matthias," I told him with more conviction than I felt, hoping he did not notice the quaver in my voice. "Nothing in life is safe. Charley will take care when she needs to. Don't you think she can keep a level-head? She's won one race against the Bentley Boys, you know."

Matthias stilled. His face drained of color as he made me relay the tale to him. I did not dare give him more than the bare skeleton. Matthias cursed roughly and looked around for Charley. It was a sign of his violence of emotion that he did not interrogate me further. I breathed inwardly with relief but it did not bode well for Charley.

"Do you know the man standing beside Charley?"

So Matthias had found her. I looked in the direction he indicated. Charley was standing in a cluster of people with James Dorsey. I told Matthias.

"James Dorsey?" Matthias repeated.

"The hero from Covent Garden who picked up my purse. Not Dr. Bommel, the other one, remember? You sound like you're familiar with him."

"I keep hearing of him. This is the first time I've seen the man. How well exactly does Charley know him?"

"He pops up from time to time. We met him on board the Mauretania, as I've told you previously. He saved Charley's fly-away scarf."

Matthias made me recite the entire history of our acquaintance with James Dorsey from the start and in conscientious detail. I knew it was a terrible idea but there was no escaping it. Matthias's ferocious scowl etched deep into the planes of his face. When he saw Baron Andre d'Erlanger approach, he took himself off abruptly, apologizing to me, because he was going to take a swipe at the man if he stayed. I watched Matthias maneuvering through the crowd towards Charley. I saw Matthias draw Charley away from James Dorsey and pull her towards a corner of the bar where they carried on a tense argument in muted tones—unhappy stubbornness on Charley's side, refusing to retreat, and insistent, burning entreaty on Matthias's.

Baron Andre d'Erlanger found them diverting to watch. "He is jealous, no?" he remarked.

"He is concerned for Charley's safety. He fears that she is unfamiliar with driving in France, and wants her to pull out of the race."

"Then he should drive," said the baron. "He is not half bad."

"You've seen Matthias race?"

"He drives a green Bentley 6.6 Liter Speed Six saloon, does he not? W. O. spoke of the driver who owned it, the respectable banker who worked for Godeffroy's, who took the vehicles for a test drive before selecting that model, said he had good potential, that it was a shame that he did not share the same obsessive passion for motor sports as the rest of us."

This was news. "What did he say about Charley?"

The baron smiled. "W. O. is still courting Charley to be our ambassador. We are all— What ho, is this a breakthrough I spy?"

I looked back at Charley and Matthias. The baron was right. Something had shifted. Matthias was still earnestly towering over her, but resignation had settled over him, a grim resolve squaring his shoulders. Charley's manner was no longer mutinously defiant. Nestled in the cocoon of his shadow, she was gaping back at Matthias in incredulity. She began to shake her head as Matthias continued speaking, each shake more rapid and emphatic than the last. Matthias placed a gentle hand on her shoulder in appeal. Charley shook her head again. I could not make out their words. I did not think Charley said "idiot" or "ridiculous", but it did look like they were squabbling.

"What do you think?" the baron asked, an anticipatory smile already curling around his voice. "Will we have our race?"

We spent the following day in preparations. The race was to take place on the morrow. Several of the Bugatti drivers from the Ritz Bar, of a like mind to Baron Andre d'Erlanger, had also expressed their interest in taking part in the race to Cannes. It had tickled their fancy, they thought it a great caper and, for the driver who arrived first in Cannes, a great victory to savor.

Poor Tilly continued to moan in terror. What would she tell my mother and Charley's aunt if—oh, Miss Charley! But with Matthias's capitulation, Tilly could only flail helplessly in dread, deaf to our words of assurance. We booked Tilly a seat on the Calais-Méditerranée Express and told her that we would be seeing her at the other end and would she mind ordering the cocktails so that they would be ready by the time of our arrival. To distract Tilly from her lamentations of doom and not rob her of a day's experience of Paris from the many cut short by this premature departure, Charley had the Meurice hire a guide and place a motor-car at her disposal to take Tilly to see the Louvre and the Jardin des Tuileries and Jeu de Paume and Musée de l'Orangerie and Jardin du Luxembourg and the poplars and horse-chestnut trees and stroll along the cobbled quais and stone parapets and bridges and banks of the Seine and boulevards and the arcades of the rue de Rivoli and visit the shops and cafes and see the Eiffel Tower and anything else Tilly wished, and bring her back in time to board the Calais-Méditerranée Express to Cannes. (Tilly's admirers had volunteered for the role but Charley deemed this a better arrangement, though she told Tilly that they could certainly join Tilly on the excursion if Tilly wished it.) "Now mind you pay attention, Tilly, you will be tested later on what you've seen today," Charley told a grumbling Tilly as the guide led her to the motor-car.

Matthias went about diligently checking and adjusting our helmets and goggles and gloves and the mechanics and oils and fluids and fuel and spare tyres and every aspect of Charley's Bugatti—despite Charley taking it to a mechanic, and the kind offer from Philippe and Suzanne Étancelin to help us. Matthias went over it all again, trusting no one. He gave us a map and showed us the best route to take and made us go for practice drives out of Paris and back (before doing a final check of the motor-car), warning us about rain, fog, problems with getting petrol and refueling, level crossings between Versailles and Lyon, bad roads and detours, burst tyres... Charley oscillated wildly between sulky contrition and impotent, worried indecision and staring daggers at Matthias's dogged patience, muttering darkly under her breath about stubborn, pig-headed idiots who should pay more attention to their own safety than those who needed no babysitting. Matthias, to Charley's great consternation (the cause of those emphatic shakes of the head), had decided he would join the race in his Bentley. He had no interest in racing but he would be damned if he did not follow us, just in case. Unable to back away from the race, Charley swallowed her irritation and showed Matthias that yes, she did know a little about making motor-car repairs and changing tyres and refused to listen to another word from him until he was able to show to her satisfaction that his own Bentley was in perfect readiness for the race, too.

"Who taught you all this?" I asked Charley.

"Diego taught me to drive and basic on-the-road repairs," Charley said. "Necessity taught me the rest."

We collected Tilly, mulishly conceding that she had been shown some pleasant Parisian sights, and drove her and all our trunks to Gare de Lyon and saw her off. Tilly leaned out out the window like an abandoned orphan child and gave us plaintive, beseeching reminders to be careful.

As dusk began to fall, we returned back to the center of Paris as the streetlights were flickering on, ready to turn in for an early night while the rest of Paris was coming out to play.

"Well, Charley?" Matthias's expression was resigned, without hope, the proverbial fool one heard spoken of in relation to lost causes.

"We'll see you bright and early at the Ritz," Charley answered.

On the morning of the race, we dragged ourselves up before dawn and drove to the meeting point at the Place Vendôme outside the Hôtel Ritz. It was cold in the pre-dawn darkness and felt somehow a degree cooler in the shadow of the silent, gloomy outline of the Ritz's classical Mansart façade from the late 17th century towards the end of the reign of Louis XIV, although "shadow" was was a poor deluded term for it. One could hardly distinguish the outline of one's own nose in the murky light much less that of the Vendôme and the Cambon rooftops from the dark sky. The outfits we had recently acquired from the Parisian ateliers and set aside from the trunks that had gone with Tilly on the Calais-Méditerranée Express were not proof against the sharp bite of the morning air—they were comfortable and versatile and elegant and acceptable for touring if not exactly for racing —but our helmets and silk scarves kept out some of the chill and the rest we accepted. The sun would soon rise and flood us with warmth.

Matthias was already waiting there. His eyes were weary and dark with concern. A tussle ensued when I made the mistake of a visible shiver. He had already begun taking off his jacket to offer it to us and was about to head into the Ritz to demand additional warm clothes be obtained when Charley told him that we had rugs in the backseat of the Bugatti and that she would make it her life's mission to lose his tail on the way if he did not calm down. We had had a basket made up for us of brioche and baguettes and cold roasted Bresse chicken and ham and cheese and fruit and four flasks, two filled with coffee, two with water, sitting in the backseat next to the rugs and extra cans of petrol and other supplies. Charley gave Matthias one of each flask and made him take half of our wrapped sandwiches for his breakfast when the sun rose, and some spare snacks for the road in case he was running late for lunch. "Bet you forgot to eat, didn't you?" Charley said. Matthias glowered back at her. He looked like he had not slept much either.

Baron Andre d'Erlanger arrived shortly afterwards in his 4½ Liter Blower Bentley (no, it was not the one he had raced at Le Mans) and bid us a cheery bonjour. Soon after his arrival, other Bugatti drivers began to trickle into the square, amassing in a motley camp outside the Ritz. In the midst of all the motor-cars and people gathered in the dim half-light of the Place Vendôme, I thought I caught sight of James Dorsey, flickering in and out of the congregation but it was hard to be certain.

"See you later in the Carlton Bar!" the baron waved to us before blowing off in his Bentley.

"We'll we waiting for you with the champagne on ice!" Charley called back above the growls of the waking engines.

I had imagined a scenic journey similar to the drive from Paris to Blois. It was a stupendously silly notion in hindsight. We were racing against Baron Andre d'Erlanger and the sun, over unfamiliar roads and terrain in a foreign country and the journey, if we did not run across mishaps, would take an entire day. We would be fortunate to arrive by nightfall.

The journey was scenic, a reel of orchards and fields and vineyards and market towns and villages and farms and woods and forest and hills and valleys filtered through the everchanging light, although I missed appreciating much of its beauties. I was too nervous and intent on reading the map and checking the road signs along the way and trying not to send us off the road or into a pond (oh, I could not get Toad's song out of my head!) or in the wrong direction or veer off a ledge on a hairpin bend or... It was terrifying being a navigator. I wanted to do my bit to help since I was unable to be a relief driver for Charley. We were very sensible about the enterprise. Charley was very solemnly adamant about winning the race in one piece or not at all. We made brief periodic pit stops to refuel and eat and check the condition of the motor-car and make sure we were on the correct path, occasionally waving at our fellow racers in the Bugattis who passed by and tooted merrily at us. Seeing them vanish ahead of us into the distance made me anxious that we were falling behind and wonder where and how far ahead Baron d'Erlanger was but Charley remained unperturbed, at least outwardly. I knew what losing the gamble meant for her, or I knew some of it; there was very likely more at stake than Charley had revealed. Charley never allowed us to deviate from the steady course. "Don't be rattled, Lucia. We just follow the road ahead and get there in one piece to enjoy the cocktails that Tilly will have ordered for us." So we followed the long stretch of road wherever it beckoned and pointed.

We never lost Matthias, our shadow. Once, he eased his Bentley smoothly down beside the road and joined us, asking if we were all right. We replied yes; and Charley felt incumbent upon her to ask if he was all right and did he want an apple, which brought a ghost of an exasperated smile to Matthias's face.

When we were on the road and had a good sense of the next section of our route south, Charley drove like a demon, speaking little, furious in concentration, almost as though in prayer, not a sign of Ingenious Mr. Toad in sight. The wind and trees whipped by us in a roaring blur as if we were in the eye of a tornado. I thought of the swift carriage, of a dark night, rattling with four horses over roads that one could not see. I had asked to come along for the ride, and Charley had said yes. I clutched at the map spread upon the dashboard and held on tight. It was, in its harrowing way, a glorious adventure.

We swiftly left Paris behind us, cut a swath through central France, passed Lyon, and broadly followed the reverse of the Hundred Days journey through the French Alps that Napoleon had taken on his return in 1815 from exile in Elba. We closed in on Provence and clung to the twisting, windy cliff roads as if we held onto one long, endless breath. As the chalky white hills tufted with lonely trees and dry, hardy grasses and rocky outcrops and the hidden mas and iron framework of village bell towers gave way—100 miles off, 10 miles off, 5 miles off—to shuttered villas and luxuriant perfumed gardens, lemon and eucalyptus, bougainvillea, jasmine, mimosa, umbrella pine, and the tender, intensified clarity of air and cloudless skies brought by the mistral—as the light began to fade—I thought I saw the glitter of the silvery-blue Mediterranean—

"Are we...? Is that...?"

"God, I hope so, I'm hungry."

Coming into the pearly dusk, the white line indistinguishable between the shore and the horizon parted to reveal clusters of tiled rooftops baked hot in the sun and old fortifications jutting through stoic dark pine forest, a glimpse here or there of an isolated beach or hithe, a thin pale strip of road, and the hues of the unblinking sea. We eased back into civilization, merging into the traffic of other motor-cars and following the long winding ribbon of the Promenade de la Croisette stretching along the shore, past the stirring of activity amongst the bright awnings and plane trees and palms and shining white yachts, until we saw the distinctive domes on the seaward corners of the Carlton Hotel.

The Bugatti drew to a stop outside the hotel entrance. Behind the wheel, Charley tore off her helmet and blew out her breath. "I could do with a drink. You, Lucia?"

As I sat on the front seat, surrounded by the noise and color and smells and balmy warmth of Cannes, at the grand hotel looming overhead and the Mediterranean across the road, no coherence presented itself to me. Only a long, breathless, strangled laugh escaped my throat.

Charley nodded. "I couldn't agree more."

We called the doorman of the Carlton Hotel to be witness to our time of arrival, and then waited for Matthias to arrive. Matthias's Bentley drew up to the hotel alongside the Bugatti. As Matthias alighted from his motor-car, his expression of guarded relief at seeing us mirrored Charley's own. We did not exchange many words but it was clear that a peace had been reached in that full, potent silence. The three of us strolled into the lobby of the Carlton together. The concierge seemed to have been expecting an influx of guests this evening and invited us to have a drink in the bar while we waited for the rest of Baron d'Erlanger's party to arrive. Did this really mean...?

We asked the concierge if Mlle Tilly Fairchild had checked in and were informed that she had and would be advised immediately of our arrival. Tilly fell upon us in tears of relief. She had booked suites at the Carlton as instructed and not done much else for the entirety of the day since she had disembarked from the Blue Train at Cannes station, too sick with worry. "I'm sorry, Tilly," Charley told her. "Are you still feeling too poorly to join us for a celebratory drink? It is after all your first evening on the French Riviera. Next time, I promise, we shall take the train and go by wagon-lit, too." Tilly's demurrals were feeble and quickly overruled.

We headed to the bar, as the concierge had suggested, to await the rest of the party even though it looked like a nap would have been preferred. There were two gentlemen already seated at the bar. They seemed to recognize Charley, waving her over and greeting her. Charley introduced us to two more Bentley Boys. Sir Henry "Tim" Birkin and M. Jean Chassagne —both familiar faces at Le Mans—greatly enjoyed the news of the race that Baron Andre d'Erlanger brought, hurrying into the bar about half an hour later, blaming his delay on trouble with a burst tyre requiring use of his only spare. (Matthias had insisted on us having two.) They toasted to our victory, increasingly impressed by our feat and time achieved as the other drivers straggled in with tales of troubles with gears or water pumps or boiling radiators or other mechanical mishap or hazard encountered on the road. Charley waved it off, maintaining that she was grateful France drove on the right side of the road and that the rest was luck, not wishing to fuel the reignited debate around the bar about the reliability and durability of a Bentley compared to the fragility of the lightweight Bugattis.

The bar filled up with the clink of ice and crystal and the rising cadence of convivial post-race chatter from the participants, still in their racing overalls—they had parked their motor-cars at the hotel entrance and come straight in to present themselves for roll-call and, not bothering to change, had settled in for a drink—standing out amidst the other formally dressed hotel guests and bar patrons. Charley and I were the odd ones out in our day clothes—to which Charley added her dash of chic—passable for a garden party, not quite fancy enough for evening nor part of the racing uniformed crowd, but none of this seemed to matter. If there was a dress code, it had been jettisoned for the evening. They built a glittering pyramid of champagne coupes and brought out magnums of Veuve Clicquot and engaged in the Napoleonic tradition of sabrage, which they felt fitting for the ceremonious occasion, filling up the tower to great cheers and set about just as enthusiastically to demolishing it with ringing laughter and more cheers, floating out the row of French doors into the indigo twilight. We were warmly feted, tugged hither and thither about the party, drifting in and out of conversations with different people, swept into numerous toasts. Matthias, being the only driver besides Baron Andre d'Erlanger of a Bentley in the race, was pulled into a pow-wow of the Bentley Boys from which his gaze flickered and met ours from time to time. It was nice to see Matthias looking more relaxed, that the tautness in his bearing had finally eased a little. Even Tilly lost her look of wretched misery and got caught up in the glamor of the surrounds, the gaiety of the celebrations and the exciting stories being shared over the flow of champagne and cocktails and spirits, her waning anxiety displaced by a shyly hesitant but satisfied pride that "her charges" and Mr. Vandermeer had beaten all the seasoned racing drivers.

For all her talk of cocktails, hovering like a beckoning mirage at the end of the race, Charley took one look at the drinks tray and asked the bartender for "Limonade...no, wait...citronade, s'il vous plaît". She claimed that she could still taste the alcoholic fumes from the cocktails she had consumed at the Ritz Bar and that she wanted to enjoy this first night under a flawless sky of stars in the South of France, that she did not intend to let the edges blur this time. The baron tsked and countermanded Charley's order of citronade for "a proper drink" and told her that she could not rely on luck all the time, Ettore or Jean Bugatti would likely be giving her a tap on the shoulder soon if they had not already done so, but best to put her faith in the Bentley that Babe would be sending her, like the dependable 6.6 Liter Speed Six Old Number One that Babe and Tim had driven to win Le Mans (and, incidentally, the same model that Matthias Vandermeer had driven to come in second place, but with a saloon body). The baron was eager for the next rematch—if the pace of today's race was any indication, the race against le train bleu would be a breeze. Charley said she was not sure that life as a fugitive from the wrath of Matthias Vandermeer would be worth it, but she would think about it, and then reordered the citronade, and wondered aloud whether Harry Selfridge's yacht was moored in the harbor.

"Hail to the conquering heroine."

Charley laughed when she turned around and saw James Dorsey. "You are following us around!"

"I tagged along with one of the Bugatti teams. It seemed too interesting to pass up."

"Oh, we didn't know you were going to be joining the race. We didn't see you at the meeting point. Why didn't you come and say hello?"

"Your friend was with you, the one who came crashing through the Ritz Bar two evenings ago and dragged you off. That protector of yours is a big, angry brute, isn't he?"

If James Dorsey had used a less jocular tone or called Matthias "a great lummox", as the Calvert cousins had once done and earned a thrashing for it, Charley might not have answered in as light a manner as she did: "Matthias? Not at all. Perhaps wrong-headed and misguided at times, but he always means well."

"Will you be staying long in Cannes?"

"I'm not sure. The Bentley Boys seem bursting with all sorts of wild ideas and riling up the Bugatti drivers. We're after a rather more peaceful sojourn, aren't we, Lucia? It might be best just to slip quietly away."

I could not quite silence my snort in time. "Oh, really, you've had enough hair-raising excitement? I quite liked the baron's suggestion of—"

"That's the cocktails talking."

"If you can manage to give your protector the slip, let me show you the Cote d'Azur under the stars."

But the Bentley Boys and Bugatti drivers came around again and bore us off into the revelry.

The party in the bar lasted until the early hours of the following morning.

Poor Charley, we found her fast asleep, curled up in a corner couch, while the party continued on around her. I would have expected Matthias to have been just as exhausted, but he chuckled quietly at the sight of Charley, out of commission at last, and picked her up gently and carried her to the hotel suite that Tilly had booked for us.

A disheveled room met us.

Tilly uttered a cry of dismay.

"Take my suite instead," Matthias said. "The hotel staff can rearrange and prepare it for you. I'll stay in here for the night and investigate. If there is anything—"

"There's no need, Mr. Vandermeer."

There was nothing missing. The clothes, hats, shoes, scarves, and books Charley had bought and been given in Paris that Tilly had carefully unpacked were flung about the room and furniture in disarray, the trunks opened and attacked, searched, ransacked, papers out of order, like a vivid artistic representation of fury and frustration. Only the ignored jars of candy from Matthias stood meekly to the side, silently apologizing for that which was not their fault. But nothing was missing, Tilly affirmed again.

"How can you tell, Tilly, without doing a thorough cataloged search?"

"I'm sure," Tilly asserted. Her gaze flickered to Charley. Tilly went to clear the space on the beds and Matthias placed the still sleeping Charley on one of them and covered her with a blanket.

"We need to report this. I'll alert the hotel management. They'll likely want to come up and interview you tonight—well—this morning. I'm sorry about this. I'll try to keep as much of this away from you as possible," Matthias said, picking up the volume of Ulysses lying on the carpet near his feet and setting it on a side table. "Lock the door behind you and check the windows too. I'll be back shortly."

We thanked Matthias and went to make sure the suite was secure.

"Tilly, how do you know for sure nothing is missing?"

Tilly checked all the doors and windows again and drew the curtains. Then she showed me.

Goodness, Charley had a devious imagination.

19

CHARLOTTE:

I emerged from a sleep so deep it was like returning from death. I would not have minded plunging back into its dark, blank depths. It was quite cool and comfortable as I was, a gentle, drifting peace. Was there any reason to move? But the surface was hovering overhead with an insistent tidal pull. I lay blinking my way slowly to wakefulness, and remembered. The motor-race. The wager with Barnato. The sea.

When I finally opened my eyes, a faint dawn was pressing against the window between the thin gap where the drapes met imperfectly. Cannes lay outside presumably. The Mediterranean. We were not in Paris anymore. There were low voices murmuring beyond the door. I raised myself up on my elbows and looked around. I was still wearing my clothes of yesterday underneath the sheets although someone had taken my shoes off and placed them neatly beneath the bed.

A knock sounded and the door opened, Lucia came into the room, also wearing the same clothes as when I last remembered her at the Carlton Bar, followed by Matthias. I would have been an idiot not to realize that something was wrong.

Lucia and Matthias bid me good morning as if I was a skittish colt.

"Do I need a drink before you whack me with the news?" I said. "Or you could just hand me the telegram."

"Telegram?" Matthias echoed.

"Charley, no, this isn't—Charley, somebody searched our suite whilst we were all in the bar last evening," Lucia cut in calmly, her eyes teeming with everything she left unsaid. "Tilly's still stubbornly trying to put everything to rights after the police came in to look about. But nothing was taken."

That jolted me awake. "Another one? Was anyone hurt? Does this mean

—"

"That you've been followed? Not necessarily. There have been no casualties. Your suite was not the only one hit last night," Matthias said. "There are reports of several others along this corridor being targeted as well as other hotels along the Croisette including the Hôtel Martinez and Hôtel Miramar. Not all of them were as lucky to escape unscathed. I'm sorry that—"

"Are there any suspects?"

Did Matthias hesitate?

"No plausible ones so far," he said. "You should all have breakfast and get some rest. And then I'd recommend thinking carefully about alternate options for securing your valuables, which I can help arrange for you, if you intend to remain here at the Carlton or finding alternate accommodation for your stay on the French Riviera. It is very late in the season to be looking for a holiday rental but—"

It was a little early to be getting into an argument with Matthias but as a matter of principle: "We have thought carefully. I have nothing of irreplaceable material value. Wouldn't matter anyway if they were lost. They're all insured. If you can offer a bank vault for Lucia's diamond necklace, however, she might want to—"

"Lucia's mother's necklace," said Lucia. "I'm sure it is insured—with Godeffroy's, I believe—but I think it is pretty safe where it currently is."

"Are you sure?"

"Mother tasked me to wear it. So I'll wear it. But I'm not having Matthias run off to get it out of a bank vault every time someone sends a party invitation. I think the state of the suite suggests that the thief was frustrated in his attempt which is a good sign of...the effectiveness of our security measures." Lucia gave me a pointed look.

A nonsensical giggle rose to my lips and nearly escaped.

"I'm not sure I follow." Matthias's brow creased in a deep furrow at us. "I'm not meant to follow, am I?"

"In good time, Matthias. If breakfast hasn't been ordered yet, may I pull on the bell-rope now before you schedule in the interrogation?"

Poor Matthias, frowning with so much perplexed weariness. He must have stepped into his protective, stuffed shirt mode and lost the way out again. His face looked gray. How long had it been since he had last slept— 24, no, 48 hours ago? I should not have been so hard on him but he needed to reminded of a sense of proportion and perspective. And naps and sustenance.

In the private moments after breakfast after everyone had been forced by me to take a nap, I ran down to the lobby to check for telegrams.

"TRANSFERS RECEIVED FROM B POSSIBILITY HUNTINGDON COLD FEET D"

The cable was scrunched up into a ball before I could master myself. Slowly, I unwound the ball and smoothed out the piece of paper and tore it up into tiny little snowflakes. I penned a reply.

"B VERY SPORTING VS AGREED HONG KONG SHANGHAI HOLDINGS PEGASUS SHOULD RECEIVE FUNDS FORTHWITH HUNTINGDON MY BLUNDER RELEASE ESPERANCE RUNNYMEDE C"

I had just come away from the front desk when I heard: "I'm sorry that this has been your introduction to the South of France."

I turned to find Matthias standing in the lobby, practically standing at my shoulder, looking only marginally less ashen than earlier and a bit disheveled, as if he had only just fallen into bed—so he could say he had fulfilled the letter of his agreement to rest—and bolted out again a second later, which he probably had. What was he doing, hanging around like a bad conscience?

"Aren't you supposed to be taking a nap?"

"You're down here," he retorted.

"I was the one who evidently slept through all the excitement last night so I'm exempt. What's your excuse?" I began to walk back to the elevators. Matthias fell into step beside me.

"You seem very unruffled by all this," Matthias remarked.

"If you were Lucia, you'd be telling me next that it is a giveaway sign of my criminal guilt." A startled, confused dismay overcame Matthias's face but that expression fled on the instant before I could examine its meaning. He pressed me to explain. "Lucia fancies herself an armchair detective." This did not seem to register anywhere near his funny bone. "Oh, for pity's sake, Matthias, your lack of sleep is addling your brain cells! Nobody was hurt. There are worse things than a riffled hotel suite."

"It may be more than that," Matthias said with gentle gravity. "I wish you'd reconsider—"

"What do you mean?" The elevator doors opened and we entered. There were no attendants or hotel guests in the elevator and I felt at liberty to return his questioning from breakfast.

"You had the same thought earlier, that the series of attempted robberies you've encountered on your trip were not isolated incidents."

"So we are being followed?"

"Possibly. Do you recall the Holyoke Masquerade Ball?"

"Are we back to that again? I told you I don't—"

"The Holyoke Ball at The Sagamore Hotel in Bolton Landing, was one of the evenings on which a burglary attempt was made on the hosts and guests to deprive them of their worldly jewels, unsuccessful as it happened, like several of the other burglaries over the past year on the East Coast of America." Matthias anticipated me before I could besiege him with questions. "The police and the insurers of the jewels have been jointly investigating the burglaries. Jewels were stolen but we don't know how except that the theft did not always take place at the events, as perhaps reported in the papers, but rather before the event. A pattern seems to have emerged. A party would take place, jewels worn to the party would be stolen. Frequently they were discarded during an apparent bungled escape or dumped nearby to be later found by police and returned to the owners. The owners of the jewels were unaware until the returned jewels were examined and discovered to be fake. Since the jewels were genuine at the time that they were insured, there is a wide window within which the real jewels could have been swapped for a copy."

"I don't see a connection. I don't understand how that is connected to the things that have happened on our Grand Tour."

Matthias's eyes flickered with a conflicted light. "So far, two potential connections. Two people who were or are believed to have been present on each of those occasions. James Dorsey was one. And the other..."

"Me?" I stared at Matthias. "I'm a suspect?"

"Not yet," Matthias answered.

"I don't understand what that means." A shiver passed through me. "Who— Where do you stand?"

"James Dorsey's attendance at the events is known to the official investigators."

"The official...?"

"The police. The insurance investigators."

"And you are...not actually on holiday?"

"I am. I was only handed this... The two matters just...coincided. To date, only I know that James Dorsey was present or within the vicinity on each of the occasions when something has been stolen or your belongings have been ransacked. Your secret business and disappearances have not helped." All the scowling and hovering and meddling would have been intolerable if Matthias's earnest concern had not been bleeding through every terse word and frown-line and gesture. "I am also the only one involved with the investigation who knows that you lied about your whereabouts in the past year in your letters. Your friends have staunchly vouched for you, Charley, but I know for certain that you were not at the Holyoke Masquerade. There is a witness. You said that there are worse things than a riffled hotel suite. What did you mean by that, Charley? What are these things?"

"How long have you been investigating me?"

"Not you. The burglaries. The stolen jewels which were insured by the company." Matthias's eyes were as troubled as I had ever seen them, his expression, the way he held himself, tortured. I thought of King Canute trying to hold back the tides. "This is serious, Charley. It's one thing to keep secrets, but getting mixed up with this investigation—"

"I see. Like the time the diamonds went missing at the Savoy party. Where Mr. Dorsey also happened to be present."

"I have attempted to broach this subject—your disappearances—with Diego," Matthias said wearily, "many times, and, diplomatically, discreetly, with Aunt Merry. I am satisfied that Aunt Merry knows nothing. Diego, on the other hand, is tight-lipped. His allegiance is clear. His testimony cannot be trusted. Which leaves Lucia and Tilly. Tilly seems to know as much about your movements as Aunt Merry, but Lucia, you and Lucia have been inseparable since you were children, she—"

Another shiver threatened. I hoped, at least, that it was not visible. "You will find that Lucia knows as little as Tilly does, so it will not be a question of trust and you will find no satisfaction badgering them, You will lose nothing by leaving them out of this. In fact, you made me a promise, Matthias, in Blois. Are you reneging on it?"

"No, but—"

"Good. The same holds for Tilly. Do whatever else you must. I shan't stand in your way."

"But you won't tell me the truth?"

"I'm not afraid. Bring on whatever investigations you like. But my business is mine to tell or withhold. You must decide where you stand on your own, whether you choose to trust me or not."

"Trust does not satisfy the burden of proof of an official investigation," Matthias growled low. "If they get hold of you, nothing that I can do or say —"

"Are you trying to be my captor or guard-dog? Do your employers know about this wavering impartiality of yours?"

"Charley—"

"I think, Mr. Vandermeer, that you are a little confused about which hat you are wearing. You cannot hang a man on circumstantial evidence alone just because you decide you dislike him more than you do me. May I remind you that Mr. Dorsey was present at the celebrations last evening when the attempted hotel room ransackings were supposed to have taken place. There was a crowd of witnesses in the Carlton Bar to testify to it."

"It has long been suspected that the East Coast burglaries were not carried out alone."

"Oh, an accomplice! Well, there goes my alibi too! And everyone else who was in the bar last night."

"Charley—"

"Where do you stand, Matthias?"

Matthias turned his eyes to me and for a long moment, I lived in the world of his fathomless amber brown gaze. I lowered my head to look away. I would have walked away but there was nowhere to go.

The elevator doors opened on a lower floor to ours. Andre d'Erlanger was waiting outside on the landing and he came bounding into the elevator, bursting with news of last evening's burglaries. His concerned garrulity kept us all occupied until we reached our floor where he accompanied me to see the suite that had been the scene of an attempted crime and argued for Lucia and Tilly and me to remain at the Carlton, despite the outrage that had taken place—a random incident, an aberration, the police were sure to get to the bottom of it soon, we must not let this black mark obliterate the delights which awaited us in the South of France!—instead of taking a holiday rental. Matthias hung back, silently watchful, and did not once intervene.

20

LUCIA:

The natural beauty of the South of France was blinding. One came away as though touched by too much of the fierce sun, filled with wonder at the magical alchemy of bright, translucent air and shining sea and sky and light. The Post-Impressionists had migrated here to soak in the light, and splashed it vividly across their canvases to inspire the world to envy.

Had we come to the French Riviera before the First World War when the fashionable abandoned the South of France during the summer months, we could have had the Mediterranean to ourselves and enjoyed a recluse's heaven. The war and the Americans changed all that.

Until Gerald Murphy (heir to the Mark Cross luxury leather goods company) and Sara Wiborg (of the wealthy Wiborg family and a printing-ink fortune, niece to Civil War General William Tecumseh Sherman) convinced the storied and luxurious Hôtel du Cap-Eden Roc in 1923 to stay open for the summer so that they might entertain their friends, the French Riviera had traditionally been a winter escape for the aristocracy of Europe, not a summer resort destination. Americans had been coming to the South of France since the 19th century, of course, but while Europe was still recovering from the war and the American dollar was strong, more and more Americans began flocking to the South of France to enjoy the fair climes and bon vivant life. Wealthy moguls and financiers and celebrities and artists and writers soon outnumbered the royal houses of Europe, the old guard aristocrats and the British. The generous hospitality and parties of the Murphys at Villa America, their villa at Cap d'Antibes, helped to turn the French Riviera into a vibrant summer haven for the new arrivals. They held lavish parties and elaborate picnics at La Garoupe, sipping sherry under parasols to the tune of the latest jazz songs on their portable Vitrola, diving at night from high rocks into the sea in full evening wear, and introduced sunbathing on the beach as a fashionable activity (to Americans at least, there was some debate over whether it had been Coco Chanel who made sunbathing fashionable in Paris when she acquired a striking tan during the summer of 1923) and became the center of a circle of artists and writers including their American friends the Fitzgeralds, Ernest Hemingway, John Dos Passos, Dorothy Parker, John O'Hara, and the illustrious figures of the European arts scene such as Jean Cocteau, Pablo Picasso, Fernand Léger, Man Ray, Igor Stravinsky and Sergei Diaghilev, fueling a renaissance of art and letters on the French Riviera which rivaled that of Les Années Folles in Paris. (It had been Cole Porter, a friend and fellow Yale alumni of Gerald Murphy's, and Porter's wife, Linda, who introduced the Murphys to the South of France when the Murphys came to visit the Porters in 1922 in their rented Château de la Garoupe, next to the Hôtel du Cap-Eden Roc at the tip of Cap d'Antibes, and fell in love with the French Riviera's deserted crystalline blue coves and lush palm-fringed coast. Despite what they started, the Porters moved on to Venice and never returned to the Cote d'Azur.)

By the time we came to the playground of the French Riviera in the high summer of 1929, the Murphys and most of their circle had gone. The hedonistic Riviera partied on as gaily as ever, attracting more of the wealthy, fashionable, famous, and curious, but the dying strains of their incandescent partying, the ravishing jazz and champagne-swilling heydays on the Cote d'Azur, echoed through Hyères, Saint-Tropez, Saint-Raphaël, Cannes, Antibes, Nice, Cap Ferrat, Monte Carlo, the dazzle of their stardust sprinkled across the warm murmurous nights, joining the whispers of the swaying palms and the milky stars and the twinkling shoreline.

The popularity of the summer season on the Riviera meant that our social diary would be as demanding as the London Season. Considering what Charley had made of the London Season, how much of it she had avoided, it seemed unlikely that Charley was looking forward to more invitations and parties and all-night carousing. The attentions of James Dorsey and Baron Andre d'Erlanger and the company of several of the Bentley Boys, who enjoyed partying as much as they loved racing, promised to make a variance to the routine, but I could not help wondering if it would all seem like a distraction to Charley from her main purpose—if she would start behaving mysteriously, getting involved in intrigues and vanishing again.

The brief spell of anonymity that Charley and I had enjoyed in Paris could not be maintained on the French Riviera. In theory, it should have been simple to laze the days away under the flame of the Provencal sun, amidst the groves of pine and cypress and poplars and olive and citrus trees, amongst the jagged rocky terraces falling away to a blazing sea or the tiny secluded inlets of pebbly beach. However, the motor-race to Cannes had made our arrival known and the invitations flowed in from many directions, including forays into high society finagled by Matthias and the letters of introduction carried by Charley, and the many activities and parties that the Bentley Boys and our new Bugatti racing friends exhorted us to attend, and unexpected hospitality from some rather august personages whom none of us had ever heard of before and perplexed us until the name of Bommel was mentioned.

Of course, facing the inevitable had never stopped Charley before. Charley held out hope for a quiet, if brief, secluded time on the Riviera. She cited Lady Russell's Portofino novel as a lotus-eater's guidebook for traveling the distance from the chattering clink of champagne festivities into the sunshine and the lassitude of the shaded grove. Instead of finding a suitable holiday rental and moving out of the Carlton Hotel or staying in Cannes or Nice, and venturing into the summer season and the world of beautiful trailing tea-gowns and the nights of foie gras and langoustine and champagne, Charley decided to, well, put all of it out of her mind—for a pocket of time—and encouraged us to do the same.

"Nobody will miss us," Charley said as she tore up yet more telegrams. And anyway, Charley did not give anyone a chance to object.

So, in the South of France, we became tourists.

We left the parties and sea behind us and headed into the hills. Matthias drove us to Cimiez, the cream and white Belle Époque resort of les hivernants, in the hills above Nice where Queen Victoria had wintered, and to Grasse to pay homage to the gardens of the late Alice de Rothschild and to visit the perfumeries and see the harvest of scent—a heady miasma of lavender, myrtle, jasmine, rose, orange blossom, wild mimosa, violet— where we encouraged Tilly to pick whichever perfumes she liked from Galimard, Molinard, and the recently established Fragonard. The fields reminded me of the linen water fragrances used in the Montrose laundry; it was as if we had come to the source, which, given that we were in Provence, we probably had. Charley chose only one Lalique crystal flacon of scent whose prime note hinted of myrtle and lavender which seemed to trail her in the following days, like a whisper of a fresh tantalizing breeze carried from a Provencal field, drifting through the elegant salons and jazzy Mediterranean night, or the teasingly elusive glimmer of the sea through a dense canopy of pine needles, a reminder of the rolling hills and their siren call of spacious freedom.

We made excursions to Marseilles, taking a ferry ride out to the island of the Château d'If, the prison of the fictional Count of Monte Cristo of Alexandre Dumas, père—"à quoi tiennent la vie et la fortune!"—"On what slender threads do life and fortune hang!"—and saw the entire harbor shoreline from the Vieux Port to the hilltop basilica of Notre-Dame de la

Garde, the highest point in the city, a beacon site for sailors set by Charles II of Anjou in 1302, a summit to which we climbed—and what a glorious view it gave!—high above the waves, within reach of the mountain peaks and the clouds, like a palace of the gods and the Provencal winds. We came back down to the water-front to lunch on bouillabaisse and drink the local wine and, later, sipped pastis with cool spring water.

Matthias took us to see the Roman temples, arena and elliptical amphitheater and fountain gardens of Nîmes and we rambled over the nearby Roman aqueduct of Pont du Gard. We went to visit Arles, immortalized by Vincent van Gogh. We admired the architecture and windows and baptisteries and serene cloisters of churches and cathedrals. We drove to Sénanque Abbey, the first Cistercian monastery founded in Provence, and walked through the surrounding aromatic lavender fields and took away some of their sun-heated scent on our skin. We strolled the streets of Aix-en-Provence under the leaves of the plane trees, as Paul Cézanne, Émile Zola and Ernest Hemingway had done, and drank coffee at the cafes, enjoying the cool of the gurgling fountains and, afterwards, armed with boxes of orange-blossom scented navettes provençale (to which we had become attached in Marseilles) and gibassier and exquisitely melting little almond cakes called calissons d'Aix, we went to visit the white former papal city of Avignon. We climbed up to Les Baux-de-Provence, on a rocky hilltop fort, to see the 360 degree views. We decided that was fun and climbed some more to Gordes, a high hilltop village facing the Luberon, where we bought delicious freshly baked fougasse bread and sausages and cheeses and cured hams and pâtés and olive tapenades and ate them in the town square before going off to explore its narrow, sloping cobbled streets and terraces. We continued to the ocher-pigmented Roussillon, perched on another hill within the Luberon valley, and took in its views and filled our lungs with the pale diffused light and air.

There were mas and bastides dotted amongst the Provencal hills, as we had seen on our race to Cannes. How wonderful, I thought, how liberating it would be to live here, so simply and contentedly.

It was tempting to continue on towards Languedoc, but we turned back, following the azure sea eastward, driving along the coast between Marseilles and Cassis, pausing to visit the dramatic cliffs ("We cannot miss seeing the falaises," Charley said) and sheltered inlets ("Or the calanques," Charley said) pounded by wild waves. And then, we resolved, we would truly head back—but still we found ourselves readily stopping along the shore—to partake of interesting regional flavors of luncheon dishes in an unassuming restaurant, or to buy bread, cheese, pâté, wine, fruit and cakes from the plentiful markets, charcuteries, pâtisseries and boulangeries to take away to a nice beach, and to lose a new pair of espadrilles to the wash of the Mediterranean when one was not paying attention (Charley, and very nearly

Tilly as well), or to wander through picturesque little fishing villages and towns and open-air flower markets and watch the locals play civilized games of pétanque or boules—slowly, oh so slowly, edging east, passing through the resort towns of Saint-Tropez, Sainte-Maxime, Fréjus, and the red rock Esterel beaches near Saint-Raphaël in returning to Cannes.

We were handed a bunch of messages by the hotel clerk of the Carlton. The number of invitations and telegrams looked like it had multiplied.

"I guess everyone is still speaking to us," Charley said.

Thus began our true debut on the French Riviera.

Baron Andre d'Erlanger rebuked us mildly for running away and missing out on the parties and promptly issued us with more invitations. Outings with the Bentley Boys turned out to be fun. They raced all over the place (Matthias always offered to be chauffeur or co-driver so we never lacked an escape from the spirited excesses) for picnics and plages and to watch yacht races off the waters of Cannes, taking us from the bustling Croisette through pleasure-seeking Saint-Tropez and Antibes and sunny Saint Paul de Vence and carnival-like Nice and Cagnes-sur-Mer and Èze, the lofty eagle's nest (like Nietzsche, except for the mental exertions of composing the third part of his cheery philosophical novel Also Sprach Zarathustra as he hiked up to the village perché), Cap Ferrat, the white sands and pebbles of Cap-d'Ail's Plage la Mala, and along the Corniche connecting glamorous Monte Carlo to as far as Menton, its stone houses clustered on a steep slope rising from the sea turning the color of honey in the afternoon light, on the Italian border. We saw so much of the beauty of the hinterland and limpid shores of the Riviera along the way. I believe I once heard Charley standing on the edge of a hill, gazing down a sheer drop of several thousand feet to the Mediterranean Sea, murmuring words that sounded like "waters" and "firmament".

"Would you like help to arrange a holiday rental in these locations that you like?" Matthias asked, as though he had nothing else to do and was not being taxed by the nervousness on the London markets (as Charley apparently was and pretended not to be) or the ongoing lack of results in the investigation in the hotel break-ins in Cannes. "I can have a listing ready by this afternoon. There is also a villa available in Cimiez—"

"No, no," Charley said, "it's all in hand."

"How?" we asked. "Where?"

"I have two addresses, fully furnished, house and grounds staff remaining, both secure and vacant for the summer, or what is left of it. One of them is soon to be put on the market for sale. We shall be doing the owners a favor in staying and airing them out. We can pick up the keys from the agent in the morning to take a look around or move in directly. One villa is in Hyères, the other in Antibes."

"Hyères?"

"Yes, old English expat watering hole. We can pay calls whilst we are there."

We joined a distinguished body of people—from Robert Louis Stevenson and Joseph Conrad to Queen Victoria and a long line of British aristocracy—in heading out to Hyères, the oldest resort on the French Riviera and for some centuries the resort of French kings, on the peninsula of Giens, beneath the pine-covered hill of Costebelle, to call on the Countess Josephine de Rouvroy for afternoon tea on her south-facing terrace, with a staggering view down to the Mediterranean, under the shade of the palms at her villa, Caravel, where she asked after the Bommels and gossiped cheerfully about her neighbors, including the American lady novelist, Mrs. Edith Wharton whose gardens at her summer villa, Castel Sainte-Claire, were quite marvelously exotic, and who often escaped her writing toils to come to tea... Oh, do please help ourselves to the sweets— but was the rumor true that two young American girls had raced a pack of Bugattis from Paris to Cannes on a wager for the chairman of Bentley Motors?

After calling on the Countess de Rouvroy, we traveled a short distance to the Villa Alba.

We came off the road and followed a path leading to the estate's high stone walls topped with wrought-iron railings over which spilled cascades of wisteria and bougainvillea. Behind the heavily padlocked gates, which Charley unlocked with the keys from the agent, was a dense wilderness of foliage and overgrown shrubbery, giving no hint of what might lie on the other side, hidden from view: we passed through the tangle of foliage and trailing blossoms, pierced by delicate shafts of sunlight, to a private walled garden inhabited by parasol pine, laurel, lemon myrtle, eucalyptus, cypress arches, trellises covered in tendrils of grapevine and wisteria, palms, olive and Judas trees, white, primrose and scarlet bougainvillea, exotic shrubs, box hedges, herb borders, a winter garden of mimosa and camellias and other plants that flowered in winter, a white pavilion, a pond with a fountain and lily pads, rosemary, marjoram, thyme, sage, oregano, lemon verbena, lemon balm, beds upon beds of Alba and other old roses, lavender, jasmine, hyacinths, gardenias, lily-of-the-valley, narcissi, tulips, lilac trees, heavy with blossom, fat heads of hydrangeas and peonies, azaleas of every vivid hue, massed drifts of floral color and scent across manicured lawns surrounding the colonnaded portico of a whitewashed villa, terracotta and bright majolica pots filled with orange, citron and lemon trees, lawn-tennis court, lido, more formal gardens bounded by the jagged cliff edge, sloping terraces connected by steps down to a boathouse and private jetty, ripples and shallows and shadows of rocks and seaweed waving beneath clear jade and turquoise waters, like a rich seam of opal revealed in a cleaved open matrix.

An elderly housekeeper greeted us at the house and showed us around, and after her, the gardener took us around the grounds. The villa had been opened up, the kitchen and larder stocked, all of the rooms dusted and aired, installed with cut blooms and laid with fresh ivory and colorful Porthault linen, ready for occupance. While we sat restfully at the table and wicker basket chairs on the wide portico, wreathed in the sweetness of the jug of lilacs, hyacinths and roses on the tabletop, sipping cool citronade that the housekeeper had brought out in a carafe with ice and glasses on a tray, she asked us if we were staying the night so that she could start preparing dinner. We looked at each other and around us at the hastening dusk falling over the beauty of the Villa Alba and the dark tides of the Mediterranean, Homer's wine-dark sea.

"What a good idea," Charley said, a hint of a smile gracing her face. "It's too far to drive back to Cannes at this time of the afternoon, don't you all agree?"

The loveliness of the Villa Alba enticed us to linger beyond our allotted time. We strolled the grounds and gardens under the heavy blossom of the lilac trees, we swam, sunbathed, aquaplaned, water-skied, knocked golf balls into the Mediterranean. (Matthias took us to Old Course Cannes-Mandelieu —the French Riviera's very first golf course created in 1891 by the exiled Grand Duke Michael Mikhailovich of Russia, the "Uncrowned King of Cannes", and designed by architect Harry Shapland Colt, set between the sea and the Siagne River—Golf Country Club de Cannes-Mougins in the hills above Cannes, and Monte Carlo Golf Club, as much for their views as for trying out the impeccable fairways.) We indulged in delicious repasts of Occitan dishes and local fruits de mer and explored an abundance of rustic galettes, roulades, compôtes and cakes made with the seasonal harvest from the villa's kitchen garden and orangery and orchard. We tried to mix the Bommel cocktails from a hazy recollection of the recipes. We read, listened and dozed, lying in beds of soft, new grass and moss sprinkled with tiny primroses and bluebells, to whatever was playing on the wireless or portable phonograph, and were habitually late to meals. We walked unhurriedly to the town and back to collect mail and buy supplies and smile back in greeting at the pleasant and agreeable locals and enjoy the sunshine. We called at Caravel for tea with the Countess Josephine de Rouvroy. Matthias and Charley tried to teach Tilly and me to drive his Bentley. Matthias chartered a beautiful yacht and we took a launch out to it and sailed to the Hyères islands and back, dropped anchor, and bobbed out there, basking, content, on the glassy, motionless sea.

We let time slip through our fingers like fine grains of sand, like absolution, without mourning its loss.

The mirage of the other villa, hovering with endless beautiful possibilities and promise, drew us back, past Cannes, towards Antibes.

The Villa Mirabeau, built during the Belle Époque, lay on the tip of the Cap d'Antibes peninsula with a panoramic view of the sea and the Iles des Lerins. It had orange and palm groves and a maze with sculpted hedges inspired by the Provençal gardens of the 18th century. Small interconnected gardens surrounded the villa like enfiladed rooms painted in a palette awash with tumultuous color, filled with specimens of marine and parasol pines, Aleppo and Canary pines, cypress, oaks, citron and bergamot and fig and almond and olive trees, arbutus, pomegranate, lavender, thyme, rosemary, eucalyptus, oleander, heliotrope, jasmine, floating curlicues of wisteria. Luxuriant rose bushes lined the crushed-stone path leading from the curved marble terrace to the languid shore of the Mediterranean, mingling their fragrance with the warm breezes that wafted over the cape. On a clear morning, one could open the French doors and stroll out barefoot over the cool stone floor to breakfast and uninterrupted views of the pellucid iridescence of the distant mountains, sky and sea.

It would have been very foolish and ungrateful not to stand there with the hills behind us and take in the view. The glide of serene blue stretched ahead of us, rising and falling in gentle curves bending to the sun. We had found an untouched piece of the Riviera, the one French writer, Stephen Liégeard, had described in his 1887 travel book, La Côte d'Azur, as a "coast of light, of warm breezes, and mysterious balmy forests".

What a terrible choice to be forced to make between two paradises. (The nearby Hôtel du Cap-Eden Roc had never really been in contention. We had been there for a party with the Bentley Boys, and it was very grand, like stepping into a 19th century château in the middle of a forest, but it was an exceedingly popular resort and one didn't really want to be always running into film stars and other celebrated people. The same could be said of the Hôtel Provençal on the Juan-les-Pins beachfront—full of British, Russians, and Americans escaping Prohibition and property taxes back home— turned into a landmark by American railroad baron Frank Jay Gould, where Winston Churchill and Ernest Hemingway—who rather seemed to get around a lot—had chugged gin in the long bar.)

I did notice that Alba and Mirabeau had one curious thing in common: the villas were cool, elegant, simple, designed according to spaciousness and comfort, sanctuaries of the same serene calm that we had found in the echoing cloisters of the abbeys in Provence rather than the magnificent marble Italianate confections which dotted the Mediterranean shores or the baronial mansions on the North Shore of Long Island, theaters waiting for a peopled audience, with their gatehouses and porte-cochères, staggering reception halls, ballrooms, guest houses, children's playhouses, pleasure palaces, swimming pools, reflecting pools, ponds, golf courses, lawn-tennis courts, stables, greenhouses, gazebos and rotundas and formal gardens, some of which had been dismantled in their entirety in Europe and reassembled on the North Shore. It was the gardens of Alba and Mirabeau which aspired to grandeur, whether a splendid Eden wilderness or an immaculately laid out parterre, always overflowing with color and fragrant verdure and roses. The observation drifted across my mind in later days, a teasing wisp that would not be completely dismissed.

In the end, we chose the Villa Mirabeau for its proximity to the rest of the French Riviera where our social engagements would lead us.

It was as easy to practice indolence and lose sight of time under the enchantment of the Villa Mirabeau as it had been at the Villa Alba. The blowing horns of motor-cars receded into the distance, muffled by the rustling vines and lacy arboreal canopies. Memories of civilization and duty and stock markets grew dim under the nodding blooms and sun umbrellas and the light filtered through shifting leaves. There was profundity to be found in the purposeless exercise of watching the excursion boats floating across the bay to the Isle des Lerins, parting the haze of soft pale light. (Tilly took a ride out one day to Île Sainte-Marguerite, the largest island, upon hearing Charley tell the legend of its fortress prison, the Fort Royal, in which the Man in the Iron Mask was held in the 17th century, and came back disappointed—reality would always be drab in comparison to Charley's spun tales—and even more terribly sunburnt than the day before when she had dozed off in the sheltered beach cove without a hat or umbrella shade.) Not even the occasional discreet disappearance of Charley into the villa's study or into town in her Bugatti on unexplained errands could disturb our languor. Tilly had quite gotten over being scandalized by the sight of Charley wearing baccarat pajamas during the day—a fashion, with convenient large pockets to contain casino winnings, launched by Frank Jay Gould's wife, Florence—although Charley's pockets were more likely lined with telegrams and rose cuttings.

If I closed my eyes, I could almost imagine myself at home at Ithaca.

"I can't understand why the owner would want to part with this lovely villa," Tilly murmured from her chair on the terrace.

"Perhaps they have margin calls to make or losses to cover?" I suggested.

"Perhaps the owner had no choice," said Matthias. "Do you know the circumstances, Charley?"

We were enjoying the warm, limpid evening outside on the terrace. Matthias had driven over to join us for dinner with a regular update on the burglaries—none of the stolen jewelry yet recovered, the Hôtel Miramar's night watchman coshed on the head still hazy on the description of his assailant—which had led to us giving thanks for the distance between those unhappy happenings and the Villa Mirabeau.

"Only that we are able to enjoy it briefly before it is sold," said Charley.

"I'll make inquiries," said Matthias.

"You—you are not planning to meddle in—"

"I'm just going to make inquiries, Charley. What sort of skeletons do you imagine will tumble out of that?"

It sometimes felt like we had entered a room in the middle of a conversation which Charley and Matthias had been carrying on for a long while, not in literal words missed but in the expressions or flash moods or arguments suddenly provoked by an apparently innocent phrase or glance. However, they got on well enough most times, no lasting hostilities, a fair amount of baiting, which was not out of the ordinary. Every now and then, though, it made me wonder if the tremors in London were reanimating, whether one day the tines of a tuning fork would be struck and the earth would belch forth a mythical beast or salamander.

The soirées we attended in Cannes, Nice and Menton were rather formal affairs. We took out our Parisian finery (Tilly tut-tutted all afternoon over Charley's extravagance in Paris on a set of fluttering silk and chiffon Doucet and Worth robes du soir and Paquin and Poiret robes d'été, robes d'après-midi and robes de dîner for Tilly) and joined Matthias, who looked very dapper, in the parade of elaborately costumed high society into the balmy Mediterranean evening bedizened by eye-watering jewelry and liveried attendants and chandeliers and vintage champagne and Baccarat crystal and Limoges service and Germain silver and full classical orchestras playing Couperin, Mozart and Beethoven. Whether armor or disguise, these evenings seemed to bring out the Charley that was "on duty" as she had been in London. She wore softly muted Augusta Bernard drapery in silk and velvet beneath her beautiful Chéruit manteau du soir, embellished with an artfully twisted rope of gleaming pearls, and was, for the most part, on her best behavior, sustaining her polite eyes and engaging smiles through the introductions and intermittent chatter. These grandees were people who knew Matthias or Matthias's grandfather or were connected in some way to friends of the Elyots or for some other reason had to be persuaded that we were not ill-bred arrivistes gatecrashing a party styled after the Duchess of Richmond's ball on June 15, 1815, on the eve of the Battle of Quatre Bras, better off tossed out on our ears than to allow such a pollution of their company to persist. Charley and I took bets on how soon someone would laughingly joke "Is there any other kind of American?" Well, the night was still young...

"Does this feel like you're being presented at Court?" Charley whispered. "Should we curtsy?"

I gave her a discreet dig in the ribs. Tilly, reverted temporarily to a precise representation of a Victorian Lady's Companion—although I knew of no Victorian lady's companion who dressed so finely in Doeuillet pale yellow crepe de Chine—frowned at us both, and Charley duly diverted her attention back to her champagne coupe in which she hid her smirk from our hosts and fellow guests and the questioning arch of Matthias's eyebrow from several feet away, standing with Louise Lévêque de Vilmorin, writer and heiress to the French seed company fortune of Vilmorin and formerly engaged to the novelist and aviator Antoine de Saint-Exupéry, and the Princess Marie of Croÿ who had been a member of the Belgian Resistance during the First World War—and, as it happened, with whom we ended up conversing for the rest of the evening.

Charley was right though, it certainly often felt like being on duty, looking presentable, behaving with impeccable correctness, without untoward effervescence and making people stare. Wearing my mother's diamond necklace all night, for which I received several pretty compliments, felt like I had an albatross around my neck. I was certain that I was not the only one thinking wistfully of our time in Marseilles and the Provencal hills and the undemanding vivacity of the Bentley Boys, and the beautiful sunlit sanctuaries of the Villas Alba and Mirabeau. Our petals were spent and wilting, like the night blooming cereus and water lily, without the glory of the Provencal sun.

The other invitations we accepted (to vary the diet) took us a little further east to some equally grand but relaxed and interesting company for cocktails at the Marchioness Vasiliki d'Harcourt's residence in Beaulieu-sur-Mer (were we thinking of staying till the end of the season, the marchioness asked us, entertaining us with stories of our compatriot, the late Mr. James Gordon Bennett, Jr., "the Commodore", owner of the New York Herald, who had lived nearby at the villa, Namouna Cottage, as flamboyantly and eccentrically on the Riviera with this sumptuous yachts and parties and erratic moods—semi-nude dancers brought out on giant silver platters, seven Pekinese dogs that roamed his villa grounds with diamond collars, lighting cigars with banknotes and tossing them, still aflame, onto the street, buying up his habitual luncheon restaurant in a volatile rage and bestowing it on a humble waiter, kicking sacks of the New York Herald's mail sent to his yacht by coach into the Villefranche harbor when hungover and going off to lunch—and munificence in Beaulieu as he had when he left New York under a cloud of scandal when he arrived late and drunk to a party at the May family mansion, then urinated into a fireplace in full view of his hosts, thus ending his engagement to their daughter, Caroline May—he was quite a motor-racing enthusiast too, established the Gordon Bennett Cup five years before Automobile Club de France held the first Grand Prix motor racing event at the Circuit de la Sarthe, in Le Mans—oh, you must try this delicious concoction, but don't tell the Bommels of this naughtiness) and luncheon at the Baroness Suzette de Hottinguer's palace overlooking the bay of Villefranche-sur-Mer (did the Villa La Leopolda, once owned by the reprobate Belgian King, Leopold II, being renovated by the American architect, Ogden Codman, Jr., have such splendid views?)

where we were plied with the most exquisite delicacies that her chef could create (oh, yes, Gordon Bennett was easily the most diverting of all the Americans who came to the Cote d'Azur—so many stories told about him —his 246-foot steamship, Namouna, caused a considerable stir when it arrived in the bay of Villefranche-sur-Mer in 1883, Lady Randolph Churchill and her son Winston were amongst the many illustrious guests that Gordon Bennett entertained on his Mediterranean cruises—but you surely must sample the rest of the desserts, the Bommels never passed on Laurent's cakes and Laurent had created these especially for the champions of the Bentley-Bugatti Paris-Cannes rally).

"I don't think this is what your Aunt Merry—certainly not my parents— had in mind for us on a Grand Tour."

"Are you cabling to Ginny, Frankie, Celeste, Belle—oh, and your mother—or, even better, your Mr. Faneauil—about all the unholy passions you are rousing here on the Riviera, all the impassioned suitors you are collecting and all the racy things you are getting up to, thoroughly corrupted by the Bentley Boys?" Charley lumbered up the honeysuckle-covered veranda steps from the gardens with a distracted air. She frequently did this, emerging from the haze of scent that hovered over Villa Mirabeau in a wide-brimmed hat tied with streamers of her silk scarves and with a sheaf of telegrams and newspapers and the odd book in one hand and a basket of cut flowers hooked over her other arm. The skin on her hands and fingers had the ingrained smell of those who worked with roses—the unique herbaceous, mildly astringent smell of rose stalks—as if she had been attacking the rose bushes with her bare hands and their essence had rubbed off on her, or, if one was fanciful, that she was turning into a dryad.

"I'm...being economical with the truth when I write."

"Then there's no harm in being lotus-eaters for the time being. You still meet plenty of edifying company, don't you think? (You know, Ginny et al seem to have the most extraordinary ideas of what we've been up to. I don't know who's been filling their heads with such fantasy.) Would you feel less guilty if we were to attend more parties at... You have a choice of any of the soirées being held in Nice or Saint-Jean Cap-Ferrat or Menton or there's the medieval-costumed dinner party that the Clews are hosting at Château de la Napoule, right here in Antibes."

"Charley, I wasn't fishing for—"

"We could distract Tilly from going native and show her the 'Once Upon a Time' inscribed on the château entrance. I'm not sure who else is attending. Henry Clews might be a former Wall Street banker but he's always been more of a bohemian artist—he named his son Mancha and calls his manservant Sancho, after Cervantes's Don Quixote. Or there is the party at the Goulds' villa in Cannes. Too risky of running into an American crowd? That rules out the party hosted by Rex Ingram then—Tilly will be disappointed in missing out on meeting movie stars although I doubt Charlie Chaplin and Mary Pickford and Douglas Fairbanks will be there. The other invitations are all very fancy. Do you think Tilly will enjoy meeting some more European aristocracy? Miss Matilda Fairchild of Montrose, New York, seems to get along with and tolerate them far better than we do."

"I think Tilly is rather more enamored of the beach. She's going to have such a fashionable tan if she ever stops getting sunburnt."

"I think Tilly rather enjoys the buttermilk baths to soothe the burn. Was it Cleopatra who...no, Cleopatra used ass' milk, didn't she?"

"In any case, those ambitious mothers on the Mauretania were right. You do know everybody."

Charley made a face. "Or maybe I just owe everybody money."

"Charley!"

"Same outcome." Charley pulled out some of the invitations. "Half of these invitations are Matthias's doing. A handful are on account of the people we met at the Dowager Countess's Savoy party, friends of friends of the Bommels."

"And the rest?"

Charley shrugged. "The owner of this villa thought we might want some amusing company."

"That's very hospitable. More than hospitable. We've had such a pleasant stay. You must give the owner—a friend of yours presumably?— you must pass on our thanks and gratitude."

"Naturally."

"It's been more than just a lovely place to stay, it's been a haven. I'm with Tilly, I shouldn't mind hiding here indefinitely."

"Really?"

"Wouldn't you? This villa is beautiful but the world outside its gates is very near and full of Americans, of New Yorkers. Didn't we almost run into Paris Singer the other morning? The gardener says he lives here in self-imposed exile in Saint-Jean-Cap-Ferrat."

"Yes, he left Palm Beach after he was arrested last year at the Everglades Club on charges of real estate fraud. The judge dismissed the charges three weeks later though I suppose the public humiliation was too much. Life hasn't been very kind to him and Isadora Duncan, has it?"

Paris Singer, one of the 24 sons of the American industrialist Isaac Singer, had been one of several tempestuous and ultimately disastrous love affairs of the late dancer Isadora Duncan. Isadora Duncan lived in Nice and Beaulieu toward the end of her career. She had been, according to the Marchioness Vasiliki d'Harcourt, a familiar figure at Nice's tea parlor La Vogade, where she apparently laced her hot chocolate with gin or vodka as a morning aperitif. Her tragic death was something of a mild sore point between Charley and Matthias. On September 14, 1927, Isadora Duncan had climbed into a Bugatti with a young race driver, on the pretext of wanting to buy his motor-car. As they drove down Nice's Promenade des Anglais, her long scarf caught in the spokes of the rear wheel, and she died instantly of a broken neck. "Don't be ridiculous," Charley had scoffed. "Do you think I will run amok the French Riviera simply because I share the same marque of motor-car, a motor-car, I might add, that you gave me?" Matthias's muttered reply had been, fortunately, unintelligible to Charley's hearing.

"Well, if not American crowds, how about the British? Some of the expat literary crowd are still here. I believe the writer Somerset Maugham hosts a literary salon at his villa, La Mauresque, on the tip of Cap Ferrat."

"A literary salon!"

"We infiltrated Miss Gertrude Stein's salon and survived, I'm sure we can muddle our way through another if we put out minds to it. Imagine, we might see Rudyard Kipling or H. G. Wells there," said Charley, supremely confident that we could pull off this very dubious idea. "We might've bumped into Mr. Wells walking through Grasse and not been aware of it... If only we'd known what he looked like. Apparently"—Charley lowered her voice so as not to scandalize Tilly's fine sensibilities nearby notwithstanding that Tilly had declared the previous day that she had grown quite more worldly since coming to France—"Mr. H. G. Wells and his current paramour, the adventurer and writer Odette Keun, had set up house in Grasse."

"Did Mr. Harry Selfridge rescind his invitations to cruise on board his yacht?"

"What? Oh no... Well, you know, another lavish party, no way of leaving except to swim... When is your Mr. Faneuil coming down to visit you?"

I had to answer delicately. Charley still had not thawed towards Vincent but her occasional offhanded remarks showed that she minded that he had gone away and not rushed back to my side, no matter that there were good reasons for his absence. "Vincent doesn't enjoy as much leisure time at his disposal as we have."

"Is he aware that the French Riviera has an abundance of precedent for couples eloping to its sunny shores?"

"Charley!"

"It's true." Charley flipped open a book, a different one to the book that she had previously been reading which was the bestselling All's Quiet on the Western Front. "You know, Mr. Forster writes here about a young woman, Miss Lucy Honeychurch, touring Italy with her cousin and chaperon, Charlotte Bartlett, and finds romance and revelations and rooms with a view in Florence. Perhaps we are in the wrong country, Lucia, perhaps the city we should be in—"

I gave Charley the disapprobation her levity deserved. "If you really wanted to cut back on the parties, you could decline the invitations from the Bentley Boys as you've done for so many of the others."

"They're different."

"Because they aren't New Yorkers? Or because of the motor sports involved?"

"They may seem like everyone else," said Charley, "but quite a number of them have military service backgrounds. Barnato, for instance, served as an officer in the Royal Field Artillery of the British Army during the war. They survived without bitterness. They party very hard but they have also known what it is like in the trenches. Life can be delightful but it isn't just a frivolous party to them. Even their motor sports—you've seen yourself how seriously they take them."

Our days on the Cote d'Azur passed by in a lovely murmur, our senses leeched by the light and the dazzling aquamarine waters and the wild and extravagant parties, flitting from villa to villa like hummingbirds tasting of the nectar of vivid flowers cascading in abundance from those verdant sun-kissed shores.

Between the opulent mansions and soirées and outings with the Bentley Boys (sometimes joined by the Bugatti race drivers—once, we had even met Hellé Nice) and visits to the botanical gardens at the Villa Thuret in Antibes and ducking into Monaco for the resplendent gardens and marinas filled with yachts and the card tables of the Casino de Monte Carlo and the Palais de la Mediterranée and the flower market in Nice, and the hours lost to the beautiful sanctuary of Villa Mirabeau troubled only by the gentle tremolo of the breeze, Charley's restlessness resurfaced. Disappearances into the seclusion of the locked study. Absences of her Bugatti from the villa's garage, often into town and sometimes to as far as Nice. (We knew because a clerk from the office of a notary in Nice had delivered papers for Charley to sign.) Belligerently silent solitary games of solitaire on the veranda long into the night, the slap of cards keeping pace to the nocturnal noises of the gardens.

James Dorsey had a knack of showing up at opportune times in his scarlet Alfa Romeo P2 and spiriting her away, diverting Charley from these moods and saving a great many golf balls from being determinedly teed off over the cliff into the seascape.

Opportune, in my view at least. Tilly, when she was not in fretful sunburnt pain, was fretful in general about the suitability of Mr. James Dorsey. We were always aware of him, his nearness and marked attentions. Unlike Matthias's steady and constant presence—and perhaps in part because Matthias seemed compelled to loom and glare and glower at the man when he was in the offing—James Dorsey's hovering always at the corner of one's eye felt like lurking danger, like being stalked by a velvet-footed predator, a sense of his dissembling, of his true intentions sheathed. Coupled with Charley's alternating droll, casual regard of him one moment and seeming easy intimacy with him the next, the uncertain situation troubled and aggravated Tilly no end.

I had once dared to inquire: "What do you see in James Dorsey?"

"He amuses me sometimes." Charley had shrugged it off with the lightest of dismissals. She had been amused enough to be persuaded to drive off with him the next time that James Dorsey, looking superbly and effortlessly impeccable from head to toe, came prowling around.

He stood apart from Charley's other admirers, offsetting his brash handsomeness against a dry, playfully self-effacing humor and irreverent charm that was perhaps more to Charley's liking than mannerly polish, but also—when he was not being playful and charming in Charley's presence—seeming harder of heart, seeming indifferent when his interest was not engaged and no apparent reward for the effort of being pleasing; a man impatient to be about the world, who knew what he wanted from it and did not allow any interference with that ambition, did not waste time in loitering or bothering with the patient and generally directed kindnesses of the nice gentlemen from London, such as Lord Mallory or Lord Trevise-Fitzgerald or Lord Hastings, whom we no longer saw. His intelligence and cultivation offered constant diversion. He spoke and listened attentively; his ready humor and smiles, carried by the conviction of his striking eyes and countenance, were always mildly amused or amusing, at just the right pitch, not rehearsed or affected, never wolfish, but they might as well have been. Was that his attraction, his singularity of pursuit, the hint at an edge of raffish danger, that he was from another world and made light fun of ours, that he was not one of many predictable, dull, respectable gentlemen with honorable intentions—was it a thrill to ride a tiger? What was it that Miss Charley saw in him? Was Miss Charley certain this Mr. Dorsey was not just another fortune-hunter dressed up in sheep's clothing?

"Whatever has James Dorsey done to be judged so objectionable?" Charley asked. "What about that evening when we went out to dinner in Nice with the Bugatti drivers after the big party at the Palais de la Méditerranée? Do you remember, Tilly? Those thugs who cornered us in the street outside the restaurant near the Place Masséna after Matthias had gone to get the Bentley and the others were wandering ahead, trying to remember where they'd parked? James stepped in and broke up the brawl. You called the other man who grabbed Lucia a ruffian amongst other names I shall not repeat—well, wasn't James the one who fought him off?" Tilly's cheeks flushed pink. It had been a brawl. Tilly had joined Charley in the thick of the fracas, trying to batter the thugs away, swatting at them with her bag. "You must give him some credit for coming to our aid before the reinforcements came."

Tilly sniffed disdainfully, and not just on account of Charley addressing James Dorsey by his Christian name. The reinforcements in the form of Matthias and our Bugatti friends and the police contingent had brought back memories of London. It had not been a fond experience for any of us, especially not the exchange of baleful scowls between Charley and Matthias in its aftermath. I had been wearing my mother's necklace that night.

"What on earth has caused this sour disposition, Tilly? You don't seem to be as uncharitable in your bias against Andre d'Erlanger or—"

"Baron d'Erlanger is a shameless flirt but otherwise harmless and a gentleman," pronounced Tilly.

"A shameless—otherwise harmless—" Charley was rendered breathtakingly without retort.

I could see Charley struggling to digest this stunning statement given Tilly's outspoken views on the ilk who were deemed inveterate playboys. "I think Tilly is trying to point out the distinction between their, er, intentions and your reception of what might not be entirely, um, sincere or honorable."

Charley looked at me, then back at Tilly. "I dare say they are not. It's just a drive, Tilly," Charley reassured her. "And who knows, perhaps my intentions are not entirely sincere or honorable. Do you want anything from town?"

That Charley did not laugh or snort and rebuke us for our silliness worried Tilly even more.

Once, I thought I had overheard Charley mutter exasperatedly to herself: "I am half-sick of shadows." It seemed puzzling and ominous that Charley would be mulling over the Lady of Shalott, if indeed I had correctly heard Charley quoting Tennyson.

I was relieved, surprised, and uncomfortably disturbed to find that Matthias met these malevolent moods and whims of Charley's with a vastly improved degree of restrained calm. One afternoon, when Matthias arrived for Le Goûter and Charley had still not returned to the villa, Tilly inadvertently blurted out her fretfulness concerning James Dorsey in the midst of apologizing for Charley's lateness as we were making our way to the table on the terrace set with silver pots of verveine, lemon balm, and linden tisanes and plates of rose macarons, petite madeleines, mille-feuilles, éclairs, mousse au chocolat à l'orange, gâteau aux fraises, savarin aux fruits, pastel-colored citron-curd financiers, pain d'épices, translucent cornelian-colored lozenges of pâte de coing, elderflower jelly, crème fouettée, dishes of fresh raspberries, scones doused in mirabelle jam, and boxes of crystallised violets from Toulouse. Tilly stopped and snapped her mouth shut in mortification as soon as she realized what she had said.

Matthias regarded Tilly's revelation for a thoughtful moment and then, cautiously, ventured: "Does she...reciprocate his feelings?"

Tilly did not trust herself to say anything more and busied herself serving the tea. I was not in any better position to answer either with wit or knowledge.

"I see," Matthias said.

Did he? What did he see?

It felt wrong to leave things so horribly twisting in the wind. Only, what was the right thing to do? Maybe that was why Matthias was apparently treading softly and letting things lie. At every turn, we would encounter Charley's darkling abstractions or airy denials—and then catch a glimpse of her looking unsettled—uncertain—hunted—no longer pretending that the world, so perfectly bright and shining and full of wonder, was not collapsing around her.

In Paris, Charley had pointed out a painting of a pastoral scene by Nicolas Poussin, Et in Arcadia ego, done in the classical French Baroque style. It had lain in the wing of the Louvre, and in memory, overshadowed by the other glories of the museum, but not unnoted or forgotten. I thought of the painting when I saw the shadows on Charley's face and saw... But no, those were not shadows, simply the change of light from the brutal sunshine of the open gardens to the dappled shade under the overhanging trees where the breezes played. The sun of the Cote d'Azur did not admit of shadows. The line of the sea and sky brushed by its bright, tender flame did not cry out the end of Arcadia approaching. There was no need to scare the children so.

21

CHARLOTTE:

"D'Erlanger says you danced with him on Señora Donna Torena de Aranjuez's yacht last night."

"Yes, he got a little tipsy on deck. It was quite amusing. Qu'est-ce qui est particulièrement bien en ce moment?"

"You had led me to believe that you were not free."

"C'est possible de goûter le Banon? Because Lucia and I had already accepted Señora Donna's invitation."

"Vandermeer was there."

"Well, Matthias was invited too. I'm sorry you were not—"

"You've rebuffed every outing with me, from the dinner party in Menton where the Rothschilds would have been in attendance to the ball in Villefranche-sur-Mer at the palace of Principessa Jasmin—"

"I'm here now, am I not?"

"I'm referring to formal invitations where one goes to the trouble of dressing up and ordering the motor around to ogle grand homes and eat other people's food."

"I had pre-existing engagements. Lady Johanna, Lady Kendi, Lady Connie and her son Sir Alex, the private musical recital held for Princess Marie of Croÿ, cocktails with that Italian marchesa who is married to the concert pianist—there is a pile of invitations sitting on our mantelpiece."

"Which you could decline as easily as you decline mine."

"Could I?"

"You made a conscious choice, Charley, each and every time. I want to know why."

"...un peu plus, s'il vous plaît. I don't really like fancy parties."

"But you accept invitations to go to all the fancy soirées with Matthias

Vandermeer."

"I attend them, yes. Oui, parfait."

"You could leave it all behind, you know, if you chose."

"Can I? As simple as that?"

"Try it."

"Hmm."

"If I hire a yacht tomorrow to sail to Mallorca, would you come along?"

"...et les tulipes, s'il vous plaît."

"Vous désirez autre chose, madame?"

"Well, Charley? Would you?"

"Non, merci! Mallorca...?"

"It's true that Chopin and George Sand had a fairly miserable winter in Valldemossa, but what I have in mind is the Bay of Pollença. The beaches and mist-hazed views at sunrise and sunset are as fine as any you will see. We could sail around to the other Balearic Islands later—Ibiza, Menorca, Formentera. Or skip over to Valencia or Andalusia."

"You want me to run away to Spain?"

"Us."

"Us?"

"Just the two of us."

"That hardly seems—"

"For once, no stuffy bores or protocol or interference or worries. More than just a few moments snatched here and there. Just somewhere where the two of us can get away from—"

"Is there such a place?"

"O ye of little faith. If not Spain, perhaps you'd prefer Italy? I think you'd enjoy driving along the Amalfi Coast. Dining in Positano. Sailing into the Gulf of Salermo, surrounded by the sea breezes, the infinite blue, the blinding iridescent sunshine..."

"It all sounds exquisite."

"Just a stone's throw away are the Sirenusas, an archipelago of little islands named after the mythological sirens who were believed to have inhabited the islands. They lured many an unsuspecting sailor, even the great Ulysses himself when he passed that way, so it is practically a rite of passage. Tell me you aren't even a little bit tempted, Charley."

"'The only way to get rid of temptation is to yield to it'?"

"That's right, Miss Masterson, look at all the flowers, all the fields of beautiful flowers that I could show you. Wouldn't you like to stray from the path, just for a moment?"

22

LUCIA:

The parties and invitations rolled on in an endless succession.

The rakishly gregarious Baron Andre d'Erlanger did his part in contributing to our amusements on the French Riviera with an invitation to a party being held by Baroness Béatrice Ephrussi de Rothschild at her villa at Cap Ferrat. He congratulated himself on the success of his exhortions for us to attend—we were, he had once complained, notoriously difficult to impress or sway. The baron was likely unaware of Charley's friendly acquaintance with the British and French branches of the Rothschilds, and he could not have known that we had already received an invitation to Villa Ephrussi de Rothschild or that it had been headed for the to-be-declined pile (Charley's excuse this time was that it would not be fair leaving Tilly behind alone to tend to her latest layer of sunburn) when the baron's telephone call intervened. Charley did not correct the baron's self-congratulations, tactfully refraining from remarking if it was not a bit, er, staid for his liking, or enlightening him as to the true reason he had been successful in changing our minds: in the end, we thought it would be nice to revisit Villa Ephrussi de Rothschild's gardens.

In 1905, following the divorce from her husband, Maurice Ephrussi, a French banker of Russian origin, 15 years her senior and a friend of her parents who was rather partial to gambling, and the death of her father, Alphonse de Rothschild, Baroness Béatrice Ephrussi de Rothschild snapped up a prime piece of real estate from Leopold II, King of the Belgians, and began construction on her ocher-yellow-colored villa, designed by French architect Aaron Messiah, on the highest point of the promontory on the isthmus of Cap Ferrat overlooking the Mediterranean. She furnished the villa directly at the Gare de Beaulieu, making her selection on the station platform from trains arrived from Paris loaded with furniture and artwork, filling it with an extensive and growing collection, including a Tiepolo ceiling and a games table that had once belonged to Marie Antoinette, of antique furniture, Old Masters and sculptures, objets d'art, and rare porcelain. The villa was given its own private zoo with flamingos, budgerigars, monkeys, mongooses, antelopes, and gazelles. She spared no expense or effort in landscaping the grounds of the villa and commissioned Achille Duchene to design the gardens. Under the direction of Achille Duchene, the French formal gardens surrounding the villa were conceived in the form of a ship, viewed from a loggia of the house, acting as the bridge of a vessel, with the sea visible on both sides. The gardens took seven years to complete.

Baroness Béatrice Ephrussi de Rothschild made the Villa her winter residence and stayed there regularly, dividing her time between Cap Ferrat, Paris, Monaco (a villa in Monte Carlo called "Rose de France" where Matthias had previously taken us, at the baroness's invitation, to tea and she gave us a tour of the villa and lost track of time chatting about art and gardens and horticulture and the cultivation of roses) and Deauville. She had not intended to come to Cap Ferrat at this time of the year but she had had good reports of the flourishing gardens this summer and wanted to throw a party in her beloved villa surrounded by the company of friends who were visiting here on the Cote d'Azur, such artistic friends as French poet Andre de Fouquières and Tamara Karsavina, the Russian prima ballerina, principal artist formerly of the Imperial Russian Ballet and latterly of the Ballets Russes, most famous for creating the title role in Michel Fokine's The Firebird with Vaslav Nijinsky, a role that was originally offered to her rival, Anna Pavlova, who could not reconcile herself with Stravinsky's avant-garde score, and who had danced one summer evening in the gardens of Villa Ephrussi de Rothschild to Chopin nocturnes in the moonlight.

The baron, I supposed, was right: we were becoming somewhat inured to these grand parties and glamorous people. In Charley's defense, she had been doomed from birth, born within the exalted sphere of Old New York into the bosom of a family who, every now and then, very courteously but firmly exerted their prerogative in refusing to conform. She had graduated from such a nursery to become a member of the Colony Club and Cosmopolitan Club, was friendly with the Trasks and the denizens of Yaddo and, as had been universally acknowledged, she already knew everybody. The blooms in the arbors she had grown up with were as exotic and majestic as any tended by royal gardeners or eminent horticulturalists. Accustomed to such things, mixing with exalted society and fame and genius and artistic temperaments was an unexceptional occurrence. Charley also did seem to have other pressing things weighing on her mind.

Nevertheless, with Tilly's blessing—poisoned by our torpor of ennui, and perhaps not as enthusiastic about gardens and artists as Charley was, Tilly professed that given the news that Villa Mirabeau had been sold and since she had already seen the Villa Ephrussi de Rothschild on the invitation procured for us by Matthias, she was content to stay at Mirabeau to nurse her sunburn, and perhaps take a dip later in the sea when the sun was not so fierce—we went along with the baron's program for amusement.

In spite of the baron's best efforts, we nearly did not make it to the Baroness Ephrussi de Rothschild's party.

The day's sybaritic amusements began early in the day (or perhaps continued on from the previous night) for the baron and others of his acquaintance who had arranged to leave their base at the Carlton Hotel in Cannes, the trunks of their motor-cars loaded up with parasols and mats and bathing costumes, and made their way to Juan-les-Pins for the Hôtel Le Provençal to join friends and lounge on its terrace, with views of the pine forests to the east, the peaks of the Alps to the north and the beaches of Juan-les-Pins to the south, and order the first drink of the day or thrash out their surplus energies at the tennis club or change in a bathhouse and claim a spot on the sandy shore under the beach umbrellas, joining the other guests of the hotel's alfresco beach club to work on their tans. The hotel was conveniently located more or less midway between Cannes and Nice, where they were talking of stopping for a late lunch, before heading for a pleasant coastal drive to Cap Ferrat, more sheltered by the mountains from the mistral than Saint-Tropez, above the blue-green colored silk of the sea. Some of them had dinner engagements to keep later in Menton, others were headed to try their luck at Monte Carlo, still others had been invited for cruises on board private yachts to sail from Beaulieu. The baron very kindly thought of us and rang up Villa Mirabeau to invite us to share in this conviviality. His first attempt failed. Charley thanked him prettily but declined. His second attempt was to send Matthias, whom he must have collared somehow, over to collect us. This did not go quite according to plan either. When Matthias arrived at Villa Mirabeau, delivering an update from Vincent of his progress on the arrangements for moving to New York, he found me attending to my correspondence, Tilly already gone, retracing her by now regular path down to the beach with a well-stocked picnic basket to make the most of the last days we would have at Villa Mirabeau, and our evening dresses set aside for the baroness's party, all ready and prepared to be loaded into a trunk, but no sign of Charley. Charley had had to make a run into town (to the telegraph office and American Express, if I was asked to guess) and said that if she had not returned by the time Matthias got there, we were not to wait for her but to join the baron's assemblage and avail ourselves of their company if we wished or otherwise shift for ourselves but, in either case, to head directly to the party at Villa Ephrussi de Rothschild where she would meet up with us.

"Charley has no qualms about ditching the baroness's party, has she?" Matthias asked.

Unless Charley was planning to run into the shops to buy a new gown and shoes and... Matthias's conclusion was not an unreasonable one.

"Something must've distracted her," I said.

We were debating what to do (I was wondering whether it would be all right to give up the enterprise and simply follow Tilly and slip down to Villa Mirabeau's private beach) when the telephone in the front hall rang. It was the baron, calling to hurry us along. Charley was already there, being obtuse, and he needed allies to help soften her up. Soften her up for what, I wondered. But of course we were on our way. The baron's third attempt had been to set out himself to find Charley and bring her over to Le Provençal but another in their search party had run across Charley and managed to waylay her. "And he succeeded?" Matthias asked and then frowned when I told him. I was of the same mind. It was unlike Charley to surrender so readily especially as she was evidently quite comfortable giving obstinate opposition to whatever the baron was proposing.

We came across Charley with the baron's party on the terrace of Hôtel Le Provençal, nursing a gin and tonic with plenty of lemon and ice and without—not for want of effort on the baron's part—the gin. The baron had grouped their chairs together and taken over the conversation, talking enthusiastically about motor-boat racing. Jean Chassagne had taken part in motor-boat racing in Monaco as part of his work in testing engine technology for Sunbeam. Would it not be amusing to—

"No," said Charley, "it would not. Jean trained as a mechanic and served in the French Navy. I may have been blotto enough to be talked into the motor-race last time but I'm not so much of an idiot as to presume to even consider trying to walk in his footsteps. Also, I find I rather like having my head attached to my neck."

M. Chassagne grinned in amusement at the baron's rebuttals and helpfully called for another round of drinks to ease the thirst they would be working up in their argument. He explained that they had spotted Charley's Bugatti at Port Vauban and caught up with her apparently just disembarking from a large white yacht berthed in the harbor. The yacht was said to belong to the nomadic tycoon, Sir Victor Sassoon of the Sassoon family, the "Rothschilds of the East", who was headed back to the Far East to open the Cathay Hotel on the Bund in Shanghai, already being heralded— with its distinctive copper-sheathed roof rising 252 feet above the ground, white Italian marble floors, and Lalique glass artwork—as the most luxurious hostelry east of the Suez Canal. M. Chassagne said that Charley had appeared startled to be met at the port by such an entourage led by

Andre d'Erlanger—as well as anyone might be—but proved amenable to coming back to Le Provençal.

I was grateful to M. Jean Chassagne for clearing up that mystery. Of course Charley had been amenable. I could just imagine the scene on the pier. She would have agreed to anything to divert attention away from being asked what she was doing there at Port Vauban. Sir Victor Sassoon, I suddenly remembered, had been another of the names on Charley's shredded list.

Matthias, without knowledge of the list but perhaps remembering Charley in London, seemed to be coming to the same conclusion as I had.

"Charley," Matthias began when he caught her eye.

Charley gave him a look calculated to cow anyone into submission. Matthias held her look for a moment, then sighed and joined in the conversation that the baron was still waging with Charley about motor-boat racing.

The talk of a motor-boat race, fueled by the drinks, rose and ballooned larger with each interlocutor joining in and adding his or her piece. The sun and morning's passive exertions had worked everyone up to wanting high excitement, an entertaining thrill, to look forward to over a cool drink. James Dorsey—it seemed that he was one of the baron's party today—was one of those whose blood was stirred by the prospect of a race and he was persistent in urging Charley to go along.

"As defending champion, you must defend your title," he told Charley.

"Oh, I thought that was based on a technicality anyway," Charley said politely. She could have been referring to anything—inebriation, pot luck, burst tyres, Matthias pulling up a bare whisker behind us because his single-minded focus had been to get us to Cannes safely—but the notable thing was that she was very polite.

Matthias, who had been disgruntledly chafing at the table at James Dorsey's goading Charley and Charley's pointed refusal to meet his eyes after that first exchange and wordless directive, saw the warning signs and leapt in.

"It's impossible today for Charley and Lucia to take part in the race." Charley looked at him in silent inquiry. "They've an appointment to see a property in Cimiez."

"Are you moving again?" asked James Dorsey.

"If this property is promising, perhaps," said Charley. "I hate to run off so soon, but we really must be going if we are not to be late."

"That's quite all right," said the baron cheerfully. "We're all headed that way. Cimiez is barely a moment away as the crow flies. You could easily join us for luncheon in Nice. You can meet up with us at the rendezvous point after your house tour."

Charley smiled like the Mona Lisa and we took our leave.

"Is there actually a property to inspect in Cimiez," Charley asked Matthias on our way to the motor-cars, "or shall we just be taking a drive up there again to look at all the self-important wedding cake hotels along Boulevard de Cimiez and find a place for lunch and then potter about Park Arènes and the gardens of the Franciscan monastery?"

"There is a villa for you and Lucia to view. It is ready for occupance and very secure," said Matthias.

We wound our way up to the palm-lined patrician neighborhood of Cimiez, following Matthias's Bentley up the south-facing hill overlooking orange tiled roofs and views to the Baie des Anges. We skirted the town center and followed the Avenue des Arènes de Cimiez and turned east into a leafy residential quarter and up to the gates of a private residence.

The Villa Serena was built in the neo-classical style in shades of white and cream, designed, like much of Cimiez and Nice, by Charles Dalmas, with ornate cupolas, balconies and decorative plasterwork, suites and galleries of stately proportions, gobelins and Aubusson rugs and Savonnerie carpet and Baccarat crystal chandeliers and beveled mirrors framed within elaborately carved and painted boiseries, discreetly gleaming of gilt and refinement and old money. It was surrounded by tall trees and neatly tended gardens, floating at its altitude aloft the clear cerulean of the Mediterranean sky and sea. Matthias took us on a tour of the villa, pointing out the amenities and the fine views over Nice and the distant bay. We murmured appreciative noises to the aspect and the staff who brought out refreshments.

In the gardens, with the Baie des Anges spread out below us, Charley drew me aside.

"What do you think?" I asked her.

"Oh, dreadful, quite the hovel," Charley said airily, barely regarding the view. She lowered her voice. "Lucia, we can't take it." She glanced back at Matthias talking a short distance away with the head gardener where she had clearly sent him on some trumped up errand.

"Why? What's the matter with it?"

"When Matthias was taking us around the garden terrace earlier, I overheard the under-gardeners gossiping. They were pointing to Matthias and whispering: 'Le petit fils, le petit fils!' The grandson. This is his grandfather's villa, Lucia. This is the first time the villa's staff have seen Matthias here."

"Oh."

"Do you know his grandmother's name? I heard 'Madame Serena' mentioned several times too. I would be willing to bet that this villa might be named for Albrecht Matthias Godeffroy's late wife. These gardens—his late grandmother's gardens."

"Oh."

"There are plenty of hotels to which we can continue our nomadic roaming. We could follow Matisse's example and shuffle around Nice and its environs. Or we could head back to Villa Al—" She abruptly stopped when she heard the tread of Matthias's footfalls returning.

"Charley, the gardener says the roses were only planted last season but have all been doing well, very robust growth. He says that they were supplied by a firm by the name of Meilland here on the Riviera," Matthias said. "Sound familiar?"

"Do you mean... Not M. Meilland?"

"The very same. He's based at Cap d'Antibes."

"Oh, how exciting! So close by to Mirabeau the whole time!"

"So what do you both think of the villa?" Matthias asked.

"It's very beautiful," I said, "but..." and looked to Charley for direction.

"It seems that the sale of Villa Mirabeau is not as certain as we were previously led to believe," said Charley.

"What do you mean?" demanded Matthias.

"Well, it seems that a new buyer came out of the blue and offered for the property at almost double the previous bid price."

"And why is that a problem?" asked Matthias. "If the sale contract was signed, your friend the vendor receives a price much higher than original —"

"Doesn't it seem odd that someone should make such a bid without even viewing the property?" said Charley.

"Its prime location—"

"The transaction is being reviewed further to ensure that it is genuine, that everything is as it should be and not untoward. So we might have a brief reprieve and continue to cool our heels there." Charley narrowed her eyes at Matthias. "Why are you so bothered about whether the sale of Villa Mirabeau goes through or not?"

"I'm not," said Matthias. "It's just unheard of for a vendor to rescind a contract of sale because the offered price was too high."

"Perhaps the vendor has scruples as to whom the property can or cannot be sold," said Charley. "In any case, it means we are very grateful to you for showing this beautiful villa to us but we cannot take it."

Matthias grimaced at this but told us: "It is available for whenever you have need of it."

We left the Villa Serena. The shaded green corridor swung closed behind us like a strange but benign half-remembered dream filled with fragmented understandings that I could not grasp. Roses, I pondered, roses.

We were driving around Cimiez and along the Boulevard de Cimiez, the main thoroughfare—passing the Belle Époque wedding cake hotels, many of which were designed by Sébastien-Marcel Biasini or Charles Dalmas, including the Riviera, the Winter Palace, the Hermitage, the Alhambra (in the Moorish style with two minarets), the Majestic, the Grand Palace, the Prince of Wales Palace, the Art Deco Valence Palace and Cimiez Palace, and the Excelsior Hôtel Régina (built with Queen Victoria in mind and where she stayed thrice, taking over the entire west wing)—when we were tooted from across the street by a familiar looking motor-car. Sitting in the box-seat of the scarlet Alfa Romeo P2—Grand Prix blessed, Charley had laughingly told me aloud to rile up Baron Andre d'Erlanger, with and 8 cylinder supercharged engine and 2 carburetors placed after the compressor —was James Dorsey. He tooted his horn again and waved at us. Charley stopped, waved to Matthias ahead, and turned the Bugatti around. We could not see Matthias's face as he followed suit but we had no doubt that he was scowling.

"I thought I'd run into you sooner or later," said James Dorsey.

"Are you here to meet a friend?" Charley asked.

"Came to make sure you wouldn't miss luncheon or the race," James Dorsey replied. I could almost hear the low growl from Matthias behind us. "There's a talk of a new rendezvous point. Hotel Negresco instead of Palais de la Méditerranée. Then, we are supposed to head out with the rest of D'Erlanger's party to a beach in Nice—Ruhl Plage—or Cap Ferrat—Paloma beach, Passable beach on the northwest side of the main peninsula, or Cro de Peï Pin—which beach being a question that has yet to be resolved."

"Oh, you shouldn't have gone to so much trouble," said Charley. "Our plans have changed slightly, haven't they? We are—"

"But surely you are still coming to luncheon? You have to eat," James Dorsey insisted.

Charley fenced politely with him for a while. In the end, in the interests of keeping the peace, we agreed to luncheon in Nice as an acceptable compromise—all the better to slip away unnoticed in the luncheon crowds, my dear...

We drove down to Nice towards the pink dome of the Hotel Negresco on the Promenade des Anglais, facing the Baie des Anges. ("Isn't that where Isadora Duncan...?" I asked Charley.) In the Royal Lounge, we ran into Baron d'Erlanger and M. Jean Chassagne and they directed us to head out to our motor-cars again. The pendulum, we were told, had swung back to the heady trinity of casino, restaurant, cocktail bar at Palais de la Méditerranée. However, when we arrived at Frank Jay Gould's monumental entertainment palace, the state of indecision remained amongst the party, several of whom were arguing the merits of the Casino de Monte-Carlo—roulette and blackjack under the gilded ceilings of the Salon Europe—no, no, far better to have a word with the croupier and move on to the Salons Privés—or book into Hôtel de Paris across the street and access Les Salons Super Privés via a secret tunnel connecting the two establishments for special guests. This discussion was becoming almost as tiresome to Charley as the ongoing debate and ribbing regarding the proposal for a race which had, by now, expanded to include any variation on the theme of racing— yacht, motor-boat, motor-car—and she lost patience, telling Baron d'Erlanger and James Dorsey, both still discussing racing, that we had to toodle off to look into taking rooms at the Grand-Hôtel du Cap-Ferrat.

"Excellent idea," was the baron's verdict, deciding that it would be an ideal venue for the afternoon—a pool and Cap Ferrat beaches on the doorstep, luncheon in the loggia dining room, and aperitifs later in the Gustave Eiffel designed La Rotonde with views of the sea over the parasol and Aleppo pine.

Charley stoically accepted the decree and we bundled off again to our motor-cars.

We followed the motorcade ahead of us, driving along the Corniche, past ornamental gardens, strips of colorful shops and cafes, distant islands squinting in the sun, bright flashes of bougainvillea and Fischer's Lovebirds, veering off to the peninsula. We drove through the wilderness of rocky coastline, dense shrubbery and vegetation, a heathen paradise into which Leopold II and the other residents and visitors to Cap Ferrat had made small inroads to penetrate and tame. We heard or saw the motor-cars head of us on the road, and at turnings, and then gradually less and less as we fell behind, steadily dropping to the rear of the motorcade by Charley's design.

"Allez, allez! Keep up!" the baron cheerfully called to us, then sped on ahead.

James Dorsey's Alfa Romeo P2 kept weaving around us to tease us onwards. He pulled in to drive alongside of us and said in a lively tenor: "You're just not trying! D'Erlanger is going to reach Le Phare and crow about it all afternoon!"

Charley replied, "Not if you reach it first!"

None of Charley's retorts proved satisfactory in repelling James Dorsey's eager taunts for us to compete in racing to the semaphore at the headland of Saint-Jean-Cap-Ferrat commissioned in 1862 by Napoleon III. Annoyed toots from Matthias's Bentley behind us broke up the conversation a few times but James Dorsey would not be discouraged or batted away for long. Twisting cliff paths overrun by stray goats could not have been more distracting. As it happened, an oncoming motor-car did come around a turning towards us. We swerved urgently apart from James Dorsey, Charley spinning the wheels away off the road, and the Bugatti went crashing through the thickets and tangled shrubland and, such was the rugged terrain, we could not avoid hurtling headlong into the closely spaced trees.

For a moment there was stillness. Then came an onrush of sounds and impressions—the hissing groans and squeals and wheezing of a motor-car in pain, a hand on my shoulder, and a voice—familiar—Charley's voice—saying, "Lucia? Lucia, are you all right? Are you in pain? Are you able to move?" and then scrambling noises, and the door of the motor-car being yanked open, and another familiar voice rising on a note of controlled panic—"Lucia? Charley?"—and someone undoing my seat belt. I blinked several times. The world came into focus.

"Lucia?" Charley and Matthias's worried eyes stared at me.

I looked down at my hands. They were not even shaking. Only my insides felt like they were knocked out of place and still churning. I touched my forehead, my face. No bleeding. My head was clear but my neck felt sore. I moved my limbs. They seemed to be in working order. I looked at the smashed up bonnet of the Bugatti pressed against the tree trunks. I looked away.

"I think I'm all right," I said. I looked at Charley, so unflappable. No blood on her either, seemingly untouched, but... "Are you all right?"

Charley's gaze roved over me again. She prodded and examined and asked me a thousand questions with input here and there from Matthias. I must have passed the examination because she smiled. "Better than our ride. Let's get out of here. Can you stand without your knees collapsing?"

"Charley, wait—" Matthias said, half in frustrated rebuke, half in concern as he helped to steady me to alight from my seat. Charley would not suffer assistance and got out on her own from the smashed motor-car before Matthias made it around to her side and glowered at her stubborn impatience. Her legs did not wobble, I noticed, but she did take gingerly light steps. Had Charley been in a smash before? Her practiced reactions seemed to suggest so. Was she hiding an injury?

"Charley," I said, "are you—"

A clamor of voices approached us. M. Jean Chassagne hurried over, followed by two men from their party, and offered us assistance.

"D'Erlanger's sent for help and a tow... Ah." He paused, seeing the state of the Bugatti. "She won't ride again, will she? A pity. Are you all right?"

"No, they are not," Matthias growled as he unscrewed a flask and handed the cap to us for a sip of water and took off his jacket to throw on the ground to make it more comfortable for us to sit on, which we declined, feeling all right to remain upright. The other men rushed to follow his example, trying to assist in any way possible. "The bloody fool! Was he confused as to whether he was on a racing circuit or carrying on a tête-à-tête in a drawing room? The road was narrow enough with the tight, narrow bends, but he had to take it neck to neck—"

"We're a little shaken but fine," Charley piped up. "Is—"

"You are not fine and neither is Lucia," Matthias said. "I'm taking you both back to Nice to get properly examined and only when the doctor pronounces you fine—"

"What of the other oncoming motor-car? Is its driver all right? Its passengers? And James Dorsey?" Charley ignored Matthias's growling.

"Reasonably unscratched," M. Jean Chassagne replied. "Dorsey and his P2 fared better than you. He sends his apologies by the way."

That put the fuse to the powder keg. Matthias's seething wrath boiled over. He was furious with James Dorsey for endangering us with his carelessness, his recklessness, his negligent—

"Thank you for the water," Charley cut in. "Shall we head back to the road to see if help has arrived? All this talking is probably going to give Lucia a headache."

Matthias immediately fell quiet and all of the men jumped in to make renewed efforts to be helpful. Their gallantry and kindness was appreciated but proved unnecessary. Charley, who accepted no fuss over herself and was waving off directives, questions and concern as fribbles, made a good deal of fuss over me, but I was also finding that after the initial shock and threatening nausea had passed, I was physically unharmed and had no need of being carried or even steadied.

I saw Charley give the Bugatti, the only fatality of the accident it seemed, a sad pat before she turned away to find Matthias's concerned eyes upon her. "I'm sorry about your gift, Matthias," Charley said.

Matthias scowled. "If you think I care about a motor-car being smashed up—"

We returned to the road and found Baron d'Erlanger waiting there beside the vehicles with James Dorsey and the other motorists, a Parisian couple who was returning from a holiday on the cape. We all rushed to exchange apologies, grateful that a major collision had been averted and everyone concerned unhurt. James Dorsey was especially warm in expressing his apologies and regrets. He implored, free of his usual urbanity, in what was to become profusely iterative invocations for Charley's pardon.

"Charley, you must understand that I never meant for—"

Charley gave a quiet nod of acknowledgment. To have expressed anything more, whether anger or forgiveness, was to knowingly court the wrath of an enraged man whose self-restraint, like low-rolling thunder, was already testing its limits. The weight of a single breath would have been enough to bring the storm down on James Dorsey's head, something that Charley seemed disinclined to do. I could not decide whether this protective gesture was merely diplomacy or a mark of favor.

James Dorsey, however, did not seem to realize the favor, or the danger, or he simply did not care, intent on gaining her attention. "Charley—" he began again, his face pulled into lines of desperate urgency.

M. Chassagne must have had a word with the baron because they became our allies in keeping James Dorsey and Matthias, whose face was tight with anger, whose eyes still glowed red and whose clenched jaw and fists still itched, as far apart as possible.

We waited for the arrival of the local constabulary to attend to the smash. We were interviewed, gave our details, and arranged for a tow of the smashed up Bugatti, before going our separate ways.

"We won't be seeing you at the Grand-Hôtel du Cap-Ferrat, will we?" Baron d'Erlanger sighed.

"Perhaps not," Charley agreed. "Matthias is rather adamant about getting the all-clear from the doctor in Nice."

"And what about tonight at the Villa Ephrussi de Rothschild?"

"We shall see."

Baron d'Erlanger, M. Chassagne and the rest of the party, including an extremely remorseful James Dorsey, held back by the baron and his friend, wished us well and hoped to see us soon.

It was a relief to be away. No amount of James Dorsey's protestations of apology and petitions for absolution could brush away the dark clouds of Matthias's anger. Too profuse, too hollow, too belated, was Matthias's view. Charley had dismissed Matthias's charges lightly to keep the peace and admonished Matthias to stop prowling about like an aggravated grizzly bear.

"If you want to pick a fight, pick one with me. I'm as much at fault as anyone. I—"

"Don't be r—"

"No one is hurt. You're insisting on taking us all the way back to Nice to prove it, so let's not waste any more time. Lead on. Drive," Charley issued in command to Matthias.

Matthias made a scoffing noise in his throat—rather obligatory to all of Charley's peremptory edicts—but was pleased to oblige. He readied his Bentley Speed Six for additional passengers and was impatient for all the leave-taking to be finally done so he could usher us away from the evil that was James Dorsey.

Matthias's surly humor cleared and became calmer as the distance grew between our automobile and the scene of the accident. Except: "We'd better not end up running into the bounder again at Villa Ephrussi de Rothschild," Matthias said.

"You are a terrible grump, Matthias Vandermeer," said Charley. "If you weren't so busy nursing your umbrage, you'd recall that we are the only ones besides Andre d'Erlanger who have received invitations to the baroness's dinner."

"Good."

"Do we have to go back to Nice?"

"Yes."

"It wouldn't hurt for Lucia to get a check-up and maybe be given a harmless tonic and instructions to rest up but I certainly don't need one.

Not anywhere battered or bruised and nothing loose inside either."

"I'm not going to see a doctor if Charley isn't!" I said.

"It's pointless arguing. You are both going to be seen by the doctor."

"You really want to give me a professional medical opinion confirming that we are fine to rub your nose in?" said Charley.

"Absolutely."

"Fine," said Charley, pouting. "It just seems a shame when this day could be spent a lot more profitably and pleasantly... M. Meilland did ask us to call on him, didn't he, Lucia?"

"Yes, he did. M. Meilland said his family grew roses in the south of France. He mentioned a place near Lyon too but—"

"After the doctor in Nice has seen both of you," Matthias said. It was obvious he would have preferred that we rested placidly for a week but between taking us to visit M. Meilland and Charley and I bolting off on our own, Matthias pragmatically accepted the lesser evil.

"Well, in that case, do hurry. Oh, wait, what if M. Meilland is not at home? And we can't arrive empty-handed."

"I have Meilland's address at Cap d'Antibes," said Matthias. "I'll ring him up from Nice to see if he is accepting calls."

"And we won't be empty-handed when we turn up at his door. There are shops in Nice. We can buy some lovely bottles of wine which should somewhat mitigate the unexpectedness of our arrival. If the shops are unsatisfactory, I'm sure the Goulds' Palais de la Méditerranée would have some fine vintages set aside in their cellar that we could raid, perhaps a Château Lafite Rothschild or Château d'Yquem. Oh dear, he was quite young, did he drink at the dowager countess's party?"

"We're in France, wine is like mother's milk! He could dilute it...or let them mature in his cellar...or the rest of his family can enjoy them."

"Then we're all set, I suppose."

"Are you both sure about this?" Matthias asked as a reluctant afterthought. "I mean, if you really wanted to join D'Erlanger's luncheon party back at the Grand-Hôtel du Cap-Ferrat—"

"Absolutely sure."

"Because of Meilland's roses?"

"Because of M. Meilland and yes, roses—a profusion of roses. Aunt Merry will be ever so pleased."

It was a lovely drive and one of the most pleasant times we ever had on the French Riviera. We submitted to a medical examination in Nice (cleared and pronounced two very lucky young women—and Charley never admitted to being involved in so much as a previous race much less a smash-up) and shopping and then followed the pleasantly meandering scenic route to the wilderness of Cap d'Antibes with the Mediterranean beside us, as fresh in impressions as the first time we had come to visit Villa

Mirabeau, an adventure, and yet also like coming home... The Cote d'Azur flew by in a vivid blur, the pedestrians ambling along the promenade and diving between the traffic, the bright awnings of the boutiques and grand hotels and the outdoor tables of the cafes heady with delicious smells. We passed rocky beaches, harbors bobbing with fishing boats and and marinas of sleek vessels, stone pine and firs, palms, mimosa, citrus trees and other lush vegetation shielding the luxurious resorts and whitewashed villas clinging to the hills with their colored tiled rooftops and pale shuttered windows, and the glittering blue Mediterranean lying stretched out alongside the Corniche, like a lizard dozing under a meridian sun, shivering silver in one moment, hazy bleached white in the next.

We passed the fairground gaiety of the Juan-les-Pins casino and resort hotels and dropped by Villa Mirabeau, running down to the beach to chivvy Tilly out from her sunbathing nook ("Change of plan, Tilly, we—no, I left the Bugatti behind on Cap Ferrat, but never mind that, there's plenty of room in the Bentley and we've a much better plan for luncheon than Andre d'Erlanger's. Matthias has discovered that our friend from London resides here on Cap d'Antibes. You're coming with us to call on M. Meilland! Yes, the Frenchman from the Savoy!") and raiding the larder for more supplies before driving on further away from the common way along the peninsula. We arrived at a modest house on that quiet, lonely cape jutting out into the Mediterranean, covered in wild tangled forests of pine and fir tumbling down to the sea.

Young M. Meilland's eyes lit up finding on his doorstep four Americans whom he had met under such peculiar circumstances in London. He gave us a warm welcome which became even more voluble when he was presented with the three bottles of wine and fresh flowers (not roses) from the Nice flower market and glossy strawberries that we had not been able to resist buying from a rustic roadside stall. We were invited into his home, whose windows looked over the rose gardens, and invited to luncheon on the wide terrace, shaded with a vine, on the side of the house looking down to the sea. Unfortunately his parents were in Tassin, the family's other rose nursery near Lyon, but M. Meilland entertained us with great charm, generosity, friendliness and conversation. We shared tales about our recent travels and our mutual friends and acquaintances, we discussed world news and events over a delicious simple meal (Tilly's remembering and mention of the round of cheese and baked tart sitting redundant in the Bentley trunk was met with unaffected garrulity, added to the luncheon feast, shared happily, and pronounced to be divinely inspired) while M. Meilland regaled us with family anecdotes and the lore of roses, especially of Empress Josephine and the gardeners of Malmaison. Towards the end of the meal, M. Meilland brought out some crystal goblets of palate cleansing sorbet ices.

"Please, try, tell me your verdict," he told us with the eager enthusiasm of a young boy.

Our exclamations of surprise at the flavors broadened his smiles.

"It smells—tastes like...like...roses?"

"This is one of the reasons why the Dowager Countess de Clermont de Montmorency-Beaumont and her god-daughter, and the many generations of their family who have passed on the precious rose petal sorbet recipe, love their rose gardens," said M. Meilland.

After luncheon, M. Meilland introduced us to his nursery.

The beauty of the rose, M. Meilland said, had inspired many deep, tempestuous and artful passions in history.

It was not difficult, coming through a wilderness behind the greenhouse into a sudden clearing, finding ourselves standing in the Meillands' rose garden—watching his face light up and listening to the animation of his voice as he showed and explained the variety of roses surrounding us, unveiling the stories of their provenance, their beauties and susceptibilities, the methods of propagation, grafting, cross-pollination and hybridization, the perpetuation of a line of desired beauty—to understand how this thorny, fussy, unprepossessing bush, of all flowers, had so inextricably interwoven itself into the existence of humankind.

"...Napoleon's wife, Josephine, loved roses. She cultivated them in her garden at Malmaison, tended by expert gardeners. One legend has it that one of the Malmaison gardeners, a Frenchman by the name of Dubois, was the first man since the ancient Greeks to have carried out the grafting of a rose. Dubois wrote in his notebook: 'Someday a man who would like to declare his love to the woman he worships will have a choice among a hundred different roses. Perhaps more. Alas, I shall not live to see that day.'"

"Oh, it almost seems as if..." ventured Tilly. "Was this M. Dubois...?"

"A man in love?" M. Meilland smiled. "Yes, supposedly Dubois' unrequited depth of feeling for the Empress provided his inspiration for the first modern rose grafting."

"How sad—tragic!"

"It's only a legend, Lucia, and if true, surely it is a moral lesson in rectitude and the greater good?" said Matthias.

"I believe that deserves a thumping. Matthias is calling you a sap, Lucia," said Charley.

We followed M. Meilland through the glasshouse and the paths of the garden, walking amidst this wondrous enterprise in the heart of a wild tangled forest, the rows of rose bushes, lined up on wooden benches behind glass or along neat parallel earthy mounds protected by shady trees standing on the periphery, glossy green leaves, dark new slender stalks blushing in purple-maroon hues holding up tight buds, branches heavily covered in blooms from blowsy pale shades to vibrant color. As we wandered along the dirt paths, M. Meilland pointed to Centifolias where asparagus, cauliflowers, green peas and beans had once grown, indicated Alba roses growing in the soil reclaimed from the fruit orchard. Matthias drew down a stem to allow us a closer sniff at an opening Damask or tea rose on its tip. Charley, Tilly and I tried to impress M. Meilland by correctly identifying as many rose varieties as we could name. Matthias showed a surprisingly good knowledge of the new hybrid teas. Row upon row of dense foliage and beauty surrounded us, brushing past in drifting, whisper-soft fragrance, as if we had trespassed into a lost Eden.

"Gifts of the most exotic varieties of rose were sent to Malmaison from powers all over the Continent, anxious, deposed and would-be potentates, adventurers, toadies, hopeful of seeking favor and alliance with the rising French power," continued M. Meilland. "During the Napoleonic Wars, ships carrying specimens for the Empress Josephine were allowed free passage. The English-born John Kennedy, of the firm Lee and Kennedy, a partnership of two families of prominent Scottish nurserymen based in Hammersmith, west of London, was employed by Empress Josephine to assist in the design of her rose garden. Despite France being at war with England, Lee and Kennedy continued supplying roses to Malmaison—in one year, the Empress ran up a debt of over £2,000 with the firm—and Kennedy was given a special permit to travel back and forth between England and the Continent, advising the Empress on the collection she was building at Malmaison. A lady will have her garden."

"I hope such sound priorities and reasoning will hold true if we ever have another war," said Charley, letting go of a delicate, drooping pink bud and moving ahead to observe another fragile cream Noisette which M. Meilland drew to our attention in turn. "It would be a dreadful shame if our bloodthirsty need to wage war should deny civilization the enjoyment of a little beauty—the scent of the Quatre Saisons and Felicite Parmentier, the intense color of a Tour de Malakoff, the cheerful brightness of this...it is a Gloire de Dijon, isn't it, a sport of Souvenir de la Malmaison?"

"Oui. During the war, no one had the time or money for roses anymore and our garden which had once been planted with rose bushes was turned to the growing of vegetables and fruit. However, Maman set aside a small part of the garden for Papa's best-selling roses for the time when the war would finally be over, when the world would want roses again. Gloire de Dijon was one of them. Maman considered it one of the best-natured roses in the world, not demanding, obligingly growing anywhere, and deliciously scented." From a bush covered in flowers in varying stages of bloom and ranging in color from creamy-buff to vibrant saffron, M. Meilland held out a flat homely pale yellow newly-opening bud for us all to take a solemn sniff. He observed Charley lingering over it, a faint, happy, almost reverent smile in her eyes. "You prefer the old roses?"

"Old roses are the cat's meow. They breath something of a poetic, gentler age, don't you agree? (Oh, be quiet, Matthias!)" Matthias had started to grin. "I apologize for Matthias, M. Meilland. It's the effect of the wine at luncheon. Our friend is not accustomed to adult quantities of alcohol."

Both Matthias and M. Meilland laughed.

"Perhaps you meant a more romantic age?" suggested M. Meilland.

"Yes, that's right, a reminder not of a gentler age but of a romantic one —well, at least, one that is easier for us to romanticize," said Charley.

"Charley likes roses she can smell. Her aunt has a garden full of old roses," I said.

"Ah."

"The new varieties are very pretty but they are often without scent— unlike these roses growing here in your nursery," said Charley in a voice low with wistful yearning. "Every year, my aunt adds a new bush to her garden. She orders them directly from Mr. Robert Pyle, the horticulturist from—oh, but of course, you know of Mr. Pyle—although she has been resistant to the modern varieties. Last year, we planted a Devoniensis cultivar, a kind gift from Matthias. Aunt Merry has yet to embrace the brave new world of hybridized roses. However, I think if she were here to see all your lovely roses, M. Meilland, she would change her mind."

"I would be delighted to send your Tante Merry a rose—a new creation —perhaps even—I, like all rose growers, dream of the unattainable blue rose—but in the meantime, there are a number of experiments which may yet produce success worthy of being included in the firm's catalog, if not precisely of a blue shade. Allow me to show you a sample..."

"That's tremendously kind of you, M. Meilland. I think Aunt Merry would faint from the honor," said Charley.

"On second thought, I have a better idea. Come, come this way, let me show you something..."

M. Meilland led us to a bench on which stood troughs of gnarly root stock, each one neatly tagged and labeled, sticking out of dark loamy earth. He pointed to one knobbly, heavily pruned bush. A tenacious climber, he said, the sport of hardy stock, resistant to disease, of vigorous growth, deep crimson in color, long lasting semi-double flowers with petals that curl out from the center, glossy foliage, very free flowering and repeat flowering, exhibiting a sweet perfume. M. Meilland said that he would be honored if Charley would lend her name to the rose in honor of the kindness she had done him in London.

Charley was stunned and touched, rendered quite speechless by the rose grower's gesture. When she had sufficiently recovered her wits—and bickered with Matthias and Tilly and me over the unfairness of her being given all of the credit and wanting to share M. Meilland's generosity, an argument which Matthias quickly ended with the pronouncement of: fine, he was more than content for M. Meilland to name the rose after Charley, what did Tilly and Lucia think?—and of course, Tilly and I agreed with him—Charley, flushed with embarrassment, thanked M. Meilland but made a small request.

The young Frenchman smiled. "You must love your tante very much," he remarked. "I shall be delighted to accede to your wish. The cultivar should be ready to be shipped very soon."

It was a quiet, somnolent afternoon—the resplendent sun clinging to a sky of almost a transparent blue, mirroring the sea, the gentle breezes chasing after the lambent afternoon light, golden and liquid and warm, in charity with the fair milieu and company, the fantasia of roses, old and new, dowager duchesses from a bygone age and the flashy new upstarts not yet revealed to the outside world, time passing by with unhurried grace—quiet and yet somehow glorious and effulgent, too, like friendship. The afternoon entered piquantly into memory, a sepia-stained pane wherein Charley and Tilly chatted away with M. Meilland and Matthias smiled, watching them, as we trailed behind at a leisurely stroll, grazing the soft nodding buds and scattered petals of the surrounding roses, such wounded splendor, and foliage and letting the sweet, exquisitely scented air settle around us in benediction. On such a day, one could dream composedly and without cynicism of a peaceful, contented life in a beautiful world.

In years to come, one could visit the trellis at the back of the garden at Montrose—and in other gardens of the world—and find again that dream of peace and beauty, surrounded by the riotous sweet scent of wine-dark Meredith Elyots.

Back at Villa Mirabeau, we dressed for the baroness's party and turned the radiantly beautiful blooms from M. Meilland's posies into corsages to adorn our wrists and gowns and pinned one on Matthias as a buttonhole. M. Meilland had sent us away with gorgeously scented posies of roses from his nursery, including the delicious Gloire de Dijon. They were the most wonderful gift. They seemed to lighten the weight of my mother's diamonds.

When we arrived that evening at the Villa Ephressi de Rothschild, our hostess and her guests all exclaimed and admired the wondrous scent and beauty and asked us where we had gotten such lovely golden roses that they had never seen before.

"Meilland?" our hostess murmured, repeating the name we gave her. She drew us aside and questioned us further about the rose grower, intent on adding to the magnificence of her gardens, quite distracted from the entertainments and feast laid out for the evening with its fine offerings of truffles and langoustine tails and caviar and champagne and Lillet.

In addition to collecting Tilly from Villa Mirabeau and convincing her to give up the beach to call on M. Meilland, we had also persuaded Tilly to bath and anoint herself in a gown (suggested by Charley and twice spurned by Tilly as too outrageous) of a splendid vermilion hue and join us for the Villa Ephressi de Rothschild. The afterglow of the afternoon spent with M. Meilland and the company and marvelous museum of a villa did the rest in turning acquiescence into smiles of radiant appreciation of the gardens and cuisine and music and conversation of the baroness's party and the pink and mauve and violet twilight of a sky dimming, shedding its gauzy raiments, and sinking into the sea.

Baron Andre d'Erlanger's expansive salutations had greeted us as soon as we arrived and met our hostess, warmly expressing his delight that the Nicoise physician had deemed us in good health and well enough to attend the baroness's dinner. He was a charmingly entertaining companion as he circled us about the baroness's guests who had gravitated into select little groups of conversation, forming and reforming like schools of darting exotic tropical fish, as the party flowed out into the night. He also informed us during the course of the evening that, by the by, were we aware that an American by the name of Tallis Lloyd-Chase had turned up in Cannes and had been contacting the grand hotels along the coast, steadily working his way through the French Riviera, apparently looking for a Miss Lucia Bernhardt who had been last known to be staying at the Carlton Hotel in Cannes?

"Tallis? Here? What on earth for?" Charley's brow scrunched up.

Our wild surmises bore no fruit and gave way to the far more tangible wonder of Tamara Karsavina in the Baroness Ephressi de Rothschild's villa gardens high above the Mediterranean, stretching out like an endless carpet, under the lyrical moonlight.

The next morning, for no discernible reason, I woke with a start. Something in the air felt different. Had there been a sharp drop in temperature during the night—had the cold mistral blown in? It was still early, no one yet stirring in the slumbering house. I felt no premonition or dread but I drew on my peignoir and let my wakefulness guide me to the various domestic and living quarters of the house, to the study (locked, no occupant), drawing room, dining room, breakfast room, kitchen, south parlor, vestibule. Last night, when we had returned from the Baroness de Rothschild's party, there had been several telegrams lying on the salver next to a large and impressive florist's sheaf from a repentant James Dorsey on the sideboard in the hall which had come during the afternoon while we were out. (Monsieur had been advised by the staff that, unfortunately, callers were not being accepted, and courteously but firmly ejected from the grounds.) The florist showpiece was still there, the telegrams were not.

I walked to the French windows of the drawing room and peered out. The terrace, hung in a pale fragrant profusion of climbing roses, and lawns and gardens, the shadows of the pines and massed flowers, the sea and horizon were quiet, undisturbed, fresh and cool, the dew still glistening upon them, just beginning to be touched by the soft, quavering coral pink flush of dawn.

And there, near a cluster of ancient rose bushes by the terrace which led down to the jetty and beach cove, stood Charley in her baccarat pajamas and a silk Redfern garden robe, bare-headed, pensive, alone, still, like a dryad, as if her feet were changing and taking root, like a bastion standing against invading armies. She was not looking towards the sea but at the gardens, or rather, with her face turned toward the gardens, she looked away from the visible world for her mind must have been somewhere else far away to be steeped in such melancholy and grim determination.

I did not dare disturb her. Someone else had no such qualms. I heard a door softly open and close, the weight of footsteps on the veranda, and saw Matthias stride out across the lawn. He stopped at a short distance from Charley and, for a time, went no further. Charley turned eventually, and saw him there. They spoke. Matthias held out his hands in a generous, open gesture. Charley shook her head. They exchanged more words. Matthias nodded, and returned to the house. I heard the considerate, muffled noises of his leaving, the rumble of his Bentley dying into the distance.

Charley left the pale stillness of the gardens and came back to the house. As she crossed the threshold, her face caught a straying finger of light and some small measure of color. She wore no scent but that fleeting, elusive breath of Provence hovered about her, as if someone had opened a window just as a singing expectant breeze whispered down from the mountains, untarnished by the stamp of the weighty ruminations in the garden.

She was surprised to find me waiting for her near the veranda door.

"Oh, you're up," she said.

"Is everything all right, Charley?" I asked.

"As well as can be expected. Why do you ask?"

"Has there been bad news?"

"No."

"Really?"

"Really."

"Charley."

"It's nothing, Lucia."

"Then is there something that can make you less sad?"

"I— What? No. It's nothing. I couldn't sleep, came out for a walk. It'll pass."

"Really? There must be something."

"Sometimes," said Charley, my bold, uncageable friend who did not dream timid dreams, "I think all I expect to be happy is a morning when I can stand quietly, peacefully, forgotten, in Aunt Merry's garden at Montrose and feel the sunshine on my face. Some days I close my eyes and it is enough."

"Are you homesick? Do you wish to return to New York?"

"I can't even if I wanted to, not just yet."

"Why not?"

Charley simply repeated, "Not just yet."

"Charley?"

"I must go where the wind blows," Charley said. "Would you mind very much if I were to leave for Cairo?"

"When? Very soon?"

"Today. This morning."

"What? Why?"

"I can't answer that just yet, Lucia, I'm sorry."

"Matthias agreed to this?"

"What has Matthias—"

"I saw him speak to you."

"Matthias has accepted it."

"Tilly is not going to be happy about how little time to prepare and p —"

"Of course I'm not going to upend your holiday here in France. You and Tilly stay and—"

"Don't be ridiculous, Charley. Of course we're coming with you. It's not so easy to cut us loose."

"There's no 'of course' about it. There's no reason why your holiday should be cut short and spoiled because you feel obliged to stick with me. Especially as this isn't the best of times to visit Egypt with the hot summer daytime temperatures and—"

"So it is all right for you to rush headlong into the Egyptian summer but not Tilly and me? Do you not want us to be there for whatever reason?"

"No, I don't want to ruin your—"

"Then it's settled. We're coming with you."

"What about Tallis Lloyd-Chase looking for you?"

"What about Baron d'Erlanger and James Dorsey?"

It took a lot more arguing and Tilly's direct objections to being left behind to settle the matter. I heard Charley sigh and mutter "Blasted Matthias" as we pared back our steamer trunk contents to the essential provisions needed for Egypt, shipping the remaining articles directly back home, and dashed off notes to our friends and acquaintances on the French Riviera to thank them again for their hospitality and advise them of our pending departure.

Matthias came back to the villa when the faint outline of the waning half-crescent moon was almost vanished against the robin's egg blue sky and the sun was climbing to its radiance, with food and tickets for the first train to Genoa. He drove us to the Gare de Nice-Ville, ensured we had sandwiches made up from the station restaurant, and walked us to the platform to send us off, waiting there until his tall figure faded, retreating so far into the distance that he—and the bright morning and the French Riviera and the sea and the mountains—was only a speck of memory.

23

CHARLOTTE:

"WHAT THE DEVIL ARE YOU UP TO CHARLOTTE ABANDON THIS STRIDING FOLLY RETURN IMMEDIATELY NEW YORK PUT THIS RIGHT NICHOLAS MASTERSON"

"NYSE TRANCHES POSTPONED POST FED RATE RISE UNCERTAIN MARKET CONDITIONS AWAITING IMPROVEMENT EXPECT CBOT HEDGES CLOSE IN THE MONEY D"

Music and Tamara Karsavina dancing in the moonshine, faint pin-pricks of stars, the beacon head-lamps and tail-lights of motor-cars ahead of and behind us in the necklace of lights tracing the inky shoreline, a blur of voices blending into the soft, warm breath of the cavernous star-filled darkness, billows of pine and jasmine and mimosa, the sighing wash of the Mediterranean, the dark and distant murmur of the tides... None of them real or lasting. All of it, vague phantasms, barely formed incantations and dreams, conjured by champagne and the night. Such faint-hearted cowards, they always fled before the first glimmers of the sunrise. Villa Mirabeau's gardens received those tentative creeping blushes of dawn like a maiden gathering rosebuds. It would be another day delivered up to the vault of a burning hot sky and sweet airy breezes: benevolent, insensate, memoryless, beautiful.

I longed for something more humble but I held my longings and grievances in the dark stillness of my heart. Perhaps in the fullness of time they might age like wine into something approaching wisdom.

I turned to head back to the house and found Matthias standing only a couple of feet away, regarding me with his steady, penetrating but kind eyes.

"Couldn't sleep either?"

"No," Matthias replied.

"Probably should've had more champagne last night."

"Charley," Matthias said in the tone that served up a world of questions.

"No," I said.

"Do you need help?"

"No."

"Charley."

"You should know that I will be leaving this morning for Genoa. Connections permitting, I shall be taking the afternoon boat to Alexandria. If your investigations require—"

"Hang the investigation. Charley—"

"If your investigations require additional communications with me, you will know where to find me. I thought you should know. I am not trying to elude capture. If you would be so good as to not volunteer or otherwise disclose my whereabouts to anyone else not connected to the—"

"Sometimes, Charley, I could wring your neck. Why this sudden flight? What are you running from?"

What was I running from? I silenced the small, vicious, mocking voices within. "Let's just agree that this is a whim of mine." And then it struck my bedeviled humor to add, "If it were done when 'tis done, then 'twere well/ It were done quickly."

"Has this to do with James Dorsey?"

"What? No."

"For certain?"

"Yes."

"Then why—"

"I'm not answering that, Matthias."

"I see."

"Good."

"When will you make this whim known to Lucia and Tilly? Are they to be roused from their beds and rushed off to the train station to—"

"I said I was leaving. Not Lucia and Tilly. I don't impose my whims on others. At least, not if I can help it."

"They would never allow that. You can't go traipsing off to Egypt on your own—"

"I can and I will."

"I wouldn't be so sure of that, Charley. Lucia and Tilly are forces to be reckoned with."

"Don't you dare interfere, Matthias! This isn't some—"

"I didn't think it was. You wait and see. Your friends will not let go of you so easily, Charley."

"You promise not to interfere?"

"I won't interfere provided—"

"Matthias, I swear, you are—"

"—provided you take care. Don't let this playing a lone hand business seduce you into something...unsafe."

I considered this. "All right."

"Have you booked your passage yet? What can I do to help?"

"Nothing."

"I'll be running the motor off shortly and passing the station. I could—"

"You just said you wouldn't interfere!"

"Help. I'm helping. It'll save you a trip if I book the tickets and—"

"Ticket. Singular. Only one passenger: me."

"Oh, I think you'll find—"

"And you say you want to wring my neck!"

"Go and pack, Charley. And wake Lucia and Tilly up. I'll get your tickets."

"You are an interfering blockhead."

"I'll be back shortly. Will you have enough time to rustle up breakfast here as well as finish your packing? I can get something for breakfast on the way?"

"That might be well-advised. I'm tempted to poison your breakfast."

"Yes, dread lord. I'm sure it'll still be tasty."

"Matthias, if you are going to meddle... There is something that you might be able to...nudge along a little."

Matthias listened intently. At the end, he said, "But you don't like him."

"Neither will her parents. Why should any of that matter?"

"I'll see what I can do."

Matthias left the garden. In his receding footfalls, he took away with him some small particle of the icicle which had lodged in my chest.

PYRAMIDS, TELEGRAMS AND ANGER

Late August-September 1929, Cairo-Luxor-Assuan

24

LUCIA:

We took the train to Genoa and, instead of lingering on the water-front or a short drive to the sunshine and wisteria of Portofino, we changed at the bustling Mediterranean port, first for a steamer which brought us to Alexandria—Alexandria!—a center of Hellenistic civilization and the capital of Ptolemaic, Roman and Byzantine Egypt for almost a thousand years, and, for several centuries, the largest city in the world, second only to Rome, home to the Lighthouse of Alexandria, one of the Seven Wonders of the Ancient World, and its great fabled library... Alexandria, we could scarcely conceive of it... And then, wonder of wonders, breaking through the commotion and swarming crowds, from the crush of Alexandria's quays to a platform teeming with people and onto another train from Misr Station heading towards Cairo—Cairo!—to tour deserts and tombs and pyramids and other wonders of the ancient world. The chaotic manner of our precipitate departure from France somehow continued to thrum and echo like a rapid, steady heartbeat in motion with the portentous rhythmic chug of the locomotives, the onrushing swell and retreat of the waves, the jostle and cacophony of the quayside, the traffic and choking fumes and discordant bustling noise of the cities towards which we traveled, hastening as if a nemesis was behind us, hot in pursuit.

The heat and fine golden dust, the aridity, away from the Alexandrian harbor and the Nile Delta, in contrast to the lushness, the green and blue and white, of the Riviera's coast and sea, hit us immediately, cutting through the fatigues of travel.

Egypt. We were in Egypt.

Tilly and I had to continually remind ourselves to stop gawking on the drive from the train station into downtown Cairo. There was so much frenetic and chaotic activity, so much energy and life, it almost seemed like a traffic jam on Madison Avenue if it had not been for the heat, the babble of foreign dialects and sounds and smells, the unquestionably exotic environs, the palm trees and domes and minarets and hazy outlines of—could it really be?—pyramids hovering on the horizon like distant rumors.

"It's surprisingly European in style—very...Parisian—and so many Europeans here, too, amongst the local Cairenes," I noted. Tilly pointed out the elaborate façades of a Sednaoui Department Store, a Cafe Riche and a patisserie coffee shop on Suleiman Pasha Street with the name of the Swiss chocolatier J. Groppi above it.

"We've yet to pass through the Egyptian quarter of Cairo. This is the European quarter, cosmopolitan hub designed by French architects—blame Napoleon and the British and the war and Egyptologists," Charley answered, distractedly scanning the passing streets crowded with pedestrians and traffic. "Here we are, this is us, I think." And then, "Oh, for the—it's full of Americans. Are we never to get away?"

I looked out of the cab window. Across the busy street, a bustling hub of activity, on the northwest corner of the Ezbekiya Gardens, facing the tourist and antique shops on Ibrahim Pasha Street, stood Shepheard's Hotel, its terrace entrance presently disgorging onto the street-front several young men whose accents were decidedly not Egyptian.

We paid the driver and, despite Charley's utterance of dismay, strode up the sidewalk and entered the hotel's main lobby.

"I was expecting it to be frequented by the French and British crowd, not..." Charley muttered as we passed silent-slippered liveried servants, granite pillars, stained glass, high domed ceilings, ornate public rooms with dark and intriguingly mysterious alcoves, Oriental rugs and tapestries, plush divans and silken cushions, great cascading chandeliers and polished silver service, and other manifestations of Shepheard's opulence. Charley's mutterings were caused by the hotel's oval-shaped long bar, otherwise known as the American Bar, stocked by Shepheard's vast wine cellars, which appeared to be popular with Americans as well as the French and the British. "We should probably have checked into the Continental-Savoy instead, just up the street on Opera Square—it was good enough for T. E. Lawrence and Lord Carnarvon. Or the Windsor... Or the National on Suleiman Pasha... Or the Semiramis on the river... Surely one of the other big hotels in Cairo must be open during the summer months... It's as well that we are only staying in Cairo a short while before we head to Luxor."

Charley lost no time in commandeering the staff of Shepheard's to hire private transport and to scurry off to Cook's tourist office to book excursions and tours and anything else that would get us away from the maddening crowds as soon as possible. Charley retired to the suite to rest (write telegrams) while Tilly and I ventured out on our own very modest expedition to the Groppi garden coffee shop that we had seen earlier to sample the ice cream smothered in creme Chantilly that our driver had recommended. It was delicious and made us eager to try the other treats praised by our driver such as the iced coffee and chocolate and freshly baked croissants and chocolate-covered dates. When we returned to the hotel, we duly reported back to Charley on the delights she had missed. Charley evinced regret and an intention to join us next time but she had that distracted look in her eyes again. It had been obvious why she had chosen not to join us on our expedition to Groppi's: the coffee shop had been bustling and welcoming, a pulsing center of the city, not the place to loiter for one who wished to avoid people and notice and prowl about in the shadows.

We eschewed the sociable lawn-tennis court, the garden restaurant and grill room downstairs and the concerts held on the large terrace and the nightly dances under the magnificent chandeliers, for which women wore evening gowns and men appeared in military uniform—de rigeur evening dress at dinner was too much effort, Charley complained, and we concurred, taking a quiet dinner in our suite and discussing the coming excursions and the Cook's touring guides and brochures that Charley's minions had brought back which were presently scattered around the sitting room along with our 8th English edition Baedekers. After our meal (which made no concessions to the Egyptian location, the printed tassel-corded menu might have featured in any stylish hotel or restaurant in Europe), Tilly and I found that our recent travels and the day's exertions had finally caught up with us and we decided to retire early for the night to recover from too little sleep—finally, comfortable, stationary beds into which to sink!—and the dry Cairo heat which seemed to linger in our pores in spite of the cooling evening air and a long bathtub soak—the vast, echoing bathrooms were the closest we had yet come to being inside the inner chamber of a pyramid— and the continuous whirring hum of the fans.

"Good night, children. Rest well. We have a full day ahead of us tomorrow," said Charley.

"Don't sound so gleeful," I said.

Charley smiled and turned back to attend to the open window, its shutters thrown open to the Cairene night, and gaze after sundown upon the city that she had snubbed during the day, as if contemplating the orbit of the constellations in the blackness or seeking for water in the blank spaces of the desert without a compass.

There was no doubt that Charley would share her mind's busy plottings with the night—and probably her playing cards as well—relying on these confidences to vanish with the sunrise. I remembered Charley at the river bank at Tessa's wedding in Oxford, Charley standing in the gardens of Villa Mirabeau, sinking under the weight on her shoulders. I recalled Charley's light-hearted letters about all of her putative frivolous goings-on away from New York, all the occasions in England and France when she had laughed and told a charming lie or gotten up to more mischief instead of bowing her head in defeat and weeping. There had been a time when I wondered who had taught Charley the ability to fight from a deficit, to smile and chatter and embrace amusement while secretly plotting away in defiance of the skies falling. I no longer wondered. Necessity must have somehow honed that innate treasure within her, forging the humor and resilience and intractable disobedience that my father had found so objectionable into a means of survival. I did not know exactly what it was that Charley faced, what all our futures held, but I had grown accustomed to this quality of Charley's—stalwart, reassuring, nourishing—it was like a piece of her knight's armor, it gave courage, the brightest beacon of hope in the darkness. She would yet set fire to the world.

"Good night," I told Charley before returning to my room, closing the door behind me, drawing out a pen and, since I had used up my own supply of stationery, took out the complimentary sheets of paper supplied by the hotel.

The following mornings at Shepheard's began predictably with a comprehensive pile of English newspapers from around the globe, to which The Egyptian Gazette had now been added, and telegrams alongside a full breakfast spread in our suite. ("Aren't you curious about what is happening in the rest of the world and the markets?" Charley had asked us. Well, the Exchange was the same as when we had left New York, still carousing on drunken high spirits, still competing for who had the greatest hubris and ambition. "The New York Stock Exchange, yes, but the London Exchange seems a bit undecided as to whether it is still happily drunk or hungover," Charley had said and turned back with a frown of concentration to study them.)

"Are those...they look like..." Tilly peered at the dishes on the table.

"You were quite right. These chocolate-covered dates are delicious," said Charley, reaching out for a pastry. "I bribed one of the staff to run out to Groppi's to, um, requisition some contraband. The hotel breakfast is excellent, I might add, but I was dreaming about the chocolate covered dates last night. I lay the blame entirely at your feet. Oh, did you either of you realize that there are other Groppi's in Cairo besides the Suleiman Pasha branch?—Groppi's Grand Rotunda seems to feature soirée concerts and dances in addition to coffee, cake and ice cream. It's a pity ice cream is not agreeable to transportation. You never mentioned that Groppi's had so many tempting flavors: Peche Melba, Surprise Neapolitaine, Morocco, Mau Mau, Maruska, Sfogliatella, Comtesse Marie..."

Rested, nourished, swathed in pale silken scarves (except for Charley's which retained their vivid color) and cool linen and roomy hats, we were able to greet our excursion itinerary in a more satisfactory, less daunted, frame of mind.

Our dragoman guide, Waleet, met us in the lobby and we drove along the river Nile, crossing the river twice on five bridges, and out to see temples and colonnades and ruins at Memphis, the ancient capital of Lower Egypt and the Old Kingdom, on the edge of the Western Desert. We continued on to the necropolis at Sakkara to visit the step-pyramid of King Djoser from the Third Dynasty and neighboring buried and unfinished pyramids and the beautiful bas-reliefs representing ancient Egyptian life in the nearby tombs of the nobles. It wasn't very impressive, Tilly said, and was told that it was the early predecessor to the great pyramids at Giza. Giza proved to be rather more dusty and less romantic than Cook's advertisements had led us to believe but the three great pyramids of Cheops, Khrafre, Menkaure and the number of smaller subsidiary pyramids and mastabas next to the broken-nosed Sphinx rising from the golden sands were imposing enough to meet Tilly's approval, although she balked at the chance to enter one of the pyramids for a small charge, her horror— despite all our reassurances—feeding on the idea of climbing inside a steep, low-ceilinged, dark passageway and rumors of the mummy's curse that befell all who had desecrated their resting place. Tilly chose instead to try a camel ride. It had looked so thrillingly adventurous and romantic in the Rudolph Valentino movies that Tilly had no trouble persuading us to join her but we had to stifle our giggles as Tilly went speeding on ahead of us into the desert sand to the terrified squeals of "Mohammedddddddd!" and, when Mohammed, the owner of the camels, finally caught up with Tilly and helped her off the beast, at Tilly fervently vowing never, ever, ever again would she mount another obstreperous, cheeky, smelly, impossible creature who would not listen or obey and would always go in the opposite way to the direction Tilly wanted and kept trying to sniff Tilly or bite Tilly or chew Tilly's hem instead of obeying Tilly's commands and would then bat her long black lashes back at Tilly's admonishments as though she had been unjustly wronged. "That's because she is an Egyptian camel, Tilly," Charley laughed. "She responds better if you talk to her in Egyptian rather than a strange American tongue. Didn't Waleet teach us the Egyptian for 'please' and 'thank you' yesterday?"

The rooms at the Egyptian Museum full of richly adorned sarcophagi and gold funereal masks and royal jewelry and mummies and statues and thrones and coins and artifacts from intact tombs, such as that of Tutenkh-Aman discovered by Howard Carter, and other exhibits from the Egyptian dynastic periods of the Old Kingdom to the Greco-Roman occupation wrung fascination from me. I finally understood why the French and British and the world at large had caught a terminal case of Egyptian fever.

Interspersed between the immersions in ancient Egyptian history,

Waleet also took us to a carpet shop and, giving us prior warning, an antiquities shop full of papyri and cartouches and other "artifacts" for purchase at bargain prices, and the maze-like Khan el-Khahili souk which was bewilderingly mesmerizing like an Arabian Night's dream and impossible, though we tried, to explore fully in one attempt, and thus we vowed to return.

Charley's appreciation for Egypt's ancient civilization and treasures did not find expression in the gushing raptures she had shared with the Bommels in London over Howard Carter's discoveries, over the Rosetta Stone at the British Museum or the Egyptian souvenirs in the Louvre and around Paris left behind by Napoleon—that fountain had been turned off quite sharply into a trickle of polite, restrained murmurings in the face of these marvels of antiquity. When asked, Charley said she was keeping her gunpowder dry for later.

"If I use it all up now, what will be left for Luxor and Assuan?" she argued. "For the royal tombs and temples carved into hillsides and obelisks and pylons and colossi and open-air museums and avenues of sphinxes? No, no, I'm a philistine until then. I'm sure the Bommels would approve of my discernment. Shall we get another set of these ceremonial pharaonic trinkets for the Misses Bommels and our friends back in New York and London?"

When we were not being led to inspect tombs and pyramids and mummies like any self-respecting tourist with a list of Baedeker-approved sights regarding which to write to those back home, or being caught up with the boisterous social activities of the international and cosmopolitan crowd who drifted in and out of Shepheard's, the Sala Badia club on Emad El Din Street ("Would you like to see some belly dancing, Tilly?") and the popular bars and restaurants on Alfi Bey Street (La Parisiana and the barrel lounge at the Windsor Hotel—former British Officers' Mess frequented by T. E. Lawrence amongst others—and the nearby Kursaal and St. James were very popular rendezvous), we directed our driver and guide to take us out of the common way—certainly far, far away from any notion of what was suitable, appropriate or edifying for a young woman while on Grand Tour according to the standards of Old New York. Hussain and Waleet led us away from the European quarter to see the Babylon Fortress and Hanging Church of Coptic Cairo, caravanserai and former palaces and mausoleums and old churches and ruins of fortifications and minarets and geometric domes and mihrab with inlaid marble and shaded arcades and private courtyards and fountains in Islamic Cairo, the Citadel, the beautiful 9th, 10th and 13th century mosques of Ibn Tulun and Al-Azhar and Sultan Hassan, the Qalawun complex from the 13th century, the wikala of Sultan al-Ghuri, and other remnants of civilization left behind by the Romans and Mamelukes and Ottomans that we had only glimpsed from within the confines of taxis as though from behind a mashrabiya screen. Being female and foreigners, we were restricted in where we could go in Old Cairo, even escorted, but curiosity (she whose name was Charley) guided—or incited—us to make the most of our explorations into the vast sprawling metropolis including heading out to Rhoda Island to see the nilometer, a memorable visit to perform purifying ablutions in a women's hammam, a quarter of the Turkish bathhouse given exclusively for women (Tilly's eyes nearly popped out of their sockets in disbelief), and traversing the length of Muizz Street with its endless distractions and architectural diversions, flanked by the magnificently decorated portals and façades of medieval palaces and mansions and mosques and markets, often leading back to Khan el-Khahili, to the tentmakers' market and cloth market and goldsmiths' market and spice market and antiques market and the street where a thousand perfumes could be found and bought, plunging into the torturous streets and alleyways whose air hung thick with the scent of incense, perfume and spices—ambergris, myrrh, frankincense, cumin, coriander, and cardamon—choosing Damascene cloth or trinkets over copious Turkish glasses of sweet mint tea, drinking potent Arabic coffee brewed from gilt dallahs and attempting to smoke apple-scented shisha from the beautifully ornate water pipes at the El-Fishawi coffeehouse, thrilling in the sense of getting lost in the heart of the maze with the reassurance that Waleet and Hussain were always on hand to lead us out again.

Tilly and I dropped into our beds each night from the sheer overwhelming exhaustion and wonder of becoming acquainted with Cairo, old and new, and the sun which beat down each day and the dead heat and gritty sand and dust that blew everywhere and got into everything. We were no match for Charley's stamina, always the first to rise for the morning newspapers and running to the Shepheard's telegraph office downstairs, always with a head full of ideas and schemes, always the last to retire, gazing out of our hotel window into the shadowed recesses of the Cairene evening scored by the muezzin calls to prayer.

In the midst of the frequently unbearable heat, Charley sought out the parks and gardens in Cairo—green oases created at the direction of Khedive Ismail—in the same way she sought out books and anonymity, in the same way archaeologists unearthed treasure: the Ezbekiya Gardens, the Giza Zoological Gardens, the Fish Garden in Zamalek, the Qanater Gardens, the gardens of the Mohammad Ali Palace... Every time Charley drew us out to a newly discovered patch of greenery, I wondered at the impetus which had caused Charley to run knowingly towards the trial of endurance in an Egyptian summer. Then I remembered the morning when Charley had stood in the Villa Mirabeau gardens. Telegrams. Always telegrams.

Upon returning to the lobby of Shepheard's Hotel on our third day after driving out to the south of Cairo and hiring a donkey-drawn sand-cart with wide wheel rims for a desert picnic excursion, we were handed a telegram which I passed on directly to Charley. She glanced down at it and handed it back to me.

"For me? That can't be right. Where are yours?"

"This one is addressed to you," said Charley.

I read the cable. "Vincent is coming to Cairo. He arrives tomorrow." I looked up in shock into the avidly inquisitive faces of Tilly and Charley.

"You'd better wire him immediately and tell him to bypass Cairo," said Charley, "to stay on the train until it reaches Luxor or he'll miss you."

Tilly regarded me meditatively. "Aren't you pleased to be seeing him?"

"I am, I am! I'm simply... I didn't expect this. He's so busy with work and all the—" Charley rolled her eyes. "Charley."

Charley snorted at my reproof. "Send the wire, Lucia. Now, since you and Tilly have been moaning about the heat endlessly, you may wish to take out your bathing costumes when we head out to Giza again for the Mena House..."

We did not unpack our bathing costumes, our trunks were packed for Luxor and, after the desert picnic, it was too much effort to do more than bath and dress in our apartments under the pulse of the fans. All we wanted was tea and a cool oasis, and we got it, sitting in the luxurious shade of the tea gardens of the Mena House, a former hunting lodge converted into a hotel (an oriental palace facing the pyramids with mashrabiya windows, medieval brass embossed and carved wood doors, blue tiles and hand-crafted mosaics of colored marble and mother-of-pearl, and a dining hall that replicated the interior of a Cairo mosque—Baron Malcolm McDonald and his secretary, Joplin Sinclair, had referred to "opulent elegance in desert nights" in their account of their visit to the Mena House in 1926) graced by such guests as Charlie Chaplin, Sir Arthur Conan Doyle and Winston Churchill and various royalty (and the actress Sarah Bernhardt too, Charley noted), and being served afternoon tea as if we were in an English manor, only with Egyptian and Nubian staff and views of Giza's golden pyramids before us as if sprouted from the hotel gardens along with the flowers and palms and eucalyptus trees, and feeling somehow cooler and refreshed by the mere knowledge of our proximity to Egypt's first swimming bath, opened at the hotel in 1890, where the water was supplied by the same spring that provided the Mena House's crystal clear drinking water.

"This is a better find than Zerzura, is it not?" Charley said.

When we had been discussing our excursion plans—when Charley had digressed and tried to lead us astray along a million other channels in search of desert mirages such as winding our way through the dark, narrow gorge in the sandstone cliffs to the rose-red city of Petra, or riding through Wadi Rum, the valley of light, airborne sand or the valley of the moon, which T.

E. Lawrence had passed through, or seeing the prehistoric petroglyphs of the Uweinat ranges, rising like medieval castles out of the desert sand, first reported in 1923 by the Egyptian explorer Ahmed Pasha Hassamein Bey, and the ruggedly beautiful remote plateau of Gilf Kebir discovered and named in 1925 by the adventure-loving Prince Kamal el Dine Hussein, two men who had answered the siren call of lost oases, lost cities and lost treasure, the quest to find Zerzura—Charley had spoken of the legendary Zerzura, called "The Oasis of Little Birds" in writings dating back to the 13th century and mentioned by Herodotus, the rumored city as "white as a dove" lost in the desert sands of the Sahara, the resting place of a sleeping king and queen filled with great riches and guarded by black giants, that had fired the imagination of the Royal Geographic Society and inspired numerous expeditions of desert explorers. It had inspired our own impulsive, disastrous fool's dream of a picnic excursion into the unrelenting heat of a desert furnace. We really should have known better than to fall under the spell of another of Charley's tales. "At least we didn't walk into a sandstorm blown in by the khamsin," Charley had said quite magnanimously on the return journey. She had voiced doubts at the start regarding our expedition to reach the Fayum Oasis, the triumph of our flights of romantic fancy over practicality and good sense, and had recommended a detour to the Mena House instead—to try out the 18-hole golf course which looked like an oasis on the edge of the desert due to its regular irrigation in the early hours of the day, or to ask the hotel to charter a caravan of camels and prepare tents, camp-beds, supplies, servants and maybe even a chef, for an excursion into the desert as Peggy Guggenheim had done—but had come along with us anyway on the hastily arranged desert picnic and swallowed as great a quantity of desert dust as Tilly and I had. (Thank goodness for our kaftan-style robes and stout lace-up desert boots and wide-brimmed hats tied with muslin scarves, fluttering about us and keeping out the worst of the heat and dust, although not quite as good as if we had dressed as the Bedouins or Tuaregs did.) It was ironic, I thought, that Charley who was known for being the reckless one should have been so conscientiously practical and sensible.

Charley's motives for suggesting tea at the Mena House were rather more straightforward and transparent than the pretty views and fresh milk supplied daily from medically-examined cows from the hotel's own dairy. All her focus since arriving in Cairo had been to go unnoticed, to stay away from the public congress at Shepheard's and popular meeting places around Cairo where she might run into someone who knew her. The Mena House seemed a dubious choice, it was scarcely a discreet backwater, but most of the hotels in Cairo were closed until the winter season and given the Mena House's clientele was predominantly British, the likelihood of bumping into a New Yorker was marginally lower here than at Shepheard's. And it was cool and the views were impressive. Charley must have been seduced by the glamor and mystery of the pyramids trumpeted by all those Cunard, Peninsula & Oriental, Cox & Kings, Thomas Cook & Son, Lloyd Triestino, Anglo-American Nile Company, Egyptian Mail Steamship Company and countless other advertising posters and brochures more than she had let on.

I thought of this when a familiar figure appeared against the backdrop of the looming Great Pyramid. He had appeared in London and Paris and the French Riviera; of course we should not have been surprised that he would magically appear like a djinn in Cairo, too, with his charming smiles and magnetic green eyes.

A stiffening of Tilly's shoulders in the midst of a discussion with Charley regarding the afternoon refreshments served on silver trays by the traditionally liveried, red tarbush-wearing Mena House waiters alerted Charley to something being amiss. She slowly turned around.

"Miss Bernhardt. Miss Fairchild." James Dorsey's charming smile swept over us. There was an edge of frustrated irritation to it when it alighted on Charley. "Miss Masterson."

Charley smiled serenely back. "My, my, what a small world. You never mentioned that Cairo was also on your itinerary."

"I didn't know either until the sudden urge to run away struck me as it did you." There it was, a subtle undercurrent which had Tilly's feathers stiffening even more at what that instinctively lowered, deepened voice and accusatory, proprietorial anger implied regarding James Dorsey's standing with Charley. "You've been sorely missed. The great mystery on the Riviera was to where you'd suddenly vanished."

"Oh, I make no secret of my fickleness," said Charley. "This fever for all things Egyptian simply claimed another victim. I dragged Lucia and Tilly along with me, highly reluctant they were, too, to leave the French Riviera but you don't know how much fun we've had since arriving in Cairo. What a good detective you are to have found us! Or was it simply luck?"

How interesting: so it was true that nobody aside from Matthias had been told about our destination, only of our departure.

Charley went on to relay to James Dorsey our excursions to explore Cairo and the pyramids and tombs and Sphinx and museums, even the foolish desert picnic, as if every minute had been a superb intrepid adventure that we were breathless to prolong and not a word voiced about the heat and exhaustion and the myriad little complaints and irritations. It was one of Charley's most outrageously ornate tales. At times it was all that I could do not to gawk or laugh at her audacious half-truths. Tilly kept her embarrassment to herself, her loyalty was with Charley; she still did not like James Dorsey but there must have been a reason for Charley's embroidered tall tales, and the speculation as to what those reasons might have been made Tilly's hackles relax a smidgen.

James Dorsey listened to Charley's account and asked, "Why isn't your protector also here?"

"Are you staying here at Mena House?" Charley replied.

"At one of the smaller downtown hotels," he answered, his lips pursing in a faint hint of displeasure at Charley pointedly ignoring his question. "Shepheard's was full. Charley, could I have a private word with you?"

"Right now?"

"Are you in a hurry to be elsewhere?"

"We do have to get back into Cairo for another engagement, one that we are rather keen to keep, aren't we?" Charley looked at us expectantly and we murmured our assent. "We've been invited as guests to the Gezira Sporting Club. I understand it is quite exclusive, else I would've extended the invitation to you as well. They have lawn-tennis and other recreations that the British seem to enjoy and, I'm told, part of the club's grounds were carved out of the Khedivial Botanical Gardens, shaded with acacias and jacaranda trees, a most important consideration. It promises a pleasant way of escaping the sultry heat of Cairo for an afternoon. We really should be leaving now if we are to get back to our hotel to dress and drive to the club on time. Are you heading back downtown for the evening or staying here?"

"Charley, are you still upset about what happened at Cap d'Ferrat with the Bugatti? I—"

("What happened with the Bugatti?" Tilly asked me.)

"Oh, have you been brooding about that? You've said your apologies, it's all forgotten about and left behind. Now, if you are also headed back downtown for the afternoon, you may come with us. We have a driver—can we drop you off? It's really no trouble at all. It will be much more comfortable than catching the electric tram to the Pont des Anglais."

We did not have invitations to the very exclusive Gezira Sporting Club. We did not have a driver either. We had thanked and said goodbye that morning to our nice guide, Waleet, and driver, Hussain, who had chauffeured us around Cairo and beyond over the last few days because we were due to leave for Luxor tonight. We had simply hailed a cab here instead. Of course, Charley's hint was quite clear. I excused myself to the powder room while Charley and James Dorsey continued to converse under Tilly's chaperonage—James Dorsey politely declining the offer of a ride back into Cairo and Charley charmingly persuading him to accept—and while they were thus engaged, I went to the hotel desk and requested a motor-car and driver which the hotel immediately arranged.

We had a very restrained, polite journey back to Cairo which Charley filled with easy chatter. She gave the impression of how much adventure and gaiety we had yet to explore in Cairo and made no mention of our plans for leaving for Luxor that evening. After dropping James Dorsey off at the Metropolitan Hotel off Qasr el-Nil Street in downtown Cairo near the Cairo Bourse and Bristol Hotel as he had requested—his intent green gaze following Charley until extinguished by distance—we drove back to our hotel. Charley told us to head to our suite and dress as though we were heading out to the Gezira Sporting Club while she ran into Shepheard's telegraph office. A short while later, she joined us.

"There's a cab waiting downstairs to take you to the Gezira Sporting Club. Don't w—"

"But—how—wait, you're not coming?"

"I sent off a bunch of desperate pleas in the hope that one of them would reach its destination and be answered in the affirmative. Colonel McGillivray came through, as did Trevise-Fitzgerald. When you arrive at the club, ask for either Brigadier Rupert Fothergill-Chorley or the Grahames (Sir David, his wife, Lady Wendy, or their son, the Hon. Matthew Grahame) when you arrive. You will be their guests. No one will bar you or Tilly from entering."

"Your Englishmen? They answered?"

"Yes, why shouldn't they answer? Certainly not every Englishman has contacts in a British outpost like Cairo within his great web of English associations but the greatest risk was really not being able to get through to them in time to be of help. There is very little time difference to take into account, only two hours ahead of London, else I would've—"

"You still correspond with them?"

Charley tilted her head and regarded us. "You shouldn't believe every rumor you hear, you know."

We were still dazed by this revelation. Charley opened up a trunk and, instead of the cool elegant linens she had taken to wearing in Cairo, she took out one of the plain outfits she had purchased from the Galeries Lafayette. Her incognito uniform. Charley was not coming to the Gezira Sporting Club with us.

"Don't worry about the luggage. I'll take care of it," Charley continued. "Just make sure you leave the club with enough time get to the train station allowing for Cairo traffic. Here are your tickets. And follow these instructions."

Tilly and I hailed a cab to the Gezira Sporting Club in Zamalek. We entered without hindrance, as Charley had foretold, as the guests of not one but five esteemed club members (Charley had mentioned only four names, hadn't she?—and yet five members had alerted the front desk clerks to expect us as their guests). Brigadier Fothergill-Chorley, the Grahames, and Captain Maddox Aldersley came out to welcome us and kindly showed us around the club's playing grounds and chatted and ordered us gin and tonic sundowners at the bar. Our impression of the club as a very colonial British watering hole was confirmed but it was certainly a very comfortable one, a refreshing respite as promised, and our hosts had been more than generous in sharing their time and hospitality with two strangers on the pretext of nothing more than a hurried exchange of telegrams. After sufficient time had passed by, we thanked and bid farewell to our hosts and left the club discreetly and hailed another cab towards downtown. We changed taxis three times and with different destinations each time, checking that we were not being tailed or noted, exactly according to Charley's instructions, and then finally headed to Cairo train station. We waited on the platform for Charley to arrive. Time ticked by. Tilly and I grew more and more nervous as the train's departure time drew closer.

"Should we wait?" Tilly asked.

"Charley said not to miss—"

A tap-tap-tap sounded behind us. We looked around the platform, at the people hurrying by around us, and finally up at the dusty carriage windows. At a face covered with a niqāb veil looking down at us from inside the carriage, head swathed in a melaya luf and an improvised blue mandil—a patterned sky blue scarf which we had chosen in Paris that was the only thing I recognized until I saw the familiar eyes peeping through the veil.

"Of all the—!"

Tilly and I hurriedly scrambled to board the train and find our compartment.

Charley sat inside the compartment, looking as mysterious as you please, quite unrecognizable in local Egyptian garb.

"Damnit, Charley!"

"Shh, not yet," warned Charley.

It was only after the train drew out of Cairo station and the compartment door closed behind us after our tickets had been checked that Charley unwound the veil, abaya robe, melaya luf, and blue headscarf from herself and threw them onto the opposite seat and deigned to change back into her Parisian tailored linen suit.

"All this fuss and cloak-and-dagger over just one Mr. Dorsey," Tilly grumbled.

"Not just James Dorsey," Charley said with a chiding smile. "I do prefer the freedom of being able to move about without others on my heel. Don't you, Tilly? Egypt seems rather a nice place to have to spoil with running into folks all the time."

"Egypt seems to be quite a small world unless you are adept at disappearing into the sands like an explorer or desert dweller. Isn't it rather a wasted effort to try to lose our tails when it will eventually be found out that we've gone to Luxor?" I pointed out.

"Ah, but by that time we will have moved on to Assuan or elsewhere," Charley said. "A reprieve is never a wasted effort. And a reprieve may be indefinitely extended..."

Charley had bribed one of the porters to purchase several trunks (thrown about several times to make them look well-worn) and several changes of wardrobe and sundry toiletries and meretricious souvenirs, which she arranged and adorned with some luggage labels transferred from our packed steamer trunks bound for Luxor, and left them inside our suite at Shepheard's, along with her copy of Baedeker and The Seven Pillars of Wisdom and a handful of other books she had bought at the Anglo-Egyptian Bookshop thrown in. The purchases had also included a set of traditional Egyptian female costume which she took with her in a small bag. She gave instructions to the hotel management that they were to hold on to the suite for us until we returned from a desert expedition. She added an advance payment against our hotel account for good measure. Then she donned her incognito uniform and collected our actual steamer trunks and snuck out of Shepheard's to hail a cab to the grandiloquent domed Heliopolis Palace Hotel in Heliopolis (the most luxurious hotel in Cairo, succeeding to the crown of the late aristocratic Savoy Hotel overlooking Qasr el-Nil Street, whose monumental dimensions and sumptuousness had inspired awe in monarchs and tycoons alike, including the late John Pierpont Morgan, who had been a regular visitor to Egypt, and the Builder Chocolate King, Milton S. Hershey, saved by Fate from traveling on the maiden voyage of the RMS Titanic, who had abandoned his plans to build a hotel in Pennsylvania "like the great Heliopolis Hotel in Cairo" at his late wife's urging when he saw the astronomical cost of such an enterprise—the Cairo hotel inside which Charley had dared not show her face for fear of running into a fustian aristocrat or some other bored moneyed gossiping crony who might rat her out to Old New York). At the Heliopolis Palace, she found a different cab and got into that for Cook's offices. From there she changed into another cab for the Khan el-Khahili bazaar. And then another. And another—in the back seat of which she took out from the small bag the abaya robe and niqāb veil and drew them over herself, adding the blue scarf as a hijab and the melaya luf to cover her head, a second layer of incognito from head to toe—until finally alighting at Cairo train station and being ushered through to the sleeping car of the train due to depart for Luxor where she ordered our trunks neatly inside our compartment and sat down to wait for Tilly and me to arrive.

If we had had any lingering doubts that James Dorsey was no longer the queen's favorite, this elaborate avoidance laid those doubts to rest. For the most part.

We did not ask the questions burning on our tongues; Charley would only have met them with evasions or apologetic half-truths. Tilly did the next best thing.

"What happened with the Bugatti?" Tilly asked.

The overnight sleeper train bore us uneventfully to Luxor. Tilly's reconnaissance confirmed that there were few people about and gave us the all clear to head to the dining car where we had a light supper in peaceful anonymity. (Tilly would ordinarily have protested her disapproval at such behavior—ladies ought not to be skulking about as though they were criminals—but the notion that such behavior might avoid further encounters with James Dorsey had Tilly playing scout with zealous alertness and dexterity.) Afterwards, we debated heading to the club car. There were a few groups and private individuals in there enjoying a quiet drink— fortunately nobody we knew—which seemed to allay Charley's concerns and she gave up the caution of donning incognito again (which at close range, I pointed out, would either have been inadequate disguise or looked ridiculously conspicuous anyway). We spent most of the evening at a table making use of Charley's playing cards. A few of the other patrons saw Charley's growing pile of winnings and came over and asked in a friendly manner if they might join in our card game. After that, Charley agreed to sharing a liking for gin and tonics (we had apprised her of the hospitality extended to us at the Gezira Sporting Club—"I was not advised of a Captain Maddox Aldersley," Charley frowned) and her winnings dwindled at a steady pace, rapidly reallocated in generous pourboire to the waiters and amongst the other players, ensuring everyone retired for the evening in good humor and in charity with each other. Tilly (rightly) thought it all highly suspicious and suspect.

"Isn't the point of cheating to win?" we asked Charley as we collected our stack of Egyptian pounds and piastres from the table (which would be redistributed again on the morrow at the souks and as bakshish) and returned to our compartment.

"Isn't it better that our fellow travelers to Luxor don't remember us in relation to a grudge they bear for losing to us at cards?" Charley replied.

"Do you want to place a wager that they'll remember you quite apart from the card game and the plentiful nightcaps, Charley?" I said. "What are the chances of running into our new Charley-Masterson-enspelled friends and being hailed tomorrow on the street or at one of the popular sites we are to visit?"

"You really have been corrupted to terrible ways," Charley observed with polite indulgence.

The rickety clacking of the train carriages kept me in a light, fitful sleep. It was still quite dark in our compartment when I came awake. I drew up a corner of the blinds expecting to see dim shadows in the blackness and was met with something like a nocturne watercolor, tinted with an ominous flavor, or perhaps that had simply been the result of my chaotic, uneasy dreams.

The glaucous dawn outside the train window, full of murky silhouettes, gave way to a sky stained with saffron and ocher gold.

"It will look much prettier when the sun comes up." Charley yawned from her berth, still grumpy from her slumber and far too relaxed for a someone who had fled from Cairo as though there had been a bounty on her head. "It will certainly be much cooler on the Luxor river-front than it was in Cairo. And when we sail up the Nile towards Upper Egypt, we really will be leaving the humid heat behind."

Our train presently drew into Luxor station. A cab took us down the palm-lined Corniche to the Winter Palace Hotel, a good deal less crowded than it was in the wake of Howard Carter's discovery of Tutenkh-Aman's tomb when the whole world descended upon Luxor. The Winter Palace looked gracious and solid standing before the Nile. Its buff and white façade seemed to assure us that nothing bad should disturb us here.

We strode up the sweep of pale marble steps into the hotel foyer and signed in at the front desk. We wasted no time repairing to our suite. Our rooms had high ceilings and vast bathrooms and views across the Nile to the West Bank and the Theban Hills. I wanted nothing more than to dive into the plush bed and sleep—or perhaps sink into the enormous bathtub and doze a while. Tilly agreed. But Charley had other ideas, dragging us downstairs again to the terrace and ordering breakfast. After coffee and sunshine and the soft breezes coming off the river, we grudgingly conceded that Charley had been right, we felt more human again.

"Good," said Charley, "now you can go back upstairs and take your nap, if you like, or we can go play tourist after a stroll around the hotel's gardens."

"What about your telegrams?" I asked.

"They can wait," said Charley.

Tilly and I exchanged glances.

"Well, they can," Charley huffed. "So are you for napping or sightseeing?"

We decided to visit Luxor Temple to take advantage of the temperate morning before the heat of the day became too overwhelming. During the stroll through the pleasure gardens behind the hotel—where we had stopped to admire the exotic plants and flowers and we had flowers that Charley praised for their beauty promptly cut and presented to us and, upon leaving, kisses blown to us in farewell from the friendly gardener—Charley had voiced many ambitious ideas and made many suggestions but this seemed to be the choice towards which she gently nudged us. Was it, I wondered, simply on account of the threatening midday heat? When Tilly and I ran upstairs to the wing where our suite was situated to grab silk shawls and parasols (Charley and her beautiful scarf-covered hats seldom parted company), I caught sight of Charley being handed a message by a clerk as she waited in the grand foyer beneath the crystal chandelier. Charley read the message and returned to the clerk a few words in reply. It made me half smile. The telegrams might ostensibly have been ignored for a while but all was right with the world if Charley and her intrigues and plots were still afoot.

We took a caleche waiting at the bottom of the steps of the Winter Palace and rode along the Corniche towards Luxor Temple. Sitting atop the open carriage brought fanning across our faces, like an angel's breath, the gentle eddies of a pleasant breeze and gave us a wonderful opportunity to see everything around us as we passed through into the heart of the town. The unhurried clip-clop of the horse's hooves ahead of the carriage set a quaint, leisurely pace to the morning venture. How fantastical it was that this little town growing around the banks of the Nile was once a great metropolis, Thebes, the vast capital of Egypt in the Middle and New Kingdom eras.

As we approached Luxor Temple, turning right at Shariah al-Montaziah, and saw the procession of sphinxes amongst the palm trees leading to two seated colossi of Ramses II and a pink granite obelisk and a 79-foot high main pylon at the temple entrance, I began to see why Charley had reserved her raptures.

"Oh, look at that," said Charley, waving at the obelisk, "doesn't that look familiar? I think we passed its twin in Paris at the Place de la Concorde."

She did not sound in the least bit rapturous. Our guide in Luxor, Ussama, however, did confirm Charley's observation when he met us at the entrance.

"When are you going admit to being impressed?" I asked Charley.

"Oh, there's meant to be plenty more to come, according to Baedeker and Ussama. There is still Karnak ahead and the entirety of hundred-gated Thebes on the West Bank," Charley said, eyes twinkling. "It's likely that I shan't feel the urge to swoon or start reciting Shelley until at least the mortuary temple of Egypt's only female pharaoh at Deir al-Bahri, the Temple of Hapshepsut—until Assuan at the First Cataract—until we reach Abu Simbel..."

Beyond the pylon boasting of Ramses II's military triumphs, we entered courts and colonnades and a hypostyle hall with single or double rows of towering papyrus-bud columns and sundry giant statues of the pharaoh. Tilly professed to feeling very small in the presence of his likenesses.

"Karnak is meant to be larger," observed Charley. "Countless courts, halls, temples, sphinxes. Every pharaoh worth his salt made sure to leave his mark at Karnak. Isn't that right, Ussama?"

Besides being a jaded know-it-all, Charley had been wandering in and out of the colonnade, peering around every column, looking up at each passing visitor to the temple, chasing after echoing footfalls, only half paying attention to the majestic statements surrounding us of a megalomaniac pharaoh.

"Who are you looking for?" I asked her.

"Oh, it's nothing. I think I lost my ticket. Silly to look for it now, I suppose, since we're already here inside," Charley replied breezily. She discovered a renewed interest in the carved reliefs and inscriptions which covered almost every surface of the temple and went to catch up with Ussama who was explaining to Tilly about the ancient Egyptians' love affair with empire building.

When we retraced our steps and emerged back out of the temple entrance, I thought I saw a desert mirage. A man was walking down the avenue of sphinxes towards us. His figure looked so familiar, yet my mind would not yield its disbelief until he came so near in approach that he was within touching distance and his identity could no longer be mistaken.

Vincent removed his hat and smiled. "Good morning, Lucia," he said.

He was not a mirage. He was wearing a pale linen suit with a touch of London drawing room still faintly lingering. Had he grown taller and more handsome since I had last seen him in Paris? Had it only been yesterday that I had received his telegram? He appeared fresh and unwrinkled as if he had just stepped off a dahabiyah, as if he had been flown here by a messenger of the gods and not been ruffled by the wind. And he was smiling at me in perfect answer to the restless murmurs in my heart of drifting and absence and missing him, of not having appreciated enough our time in Paris.

I had just enough of my wits about to realize that Charley was behind me, whispering to Tilly, "We could go see the Luxor Museum before tackling Karnak. They have to keep the mummies and treasures cool to preserve them so the museum will be nice and cool inside. Ussama..."

I had suspected that Charley had been up to something—up to many somethings—but not this! For someone so averse to the romantic, Charley certainly let her imagination and her notions of courtship roam wild.

"Your freckles have multiplied since I saw you last," Vincent said, smiling, tracing them on the bridge of my nose. The visible souvenirs of a nomadic sojourn on the French Riviera and scrambling about in the desert, chasing oases. What other changes would be found inside me?

"Too much sun," I agreed. "I got your cable but I didn't expect you to arrive so... Well, it's just... It seemed too wonderful. I didn't want to raise my hopes." My heart was too full, perhaps my face was transparent enough to speak for it, to ask how he was here, to show how my being was filling with wonder and joy.

"I couldn't stay away any longer. I kept hearing about your adventures with that mad whirling dervish, Charley Masterson. London misses the two young Americans who simply vanished one day into thin air and turned up on the Continent."

"Does it?"

"Do you doubt it?"

"I'm sure society has moved on to other more interesting subjects of gossip. We've been gone for a while."

"Oh, Lucia, I've missed you most of all."

Karnak, royal seat of the mighty pharaohs, passed in a golden blur of statuary and monuments and a sacred lake and massive pylons and temples flanked by colossi ("Oh, look, is that Ramses II again?") and a forest of soaring columns in the Great Hypostyle Hall and obelisks and shrines and courts and colonnades and chambers radiating out from the Temple of Amon at the heart of the complex, awash in rich reliefs and wall carvings and murals, as grand and immense in scale as Charley had said, and yes, it had its own avenue of sphinxes on approach like the one Vincent had strolled down towards us at Luxor Temple, except the Karnak sphinxes were ram-headed rather than resembling the mythical creatures couchant with the face of a man wearing pharoanic headdress. Did we absorb much of the history of this home of Egyptian gods and pharaohs and the priestly ruling caste? What a silly question. I remember Karnak as golden, monumentally beautiful, a sublime blur.

Tilly and Charley disappeared with our guide Ussama somewhere around the Seventh and Eighth Pylons south of the Cachette Court, presumably trusting that at least one of the abundance of Egyptian deities would take pity and guide our steps in retracing our way back on our own. Vincent did not give away any involvement on Charley's part in his coming to Luxor but he could not hide his small conspiratorial smile when he spoke those denials. I did not care. I didn't need confirmation of what I sensed to be the truth. I was too overwhelmed by the sweep of happiness which filled me at his being here, at his voice and warm presence and the hope of a future that had seemed stalled and an impossible hope and yet was now rapidly taking shape as he spoke of New York and a job—the announcement expected to be made very shortly of an appointment as an associate in a joint commercial venture backed by two established banks— and relocation arrangements being finalized and... New York, Luxor, Karnak and the golden pillars and shifting sands and desert heat of Egypt, it did not matter, they were one and the same cup filled to the brimming.

"It won't be too long now, Lucia," Vincent said and squeezed my hand. I smiled back at him and believed.

Time floated by on a languid river. When the afternoon sun's beams lengthened and began to turn the temple stone and the Nile a beautiful pink hue, Vincent and I wandered out of the complex and returned to the porte-cochère of the Winter Palace by caleche. I watched the calmed waters of the Nile and listened to the soothing tempo of the horse's hooves along the Corniche and sighed in contentment. At the front desk, I was reminded by the manager of my table reservation for dinner in the hotel's 1886 restaurant—a reservation I was not aware of having made—and that formal dress was required for the dining room. Vincent also had a suite reserved for him at the Winter Palace so he and I quickly decided to run upstairs to our rooms to change. We met up again on the Nile-facing front terrace in time to have a drink while watching the sun go down behind the Valley of the Kings just before dinner.

I did not see or hear a peep from Tilly or Charley all evening. I went looking for them following dinner, after Vincent walked me back to my rooms, to thank them and failed. They had made themselves scarce and were nowhere to be found within the sprawling hotel or its grounds or amidst the clipped lawns and topiary shrubs and date palms and bougainvillea and fountains of its lush pleasure gardens, but then I suppose I should not have expected Charley to be anything less than thorough in executing one of her hare-brained schemes.

That night, my first night in Luxor, my sleep was untroubled by dreams.

It was not the sun slanting through the curtains which woke me the next morning but a rap on the door bringing a hotel attendant and a note from Vincent. Would I meet him for breakfast on the terrace?

I hurried to bath and dress.

I had overslept without the regular morning rituals of my two traveling companions rousing me to the sunrise. Usually, Tilly would be bustling about and tut-tutting over the evidence left behind of Charley's early morning rising and labors. This morning was different. It was unearthly quiet in the suite. No sign of Charley or Tilly. Our trunks had barely been touched since our recent arrival. None of the few items of clothing and toiletries and other belongings that they had taken out had been moved since yesterday. Their beds had not been slept in. It did not appear that they had returned from Karnak to the hotel at all.

I was trying to contain the chill seeping into my heart when another brisk knocking sent me flying to the door in the hope that it was Charley and Tilly. It was the same smiling attendant, bearing another message: if madam was not otherwise occupied today, would she please send word to her friends, to be left at the front desk, on her thoughts on riding out to see the Valley of the Kings?

I closed the suite door after the attendant left and collapsed in relief against it. Fearful, doubting ninny Lucia, mistaking delirious dreams for wakefulness.

The Nile was bright and shimmering in the morning sunshine, purring tamely past the proud imperial splendor of the Winter Palace on the East Bank. When Vincent and I finished our breakfast and went to the front desk, the manager directed me to the river again. I was puzzled but went outside to the terrace to look. There, amongst the other sail-boats moored in front of the hotel, low to the water, was an elegant dahabiyah with striped white and yellow sails. And stepping out from its deck onto the landing stage was Tilly. Behind her came Charley, chattering and gesticulating animatedly to the Nubian boatmen of the dahabiyah as if sketching her grand and colorful ambitions were a little beyond her basic Egyptian and charades. When they chanced to look up from within the midst of motor-cars and charabancs lining the Corniche at the hotel, squinting and searching, and saw me, they both waved.

"Good morning," Tilly said.

She and Vincent exchanged very cordial greetings and pleasantries. Vincent seemed impressed by the dahabiyah and a tad puzzled by the onset of my irritable, strained temper.

Charley smiled briefly at Vincent and assessed me with a critical eye. If I had not been so fretful, I would have been afraid of the conclusion she reached. "Good morning," she said finally in a voice as cool and unreadable as her smile. "Are they still serving breakfast on the terrace?"

"Where have you been?"

"On the Nile," Charley answered.

"What do you mean 'on the Nile'? Where on the Nile?"

"Well, I'm not sure exactly. Did we make it to Esna, Tilly?" Tilly shook her head in disapprobation. "No, I suppose that would have been too ambitious. Tilly initially wanted to scour the bazaar up the road from the hotel for spurious antiquities and painted scarabs and perfumed boxes inlaid with slivers of ivory and mother-of-pearl and gold and silver cartouche with hieroglyphs, but the river looked so inviting. So we ended up sort of drifting leisurely."

"Drifting? You mean you and Tilly—"

"It was very pleasant. Lots of chilled karkade—a most deliciously tart hibiscus-flower tea. The berths and quarters were not at all ramshackle as Tilly feared. Quite the reverse. We went through a dozen before we were satisfied with one that was suitable. And it came with a bonus—a most conscientious cook!—he fed us and fed us—my goodness, we were stuffed with true Egyptian and Nubian fare!—it will take some getting used to to go back to our usual cuisine."

"You both spent the night on that boat?"

"The white sail-boats looked so pretty gliding up and down the Nile. Even Tilly agreed it looked like fun." Tilly shook her head again in resignation. "Do you want to step aboard for an inspection? It's very spacious and excellently stocked. You could sail it all the way up the Nile to Assuan if the whimsy took you. Some people, Cleopatra and Caesar, for instance, might call that romantic."

My head spun and ached. Charley had gone to the effort and expense of searching out and hiring a dahabiyah, and she and Tilly had skulked about and spent a night on board the vessel instead of showing up at the Winter

Palace and disturbing my evening with Vincent, and now—my poor blushing cheeks—she was offering it to us and encouraging, no, scrupulously conspiring at a romantic cruise, without any sign that her approval of Vincent had improved from her last assessment? What was Charley about? Was she suffering from heatstroke?

"Well, if the two of you have nothing else planned for the morning, would you like to head over to the West Bank?" Charley said, quite unperturbed. "Tilly and I ran into a Professor Anita Natarajan at the Luxor Museum yesterday. She's supervising several local excavations, worked with Howard Carter too. If we run into her at the Valley of the Kings, she might even take us into one of the tombs closed to the public."

Vincent turned to me with a relaxed, unsuspecting smile that said he was already won over without any arm-twisting at all. "What does your spirit of adventure say, Lucia?"

"We can take the dahabiyah to cross the river," Charley continued. "The crew won't take long to get ready. Ussama is meant to meet us in the hotel lobby. I might just also take the opportunity to duck inside for a moment to confer with the front desk..."

Telegrams. Of course. If ever there was a constant in our world, it was that.

"All right." I allowed my arm to be twisted—it would have been futile to put up any resistance—and what was at the root of my resistance if not merely irrational petulance and confusion, the tapering aftershocks of finding my fears unrealized? I reminded myself that Charley and Tilly had been trying to be generous and kind, not trying to give me a heart-attack. My fragile, feverish nerves grasped onto that straw and tried to settle down. "Why not?"

Charley beamed beautifully but her eyes danced with evil mischief.

"My favorite words in the whole wide world," I heard her murmur as she turned and headed towards the sweeping white marble steps of the hotel terrace, leading the way.

Tilly patted my arm in sympathy.

It appeared that Charley still had not shared her less than complimentary opinion of Vincent with Tilly, who chatted pleasantly with him on the way up the terrace steps. Tilly turned at one point and came to walk beside me.

"We had been expecting... We were hoping for an announcement," Tilly confided in a conspiratory whisper, smiling kindly and patting my arm once again. "Patience, Miss Lucia. Some gentlemen cannot be hurried even with Miss Charley pulling the strings."

While Charley went into the hotel to speak to the clerks at the front desk, Tilly ran up to the suite to fetch a fresh shawl and hat. Tilly returned soon thereafter to join us on the terrace. We waited for Charley to come out. Minutes passed. Charley seemed to be an unusually long time. I went back inside the hotel to check on her.

Charley was not at the front desk. Looking about, between the shifting people and pillars and other decorative stationary objects in the way, I caught sight of her in a corner of the grand foyer area which had been furnished to Victorian taste with polished walnut furniture and couches and armchairs and velvet drapes and tasseled curtain ties and potted ferns and flower arrangements. She was standing beside a pillar, drawn away from the busy foyer traffic, in conversation with a gentleman. It seemed to be a rather terse exchange, not heated nor exactly unpleasant, but I recognized the stiff, tightened stance in which Charley held herself, the civil and closed expressions passing over her face as she spoke, the way her lips seemed to bite words off in sharp, clipped volleys. Her interlocutor's back was turned to me, partially obscured by the pillar and fern fronds, so I could not see who the man was, and what I did see of him was unremarkable and indistinguishable from any other well-heeled foreign tourist visiting Egypt. Charley broke away in a momentary tremor of agitation, then returned and said something that seemed like an imperious command, ending the conversation. The man bowed, turned, and left—oh, I wished that I had been in a better position to see, that my view had not been continually obstructed by the milling guests and staff moving about the foyer! When these obstacles cleared away, the man was gone and Charley stood alone by the pillar, starring in a fixed direction—perhaps the direction that the man had exited?—or merely starring blindly into arbitrary space.

Presently Charley smoothed out the displeasure from her face and stalked away from the spot by the pillar to the front desk. She collected and read her telegrams, and came back towards the terrace entrance doors. On her brief journey across the carpeted floor, she squared her shoulders and gathered calm to her face and manner.

My inimitable friend, who could look an adversary in the eye and continue smiling. There but for the grace of God...

I hurried back outside to ensure that I would return to Vincent and Tilly ahead of Charley, that there would be no awkward questions or explanations required. It was clear that Charley had added another secret to her treasury that she did not intend yet to share.

"Oh, there you are!" exclaimed Tilly. "We were beginning to think we'd lost you both."

Our guide, Ussama, had also arrived.

"She'll be out shortly," I said. "Charley and her endless telegrams." I had the relief of seeing Tilly and Vincent and Ussama readily accept this glib lie.

Even with the evidence of my own eyes, I was liable to doubt what I had witnessed when Charley returned to join us on the terrace, so effortlessly unruffled, so blasé and ready to find adventure in the desert. Her armor was perfect and unassailable and glistened in the sun. Neither

Tilly nor Vincent nor Ussama had any notion to guess that her delay had been caused by anything besides delinquent dallying, that she had passed through such a mysterious episode. If I had not been watching Charley earlier in the hotel foyer, I would not have cherished that tiny, restless kernel of disquiet within me. Et in Arcadia ego, I thought, look for me even in the midst of paradise.

Our party crossed the purling blue waters of the Nile in the dahabiyah and, under Ussama's directions, rode out part of the way by motor-car and part on donkeys (Tilly pouted and made faces but her mount proved to be a docile creature, nothing like the recalcitrant camel at Giza) to explore the remains of the size and power of ancient Thebes, bathed in brilliant, unclouded sunshine. We saw the Colossi of Memnon rising from the plains, black granite fragments of what were once colossal statues of Ramses II, most notably his head, missing the nose, lying on the ground of the Ramesseum, and descended into the Valley of the Kings at Biban el-Muluk to visit two lit royal tombs—we were forced by limited time and the scorching sun to ration—No. 17, the tomb of Sethos I, or commonly known as Belzoni's Tomb from its discoverer in 1817, which housed the best preserved and most surpassingly beautiful reliefs on its walls, and, of course, No. 62, the tomb discovered by Howard Carter in 1922 of Tutenkh-Aman, with the mummy of the famous boy king lying inside a gilded sarcophagus, and then later in the afternoon—to avoid the oppressive rays of the sun which reflected off the rock with extraordinary intensity—we took the scenic zig-zagging path down to the ravine of Deir el-Bahri and the great terraced mortuary temple built by Queen Hatshepsut, hewn out of, and framed by, the golden rock of the precipitous mountainside which was turned by the afternoon sun a haunting ocher-red against the stark violet-blue of the sky.

I had initially thought that Charley would be spurred to invoke Shelley from the summit of the path from the desolate tombs in the Valley of the Kings to Deir el-Bahri, looking out upon the view of the steeply projecting mountainside, with the dazzling structure of Queen Hatshepsut's temple in magnificent relief, to the green, fertile plain below, spread out like a spacious theater dotted with palms and gigantic temples, on both sides of the Nile. Or perhaps to wax lyrical while standing on the third and uppermost terrace of Queen Hatshepsut's temple, gazing out towards the point on the convex horizon where the sky and the plains and the Nile met.

"Nothing?" I came up to stand next to Charley on the terrace. "Surely this," I swept an arm over the view, "would elicit more than silence?"

"Hmm?" Charley turned from the view. "Oh, I see... Well... Ozymandias would be the name of the wrong pharaoh to shout out. It would be a discourtesy to Queen Hatshepsut and her architect if I were to..." She trailed off, her eyes wandering that vast horizon.

Since the morning, Charley had not uttered an exclamation or word of praise that was not conventional and lackluster compared to her usual arsenal. She had been an irreproachably agreeable and pleasant traveling companion, ready with laughing smiles and light remarks, discreetly continuing her conniving and maneuvering to give Vincent and me every chance at quiet interludes and privacy—but irreproachably agreeable and pleasant was a tremendous difference from Charley in her splendor. At every location on the West Bank—taking the passageway to the royal tombs, around the courts and pylons and ruins of the Ramesseum, ascending the inclined planes from level ground up three levels of terraces to the colonnades, shrines, halls and chambers of the temple at Deir el-Bahri—I had caught sight of Charley quickly glancing about and behind her as if she had a suspicion of being followed. Perhaps I attributed to her distraction a more sinister meaning than was the case. Or perhaps she was simply saving her panegyrics for Abu Simbel as she had previously said. Regardless, Charley seemed wary and subdued beneath her smiles, and it worried and distracted me.

Tilly and Vincent, however, more than made up for our distraction. Tilly, for one, was more than satisfactorily awed by Deir el-Bahri and lavished upon it a plenitude of rapturous transports which did not dry up even as we reached the East Bank again.

As we were stepping off the dahabiyah, Charley—having listened to Tilly gushing through the entire crossing—decided it would be amusing to point out to Tilly that Tilly had not expelled so much appreciative breath in wandering all of the great museums of Europe than she had spent in one day exploring what was essentially the ruins of a city devoted to the dead and the afterlife, was that not a tiny bit morbid?

Tilly's retort was interrupted and drowned out by a familiar sounding laugh from the shore. We looked up and saw Matthias standing a mere few feet away on the quay.

Matthias held out his hand and helped Tilly alight down the gangplank, then he helped the rest of us come ashore. He handed over a box—he never neglected to bring us candy—of peppermints.

Charley overcame her surprise and scoffed, "You again! I might've known our uninterrupted peace was too good to last."

I said to Matthias, "How did you know we'd—?"

"Cleopatra," Matthias told us, "used to soak the sails of her feluccas in perfume so that her arrival would be announced by the wind as she sailed down the Nile." Then, turning to Charley, he grinned. "Your voice carries in much the same way."

It was well that Matthias added this clarification else he might have been in real danger of earning scorn for being a sentimental sap.

(Charley, I thought, sometimes still carried a whiff of lavender, myrtle and lemon verbena trailing about her person. The bottle of perfume—that magical memory jar from the Provencal hills—must not have run out yet.)

Matthias greeted us all properly as we filed into the Winter Palace to take tea on the terrace. He did not seem the least bit surprised to see Vincent in Luxor which raised my suspicions immediately but I stored it away to mull over and quiz him about later.

Tilly was more than chuffed with Matthias's unexpected arrival and, forgetting all about her squabble with Charley, went on to bombard him with questions and relaying to him our day's sightseeing on the West Bank throughout refreshments on the terrace.

"What have you planned for tomorrow?" Matthias asked us. "Taking another excursion out to the Valley of the Kings to see the remainder of the tombs? The Valley of the Queens?"

We all automatically swung our faces towards Charley. She had been quietly inattentive to the conversation, looking towards the darkening river, perhaps trying to distinguish the yellow and white sails of the dahabiyah, until she felt our gazes directed upon her.

"Is it time for a round of gin and tonic?" she asked. "Do we have time?"

We all laughed. Vincent raised his hand and asked the waiter who appeared a few seconds later to bring more drinks.

"No, Charley," I explained. "We are looking to you for direction. You're the one always bubbling with ideas that we have to sift through to find our adventures."

"Oh, well, one needn't always be finding adventure," Charley answered. "Wouldn't you rather a pleasant interlude of sloth and relaxation this evening after the day we've had?"

"Not for passing a few hours this evening, Charley," Matthias said, smiling. "Where will you all be headed—what intrepid plans have you for tomorrow?"

"Oh." Charley responded to Matthias rather as she had done to me earlier in the day with: "On the Nile."

We waited for her to elaborate. Charley looked back at us uncertainly. Then Tilly and I gasped.

"Oh, Mr. Vandermeer, your surprise arrival made it slip my mind completely!" Tilly cried. "Oh, I shall run up to the wing now and—"

"Tilly, what's the matter?"

"The trunks—the packing—I must—"

Before Tilly rushed off in a flurry, Charley said, "Sit back down, Tilly, and finish your drink. There's no need to fuss and flap about. I arranged for them to be sent to the steamer this morning before we left. It was all very straightforward. Our luggage had hardly been unpacked since we arrived in Luxor."

"What's going on?" Vincent asked. "Are you leaving?"

"I forgot it was scheduled for this evening," I said. "Your surprise arrival made me lose track of time... We're supposed to be leaving by Nile steamer for Assuan tonight."

"Well, you needn't if you don't want to," said Charley, looking between us at all the chaos. "There's no reason why you cannot take the dahabiyah whenever it suits your fancy."

"How long have you chartered it?"

Charley shrugged. "How long do you want it?"

"Charley!"

"Which steamer are you taking?" Matthias asked.

"The Rosetta. Why?"

Matthias questioned us until he was satisfied with the information. He rose from the table. "Faneuil, are you coming?"

"What are you doing?" Charley scowled pugnaciously up at Matthias as if she already knew the answer.

"It's the low season. It's unlikely the steamer is fully booked. Shouldn't be too difficult to secure a berth." He returned Charley's scowl with a grin. "You'll have to try harder to run away next time. I have more questions for you later."

We went to our hotel suite, changed into fresh clothes and collected our few possessions and Matthias's box of peppermints, then left the Winter Palace for the jetty. We were one of the last parties to arrive. Matthias and Vincent were already on the Rosetta, leaning over the railing, having both obtained accommodation on board. Very shortly after we had boarded, the steamer Rosetta set sail.

"We should've stayed on board the dahabiyah," Charley muttered as we were being shown to our accommodation and saw the yellow and white sails pass by us on the river.

"Where do you think it's going?" I asked.

"Towards Qena—there is meant to be a very well-preserved temple in Dendara, a few miles south of Qena, dedicated to the sky goddess Hathor, she of the cow horns or bovine likenesses. Perhaps as far as Asyut. The opposite direction to where we are going." Charley sounded very definite.

"Wait, you mean it's still sailing under your charter? But if we are taking this steamer to Assuan, why..." And then I remembered the myriad of diversionary cab rides on our last afternoon in Cairo. To throw others off our scent. "Is it still necessary?"

"Better to err on the side of caution," Charley replied glumly.

We were given what the steward assured us were the best cabins adjacent to each other on board the Rosetta. I had no doubt of it given how liberally Charley was dispensing bakshish. Our luggage had already been deposited inside the portside cabins on the promenade deck, however, since the Nile steamer was not, as Matthias had predicted, fully booked, we were also offered the choice of changing if we were not satisfied with our cabins, which we declined. Besides comfortably-sized cabins, the steamer had several saloons on the lower decks as well as an open observation saloon at the front of the promenade deck like a spacious veranda where, we were told, many passengers had found it very pleasant to recline and take afternoon tea watching the Nile unfold before them.

Charley and Tilly were old hands at it by now but it was the first night that I had passed on the Nile. Its gentle waves cradled and glided smoothly into the darkness as we sailed upstream, the verdant green palm-lined banks fading into inky shadowy outlines and soft breezes.

Dinner was not as lavish on board the Rosetta as at 1886, the French restaurant at the Winter Palace. However, Tilly made sure we were presentable in our evening dress as we entered the dining saloon on the lower deck and were shown to a table where Matthias and Vincent were already seated, waiting for us. They rose to their feet when we arrived. As we took our places, several other passengers entered the dining saloon and were shown to nearby tables. They stopped and greeted us when they passed by, exclaiming in recognition, the excited tremor in their voices and faces rising without abatement.

"Renfrew and I thought we'd spotted you yesterday at Karnak," said Mrs. Perceval.

"The great card sharps!" said Mr. Tainstel-Tarsted. "Are you interested in a game in the smoking saloon after dinner?"

"What a lovely surprise to run into you again!" said Mrs. Draycott. "How long will you be staying in Assuan?"

Tilly glanced at Charley. I did the same. I could almost hear Charley's inward groans.

"Planning on cheating at cards again tonight?" I whispered. A soft titter escaped from Tilly.

Charley glared back at Tilly and me. "I knew we shouldn't have gone to the club car," she muttered.

A faint line of puzzlement appeared between Matthias's eyebrows. As dinner progressed and the friendliness between the tables of our fellow passengers and ours continued, it became evident how we had become acquainted.

There was not much Charley could do to avoid all the calls for her to take out her playing cards after dinner and combine them with the set the Percevals had bought in the souk in Luxor. The friendly civility which had begun in the dining saloon spread to the other passengers on board the Rosetta who had also decided to spend the remainder of the evening surrounded by the passing Nile scenery in the less formal atmosphere of the observation saloon, and several wicker tables and chairs were pulled together to seat all of the company of card players and hangers-on.

At first, a relatively tame game of bridge was played. Our friendly fellow passengers with whom we had become reacquainted over dinner, however, had had their taste whetted on the train from Cairo to Luxor and called for something more exciting and more players joined in. The attendants to the observation saloon ran back and forth to answer the bell and the loquacious thirst of the players and observers of the card game and all the other passengers enjoying the cool breezes coming off the river as a refreshing antidote to the sultry night. The stakes of the game were not raised very high but Tilly won and Charley lost spectacularly. The result put everyone in a good mood, congratulating one and commiserating with the other and calling for another round, and the bell was rung many times and more drinks were ordered.

Mr. Tainstel-Tarsted had been fueling the evening's relaxed camaraderie in the observation saloon by trying to emulate the drink orders called out at Shepheard's American Bar in Cairo: Scotch and plain water for the British. Gin, lime juice and water for the colonials. Bourbon or rye and soda for the Americans. And for everybo—

"Gin and tonic, please, with a slice of cucumber and a dash of black pepper if possible, for these three Americans, and also a carafe of karkade on ice," Charley cut in. She looked to Matthias and Vincent for their orders.

"But of course, I forgot, you've been shockingly turned,"
said Mr. Tainstel-Tarsted.

As the boat pressed up the Nile and the night unwound, the evening breezes turned surprisingly crisp. I briefly left the observation saloon to run to my cabin, which was two doors down from Charley's and Tilly's, to find a shawl to wrap about my shoulders and ward off the chill. Vincent had offered me his dinner jacket, but I didn't want him to be cold too, and Tilly had risen to fetch one for me, but I didn't want to interrupt her winning hand either.

I was rummaging about in my cabin when I heard low, furious whispers outside my window.

I knew Charley had withdrawn from the game earlier to go to her cabin, citing a sudden hankering for peppermints. That had been a little while ago.

It was Charley's voice that I recognized outside my cabin. The other voice was also familiar to me—and even had it not been so, had it been somehow disguised, there was only one person with whom Charley bickered so fiercely: Matthias.

"...Andre d'Erlanger's fault, people would be chasing gondolas down on the Venetian canals or inspecting all the young women admiring statues of naked Greek gods and demi-gods and heroes in the Piazza della Signoria instead of—"

"You didn't tell him?"

"You're the only one who knew and only because—"

"Does this mean the cad is no longer in your good graces? It's about time."

"There is no need to be churlish. And who says he is?"

"Then why were you running—"

"I run from everyone. It isn't personal."

"Is he or isn't he?"

"That is my business. But it doesn't mean I want every Tom, Dick and Harry to know my whereabouts."

"I certainly didn't tell him. Did my damnedest trying not to be seen when I walked into Shepheard's and saw him at the front desk. I'm a bit too old to be shuffling between columns and attempting to hide behind a ridiculous pot plant. He was asking after you. How many hotels in Cairo did you leave your calling cards?"

"Well, I wouldn't have had to take those measures if your boy hadn't—"

"Stop calling him that. Just because—"

"When can I expect him to stop following your lead then?"

"What—"

"Your boy has been trailing behind your coat-tails since Ginny's wedding. Why does he need to rely on you to get things done? Doesn't he have any steam of his own to sustain him?"

"You're just miffed that you were tracked down to Cairo, but that doesn't mean he was responsible."

"If you were careful and we were careful, I don't see who else it could've been. It's a little too convenient to blame everything on luck. Reservations at Cairo's hotels weren't the only red herrings I left behind. For all the good they did."

"Yes, I know. Your trail of bread crumbs spreads far and wide. Aldersley said that he was redundant, that you'd already had an entire welcoming party lined up at the Gezira. Is this what you were doing during your year away from New York?"

"You were responsible for Captain Aldersley? I didn't think my cable reached you."

"It took me a while to find Aldersley. I'm a bit out of practice pulling rabbits out of a hat at short notice but I figured you must've been in the same situation and desperate enough to be asking for my help."

"Should I have asked your boy instead given that he was already on his way?"

"Will you stop—"

"All the ruses and contrivances in the world can be undone by a moment of carelessness. Your boy could've led—"

"Well, even if it was him, what are you going to do? Send him before a firing squad? If it was done inadvertent—"

"What exactly is your boy waiting for now that he is here? Gee, you sure can lead a horse to water but you can't make him drink. Does he need someone to give him a swift—"

"What do you know of Rhys Hadden?"

"Who?"

"All right, we can pretend you don't know him, but he knows Diego. A thorn in Diego's side apparently, persistently trying to seek an interview with the man regarding the welfare of a Miss Lottie Fairchild."

"You seem to be quite au fait with this matter, why are you bothering to ask me anything?"

"You're dying to know how I know and how much I know."

"If you say so."

"Would it be so horrific to just confide in me, Charley, to trust that I—"

"Your hats, Mr. Vandermeer. And you assume that I know anything to confide."

"Charley."

"Careful, Matthias, you might sprain something in your brain."

"Fine. Do you remember what D'Erlanger said about Tallis Lloyd-Chase at Baroness Ephressi de Rothschild's party? Well, Tallis Lloyd-Chase found me shortly after you'd left France and asked me the same thing he's been asking everyone: where could he find you? He has been trying to track down Lucia and since you and Lucia—no, of course I didn't give you away. I did some digging after you left Antibes. The Hadden fellow wasn't the only one hanging about Diego's office trying to catch Diego for an interview. Tallis Lloyd-Chase had been sniffing around Diego too, according to my agent, with about as much luck. This was before talk reached New York about Lucia in London—all the tabloid speculation you put her in—then suddenly turning up in the South of France after the race to Cannes. That is what had Lloyd-Chase crossing the Atlantic and chasing all over London and France to the French Riv—Charley? Charley, what's wrong?"

"Who's your agent? How long have they been spying—"

"Damn it, Charley, who else has followed you here?"

"No one."

"Charley—"

I dropped my hairbrush. It clattered over the floor of my cabin and came to rest near the window. The sound of its fall extinguished the voices outside my cabin. Fear beat in the narrow space between one second and the next. Shortly afterwards, I heard footfalls moving away on the promenade deck and then silence.

When I returned to the observation saloon with my shawl and two extras for both Tilly and Charley, I heard Charley explaining to Mrs. Draycott that unfortunately she had no peppermints to share because she had forgotten that she had handed the peppermints to Tilly earlier and Tilly must have put the peppermints away in her own cabin and, in any event, peppermints did not really go down well with cocktails, did they? Matthias watched Charley meditatively all night.

The Rosetta passed through the lock at Esna and continued its journey south. We moored briefly near Edfu and disembarked to visit the temple honoring the falcon-headed god, Horus, freed from the desert sands through the efforts of the French Egyptologist, Auguste Mariette. Like Karnak, it was grand and imposing and retreated into the background of our lovely time together. Happiness bled from one moment into the next and flowed onward with the blue waters of the everlasting Nile.

On the second day, we continued on to Kom Ombo and the ruins of the symmetrical temple carved out of golden sandstone overlooking the Nile, its vestibule, courts, halls, sanctuaries and chambers dedicated in the northern part to the crocodile-headed god, Sobek, and in the southern part to Haroeris, Horus the Elder, covered in murals and reliefs and friezes and beautiful details on all of the giant papyrus-bundle columns, even the stumps missing their palm and lotus-flower capitals that were as thick and immovable as the legs of a prehistoric mammoth. (Tilly wrinkled her nose up at the mummified crocodiles.) In my memory, the temple's colonnades echoed with our sunny laughter.

It was indeed very pleasant traveling up the Nile by steamer, strolling the deck or relaxing and taking tea while views of the desert and the everyday life on the river and its surrounding banks passed by us, and stopping at regular intervals to be impressed by exquisitely preserved temples and archaeological finds. The days were bright and warm and golden and new and the evenings lazy and equally happy. We were fortunate to have been in the company of an agreeable set of travelers on the Rosetta and not in so large a number in comparison to the size of the steamer as to make the accommodations and journey feel crowded. The situation really could not be faulted for nearly driving Charley—nursing her secret sorrows, straining for freedom—mad. She was smiling and engaging enough in company, enchanting the staff and natives as thoroughly as she had done our fellow passengers, but as much as she was tempted to give in to her funk, the riverboat was too small for Charley to stay inside her cabin to play hermit for the entirety of the cruise. (Although one unfortunate gentleman apparently had been laid up in his cabin the entire trip—according to Mrs. Draycott whose neighboring cabin was also on the starboard side—an American, poor thing, who had yet to grow accustomed to the heat and food.) Charley hoarded and pored over the newspapers that she had managed to obtain at only a few days' delay through her ready dispensation of bakshish.

Buried behind the older headlines of Prime Minister Ramsay MacDonald's address regarding the armament negotiations between Britain and the United States, the crash of a Transcontinental Air Transport plane in New Mexico during a thunderstorm, with the loss of eight lives, alongside Graf Zeppelin's triumphant completion of its ocean crossing, tales abounded of the volatility on the London Stock Exchange and of Wall Street's continuing vilification of investor Mr. Roger Babson following his speech at the Annual Business Conference in Massachusetts on September 5 where he had proclaimed that "a crash is coming, and it may be terrific. ... The vicious circle will get in full swing and the result will be a serious business depression. There may be a stampede for selling which will exceed anything that the Stock Exchange has ever witnessed. Wise are those investors who now get out of debt". News of Mr. Babson's speech had reached Wall Street by mid-afternoon and caused the Exchange to retreat by about 3 per cent. Wall Street had not been amused. Indignant rebuffs from numerous economists and Wall Street leaders had been published in the papers. Mr. Babson's patriotism had been called into question. Yale economics professor Irving Fisher had declared: "There may be a recession in stock prices, but not anything in the nature of a crash." Financier Bernard Baruch had apparently cabled Winston Churchill: "Financial storm definitely passed." Americans had been assured by President Hoover that the market was sound. Charley thought this was persuasive support for the maxim that one should never believe anything until it was officially denied. I pointed to the subsequent upward bounce in the Exchange, on the very next day, and asked Charley how the "Babson Break" was any different, as an academic or a real world dilemma, from the Federal Reserve's warning earlier in the year or any of the other bearish forecasts of doom following which the Exchange always rebounded, irrespective of whether it should? How could one tell if this was the long overdue day when everyone came to their senses and everything would fall off a cliff? What were the prominent speculators Arthur W. Cutten (profiled in Time magazine's December 1928 issue as one of the leading market bulls) and Jesse Livermore (more often bearish) doing? Had not Goldman, Sachs & Company backed the bulls by sponsoring the Blue Ridge Corporation, an investment trust which offered to exchange its stock for those of the leading "blue chips" at the current market prices? Charley responded by taking to the promenade deck once again and likely sending more telegrams.

The occasional stops and land excursions on our riverboat itinerary provided little relief for Charley—coming back to the boat usually entailed coming back to a fresh attack of telegrams waiting for her which merely added an edge of apprehensive frustration to her condition—and Charley prowled the decks even more restlessly than she had on the much larger RMS Mauretania when she had had a Mrs. Stuyvesant and a Mr. Ned Irving from whom to run.

Matthias joined her on these laps of the deck; whether he was welcomed or tolerated, I was not entirely sure. Matthias had his own batch of telegrams awaiting him on board, sitting alongside Charley's, the sight of which made Charley clench her teeth and set off on another prowl about the promenade deck. Matthias's mouth gave a hint of the mood into which the telegrams put him—a silent, thin, straight line with the corners turned grimly downward.

Tilly gave up watching them in bemusement. I tried not to brood on the conversation that I had overheard outside my cabin on our first night aboard the Rosetta. When Vincent asked whether Charley was feeling under the weather, I told him that Charley didn't like being stuck on boats, which was true enough.

"Charley, is there anything I can do?"

"No," Charley said, losing a measure of her misery to smile at me. "Nothing."

Charley's playing cards were no longer enough of an escape or distraction given how much company they now attracted. I think Charley missed her golf irons; there would have been as many balls knocked into the Nile as there had been lost to the Mediterranean if she had had her druthers. Whether she missed James Dorsey... Of that, I was not entirely sure either.

On the third day, we arrived in Assuan.

After a typically chaotic and noisy disembarkment from the Rosetta, the porters transferred the assortment of luggage from the steamer to the landing place—where our guide, Ussama, who had taken the Luxor-Assuan train instead of arriving by Nile steamer, stood in welcome—and from thence to carriages lined up on the riverside street, waiting for a destination to be named. We joined several of our fellow passengers in heading a short distance down the Corniche to the Cataract Hotel, a striped maroon and white building which sprawled across a granite bluff overlooking a rocky stretch of the Nile which formed the First Cataract. The interior of the Cataract Hotel was lavishly decorated in Moorish style and it had a terrace which looked out across verdant tropical gardens and eddying blue waters dotted with white sails to the sandy golden peak of the distant hillside, crowned by the Aga Khan Mausoleum, on the West Bank behind the luxuriant palms of Elephantine Island.

Some of our fellow travelers from the Rosetta retired to their hotel rooms to settle in and rest. Mr. Tainstel-Tarsted departed on an expedition arranged for him by the hotel at his request to see the granite quarries and tombs and the Monastery of St. Simeon on the West Bank. The Percevals and Mrs. Draycott joined a party led by Ussama venturing out to head back up the Corniche to explore the colorful souk. We decided to hire a felucca and passed a few peaceful hours sailing around the islands. We were dropped off on Elephantine Island, immediately opposite the hotel, to see the Nilometer, and later, on Kitchener's Island filled with groves of palms, oleanders, pomegranates and other exotic plants and flowers planted by General Horatio Kitchener, a keen botanist.

By the time we returned to the hotel, the Nile and its islands and the sandy slopes on the West Bank were turning a beautiful rosy hue bracketed by lush date palms and tropical vegetation and the terrace was set for tea. Vincent and I strolled down through the gardens to the river. It was all so poignantly beautiful. We agreed that it was very near perfect a setting to announce an engagement. When we returned back up the path to the terrace, we did just that.

Tilly exploded and fizzled in a voluble outburst of congratulations. Matthias clapped Vincent on the back and had the attendants bring champagne out to our table along with carafes of chilled karkade, the tart hibiscus-flower tea we had grown so fond of, and the selection of sundowners he had ordered. Charley barely said a word, she just sat in her basket chair and smiled at me, and I was glad. The world, it seemed, had righted itself on its axis.

Gradually, our friends from the Rosetta began to arrive on the terrace, including the returning Percevals and Mrs. Draycott and Mr. Tainstel-Tarsted. They were thrilled about the news of the engagement and their excited heartfelt goodwill enlivened and enlarged our celebration, expanding and threatening to invade the entire terrace and demanded that tonight's dinner be in honor of the felicitous occasion. They asked after details and squealed with delight and laughed and shared with us their day's adventures —"Far less thrilling and romantic, sweetheart, I can assure you"—and showed us their stories and finds from the souk—Mr. Perceval had apparently been offered three camels to have his wife taken off his hands whilst he was haggling over postcards and fine woven shawls and lapis-lazuli trinkets with one of the souk vendors—and talked of expeditions to Philae, Abu Simbel and heading further up the Nile to Wadi Halfa and Khartoum.

When the drinks were served and the terrace had begun to fill up, Charley and Tilly started giggling behind their hands about another guest, a barrel-chested, middle-aged gentleman who had arrived for tea and seated himself at a table on the terrace under the covered area near the glass-paneled doors: with his white walrus mustache and calabash briar pipe and khaki service dress uniform, he did look comically like a British colonel for whom time had stopped at the Boer War.

"Do you think he's real?" Charley said.

"I dare you to go up and speak to him and find out," Tilly—giddy—uncharacteristically and unwisely replied.

An evil smile trembled on Charley's lips. Charley rose from her seat and took several steps towards the "colonel", then her eyes froze in horror and she bolted around the terrace tables and up the steps and disappeared into the hotel.

Nobody knew what had happened or where she had gone. When we finally came across Charley, she was at the front desk harassing the clerk, frantically issuing instructions and handing over cable forms to be sent.

"Charley?"

Charley became very, very still.

"Charley, what on earth is the matter? Who did you see?"

Charley turned around. The turbulence of emotion in her eyes was frightening.

"I'm sorry," she said. "I shouldn't have taken off. I didn't mean to cause alarm. It's a nuisance I should've attended to sooner and didn't and I've realized belatedly what needs to be done, only there is no time and... I'm sorry. Forgive me, Lucia."

Charley was calm, her voice steady, her words carefully chosen, nothing betrayed her except her eyes. Haunted, hunted eyes.

Matthias would not let it stand at that vague apology, but Charley's eyes reminded me of the night that she had gotten drunk in Paris, of the river bank at Oxford, of the garden at Villa Mirabeau, of every stricken unspoken plea since the first time I had seen her in a year on board the RMS Mauretania, trying to hold the skies up, straining for something just beyond her grasp.

"Is there anything that we can do, Charley?"

"No. Nothing. I'm..." Charley paused. "I'm waiting on a telegram."

I nodded. I understood the concession in her revealing that much.

"We'll leave you in peace. We're heading into dinner in the hotel restaurant. Come and join us when you have news?"

"Yes." Charley's eyes burned again with that haunted look. "I'll do that as soon as I hear."

I drew the others away from Charley. It took some effort—Matthias gave fierce resistance—but I managed in the end to persuade them that it would do no good, would be of use or no help, to compete with Charley for stubbornness.

"We're Charley's friends and we trust her, don't we?"

Matthias glowered. "You can't pull that one out every time, Lucia. Haven't you heard of the boy who cried wolf?"

"Just because Charley hasn't told us anything, doesn't mean she is being careless or unthinking. Just because she hasn't told us anything, doesn't mean she isn't telling someone else and getting help from...others. She's sending telegrams! Everything she does... Charley is not reckless. Let her take care of this as she sees fit."

"Are you aware that that Esperance and Runnymede have been put up for sale?" Matthias said.

"What? Where did you hear this?"

Esperance in Old Westbury and Runnymede in Oyster Bay were two Masterson residences that I had visited in summers past with Charley, the residences that Charley's father had built for her mother, just as he had named his business empire for the Elyot home, Montrose.

"It's been whispered all over New York. If you aren't aware of that piece of news, then you probably don't know about the other properties in Newport, Nassau and Suffolk counties and East Hampton, St. Augustine and Palm Beach which have been sold. Or that our old friend Miles Calvert is spreading careless talk about Charley sneaking out of the Biltmore and Commodore Hotels with the likes of banker George Foster Peabody, John Moody, owner of Moody's Investor Services, and Adolph Ochs, publisher of the New York Times, during the time when she was supposed to be anywhere but in New York? What else is Charley hiding? Do you think you can still trust Charley not to be in trouble, Lucia, that Charley doesn't need our help?"

I told myself there was absolutely nothing untoward to be read into Matthias's revelations. George Foster Peabody had been friend and business partner to Spencer Trask. Trask and Peabody had been leaders of the investment group that had bought and rescued the New York Times, financially crippled by the Panic of 1893, from bankruptcy in 1896 and installed the former owner Adolph Ochs as publisher. Eleven years after Trask's death in a railroad accident in 1909, Peabody had married Trask's widow and, after her death in 1922, graciously continued the Trasks's legacy at Yaddo. The Elyots and Mastersons had been friends of the Trasks and welcomed guests at Yaddo. Charley... Her acquaintance must have included Peabody and Moody and Ochs and expanded to others within their business, philanthropic, political and social circles... Hadn't John Moody worked for Trask and Peabody before launching his own bond rating business? Wasn't the current Governor of New York, Franklin D. Roosevelt, one of Peabody's friends? Charley was the Montrose heiress, coming into her own, what was so surprising about her mingling in these circles? Miles Calvert had to have been spreading pernicious lies...

I gritted my teeth. "You're assuming Charley doesn't know what she is doing—if this is her doing."

"You know this is Charley's doing. And you're terrified that Charley is in over her head even if you won't admit it."

"My ignorance and terror are mine alone. I won't let that overpower my judgment. Charley has her methods and she is so very far from reckless, Matthias... It's no use pushing Charley when we are in the dark like this and there's nothing that we can do to be of help. Fumbling about, interfering when we think we are trying to help may turn out to be more obstructive or damaging than helpful. Give her tonight at least to do what she needs to do.

Charley's methods and her madness have yet to fail her—or others. We're her friends. Don't make me fight you on this. You told me last time to guard her. Well, I will do it if I have to, even if it means it's against your best intentions."

"Lucia—"

"Mr. Vandermeer..." Tilly's diffident, plaintive plea gave the deciding vote.

"Until tomorrow," Matthias conceded in arduous, begrudging defeat.

It took a supreme effort for all of us to proceed beneath the Moorish arches of the restaurant to join the celebrations that our friends had arranged without glancing back to check on Charley.

Charley did not reappear. However, the 1902 restaurant that evening was flooded with the pop of champagne corks and the scent of flowers— vases and arrangements of every beautiful imaginable bloom were brought in and set around the dining room and an enormous bouquet presented to every guest—a cloud of heavenly scent to bind and uplift and infuse the night with the happiness and blessings wished upon us by our friends and carry them away with us to every corner of the earth. Mrs. Draycott patted Matthias on the arm and told him delightedly what a wonderfully sweet gesture it was. Vincent warmly thanked him. Matthias was about to disclaim the praise in embarrassment that someone had beat him to doing something generous but I stopped him, knowing that the one responsible would not have wanted it widely known. As soon as I had seen the flowers, I knew. My throat swelled thick with gratitude.

Charley did not reappear that night, she kept her fraught, lonely vigil, but in the scent of the flowers pervading the night and in a thousand other ways, she never strayed far from us.

25

CHARLOTTE:

"I met a traveler from an antique land
Who said: 'Two vast and trunkless legs of stone
Stand in the desert... Near them, on the sand,
Half sunk, a shattered visage lies, whose frown,
And wrinkled lip, and sneer of cold command,
Tell that its sculptor well those passions read
Which yet survive, stamped on these lifeless things,
The hand that mocked them, and the heart that fed:
And on the pedestal these words appear:
My name is Ozymandias, king of kings:
Look on my works, ye Mighty, and despair!
Nothing beside remains. Round the decay
Of that colossal wreck, boundless and bare
The lone and level sands stretch far away.'"

I turned my eyes from the river and the sunrise washing the temple hewn from the rock cliff-face to burnished color and looked behind me to find the speaker of those words.

"I found your ghost," Matthias said, and turned to the man who had strolled up the terrace forecourt of Abu Simbel alongside him, glibly spouting Shelley.

"I overheard you speaking to Lucia at Deir al-Bahrir."

I had known in my heart that I had not been hallucinating, that someone had been following us. He had been the ghost at the Cataract Hotel. He had been the American hiding away in his cabin aboard the Rosetta. He had been the one who had agreed that he would leave Luxor and broken his word.

"So you got bored and decided it would be fun to pair up and conspire with Matthias?"

"Oh look, sure, the new Godeffroy's heir, consorting with the enemy, absolutely—that would go down real smooth with my father—he would be so chuffed—please don't stop, Charley, what's another accusation lobbed my way?"

"Well, you are here instead of being invisible as you'd promised to be."

"Matthias found me. I was told resistance would be futile. Do you two sing from the same hymn book or did he simply take a leaf out of yours?"

He handed me a telegram.

"Do you steal cables too?"

"It's unopened. I assume that this is the urgent reply you stayed up waiting all night for? I merely came here with Matthias to deliver it. I know you said to keep out of sight but there seems little point to the pretense now. I received one this morning. I'm sure yours contains a similar message as mine. I have also brought the other one that arrived at the same time for Lucia."

I tore open the telegram.

"CONFIRMED LILA BERNHARDT"

I closed my eyes. I did not want to look towards the entrance of the Great Temple, flanked by four 65 feet tall colossi of Ramses II seated on their thrones and wearing the double crown of Upper and Lower Egypt, into which Lucia and Vincent Faneuil and Tilly and the Percevals and Mr. Tainstel-Tarsted and several other tourists had passed at Ussama's direction. I wished that the sands under which Abu Simbel had once been buried would sweep in again and cover us and that we, like the original designation of this temple complex, would be lost and nevermore be disturbed by young boys named Abu or desertcombers seeking treasure.

"We can't keep this from Lucia forever."

"Can't we?"

"There's only so much you can do to protect her now."

"There are a great number of things that can be done. I have a priest and notary ready at the hotel who can marry Lucia anytime she says the word. There are cities and houses and so many, many places where Lucia can find sanctuary if she doesn't wish to return to slavery in New York. This is not a foregone conclusion. She is not a pawn. She will not be cowed in this intolerable fashion. There are means and ways—"

"We're all pawns, Charley."

"Pawns don't have to remain pawns. If you'd been content to remain a pawn, you wouldn't be here in Egypt, trying to change the foregone conclusion arranged by your parents."

"By our fathers. Lucia's mother and mine had nothing to do with this.

And neither of them would recommend Lucia to the escapes that you've suggested. You know they mean exile."

"From Old New York? Is that so awful?"

"It's not your choice to make."

"I know that. But neither is their foregone conclusion."

"There is another idea which you might be willing to entertain."

"I and not Lucia?"

"The foregone conclusion cannot be accomplished if none of the parties are available nor cooperative. According to society gossip, you've been very popular, Charley, but have you contractually promised yourself to any particular party? If not, we can walk out together. If Lucia isn't at liberty and I'm not at liberty, there goes the paternally-blessed foregone conclusion. It may, in fact, throw a more favorable light on her current choice and make that prospect appear very reasonable and acceptable. Provided that her current choice is actually accept—"

"No," said Matthias, "that is an absurd plan."

"It is not an absurd idea at all. It doesn't have to work forever, it merely has to scupper the current merger and buy us all time for Lucia's choice to be accepted as a fait accompli. Why, it—"

"Nobody is going to believe it for a minute and it won't prevent Lucia's father from forcing her—"

"Oh, don't be such a wet blanket, Matthias. I rather think half of New York will swoon over how romantic it is to be chased all the way to Egypt and becoming engaged."

"It doesn't matter what all of New York thinks if Lucia doesn't agree to it."

"Ah, but Matthias, that's exactly why its fiendish simplicity will be effective. It isn't Lucia's choice at all, but ours. Neither of us are in same position of being vulnerable to parental coercion and our reputations—"

"And what about your other schemes, Charley? How will you feel about the scrutiny that will be applied to those when you bring New York's attention your way?"

"What's he talking about?"

"Nothing. They are of no concern or relevance."

"It sounds so easy, doesn't it, spinning this fantasy happy-ever-after?" Matthias said silkily even as the lines of his face tightened into harshness. "But it will be a brave man—or woman—who breaks the news to Lucia."

I closed my eyes against his expression. Men have been hated for uttering lesser truths.

"Do you have a better plan?" I asked.

"Tell Lucia everything," Matthias said, "and let her decide her own fate. And be there when she asks for your help."

26

LUCIA:

The night had not passed swiftly or easily.

When I awoke in my hotel room, the hour was early and still heavy with a blackness without shadows but the scent of masses of flowers clung to the air like a sweet, forlorn, stubborn hope.

Despite the great anticipation engendered by Charley's remarks about Shelley and Abu Simbel, the anxiety arising from our first evening in Assuan overshadowed any enthusiasm we might have had left for sightseeing activities. In addition, none of us were particularly keen to wake up before dawn to virtual darkness to travel to the Second Cataract where the sacred site was situated but our guide Ussama had persuaded us on the previous day that viewing the sun rise over the temple complex of Abu Simbel—watching the gray of the rock temples emerge from the darkness and come alive to a breathing rose-gold by the bright Nile waters—was not something to be lightly bypassed. And so we had committed to the expedition. And had to rise before dawn.

I was grateful to have been persuaded by Ussama to undertake the pre-dawn journey. Everybody jolted awake, truly awake, when the first colossal stone head came into view. We had never seen such stupendous monuments in Egypt—such gigantic edifices carved into the mountainside! —the Great Temple standing at 98 feet high with its four seated colossi of Ramses II and the adjacent smaller rock temple dedicated to the goddess Hathor and Ramses II's favorite consort, Nefret-ere, standing at a height of 40 feet, adorned with six upright colossi depicting the king and queen, before a spacious open forecourt and the flowing blue waters of the Nile— such grandeur as a symbol of Egypt's majesty and power—it was breathtaking! Weeping was the least that one might do when looking upon such works.

Curiously, Charley, but not Matthias, turned up for our early morning expedition to Abu Simbel, meekly following behind Tilly as if in atonement for missing the previous evening. We held our truce in Matthias's absence and exchanged only quiet looks in ascertaining that the other was, at least outwardly, well. I knew that there were matters still simmering away on Charley's mind, but I was glad of her company and that she was not going to miss the great spectacle of which she had spoken, and promised, so much. Everybody on the expedition waited together on the terrace forecourt to appreciate and aww and ahh in wonder at the thin, wispy pinpricks of dawn light growing and surging forth in robust beams, transforming the façade of Abu Simbel to fierce golden splendor, but while we trooped off afterwards behind Ussama to enter the temples and view the exquisite reliefs and statuary of its interior halls and chambers and sanctuaries, lit up with a soft intimately flickering glow like cave paintings illuminated by torchlight, Charley remained outside beside the river, alone, like a night watchman guarding something precious, and yet, the direction of her gaze... She seemed lost in a daze, staring, as if she was, well, looking across something. Charley never spoke Shelley's words, but I knew that witnessing in that hushed amphitheater the elemental phenomenon of a day being born and seeing the creeping gleams of sunlight bathing the cliff-face, like a paintbrush dipped in gold, had moved her.

I was wandering out from the entrance of the Temple of Hathor when I saw three people coming across the open forecourt. Not loitering or leisurely strolling but striding with purpose. A sense of foreboding constricted my chest. As they came nearer in approach I recognized Charley and Matthias and the third man as Tallis Lloyd-Chase. Tallis Lloyd-Chase! Tallis, whose easy-mannered charm had taken him from college playing fields to his father's bank, who graced New York's drawing rooms and boardrooms with the same benign, lackadaisical affability that endeared him to one and infuriated the other... Rumors of Tallis outside the set-square and compass of New York and wandering around the French Riviera were strange enough, but Tallis, here, in Egypt!

"Lucia, could we speak privately, please?" Charley began earnestly, drawing me aside without any preliminary greetings. The feeling of foreboding increased a hundredfold. "A telegram has come for you. Before you read it, you should let Tallis tell you why he has journeyed here."

Tallis smiled politely, took off his hat and said a quiet good morning. Matthias added his behind them in the subdued pantomime.

I regarded Charley, and then Tallis. It was not Tallis's appearance but rather the way Charley looked—the set of her shoulders, the fierceness lurking beneath her cool impassive gaze, her hands curled unconsciously into fists in denial, rigid and apprehensive and defiant—that brought back the memory of the morning in Luxor and the sudden recognition.

"You're the man speaking to Charley in the foyer of the Winter Palace Hotel in Luxor!" I gasped.

"You saw us?" Charley exclaimed. "You didn't say a word!"

"I couldn't see who it was. And I thought that it was about—that you were... Never mind. It never crossed my mind that it was Tallis, that he had caught up with us."

"I'd only just arrived that morning in Luxor and, by a great stroke of luck, saw Charley in the hotel foyer when I went to inquire at the front desk," Tallis said.

"Why didn't you contact us directly if you wanted to see us? We weren't hiding in any out of the way place."

"Hiding, no, always in plain sight, yes, but still stubbornly elusive. Intentionally so, I believe." Tallis's gaze met Charley's. "I'd resorted to trying to find Charley, your touring companion who had been quite the talk of London town, because in finding Charley, I reasoned, I would by extension find you. But finding Charley proved to be a Herculean labor in itself. I met false ends, misdirection. There was a lot of talk but nobody could give me an exact location, or if they did, you were no longer there when I tried to make contact. Those whom I suspected could give me precise directions, refused. By the time I'd heard about the motor-race from Paris to Cannes and followed you to the French Riviera, you'd slipped away from France and everybody I questioned had different ideas about your whereabouts. I'd noticed, however, how Matthias Vandermeer's name continually came up in association with your travels. He was still in Cannes and I sought his help in locating you. Matthias was not in the least bit forthcoming, but while I was questioning Matthias, I saw another man, a friend and associate of Matthias's who'd arrived from London. I initially thought this man was merely a colleague from Godeffroy's London office, reporting on the unsavory rumors circling about regarding the hitch in financing holding up the highly anticipated merger of Clarence Hatry's steel and iron concerns into the United Steel Companies—they have a large insurance and lending book, they presumably must've had some exposures —but his arrival and purpose there, apparently neither for business nor staying there for personal recreation, seemed odd and unexplained. Whereas Matthias lingered behind on the Riviera, running around on all sorts of errands, this man continued on to book passage from Genoa, not to Italy or any of the other destinations that you and Charley were allegedly touring but to Alexandria. I knew that Godeffroy's didn't have a branch office in Egypt so I took a calculated gamble and followed him to Luxor."

A loaded look passed between Charley and Matthias.

"And you followed us to Assuan?"

"Yes. After meeting Charley, I was intending on leaving. I'd promised

Charley to leave you alone." Tallis glanced at Charley. Charley scowled fiercely back at him. "But as I was departing, I saw you on the hotel terrace with the same man I'd followed to Luxor. Vincent Faneuil. You see, one of the reasons Charley gave for not disturbing you—'hounding' was how Charley put it—was that you were already engaged but she never mentioned the name of your fiancé. The way you stood together with this Mr. Faneuil... It made me wonder."

"Charley lied to you," I told Tallis. Charley continued scowling.

"In respect of a few days timing, yes," Tallis conceded diplomatically. "She made it very clear that you were attached, that you were not available, that no one should put asunder... Ah, let me explain. A short while ago, my father called me into his study and made it known that it would be his heart's delight to see his son and heir betrothed to the daughter of the Bernhardts. He and Victor Cabot Bernhardt had come to an agreement which would merge our families and business interests to their mutual satisfaction. He made it clear that he would brook no opposition. A joint formal announcement would have been issued but you were away on a Grand Tour of the Continent. I volunteered to go find my promised fiancée and bring her back to New York."

I looked blankly from Tallis to Charley.

Charley sighed. "It was a ruse to keep the fathers happy. Tallis came to warn you. And to get out of the way of his father's displeasure."

"I'm not in the habit of jumping whenever my father says so," Tallis said. A wry smile lifted the corners of his mouth. "But nor do I enjoy being an audience to his ire. Thought I'd put a bit of distance between us and let him cool down a bit in my absence... Thought you might appreciate a forewarning, too, in case you didn't agree with the ruling or had alternate plans. Not that it would do much to change the course of whatever the patriarchs are planning back in New York but I thought you would want to be informed. Charley's warning caught me by surprise. You can imagine the sort of reception the news of a prior engagement on your part would have had back home."

"Then why did Charley send you— Why did you hide?"

"Charley said that my showing up and sticking my nose in where it had no business would only upset you and complicate everything and serve no beneficial purpose. Since your parents—or, to be precise, your father, I don't believe your mother was any better apprised of the matter than mine had been—since he hadn't deemed it fit to inform you of this important decision which would have something of an impact on your future, Charley was of the view that that was sufficient wherewithal for you to act independently of it all."

"Charley!"

Charley looked unrepentant.

"What changed your mind, Tallis?"

"...untrustworthy, infernally meddling busybody..." Charley muttered.

"Tallis?"

"Vincent Faneuil's name was not unknown to me. He'd been touted as a potential appointment to the ranks of junior associate in the merger discussions. I didn't know how he fit in if he was your fiancé. I was there at the hotel yesterday when the terrace chattered with the excitement of your engagement to Mr. Faneuil. That's when Charley saw me and gave chase. She threatened all sorts of retribution if I didn't... But new developments had arisen since Charley and I had last spoken in Luxor. I'd received a telegram that afternoon confirming several items of news. One, that the announcement of the betrothal, our arranged betrothal—evidently our fathers had run out of patience—had been made, to consolidate the Bernhardt and Lloyd-Chase houses and banking empires, and two, that a Vincent Faneuil had been confirmed as one of the associates in the merged bank. Charley refused to take my word for it and cabled New York to obtain her own confirmation of the news. The reply came today. A telegram also came for you."

Tallis handed me the envelope.

"JEFFERSON LLOYD-CHASE AND YOUR FATHER CONFIRMED CONTRACTUAL AGREEMENT BUSINESS MERGER AND YOUR BETROTHAL TALLIS LLOYD-CHASE YOUR FATHER EXPECTS YOUR RETURN WITH TALLIS TRAVEL SAFELY"

I stared down at the telegram. Charley and Tallis and Matthias also stared at it as if the letters were hieroglyphics.

"Expects?" said Charley. "Not 'hurry home immediately'? Not 'return New York next crossing'? And 'your father' and not 'we'? Is 'travel safely' code?"

"I don't think Mrs. Bernhardt approves of me very much," said Tallis.

"Tallis, you idiot, none of the mothers with daughters of a marriageable age can abide you. Don't you see that this is implicit permission for Lucia to disregard the ridiculous announcement?"

"Charley," said Matthias, "calm down. That isn't necessarily—"

"Lucia's mother must've suspected something was in the works and that's why she sent her on this Grand Tour to find a husband. So Lucia wouldn't be lumped with a lousy one chosen by her father!"

"Charley," I said, seeing the strangely sheepish, almost abashed, look cross Tallis's countenance and his lack of protesting rejoinder, "that isn't very charitable to Tallis."

"Oh really? I thought—"

"Charley."

Charley suddenly deflated, her eyes deepened into dark, grave pools, no longer churning and set ablaze by fury and defiant bravado but chilled by fear. "Tallis and I will be having further words later. Right now, tell me what you want to do, Lucia, and I will—we will—move whatever needs to be moved to ensure that you will have the freedom and the means to do it."

"Thank you, but all I want is some time. Give me time to absorb all this and think and talk to Vincent." I looked back to the temple entrance where the other tourists were drifting out with expressions of carefree wonder and delight on their faces. Vincent and Mrs. Draycott and Tilly came out bringing up the rear. "If this is what you've all been stewing about all morning, you should probably run over to take a look inside the temple caves before we have to leave. They are beautiful."

Charley and Tallis and even Matthias looked a bit uncertain and lost. Men—and woman—of action, I supposed, at a loose end because they had been deprived in their need to be useful.

"We'll just..." Charley gave me a tight smile. "You go and talk to your Mr. Faneuil."

BLUDGEONED

September 1929, Assuan–Cairo

27

CHARLOTTE:

Lucia walked back to Tilly and Vincent Faneuil, took his arm, whispered some words to him, and they joined the group of tourists in heading to the boat. Stoic, civil, measured, and composed.

Lucia had always been a sober child.

We followed behind like broken marionettes.

From Abu Simbel, the group proceeded on up the river to an expedition of the island of Philae. Once we had alighted from the launch and stepped onto the island, Ussama guided through the kiosks and colonnaded courtyard to the temple of Isis. It was picturesque, this pearl of Egypt, so stately, standing in the midst of the Nile waters in the clear, sparkling sunshine. As we wandered around the site, Ussama relayed to us the alternate name of the isle used by the natives, El-Qasr or Geziret Anas el-Wogud, after the hero of one of the stories in the Thousand and One Nights, a tale of love conquering all. Ordinarily, I might have scoffed at the extent of romanticism requiring the interference of anthropomorphic beasts in such fairy tales, but on this occasion, it stirred a dull ache within me.

"I'm not going inside," I told Matthias. He looked at me askance. "I'm just going to stay out here for a bit and enjoy the view."

"Are you all right, Charley?"

My insides boiled with impotence and dread. To be so far away from New York and yet a slight tug of the chains was all it took to send our futures spinning.

"The temple looks prettier from here in the sunshine," I told Matthias.

I found myself a column overlooking the water and settled myself against it. Obstinate mule that Matthias was, he came over and settled himself against the one next to mine. We watched people drift in and out of the courtyard. Tallis was one of them, strolling listlessly about, kicking up pebbles and dust. Tilly looked up periodically from whatever reliefs held her curiosity to shoot us mystified, inquiring looks.

I smiled back at Tilly who frowned, shook her head and turned back to the reliefs. "I wonder what Jefferson Lloyd-Chase will do when he learns that his flesh and blood is defying him. I wonder what Victor Cabot Bernhardt will do when he finds out that his daughter is eloping with your boy."

"Charley, will you stop—"

"I'm going to take a nap, I think."

"Aren't you afraid someone might take advantage of your inattention and stick a scorpion in your shoe, Charley?"

"That's quite all right. I'll just return the favor and give him a shove into the Nile and let the crocodiles take care of him. There are still crocodiles in the Nile, aren't there, Matthias?"

A low rumbling chuckle answered me.

I closed my eyes.

Behind my burning lids, I saw a shadow-play. I heard faint tinkling laughter and voices. Hieroglyphs and ancient deities danced before me. A great temple rose from the Nile waters and desert sands. The billowing white of a woman's dress and a man's shadow flickered between a forest of golden pillars...

But the click of heels upon hard stone woke me up and I opened my eyes to the harsh, cruel glare of the day.

Matthias had risen to a stand from the column against which he had been leaning, his head turned in sharp alertness towards the stone steps, the laughter faded from his eyes. Tallis was rooted to the spot, facing the same direction like a pointer spaniel.

Nobody bothered to explain. None of us, I supposed, comprehended enough to explain. But what we saw was enough: Lucia running down from the temple and Vincent Faneuil emerging from the pillars and striding after her.

28

LUCIA:

I did not know what to do when I got down to the landing place. The river was ahead of me and the only vessel docked there was the launch which had brought us to Philae. There was no other way off the island.

Panic seized me when I heard hurried footsteps behind me but when I spun around, it was only Tallis Lloyd-Chase.

"Get on the boat," Tallis called out to me.

"What?"

"Get on the boat," Tallis repeated.

"But—the group—"

"Don't worry about the group. Just get yourself on the boat, Lucia." Tallis had begun speaking to the boatman and pushing wads of Egyptian notes and coins at him. "Charley and Matthias are taking care of it. Once we get you away, the boatman can come back and collect the others."

Tallis and I sat on the boat ride back without exchanging a word of conversation. Tallis had always been such a genial, light-hearted person and yet here he was, as grave as Charley had been, tense and ill-at-ease, sunk by the weight of all the things he looked like he wanted to say and did not. I felt his scrutinizing gaze upon me like a physical touch but he did not demand more from me than silence. I was grateful and mortified by the kindness and pity in his eyes.

When we returned to Assuan, Tallis accompanied me for a walk in the shade of the public gardens. The hotel terrace, as pleasant a spot as it was, was too fraught with memories of recent events. We kept walking as far as the souk.

As we wandered around the many kiosks of the souk displaying their richly colored and exotic offerings, surrounded by the squawking noise and

221

the smiles and lures of the vendors, trying to hawk their wares, and the hopeful young boys peddling postcards and donkey rides and paste beads, and various other hangers-on, some of the men called out to Tallis offering him various things—a camel, a donkey—in exchange for me.

"Not even worth three camels," I noted. The shame choked and burned my throat once more.

Tallis turned his head sideways to look at me. His eyes searched mine. I reddened, realizing then that Tallis probably had not heard the Percevals' chortling over the tale of the highest bid price offered to Mr. Perceval for his wife. Charley had chased Tallis off from his spying place near the terrace only a day ago.

"Because you are without price?" Tallis said after a long moment.

It was one of those laughing remarks he might have made at a party and promptly forgotten about, but the way he said it made it seem a gift of kindness that both chipped away and added to the hard, bitter crust around my sore heart.

"Lucia," Tallis began hesitantly after another long silence.

"Miss Bernhardt!"

I turned around. Mrs. Draycott waved gaily and weaved through the souk crowds until she reached us. She had been laid up feeling unwell this morning—it must have been the suspect juice she had bought yesterday at the souk—and missed today's expeditions. The episode with the juice had not, however, prevented her from returning enthusiastically to the souk to search out more pretty treasures in recompense for missing out on Abu Simbel and Philae.

"Oh, hello, goodness, it is a small world, isn't it? I'm so glad you're doing much better on dry land, young man," Mrs. Draycott said to Tallis, who had tipped his hat in greeting to her. "I've been slightly indisposed myself but I've taking advantage of it and written to friends about the extraordinary time I've had so far on my holiday, all the lovely fellow travelers..." She turned to me. "Oh my dear, the Percevals and I were talking at dinner last night about your engagement—oh, those beautiful, beautiful flowers!—and I couldn't shake the feeling that you reminded me of someone... I cabled an old friend of mine from New York last night. She cabled me back immediately. Oh my dear, the penny finally dropped—you're Lila St. Clair's girl, aren't you! I wasn't closely acquainted with your mother but I remember her as a debutante before she was married. So beautiful and gracious and glamorous. How we all admired her and her close circle of friends, Ellie Brown and the Elyot sisters! Why, you're the image of your mother as a girl! My friend did mention something quite puzzling in her cable. I'd included your exciting news, of course, and she said that she'd heard something of the sort in New York too, only the name —your young man's name—you did say it was Vincent, didn't you?"

I flinched. Not imperceptibly enough, it seemed, as Tallis's gaze flew to me.

"Yes, Mrs. Draycott."

"That's what I thought. But Abigail said it was something like Thomas or Tobias Lloyd-Charles... Very similar sounding to yours, dear... Oh, I should've brought the cable with me... And where is your young man, Miss Bernhardt?"

"With the rest of the group at Philae. I came back early—"

"You're not feeling unwell too, are you, dear?"

"Just—"

I felt like a train had rammed into me. Mrs. Draycott screamed. Shrieks and shouts and cries rose to the skies around us. I tried to push myself off the ground. Someone grabbed at me and tried to drag me away into the befuddling crowded mass. I struggled against the fast grip but then I felt another rough tug and a grunt as if something else had landed an impact, and another, and then another, until the grip on me loosened and I fell to the ground again. I tried to scramble to my feet. Several hands came to help me.

"Oh, dear, are you all right?"

"He got away."

"Lucia?"

I looked around at the voices emerging from the melee that had surrounded me in the souk. Mrs. Draycott's worried face stood out from the crowd of onlookers. Tallis's, dark with violence and fury, while his hands held me upright. And—my heart pounded an erratic beat—James Dorsey's.

29

CHARLOTTE:

When we returned from Philae to the hotel and came into its foyer to the news of a scuffle which had broken out in the souk, it felt as though all my sins and failings and lies had caught up with us to spite me.

Our group quickly gathered around Mrs. Draycott in the foyer by our group as she, still atremble from the traumatic experience, relayed to us what had happened. Mrs. Draycott said that she and Lucia and the young man from the Rosetta had been set upon in the souk. That the assailant had tried to mug them and abduct Lucia. That another kind young man had stepped in and helped them. That, unluckily, the assailant had gotten away.

"Where is Lucia?"

A doctor had been called to attend upon her and declared her unharmed.

"I want to see her," said Vincent Faneuil, evincing concern before the gathered crowd.

I was on the verge of telling him where he could stuff his "I want" when Matthias suggested that we ask the doctor who, if anyone, Lucia did or did not wish to see. Everyone murmured in agreement and sympathy.

Vincent turned to me, aggrieved. "I still care about her." He had lowered his voice so that the people around us could not hear.

"Your actions certainly attest to that."

"Judge me all you like but you cannot deny that it was pragmatic—the best outcome one could hope for under the—"

"For you, for appearance's sake, for whatever other considerations that you feel are important, yes—but not for Lucia."

"You would have us go up against her powerful father? You'd have her disavowed and both of us made pariahs? You have no idea what it would mean if we—"

"It was cowardice. You can deny and squirm about in all your self-justifications but you can't hide from it. Lucia would've been ready to take on the world side by side with you but you tucked tail and ran at the mere mention of someone big and scary approaching. Tell me, Vincent, are you a man or a mouse?"

Vincent's face and neck flushed a deep crimson. He hissed back: "You don't know what you're—"

"That's enough. Vincent. Charley. Have a care. The doctor is back," Matthias said severely, stoppering our row.

The doctor approached, accompanied by Tallis. Tallis was scowling. A moment later, I found out why.

As Lucia's putative fiancé, Vincent Faneuil undid all our earlier efforts to waylay him and was given permission to visit the convalescent in her room. Lucia had given permission for us and Vincent to visit her in her room? It defied reason.

Shooting us warning looks, Matthias urged Tilly to see Lucia first along with Vincent. As chaperon and to keep the peace, he told Tallis and me, suggesting that we had best visit Lucia in turns.

I wanted to draw blood. I would have argued with Matthias—I was going to argue—but Matthias put a restraining hand on my forearm.

"The young man who'd stepped in," he said quietly.

I followed his gaze.

There across the hotel foyer stood James Dorsey. There had been too many people gathered around us and Mrs. Draycott, listening to Mrs. Draycott's recounting of the attack in the souk, for him to approach close enough to speak but he had seen me.

I knew a moment of unreasoning panic. In that brief second, Matthias's steadying hand was under my elbow, firm and warm, steering me aside. He murmured a few words to Mrs. Draycott, and immediately spirited us away.

It was difficult to recover one's honor after scurrying away in pusillanimity. I was still too incensed by everything that had happened to argue why retreating to my hotel room to hide was an act of cowardice—after I had just told Vincent how cowardly and pitiful he was—instead of the tactical retreat that Matthias tried to convince me of, but I felt it.

"Both of you need to calm down," said Matthias. "You're no good to anyone like this."

I knew Matthias was right. I should have set reason loose by now to rein in my quick temper and whatever other untidy emotions were flying around. But this tailspin involving Lucia... My mind was not clear enough to reason or question why or find logic in sifting through today's happenings, to consider the attempted attack in the souk or to face how James Dorsey had appeared in Assuan. Of the three of us, only Matthias could have been properly considered in his right mind. Still...

"You just made me a hypocrite before Vincent Faneuil."

"Do you know why James Dorsey is here? Did you contact him and ask him to come to Assuan?"

"No, but that—"

"Then you're in no state to deal with him. You can thank me later, Charley."

"I will—"

"What do you have against this James Dorsey?" Tallis asked. "He helped beat off the attacker."

Matthias's mouth turned into a thin, angry line. "This is the—third?—time he's stepped in and allegedly helped. He's a cad and isn't to be trusted."

"He isn't the only one but we trusted him just fine. You practically ushered him into—"

"If Lucia agreed to see him, she would've had her reasons. She is not unprotected. Tilly is there. You would've beaten him to a pulp if you were in the same room. That's hardly—"

"And he would've richly deserved it!"

"Regardless, Lucia is capable of managing her affairs without any meddling from us unless she—"

"Meddling?" I plucked a cushion from the couch and threw it at him. "Now you talk about not meddling?"

"Charley—"

"You handed him everything on a platter—you got him the blighted appointment—you can take it away."

"Charley, you know that isn't how it works—and it won't help. Do you really want to stoop to that sort of pettiness?"

"Yes, yes, I do! By fair means or foul, I don't care! That pathetic excuse for a man can get himself another job. Why does—"

"I wish I had a shotgun," Tallis said, black as a thundercloud.

I did not know if Tallis was thinking about his father or Lucia's father or Vincent Faneuil or the assailant who had tried to abduct Lucia in the souk or fate in general, but I found myself almost agreeing with him. Powerless inaction felt as sour and noxious on my tongue as cowardice.

Yes, a shotgun would have been mighty handy. Far more satisfying than throwing things or kicking over tables.

"I'm sorry. I didn't know about Jefferson Lloyd-Chase and Victor Cabot Bernhardt planning on arranging a marriage to consolidate the business alliance," Matthias said. "I didn't know that Vincent— If I'd known, I wouldn't have... Things would have been done differently."

Damnit. I slumped back against the wall in defeat. What good was a shotgun against a belly full of guilt and regrets?

Which left me cooling my heels with Matthias and Tallis in the sitting room of my suite, waiting, pacing, sulking, afraid to go out onto the balcony in case someone was below...in case someone saw...and, since I could not give in to hysteria or rage or madness, picking fights with Matthias.

"Mrs. Draycott knows about the arranged Bernhardt-Lloyd-Chase engagement," said Tallis, pausing in his long, impatient strides around the carpet. "She has had the news by telegram from her friend in New York. She is still hazy and confused but she knows my surname and it is only a matter of time before she puts two and two together and starts asking questions."

30

LUCIA:

I could not speak. My throat ached and throbbed. If I spoke, I would have begun to cry.

31

CHARLOTTE:

It was late in the evening when Tilly sent for me.

"I put her to bed," Tilly whispered. "She's had a stream of visitors in here after Mr. Faneuil. They were kindly and well-intentioned but... I called the doctor in and he ejected them."

"I'll sit with her, Tilly. Go and rest. You've had a long day too."

"I do not wish to speak out of turn but... I never would've imagined it of that Mr. Faneuil," Tilly said, shaking her head.

Lucia's bedroom was darkened. A hesitant sliver of moonlight escaped through the diaphanous curtains to draw patterns on the walls and animate shadows lurking around the perimeter: furniture, ornaments, an abundance of flowers throwing out their redolent perfume.

I was about to settle into the corner armchair for the night when a light was suddenly switched on.

Shadows and moonlight flew away pell-mell.

Lucia sat up in the bed, not caring about the creases made in her flowered gown. There was a crushed posy of white flowers in her lap and some lost petals drifting about the foot of the bed. Her eyes were red but dry.

"Tilly said... I thought you were resting."

Lucia slowly shook her head.

"Do you... Are you hungry? Thirsty? I can go if you don't want to be disturbed?"

Lucia shook her head again.

"Do you... Lucia, I'm so sorry."

Lucia plucked at the scattering of flowers. "He said that too."

She began to cry—she cried and cried, crumbling up the white narcissi and roses and lilies till they fell from her fingers like snowflakes.

"Lucia, tell me what I can do."

Lucia hiccuped.

"Gin?"

I stared. "Are you sure?"

Lucia shrugged. "Pity we don't have any marmalade."

I felt the weight of all my failings, my lack of wisdom, my regrets, my ineffectual hopelessness reflected in the dull, extinguished light of Lucia's eyes. In those vacant orbs, freedom had flickered before being crushed.

I did not think it a good idea to drag Lucia down to the hotel bar or terrace. I was not even sure if they would still be open. However... I put through a call to room service and then went to open the balcony doors to let the fresh, cool evening air take away the scent of the dying flowers.

There was something unreal about the night, downing cocktail after cocktail on the balcony to the indifferent splash of waves against the rocks below and the melancholy nocturnal silences of Elephantine Island and the black distant silhouette of the mausoleum on the West Bank hillside.

Time leaked away between the sparse conversation and the passing of the gin and the refilling of glasses, the waves and the desert moonlight and the black rocks and the black Nile, Lucia drunk, possibly for the first time in her life, crying spasmodically, hiccoughing, a ghostly light flickering in the east...

I was drunk too but with Tilly's reports of Vincent Faneuil's last interview seared into my brain, I managed to piece together her soft ramblings...same quarrel...pointless...no more hiding...why wouldn't he fight for me...hopeless...failure...it rankled...useless apologies...refuse to try...not worth the risk...more important...how did I...stupid, stupid, stupid...it rankled...suddenly   saw   through   him...walked away...rejected...leaving...home...

"I'm sorry. I'm afraid I'm...slightly drunk."

"Not really," I murmured soothingly.

"Not really," echoed Lucia into her glass.

She had fallen asleep a dozen times that night, half dozing sometimes, staring drowsily at her empty glass while I rummaged about for ice chips and lemon juice and soda and the bottle of gin, until she finally laid her head down on her forearms and was quiet.

With considerable effort, I managed to haul her off the balcony and back into her room. She was mumbling incoherently into the bed sheets when I dropped into the armchair beside the window, unable to keep awake any longer.

But sleep did not come, only a restless Morphean repetition of a night passed amidst darkness and perished flowers and drowning in gin cocktails, voices swimming round and round my head like fragments of shattered crystal...a giant shattered colossal stone head...a white narcissus...or was it a lotus flower...hanging in an oasis in the air, forever out of reach...

Our heart is a treasury, Balzac once wrote, if you pour out all its wealth at once, you are bankrupt.

32

LUCIA:

I woke up to a thundering headache and the sound of Tilly's lowered voice nearby, curtly whispering—though seeming like it was magnified to a painfully loud pitch—giving somebody a sound scolding. When I opened my eyes, they confirmed that Charley, curled up in an armchair, was the passive recipient of the sharp reprimand, and the gin bottles and glasses that Tilly was methodically removing from places around the suite and balcony were the cause.

"Good morning, Miss Lucia," Tilly said when she noticed me stirring about the bed. "Are you feeling any better today?"

I smiled weakly back at her. It was an effort. By the looks of Charley, she was in a much worse condition.

Tilly harrumphed and announced that breakfast would be brought in shortly. She then turned and gave Charley's shoulder an expectant poke.

"Oh God, Tilly, please, no," Charley groaned, "have some mercy."

"You should've thought of that sooner, Miss Charley. Nobody else to blame," Tilly retorted. "Come along." And she nudged Charley out of the armchair and half-hustled, half-shuffled a whimpering, feebly protesting Charley out of the room.

A short while later, Tilly brought in Matthias and Tallis who had dropped by to visit. Matthias handed me a new box of peppermints. Unlike the hangover cure that Tilly had made me swallow earlier, the peppermints were welcomed.

"How are you feeling?" Tallis asked.

It was a relief to find that his voice did not send shafts of pounding agony shooting through my skull as Tilly's had done earlier. Perhaps Tilly's hangover cure had some efficacy.

Matthias picked up the carafe of chilled karkade and refilled my glass. I had not been able to stomach the idea of food but the tartness of the tea had been settling on my churning insides and the constantly threatening urge to retch.

"Never again." I opened the box of peppermints and offered them around the room.

"That has been remarked a lot this morning," Matthias said, smiling. "When will you learn, Lucia, not to put yourself in Charley's hands?"

"How is Charley? I imagine she is suffering horribly. Where is she?"

"Charley has been banished to her room. She is apparently dying a slow and agonizing death and Tilly has not a bone of compassion in her body. Tilly is of the view that Charley got her just deserts. Irresponsible and criminal overindulgence might've been mentioned."

"But she doesn't deserve that censure. Charley was quite the reverse—a restraining influence, though I didn't realize it until this morning."

"Charley?" Tallis looked at me incredulously, Matthias with more curiosity than disbelief.

Everything hurt, everything was in revolt, but gradually less so. It had made me wonder about the astonishing quantity of cocktails I had poured down my throat—the number of cocktails that Charley had made for me had been too numerous to recall, but evidenced by how much mess Tilly had cleared away—compared to the fact that I was still conscious and recovering surprisingly well. And that was when I made an interesting discovery: the same could not be said for the plants and flowers around the suite. Or, evidently, for Charley.

"I'm afraid it seems I'm a bit of a lightweight when it comes to gin," I confessed. "Charley must've diluted all of my drinks and either tipped the cocktails into the plants when I wasn't paying attention or downed them herself. That must be why I'm still alive and all the plants and flowers—and Charley—are...suffering."

"That may be the case but it won't change Tilly's opinion that Charley brought this upon herself." Matthias chuckled. "Are you... How are you otherwise?"

An awkward moment passed.

Memories of yesterday skittered back across my mind and squeezed like pincers. It had not struck me until then: my throbbing head, my burning eyes had not been from the same eruption of inarticulate pain or tears as yesterday when I had dared to hope and that hope had turned to dust. The physical suffering had distracted me, had actually made me forget, and replaced for a short while the other suffering.

The look on Matthias's face showed that he had regretted his words in reminding me of the events of yesterday.

"I'm sorry," Matthias said. His eyes were pained and sincere. "He is booked to leave on the mid-morning train out of Assuan."

I knew Matthias meant to be kind but the news still brought a wounding stab. I gave Matthias a reassuring smile. "A hangover has its silver linings. It certainly brings a different...perspective to pain."

"It was Charley's dying wish that we take you down to breakfast and for a walk to soak in fresh air and sunshine," Tallis said, attempting lightness. "She has been very protective of your welfare." The unspoken lingered in the air. As my fiancé ought also to have been...

I looked at the drooping plants and dead flowers. All the routine things that I had done this morning, forced to comply under Tilly's supervision and firmly taken to task whenever I slacked off: getting up out of bed, bathing, brushing my hair, dressing, swallowing down Tilly's vile potion that was supposed to cure my hangover. Had this all taken place under Charley's direction? Forcing me to go through the motions as though what had happened yesterday to splinter my heart had never taken place? And now being sent forth to walk into sunshine and clean air as if I was reborn whole as the new day? Charley and Tilly could not possibly have believed that it would be that simple. And it was ludicrous to think of Charley conspiring— Charley who was unlikely to have been capable of much more this morning beyond moaning in bed with a crippling hangover. And yet...

My ribcage felt uncomfortably tight. I thought of the night past when I had lain in the solace of darkness and Charley had accompanied me in drinking myself into a stupor, when, unbeknownst to me, she had imbibed the heavier burden of poison, pillowing my wretchedness and softening the fall.

With a pang, I realized that I was again witness to Charley trying to prop up the skies, grasping desperately at straws.

My chest filled with an unbearable pressure. This, I forced myself to face the harsh truth, was why it was for the best that Vincent and I were no longer together, when a friend—when several friends—so matter-of-factly and without hesitation, had tried to halt my unspooling, had tried to rebuild my fractured world, showing more careful, selfless kindness to me than the man who had once sworn I was his everything and then did the opposite.

"Not the terrace or gardens," I told Tallis. The hurt was still too raw to return there.

"Of course, sunshine and air can be gotten in any number of places," Tallis said. "Would you care to revisit the scene of the crime and have breakfast on your balcony instead?"

I nodded. That sounded like something I could successfully attempt without casting up my accounts.

"Afterwards—if you feel up it—how about a felucca ride to the West Bank or one of the other islands?"

"You can decide later," Matthias said. "But you have no need to worry about visitors today. They've been told that messages and other deliveries for you are to be left at the front desk until you are pronounced to be ready to accept callers. We picked them up for you on our way here."

Breakfast was brought out to the balcony. The view across the Nile to the hills and Western desert on the West Bank looked very different in the morning sunshine. The waters were dotted with the little white sails of pleasure-seeking feluccas amidst the rocky outcroppings of the First Cataract. Gentle. Serene. Soothing. So was the company. Tilly tried to tempt me with slices of fresh fruit and pastries. I managed another glass of the karkade and nibbled some dry toast. The breeze dispersed away the smell of the cooked portion of the breakfast spread which offended my extra sensitive nose. Matthias and Tallis demolished the rest.

An hour passed more pleasantly than I had any reason to hope for.

By the time breakfast was finished and we came back into the sitting room, the plants and flowers and all the evidence of the previous night's debauch had been cleared away and the suite was left once again smooth and immaculate. It was, I supposed, an example to live up to.

33

CHARLOTTE:

"Go away."

All I wanted was my shaded bench in the hotel gardens by the river and my cool glass of iced tea in front of me. Was that so much to ask?

A light wind picked up and brushed against my face. The smell and sound of the rhythmically lapping and purling waters hit me. I tried to ignore the piercing light behind my eyelids.

Footsteps coming closer forced me to open my eyes. Even from the shade, the sun still hurt like splinters in my eyeballs. I glared at the intruder with intense loathing. "Leave me alone to die in peace."

"Charley?"

The blinding haze of light parted a little. A man who looked like James Dorsey stood in the center of the light, frowning down at me. Was Fate so pitiless? Yes, the unforgiving stabs of pain affirmed it, a thousand times, yes, foolish human. I wished I had had the foresight to drown myself in the Nile earlier instead of coming down to the hotel garden and entertaining all of Lucia's kind well-wishers who had seen me and drifted over and given me their messages to pass on to her. There had been a reason for Prohibition, hadn't there? Never ever, ever, ever again. I took a long sip of my iced tea and lifted my gaze once more to test whether the man had been a mirage. I met a distinctive gaze of intense green. No, my penance was not yet over. It really was James Dorsey.

"Hello," I said.

"Are you all right? You seem a bit..."

"Too many parties, injudicious gin consumption, not enough sleep. It's all catching up with me."

"Are you sure?"

"What brings you here?"

He gave me a long look, one part assaying, one part irritation, two parts unhappy. Finally he said: "I thought we had an understanding, Charley."

No, my penance was most definitely not over. "Did we? What understanding was that?"

"You're joking. Are you being like this because you are still angry?"

"At present, you have me at a disadvantage and I would appreciate you explaining things to me so that I may understand too and be clear what it is that I am answering."

He made a vexed gesture with his hand. "When I'd found out that you'd left the Riviera— If you knew how much I regretted the accident at Cap d'Ferrat—"

"I do know. Your apology was accepted. Why do you continue to bring it up?"

"Because you haven't truly forgotten or forgiven! Charley, don't pretend —"

"I'm very sorry that you feel that way. I thought our friendship was a little more robust and sympathetic than that."

"Friendship? You know it was more than that. You ran all the way to Egypt and then went to the trouble of losing me in Cairo to escape it." His expressive green eyes blazed at me. My head throbbed a bit more painfully.

"There were reasons why I left the Riviera in a hurry and, equally, Cairo," I said. "Those reasons had very little to do with you."

"In light of your actions, I find that difficult to believe, Charley," he replied, his low, roughened voice coated with strained resentment. "You may try to erase from your mind everything that happened between us, but that doesn't change the fact that it happened. Something changed after the night you arrived in Cannes. After you went missing for a week. You came back more distant, guarded. You blew hot and cold but you didn't turn me away. We had an understanding, Charley, it wasn't imagined. But then the accident at Cap d'Ferrat—and you ran."

"Well, I suppose a lot of things did happen on the French Riviera."

"You know what I'm talking about."

"I don't believe I do."

He pinned me with his fierce eyes. "What happened after your arrival in Cannes, Charley, that made you withdraw—that is still driving you away?"

"Withdraw?" I rose from the bench. "I'd never played on the French Rivera before. I got carried away. I suppose in that regard you might have a valid complaint. But I've never made any bones about being flighty or capricious."

"You're being deliberately obtuse. Why do you keep denying—"

"What an extraordinary accusation! I had no more expectations of you —or Andre d'Erlanger or anyone else for that matter—than you should've had about me. I would never have held you to account for anything that was said or done in the whimsy of the moment. I'm not a fan of easy promises. They are far too easily regretted and broken."

"Charley—"

"If I've misled you, I apologize. It was not intentional. I would hope that a man of the world such as yourself would understand that a nice summer does not an understanding make."

"You're lying," he said, low and savage, "to me and to yourself!"

"Surely you cannot to expect me to be naive enough to be thinking of weaving that into something greater than what it is? Why me? Why should you care—" James Dorsey's shoulders heaved with pique, it rolled off him in waves. "You can't possibly find fault with me for being distracted in the South of France! It is expected that one's head is turned by all the available diversions and attention. It is impossible that I somehow made you feel neglected!"

"It is galling," he rasped through clenched teeth, "to know that you have shared a deeper connection with someone and yet have that woman deny it as if the entire shared past had never happened. The feelings endure. I haven't forgotten, Charley, not one second of it." He reached out to touch me and I stepped back, earning an incensed glare.

"Don't lay claims on me that never existed. I enjoyed the Riviera very much. It was exciting and new. I had a lot of fun, and you contributed to that. But people pack up and go home after summer ends. They go back to life and reality."

"Why do you insist on either-or? Who is to say we can't have both? The only one standing in the way of that at the moment is you."

"You're very easy company, James. You know how to charm and please. I'm sure you will never want for popularity. But this role as a romantic doesn't sit right. I'm sure you understand that life demands a good deal more sustenance beyond those things. Sooner or later, we all have to pay our dues. A friend of mine is, at this moment, suffering because she had relied upon such a man for the making of her happiness. She had done her best to be prudent and sensible but she didn't truly know him, she hadn't seen his true nature because it hadn't been tested. It would be rather foolish of me to ignore that cautionary example. What do we really know of each other? What makes you willing to throw your lot in with me—that is what you are suggesting by an understanding, isn't it?—when you barely know me? Or perhaps I am wrong, perhaps you do know all about me?"

His nostrils flared, promising violence. "What are you saying?"

"Why are you here, James?"

"For you."

"I'm not a romantic any more than, I think, you are, so let's lay our cards on the table, shall we? You are no stranger to indulging in the pleasures of leisured society and the company of heiresses and young ladies made charming by the endowment of worldly goods. Our favorite Mrs. Stuyvesant was very chatty, I'm afraid, but the facts about the Fabens girl and others have been separately confirmed. I'm sure you're familiar with such precautions. I don't hold it against you. We all have to make our way in the world in accordance with societal constraints. You're not the only one who treads this path, and if you and the lady are both willing and agreeable... However, I prefer my friendships untainted by such concerns. It is a question of trust. When you insist on an understanding between us, well, I think it is reasonable for me to ask: would you have been anxious to cultivate my company if my name hadn't been Masterson, if I'd just been Charley?"

"It's bloody offensive to be accused of being mercenary when I have followed you across the Continent and put up with your shenanigans to throw others off your scent, thinking that we—"

"It is of no use being thin-skinned around me. Be offended, if you must, but please answer me candidly."

"It's that Matthias Vandermeer, isn't it? He's poisoned your mind against me."

"It is true that Matthias doesn't like you very much. He is rather dogged. When he gets hold of a bone, he doesn't let go."

"But are you—not Matthias, not your advisers—are you telling me no?" He advanced to close the distance between us, and I pranced back another few steps.

"I like you well enough to advise you against continuing this pursuit. It will come to no good end. Whether Matthias is justified in his dislike of you or not, I'd rather preserve our friendship as it is. It is foolish to aspire to anything more."

"That's cowardly, Charley. And it assumes I will fail if put to the test."

"It's pragmatic. We spent some pleasant times together over one summer. Don't make it out to be a love story for the ages."

"Charley—"

"You should've accepted the graceful exit I gave you and bowed out when I lost you in Cairo, or better yet, the Riviera, confused like everyone else by Charley and her shenanigans, instead of coming here and forcing this awkward conversation."

"You want proof that I don't care about your money? I'll fight whatever Matthias Vandermeer wants to throw at me so long as you stop listening to the lies he's spewing in your ear." He stalked towards me, caught my arm and jerked me against him. He ran a possessive hand through my hair. "I'll do anything you want, Charley."

"Anything?" There was a faint rustling behind the nearby rocks.

James's eyes turned wary, edged with tension, but he did not let go.

"Yes."

I leaned away. "Then leave me alone. Leave Egypt. Go back to your own life. Come back to me in a year and we'll see if you still feel the same."

"Are you serious?"

"Yes."

"What are you planning to do between now and a year's time?"

"That's not your concern."

The thick band of his arm tightened around me. "It is if you are—"

"You said you'd do anything I told you."

"You're testing me?"

"If you like. You may not believe me but I'm trying to be your friend." There was another rustle.

"How? This is the test where I will fail if I agree, and leave you to his lies, and still fail if I disagree with the same consequence. Matthias Vandermeer will win either way, won't he?"

"This isn't about Matthias. Why do you—"

"I don't trust him," he snapped. "I don't like it that you allow him to work his influence with you against me. Ask something else of me. I can't —I won't leave you alone with him for a year."

"Then we don't have an understanding, do we?"

"Charley, you can't—"

"You can come out of hiding now, Matthias, I know you're there. Your ears must be burning!"

James Dorsey turned outraged, startled eyes towards me when Matthias emerged from the rocks overlooking the Nile. Matthias's jaw was set in a furious line. "No," I assured James, "it isn't a conspiracy. I'm a tad annoyed myself."

"Annoyed—!"

"Charley," Matthias said, striding up swiftly. He looked pointedly to where James's hands were, wound around me and resting on my head. James tried to snake his arm tighter around my waist to pull me to his side away from Matthias. Matthias glared, radiating challenge, demanding satisfaction. James glared back at Matthias. I snatched at the instant of distraction to slip out from James's hold and edged away from both of them to a neutral place, which pleased neither man. James made an attempt to draw me back but Matthias stepped in front of me and used his not inconsiderable bulk to deflect any more lunges from James.

"Charley, come on, let's go." James held his hand out and motioned for me to rejoin him.

Matthias turned his gaze towards me in infuriating silence.

"Matthias, if you've finished your lurking, please leave us."

Matthias ignored me. He and James faced one another in fighting stance, several paces apart and circling closer, all pent-up aggression

240

threatening to be released, staring each other down. I was forced to step back in between the two idiots to prevent it all escalating into war.

"Matthias—"

Matthias planted himself between James and me again like a fortress wall. "If you're done here with Mr. Dorsey, would you be so good as to come with me so that we can discuss Lucia?"

James sneered. "That's the most puny—"

My head throbbed viciously. I wished that the earth would open up and swallow me.

"It happens to be true. I'm sorry, I have to go," I told James.

James's face darkened to a deep, angry shade of red. "Charley, you can't —" He tried to catch my eye. "Charley, please."

"I don't think that there is anything more for either of us to say. You know what I ask. I have to go." I turned around and made for the path even though each step sent a dagger-like jolt to my head. I could hear Matthias moving behind me, keeping a protective guard, the landing of his long steady tread against the stone smoothing out my strident pounding steps. I did not care to glance back and see the fuming look of disbelief and betrayal on James Dorsey's face.

Notwithstanding the increasing distance from the water, Matthias continued to glare fiercely back to ensure that James Dorsey kept away as we followed the path up to the hotel. I kept my eyes on the path ahead, I was not going to tempt another fight.

"I cannot believe you eavesdropped on me!" I hissed at Matthias. "And hiding? Behind rocks?"

The veins in Matthias's temple pulsed. "I heard voices." He made no attempt to conquer his scowl. "It was too late to leave when I realized to whom those voices belonged. You," Matthias pointed at me, "were warning him off."

"And if he is guilty and wise, he will leave. If he is innocent, he may stay despite—"

"If he is guilty, he may run or stay to finish a job."

"Precisely! He may do this, he may do that. A dozen possibilities, no certainty either way whether he is guilty or innocent. Just like all that precious circumstantial evidence pointing in a myriad directions, open to your interpretation or mine. You," I jabbed a finger back at Matthias, "shouldn't judge prematurely based on insufficient proof."

Matthias paused on the steps. "Was it your sense of fair play that moved you to send Dorsey away—or the understanding you share with him?"

"Fruit of the poisonous tree, Matthias!" I pushed past him, stomping into the hotel.

"Well?" His long strides quickly brought him up alongside me and he kept apace as I crossed through the public areas of the hotel.

"It is irrelevant. Put it down to whatever you like. Neither bode well for my suspected complicity, do they? Well, I don't care, I would've done it regardless. My conscience is clear. What are we discussing about Lucia?"

"It can wait. Everything is in hand. Tilly and Tallis are babysitting Lucia in her room at present. She is recovering relatively well. They are playing cards and deliberating on whether to take a felucca ride or not after lunch. I just needed an excuse to get you away from Dorsey. He seemed like he was straining your patience and adding to your hangover."

"You—an—you—"

"Well, which one was it?"

"I've a mind to turn around and walk right back down to the garden!"

Matthias put his hand out to stop me.

"Charley," Matthias sighed, "don't let him take advantage of your nature."

Something leaden dropped to the pit of my stomach. I snatched my arm away. My skin burned in the place he had touched, as if he had scorched it with fire instead of gentleness. How could he have seen—how could he have understood—if James, who did not want for intelligence, had not? "You are taking advantage of my rapidly shortening patience right now, Matthias. You'll forgive me if my hangover forgets its manners for a moment and hits you in the face. What did you need to talk to me about regarding Lucia?"

"Do it then, if it will make you feel better." He turned and spread his arms to make it easy for me to take a swing at him. I glowered back. "There's no need to be overtaxing yourself like this. I came down to find you and check on whether you were all right since you didn't show up after returning from Assuan station."

"I don't know what you're talking about."

"Charley, I spotted you there, hiding on the platform when I saw Vincent off. I knew you'd be there to make sure he left on the train and I had an idea of what to look for in the crowds and racket of the station. Tilly told me all about the get-up you donned fleeing from Cairo. I thought there was a high chance you'd use the same costume again."

Silence.

"I needed to make sure he was gone."

"I know."

"He's lucky you were there. I might've been tempted to push him off the platform into the path of the incoming train."

"I was aware of that too. I'm sure you will be entertaining many more schemes to hasten his demise."

"He folded so quickly. I'm not sure it would be worth the effort. It wouldn't give any satisfaction."

"Bankers are cautious by nature and training—"

"Don't you dare defend him!"

"Not defending, just trying to understand and explain, Charley. Even the titans of Wall Street would hesitate to consider going up against Victor Cabot Bernhardt and Jefferson Lloyd-Chase. For an ordinary man without comparable backing or resources of his own, whose livelihood is dependent on the very men he is looking to challenge, the chances of success by any objective assessment—"

"It was not a foregone conclusion! It still isn't. Aut inveniam viam aut faciam. Someone should brand that onto his forehead so that he sees it in the mirror each morning and never forgets. I shall either find a way or make one." Dratted Hannibal. He only had to contend with warmongering Romans and elephants and snow-covered Alps, not the heart of a friend betrayed. "The only thing that is foregone is that he is a coward. Even if he'd had no courage of his own, even if he'd thought it would fail, if he'd loved Lucia, he would've tried—for her. It was his own ambitions that he couldn't set aside..." I bit my lip, too angry to speak.

"When I first arrived in London at Godeffroy's, Faneuil befriended me and helped me learn the ropes," Matthias said. "He isn't a bad man—"

"Just a selfish one." I snorted. "Splitting hairs."

"Charley."

"Did it ever occur to you that he might have befriended you because he thought it would give him an advantage in the future? The more I've come to see and know of him... Lucia thinks he didn't know she was a Bernhardt when they first met at Ginny's wedding, but I wonder. When Ginny came to ask us to help rescue Lucia and Miss Latimer from that double-dealing fiancé, she meant for you to help. But Vincent Faneuil was there, wasn't he, when Ginny spoke to us? Did he seize that as a golden opportunity to jump in and be the knight errant for Lucia to witness? 'The prince of darkness is a gentleman.' So many little things that in hindsight... What will we find if I set a private investigator to look into his relationship with Lady Georgiana Charteris? I know you consider him your friend, Matthias, but he must now have surely plunged low in your estimation. He's an opportunist, isn't he? They seem to come a dozen for a dime. Quite inoffensive, even decent ordinarily, until it comes to a choice between what serves his interests or another's?"

"That isn't proof, only speculation," Matthias said sadly.

"I'm not a court. Only Lucia's friend. And he did more than enough to justify me wanting to push him before a moving train." I turned away. "Stupid, short-sighted man. He miscalculated, didn't he? He assumed that you would side with him because of your friendship, that you would countenance a wrong because of it. Didn't he see in all his calculations that he wasn't standing alone in his corner if he'd only stood by Lucia?"

"Strangely enough, if I hadn't known you were there on the platform... I might've done something like that myself," Matthias admitted.

"Oh." I pondered his confession. "If you knew I was there... You followed me back to the hotel?"

"I thought I'd let you cool off on the ride back from the train station. Didn't think you'd appreciate any company."

"Oh."

"Do you feel any better?"

"No."

"Punishing him and helping Lucia are not necessarily one and the same thing."

I tasted the bitter breath of defeat. "I've been phenomenally successful at neither."

"Come on, Charley. The battle might be lost but not yet the war." Matthias tugged at my wrist to follow him away from a group of people drifting vaguely in our direction. "There was no need to drag yourself down to the hotel garden straight afterwards as a decoy. Lucia's callers were already dealt with."

"Don't be ridiculous. I thought I wouldn't be bothered down there by the water. I thought I'd get some fresh air and peace. Was that too much to ask?"

"I'm sorry you've been put in this position and that he's such a nuisance. You were uncommonly gentle. If you'd let me deal with him earlier..." Matthias ignored my glare. "This won't be the last we see of James Dorsey. I doubt your well-meant advice will weigh persuasively against the lure of your rumored fortune. Interesting how you argued the evidence of his gold-digging yet you'd scoffed when I had shown it to you. What are you planning for in a year's time—or was that just a bluff?"

"Matthias!" I did then punch him in the arm.

The jab glanced off him. He barely noticed the impact, but it did turn his gaze back on me. "You've had quite a full morning. Haven't you run out of steam yet, Charley?"

I shrugged. "No peace for the wicked. Isn't that what they say?" I fished out the key to my suite. "I prefer to get unpleasantness over with but if we aren't going to discuss Lucia's situation, go away, please, so that I may crawl back to my room to die in peace."

34

LUCIA:

When Matthias returned at midday and reported that Vincent had left Assuan, a slight pressure eased within me. I still chose to keep ignominiously to my rooms. So many well-wishing messages from our traveler friends, so much genuine, unsought for goodwill and kindness. It burned me with shame to avoid and hide from them. I could not avoid or hide from Tilly and Tallis's kindness though in guarding and keeping me company throughout the day, despite my being unfit for company—Tilly's unflagging efforts to be cheerful, Tallis's mask of lightness slipping unwittingly, the expression in his eyes firm and unforgiving, before it smoothed out again. My gratitude grew in proportion to my mortification. The past stabbed at me. I wanted to shrink into nothing, to be spirited away to some dark, isolated place in the desert where I could play hermit, where I would not trouble these kind friends, until such time that I could bury the scarlet brand of my shame deep enough and muster sufficient bravery and whatever tatters of poise and self-possession that remained from my upbringing to face the world again.

When Matthias returned for the second time, he brought Charley with him. Charley shuffled in looking as uncomfortable as a truant schoolboy facing chastisement. I offered her peppermints in sympathy. We did not speak of the previous night or Vincent. We all resumed playing cards until the sun went down. Dinner was ordered. More messages were brought in by a hotel attendant. We continued playing cards. And so it went until the moon rose high over the desert outside the balcony doors and Charley and Tilly and Matthias and Tallis, lingering hesitantly, anxiously glancing at me, glancing at each other, before finally bidding me good evening and retired for the night.

I looked around at the suddenly desolate expanse of my empty suite. A long night yawned ahead.

A knock interrupted my ruminations on what exactly I was going to do with the hours before me, alone with my shame.

When I opened the door, I found Charley standing outside. She held up two packs of playing cards.

"Tallis did cheat. I've fixed up the decks now," Charley said. She looked around at the suite from the doorway. "You've not turned in yet? Want some company?"

I stepped aside from the door to let her pass.

"What do you want to do?" Charley said when we sat down again at the table in the sitting room and she laid out the cards. I did not think she was referring to a new card game.

"What would you do?" I asked.

Charley laughed mirthlessly and tackled the chilled lemonade which had replaced the karkade. (We had been informed by the kind hotel attendant who had brought up our third carafe that excessive consumption of the hibiscus tea had side effects.) "I heard about a grand hotel opening on the Bund in Shanghai," Charley said. "It seems to be attracting a lot of attention from the rich and famous and Hollywood stars to boot. That might be an interesting city to visit. The Paris of the East. (I thought that was what one called Cairo?) One big endless party, jazz and ragtime and champagne, opium too, I believe, and plenty of other vices for those who seek it out."

"You're thinking of running away? All the way to the Orient?" My heart raced wildly. Had another telegram arrived? It was easier to seize at this mystery of Charley's like a drowning man at a lifeline—almost like an old friend to me now—than to endlessly circle and lurch about the hellish mire inside my head.

"It is not so very far. The Earth is round after all, so in a fashion, it would actually be heading closer."

"Sir Victor Sassoon." The name escaped my lips before I could catch it.

Charley's eyes snapped to me. Then she laughed. "Dratted D'Erlanger!"

"He was on your list." I felt like a child daring to step out onto a shaky ledge. "It's his Cathay Hotel that you're talking about, isn't it?"

"It's said to be quite spectacular," Charley drawled. "But I was only wool-gathering. You can't be seriously contemplating it?"

"Is it better to stay or run away?"

I saw Charley's self-command falter, a flash of helpless desperation crossing her countenance, before she recovered. She mused reflectively, perhaps indecisively, for long moments, as if reaching inward, then said in resignation: "They can sometimes feel interchangeable, as if you aren't achieving either. It's good to have purpose, any purpose, no matter how wrong-headed. It can act as a ballast. Or it can carry you away as far and as quickly as running can."

I nodded. "You run. I don't believe you lack for purpose."

A flinty glimmer came into Charley's eyes. "You shouldn't believe everything you see. Sometimes we delude ourselves into believing it is a means to an end. Either way, it's keeping busy and out of mischief." Her expression softened. "Horrible things pass, Lucia. You're strong and sturdy and stoic and disciplined and patient. You'll heal. You'll grow old and wise and happy and far too good to associate with the likes of me."

My eyes stung. Words welled up and tumbled out of me in a rush. "Oh, Charley, what a warped fairy-tale view you have of me! If only if it was true. If I could only step through the looking glass. I know logically that this isn't the end, but it feels like it. Don't you think life begrudges us beautiful things like happiness? I was so afraid for such a long time to hope, fearing it would tempt Fate, that if I began to hope, it would scare and crumble away. But, recently, things seemed to be happening and coming together of their own accord, and I thought... When I finally gave in, it turned out to be just as I'd feared, a mirage, another failure. I thought I was being careful, sober, rational. Even when it hurt so much to face him the second time, I thought there might have been a chance that I'd just been rash and upset and mistaken— I'd hoped— It was worse than the first time, so much worse to confirm— He suggested keeping our engagement secret, to try stalling the arranged marriage in the hope that in time he might win my father's favor —any deceitful subterfuge to—to have his cake and eat it. He made it sound reasonable, even sensible. He'd put a good deal of consideration into it and—I—I couldn't do it. It was horrifying. In an instant, everything just —wavered and—I saw him clearly. Vincent hadn't changed, he was the same man. It made my heart ache. How did I not see it before? How could I have been so blind? He knew how to hold on tight and not let go—he held on for dear life to the position he was offered in New York—that was the brass ring worth grabbing, worth fighting for—but we were not—I was not. I was disposable, just an expedient pawn—my name, my family connections, access to the wealthy and powerful—on my own, I was of no value compared to what my father offered. I could not hope to outweigh the things that really mattered to Vincent. 'Love alters not with his brief hours and weeks, But bears it out even to the edge of doom.' God, what a chump I've been to believe that! It's all been such a pointless waste. After Nate, I took such pains to be careful, to— I thought I— I might as well have just accepted from the outset one of the proposals approved by my father. It would've saved so much time and effort, don't you think? Poor Hamilton. I deserve this for what I put him through. I turned down a good man, believing... Why can I not hold onto anything? Why do things appear to be within reach and then everything ends up falling apart? Is there any point to keep on going through the motions? How do you move on from the hopeless? How do you push yourself to climb out of the pit?"

"Oh." Another stricken flash. Charley inhaled deeply and gulped down an entire glass of lemonade. "Wait." Charley got up, went to the bell-pull and, when the attendant arrived, ordered another bottle of gin. She came back and sat down again, still looking uncertain. "Well." She inhaled. "Without hope, you have nothing to lose. Nothing to be afraid of losing. No expectations to live up to. So, really, it's quite liberating. You can do anything you like and not be afraid. So hopelessness is actually a blessing in disguise."

"Who taught you that, Charley? Who was there to drag you out of the pit?"

"You know I made all that up. There's nothing so bracing and causes a girl to wax nonsensical as an endless supply of gin for a bout of hopelessness. Give me enough gin and I can cobble together—"

"You're such a liar, Charley. I look at you and I feel so ashamed. I keep...disappointing."

"Don't be an idiot, Lucia."

The bottle of gin arrived. Charley looked at it and sighed, putting it out of my reach. She poured another glass of lemonade for me and one for herself and glared at the lemonade like it was an arch enemy.

"You shouldn't listen to me twaddle. You know perfectly well I'm not a good influence. Tilly would—"

"It's all a matter of perspective, isn't it? Anyway, I don't need a good influence. I prefer your kind of medicine."

"You're not getting any more gin. I'm not that unconscionable."

"You're going to drink the entire bottle of gin by yourself?"

"No."

"Then who...?"

Charley sighed again and put the bottle out of both our reaches on the side table, where it sat in neglected wallflower loneliness all night.

"I don't understand the point of that at all."

"A test of willpower. And trying to avoid another scolding from Tilly. Belated wisdom is still better than stupidity. It is never too late to remedy the error of one's ways, is it?"

We contemplated the view outside the balcony, of the black Nile and islands and the desert in silence.

"I feel his presence more now when he is gone than when he was here with me. I can't get the thoughts of him out of my head. It eats at me like a disease."

"It's fresh. It won't be forever. Also, the cocktails..."

"I think the hangover actually took my mind off him for a bit."

"Well, like the gin, it will work itself out of you in due course."

Breezes rippled silkily against the darkened night and stole into the room. Charley began to deal out the deck of cards.

"I asked Tallis about the merger," I told Charley. "He wasn't particularly keen to tell me at first. He thought it would upset me again to think on what Vincent would be involved in building back in New York."

"Did it?"

"It did. But... It felt... I'm not sure why I had a manic need to know— it's like picking at a scab and making it hurt and bleed—except I couldn't sit with Tallis and Tilly and Matthias feeling sorry for me and doing nothing all day but play cards and think about what happened. You know, I think Vincent might be right. I don't have an intrinsic value. Everything of mine belongs to my parents. I have no assets. I earn no income. I have no purpose. What am I good for except as a pawn?"

"Lucia! You of all people should know not to mistake intrinsic value with fluctuating market values."

"Oh, Charley, that's kind but I'm not naive enough to fall for that. Tilly should be out seeing Egypt's glories. I don't know what possessed Tallis to abandon New York and his career and pursuits and embark on this mad mission, he could've just sent a letter or telegram. Matthias shouldn't feel obliged to step away from his responsibilities and worries over what is happening on the London markets. I know you've got a stomach full of secrets and concerns and a pile of telegrams that you haven't opened, all of which you put aside to follow Vincent to the station—it's no use denying it, Charley, Matthias suspected and grilled Tilly and—well, Tilly didn't mean to give you up. You've all got occupations that you should be attending to instead of babysitting me while I do absolutely nothing except go quietly mad. So I thought... Well, if I'm going to be going mad thinking about it anyway, I might as well find out about something concrete."

"That sounds reasonable."

"Really? Are you just humoring me?"

"No. I'd get bored too. You're not a mentally lazy sort, but I'm still impressed you managed it while impaired by alcohol poisoning. What did you find out?"

"Tallis confirmed what I expected: a merger between two banking behemoths to try to intimidate and swallow up the rest of the market. It will combine the two private banks, their commercial banking and investment banking businesses. Do you think Matthias, as heir to Godeffroy's, will have to contend with the increased competition from this new bigger player as another headache added to his plate?"

"Matthias must be monitoring the situation but he seems more worried about what's happening on the London markets. Perhaps Volker Godeffroy is the one who gets to have the fun of tangling with your father and Tallis's in respect of the merger."

"It's possible that the tangle might be short-lived. Tallis seemed to agree that there is a good chance of Senator Carter Glass—the Democrats senator from Virginia—Senator Glass's talk of banking reforms finding broad public support, that Senator Glass will make inroads into shaking up and reforming Wall Street, including an end to ownership of investment affiliates by commercial banks and a prohibition on direct bank underwriting. There is little love or trust lost between the public and the financiers of Wall Street, certainly little after the Pujo Committee investigation into Wall Street confirmed that its consolidated control over American industry had been gained through an abuse of public trust, even if the investigation's findings did lead to the ratification of the Sixteenth Amendment, the passage of the Federal Reserve Act, and passage of the Clayton Antitrust Act. Tallis's father is strongly against any banking reforms, as you'd expect. The reforms would mean the separation of commercial banking and investment banking to regulate the flow of capital between the two operational sides. It would be a revolution in industry and trade and finance—it would change the face of banking and market mechanics, so many banking houses would be affected—the House of Morgan for one would structurally—it would break up so many great entrenched powers and fortunes—it would require the break-up of the First National Bank of Manhattan and the North American Charter Bank of New York as they stand now—but, in particular, it would destroy the basis for the Bernhardt-Lloyd-Chase merged bank."

"Are you saying you've found the silver lining, Lucia? I'm glad the fire in your belly hasn't entirely been extinguished."

"What do you mean? I... Why do you have that look on your face?"

"What look?"

"You're plotting something."

"Merely dreaming about retribution."

"Charley, don't! That isn't why I— I don't want you to—"

"Dish best served cold, yes? Oh, come on, Lucia, do you imagine that I could somehow influence that political outcome? That with one snap of my fingers, Wall Street would be separated from Main Street and the merged bank would bite the dust? It's not in my hands. My name isn't Morgan or Rockefeller. But what a lovely dream. Force majeure—a judgment from on high—the best sort of retribution."

"You're rubbing your hands over the potential dilution and collapse of Wall Street's banking empires? For the sake of getting back at one man?"

"I wouldn't be the first or last person to do so. The public don't like bankers and robber barons, remember? So why shouldn't I entertain the possibility in my head? It doesn't hurt anyone and there are no dire extended repercussions. That's the great advantage of daydreams."

"Well... Just so long as you don't do anything."

"I wouldn't dream of being so bold."

Ha. "No plotting, Charley."

Charley huffed. "Did Tallis offer you a job?"

"What?"

"You were wondering why Tallis is at a loose end. He and his father haven't been seeing eye to eye for—well, for quite some time—I'm not sure they ever have seen eye to eye, but he is not really keen to take over the reins of the bank under the terms stipulated by his father—the arranged marriage being one of those terms. Tallis has been looking around for investment partners to start his own enterprise. He approached Montrose —touted his idea to Diego, to be precise. Diego told him quite bluntly that he had useful experience and all the right connections and a reasonable pitch but needed a better financial and coolly analytical brain on board for starters."

"What does that have to do with offering me a job? I've never been near a—"

"The brain Diego was referring to was yours. Do you think I kept all your pearls of wisdom to myself? Diego's always thought it a waste that your father never made use of your abilities in his bank. But, the world being what it is—although it is advancing rapidly towards the future—so perhaps, one day, humans will become redundant because there will be machines that do everything and men will come to understand what being denied purpose and usefulness and recognition and esteem feels like."

"Charley, that's... I..."

"So Tallis didn't ask?" Charley frowned. "He's quite a bigger idiot than I thought. Shouldn't he be making haste to beat the offer that Mr. Grenfell made you? Well, Tallis does have more delicacy than I have, perhaps he's just waiting for a more opportune time. Easily rectified."

"No. No plotting, Charley, promise. And I'm sure Mr. Grenfell has quite forgotten all about me."

Charley did not answer either way. "So what else did you do today besides playing cards and going mad and interrogating Tallis?"

"That's the trouble, isn't it? I'm back in limbo again, just waiting for... Nothing."

"What do you want to do?" Charley asked once more, throwing down a queen of spades.

"I don't want to stay here. In limbo, I mean. I want to run away home but does home exist anymore? When I return to New York, I'll have to face my father. I don't know what will happen given that Tallis and I aren't cooperating with what our fathers want but I'll still have to face the disappointment and judgment, the gossip and shame of being whispered about, of being invited or received in decent society on sufferance or in pity. What a mess. Secret engagement to a previously betrothed man, jettisoned after barely a day, concurrent arranged marriage, the pawn that nobody wants except as a bargaining chip. I've obeyed and avoided scandal my entire life, Charley, only to walk straight into this—this— What an utter shambles. If I ever survive the confrontation with my parents, I'll still have to go about New York knowing that I may hear about Vincent, that I may run into him on the street or at functions, that I may even see him with a new fiancée whom he actually cares for and they'll look back at me with contempt... Oh, I know I'll bear it. What else can I do? But I don't want to. I don't want to be reminded of how I've allowed everything to go to spoil, of how easily I've been discarded. I don't want to shrivel up in bitterness waiting for the next candidate my father chooses. I don't want to be entombed alive. I..." My lungs threatened to seize up but I could not stop. "Sorry, Charley, I'm raving, I know I'm raving like a demented lunatic. I don't know why this is all gushing out now. I should have more patience, more restraint, but—I can't control it. It's driving me to distraction. If I try to contain it any longer, I'll burst! I don't know how to stop myself unraveling like this. I don't want to stay in this limbo but I don't know what to do. I envy you and Tilly your independence. I wish I could act in my own name in the same way but where do I begin? I'm not fit for anything. I can't save myself. I can't hide. I can't run the other way. It seems like everywhere I run, the abyss is ahead of me, stretching open its jaws. I'm terrified, Charley, of going home, of falling in—"

"Don't be." Charley lifted her head and met my gaze. "If running towards the abyss is the only possible way, if there is no other alternative to standing still in the spot you despise, then run. Falling in might not be so bad. And you don't know what you might find when you reach the bottom. It may be fun. You might enjoy it. Or you might not. It doesn't matter if you flounder. The important thing is that you will no longer be in that hateful limbo and since you've proven that it is possible to move from one horrible place to another, you can do so again. The first fall hurts the worst. The rest are only echoes."

I stared at Charley. Charley shrugged and poured two more glasses of lemonade. "'Le Prince d'Aquitaine à la tour abolie'," she quoted as she tapped her glass against mine in a toast. "'These fragments I have shored against my ruins.'"

I could not fathom the idea of embracing such freedom, such terror, of running towards that black abyss and voluntarily leaping in. Charley had said it so nonchalantly but also without flippancy as if she had faced the Gorgon, as Perseus had done, and not only survived but slain the monster and was busy exterminating the vipers and monstrous creatures born of the drops of spilt blood from the Gorgon's severed head. I thought of the dark moods that the arrival of certain telegrams had put her in, the unguarded moments when I had caught her ensnared in bouts of despair. Not for Charley the false hope and comfort of some tiny shaky ledge to climb, to which to cling above the chasm. Charley, I supposed, had taken the logical, the only course open to her mutinous nature and charged full tilt ahead into her abyss. She was still punching and kicking and wrestling and tussling with it on the way down, it seemed, but alive and herself and able to sit composedly here and advocate for me to consider trying the same course. Advocating without regret, without knowing whether the outcome would be good or disaster. Very, very foolish or very brave. Could I do the same?

"You'd best get a second opinion," Charley added, "before you hurl yourself off the cliff."

In my disturbed state of mind, and issuing from Charley, those sensible words sounded like a challenge. In my disturbed state of mind, I was just deranged enough to take it up.

"A cliff?"

"After considered thought and a second opinion."

"Essentially, a purpose?"

"Um, I suppose you could view it that way. Again, second opinion highly advised."

"So... Where am I to find a cliff?"

"Lucia, stop being so literal. It doesn't have to be a cliff. It doesn't have to be ambitious. It can be anything. Little steps, one at a time, one after another."

"Such as just going through the motions?"

"Yes—until they come to have meaning again or you find something new." Charley peered at the deck of cards lying face down in the center of the table. It was her turn to take a card. "If I don't choose, I'll never have to face whether my choice was a poor one. If I take a card, it may make a winning hand or losing one, but I at least have certainty and can move ahead to the next game." Charley picked up a card and held it out for me to see. It was not a favorable selection. She folded her hand. "It may be disadvantageous to be rash, but it is quite as infelicitous to fall prey to the fear and paralysis of impossible choices." A ghost of a droll smile quivered over her features. "And sometimes, if one is so inclined and the circumstances deem it appropriate, one might even consider cheating."

The meticulously plotted path of my life hovered, suspended in midair, vaingloriously conscious of its consequence, mocking Charley's words, mocking me, biddable daughter of Old New York, daring me to mess up the familiar harmonious pattern, to sweep all of those orderly stacked checkers off the board. I thought about the dare as Charley reshuffled the deck. Her notions of freedom and antidotes to hopelessness were more terrifying than they were comforting—no bromides for Charley—but there was no doubt that they offered me a say in my own future, theoretically, for better or for worse, which was more than I had before. How funny, I thought, that Charley wove such tales of fantastical enchantment but her medicines came without sugarcoating. Diego, I remembered Charley once telling me, preferred brutal honesty in his evaluations, no fudging of truth to spare hurt feelings, no feeding of platitudes, only crisp, sharp, clean incisions to cut out the diseased flesh. I wondered if Charley found them as hard to deliver as they were to receive.

I thought of the pound of flesh I would have to surrender upon returning to New York and shuddered, still not brave enough yet to do battle with it. The thought of taking that first step... Even with Charley's encouragement and calm reassurances, the prospect held an overwhelming terror. I may have hated my captivity but the bars of my cage were all that I had known. I had not Charley's obstinate courage and artfulness to impose my will on the impossible. How was I to survive on the outside? "We could complete our Grand Tour before heading back to New York," I decided. "I think I'd like to see Constantinople and Greece and Italy and the other places we'd planned to visit. This might be the only chance I'll get before I have to face reality. The Golden Horn of Byzantium—the Grand Canal—the Seven Hills of Rome—wisteria and sunshine—the treasures of the Renaissance—"

"Oh yes," Charley said, accepting my cowardly temporization, "Florence, banking capital of Medieval Europe, political skulduggery, birthplace of the gold Florentine florin, ruled by the Medici for over a century. No resemblance at all to New York."

"We'd be tourists, not contending with Medici ghosts brought back to life."

"Shame. It would've been interesting to shoot the breeze with Lorenzo the Magnificent and Machiavelli."

"You'd rather spend time with a banker and politician than the greatest artists and sculptors of the Renaissance?"

"Didn't you once say that banking formed the crucible for the Renaissance? Without one, there wouldn't have been the other. And as you may recall, the artists we've met so far haven't been nearly as interesting and attractive as their works, which is probably as it should be. Wouldn't it be a sad indictment of an artist's output if their own life was considered more fascinating?"

"In Mr. Cole Porter's case, that would be your fault. If we do happen to run into the Porters in Venice, you'd have a lot of explaining to do."

"No idea what you are talking about, Lucia." Charley began to deal out the cards. "I'll start making inquiries at the tourist office tomorrow."

I sat back and marveled. "Is everything always so straightforward, Charley? You make it seem so easy."

"The doing is easy when someone else has done the hard work of thinking. That would be you in this case." A smile was playing around her mouth; it was tiny, but imbued with warmth and encouragement.

"Oh, wait, I forgot! An invitation to tea came with the other messages this afternoon. From three sisters, the Misses Catherine, Cesilia and Michelle Denholm-Kirby-Gamil. Their address—Zamelek?—seems to be in Cairo. Apparently they know the Bommels."

"That is impressive reach."

"Do you want to go? I was considering declining it earlier but now I guess you'd include this as part of going through the motions."

"Only if you want to. It's your life, Lucia. Do with it as you wish." Charley refilled our glasses with lemonade. "And I might add that the best retribution is simply to be happy."

We played another two rounds of cards. When I caught Charley smothering a yawn, I folded and sent her away.

"Are you sure?" Charley asked, pausing in the doorway.

Nothing had essentially changed. A distant shadow of my hangover still throbbed in my blood, the same fate still awaited me back in New York, and yet I felt something tangible within had emerged unsummoned and shifted everything without. "Go get some sleep, Charley. I'll see you in the morning."

After I closed the door behind her, I saw that Charley had stolen away with her the bottle of gin.

When I crawled into bed and my mind quieted, I finally remembered the one thing I had been meaning to ask Charley, about the man whose face I had seen at the Assuan souk, the man we thought we had left behind in Cairo who had turned up here in Assuan and was bumped and jostled and lost again to the crowded upheavals and confusions and uncertainties of the last two days, swimming in and out of the haze of gin and waking nightmares.

35

CHARLOTTE:

"ALL TRANSACTIONS CONCLUDED PLEASE ADVISE FURTHER INSTRUCTIONS EDWARD GRENFELL"

"HUNTINGDON WITHDRAW CONFIRMED BAYARD"

"MY DEAR TROUBLE HOPE YOU ARE ENJOYING PYRAMIDS SHOCKING HASTINGS AND TREVISE-FITZGERALD DEFECTIONS ONLY MALLORY REMAINING FAITHFUL WHY WHAT IS GOING ON WITH LUCIA ALL THESE STORIES NEED TRUTH HORSE'S MOUTH WHEN ARE YOU RETURNING LONDON GINNY"

"NY NOT SAFE YET STAY YOUR COURSE D"

I stuffed the rest of my telegrams and the note from James Dorsey into my pocket at the sound of approaching steps on the stone floor of the foyer.

Matthias asked: "Tilly says you're returning to Cairo?"

"You need to leave Tilly alone. If you have questions, you can ask me directly."

"You never answer any of my questions."

"Exactly. Stop bothering Tilly."

"That's me told then."

I suppressed a growl. "Lucia wants to finish the Grand Tour before returning to New York. A change of scenery would be helpful."

"I'm starting to wonder if there is an end to this Grand Tour. Do you ever plan to return to New York?"

Would I ever return to New York?

My eyes slid from Matthias to the surrounding vestibule area and the view peeping from outside. So very distant from home.

The Percevals appeared from a doorway across the foyer. They must have just finished an early morning stroll before heading to breakfast on the terrace. Their eyes lit up when they spotted Matthias and me. They waved and began making their way towards us.

I glanced back at Matthias, at the familiar frown that marred his face. "When the money runs out."

36

LUCIA:

"Let her go, let her go, God bless her,
Wherever she may be,
She can look this wide world over,
But she'll never find a sweet man like me..."

Dawn peeked through the curtains.

Another night had passed in a haze of feverish dreams whose wretchedness leached into my bones while the memory of them receded with the coming of morning; dreams tainted by the voice of Louis Armstrong, filled with a chaotic press of past and future, of the relentless chug of a locomotive over precarious mountain ledges and unseen tracks into nothingness, of running and searching, of being pursued, of desperately trying to escape the horrors which stalked the night—whether chasing or running away from, it had not been clear, perhaps both—teased by monsters who hid behind friendly smiles, teased by phantoms who sometimes looked beguilingly like Vincent or my parents or Tallis or James Dorsey or Matthias or Charley or Tilly and sometimes turned grotesquely into Nate—teased by a turmoil of emotions, torn between loathing, hope and longing, teased by a clawing need for—what? Was it hunger? Fear? Loneliness?—searching for something vital that wavered like a mirage and dissolved into a heavy, clammy, gray emptiness, a phantom weight grown to the size of a mountain, which felt cold and lost and alien.

I woke up with a sense of impending doom. I kept my eyes closed and concentrated on my breathing—or at least tried to breathe—recalling Charley's level voice calling upon me to be brave in running towards the abyss.

Slowly, the suffocating heaviness of my dreams lifted from me. I opened my eyes and noted that no pain pricked when they met the pale sunlight streaming through the window, and the sour stew of shame and humiliation had abated somewhat. It was still early.

I became aware of a faint shuffling noise which seemed to be coming from the other side of my bedroom door as though someone was stealthily moving about the suite. It must have been this disturbance around the edges of my consciousness which had drawn me from my wakeful dreams.

"Hello?" I called out. "Is that you, Tilly?"

A shroud of silence suddenly descended over the morning.

"Tilly? Charley?"

There was no answer.

My heartbeat thudded loudly in my ears. I rose out of bed, quickly pulled on a robe and padded barefooted to the adjoining room.

It was empty. Everything in the suite appeared to be in the same place as I had left it last night, neat and orderly, no hats or scarves or shoes or books or candy strewn about as it would have been in Charley's suite in between Tilly's guiding hand. A strange sort of alertness kept me riveted to the spot. I gave a second apprehensive glance around the room, waiting for my senses to register...

Nothing. Perhaps I had mistaken the direction of the sound's source?

I was turning back around to head back into the bedroom to try to work out where the sound came from, or if I had imagined it, when I was roughly shoved aside as a body leapt out from behind me and brushed past, sprinting for the exit. I heard the sound of the door swing open with such force that it banged against the wall, then swing back and slam shut again. More sounds followed—fleet stomping footfalls, possibly a collision, forceful thumps, something heavy falling—muffled by the walls.

I tried to untangle myself from my robe. I had lost my footing when I had been shoved out of the way, tripped, snatching at air, and fallen down beside the couch. When I pushed back on my hands and knees and looked for the intruder, I found that everything had resumed its placid stillness. I scanned the room again to find something with which to arm myself. A parasol seemed the only thing that even marginally resembled a weapon. I picked it up and gingerly opened the door to the corridor.

There was a man slumped on the carpet a half dozen steps away from my suite. I raised my parasol in readiness as I approached to take a look at him. He was lying prone on his side, facing away from me. His shape and size looked familiar. I used the tip to poke his ribs. He gave a low groan and rolled over.

"Tallis?"

I knelt down by his side.

"Tallis, are you all right? What happened?"

He was slow to stir back to consciousness. I took the chance to run back into my suite to ring up the front desk and Charley for help. When I returned to the corridor, Tallis had pulled himself up to a sitting position, rubbing groggily at his head.

"Tallis?"

Tallis looked up, then around at the empty corridor, and swore ruefully. "Damn! He got away."

"Who got away?"

Thumping sounds, like the gait of a galloping baby elephant, resounded along the thick rug covering the floor announcing Charley's arrival as she came barreling towards us, closely followed by Matthias and Tilly. Tallis had recovered his wits by the time they came to a standstill before us. He seemed unfazed by being suddenly surrounded, calmly answering (dismissing) their concerned inquiries after his well-being.

When it became apparent that Tallis was not dying, Charley launched into a frenzy of blunt questions until, remembering that she had been carefully schooled in the niceties of polite society and her tornado-like intensity sometimes startled people into silence, she pulled herself up and let Matthias take over while she gave herself free rein to observe and sniff about on the sidelines.

"I was heading down the corridor when a man ran out of a door and ploughed straight into me. I would've tackled him down if I hadn't been so taken by surprise. He had the advantage of me, I'm embarrassed to say, and must've run off after I went down. His panicked manner and violent urgency to get away clearly indicated that he had been up to no good. The door he came out of belonged to Lucia's suite." Tallis turned his eyes to me. "Are you sure you are all right, Lucia?"

I nodded, though it was doubtful it gave Tallis any more assurance of the fact than the previous times I had given him the same answer.

"Was anything taken?"

"Nothing to take." I paused and reconsidered Matthias's question. "Nothing important was taken. My mother's diamond necklace hasn't been in my possession since—well, since the night I wore it to the engagement dinner in the hotel restaurant—and Tilly took care of it afterwards. As to whether anything at all was removed from my suite, I don't think so but I can't be sure until I do a more thorough inventory. I heard someone moving about the suite when I woke up. He must've been searching the room when I interrupted him. Tallis, we should get some ice for your—"

"No need," Tallis replied. "Is this— Has this happened before?"

"Not exactly. We've never met the perpetrators face to face before. And they weren't so neat on the previous occasions." I had thought we had left the attempted robberies behind us when we arrived in Egypt, but they had followed us here.

"What—"

"Ice and doctor and breakfast are on its way along with the rest of the hotel and local police palaver," Charley broke in. "Did you see the man's face, Tallis, before he knocked you out cold? Would you recognize him again?"

Tallis grimaced. "I can't guarantee it but I can certainly try. He wasn't one of the hotel staff or a native Egyptian. He was European. I think he was surprised into swearing an oath in—well, it might've been an English accent. There was something about the inflection. Not the Prince of Wales. More like the common Englishman that one might meet on the streets of London, although—"

We all stared at Tallis.

"Tallis, do you realize how many dialect variations there are in London, let alone the British isles? How—"

"Charley."

"All right, I'm a clueless New Yorker," Tallis said in defense as he lumbered back upright from the couch where he had been sentenced since the doctor's examination, eschewing proffered help. "Happy?"

"Pig in mud." Charley did not look the least bit happy.

"About these previous—"

"Glorified pickpockets, standard hazard of travel. Magpies love collecting bright sparkly baubles."

"But—"

"And there is nothing quite so sparkly as Asscher cut diamonds."

"If this incident is connected to what happened in the souk, then Lucia —"

"Coincidental circumstance is not causation, Tallis. You shouldn't jump to hasty conclusions. But you're right, we need to be more guarded and careful. Perhaps paint a different target—supposing your speculations are correct." Charley turned aside to whisper to Tilly.

"You did well, Tallis," Matthias said.

With Charley silently bridling, Tilly anxious, Tallis exacerbating them both with his unconcern over himself and excess concern over my part in the ordeal, Matthias's calm, emollient voice was an anchor in a turbulent sea. That Matthias was intervening instead of participating in the wrangle suggested that there was an entire conversation between him and Charley to which we had not been privy. And it made me curious. Anything that made Charley so prickly was worthy of curiosity. But as with many other Charley-related mysteries, I set it aside to attend to later.

I thanked Tallis. We had all been so busy attending to the practical things, gratitude for his help had been taken for granted rather than effusively expressed. He brushed off the thanks, more sheepish and embarrassed than he had been when Charley had attacked him with questions.

When the swarm of hotel management and police officers arrived to investigate the incident, we went through the same line of questioning. My suite and the surrounding areas and exits were searched, other guests in the neighboring suites interviewed, various attendants questioned. Nobody had seen or heard anything, no obvious sign of anything disturbed or taken, no witnesses to the incident except Tallis, no description of the intruder apart from the one that Tallis had given.

The hotel manager extended his apologies for my suffering such an unfortunate experience in his hotel and offered me another suite. I declined. I would remain here in my suite. It was unlikely that there would be a subsequent breach of my suite. It would be too risky for the thief to come back to the scene after raising the alarm like this and alerting the hotel to an increase in its surveillance and security. Furthermore, if I had missed something in my earlier inventory, staying in this suite might prompt my recognition later. In any case, we were shortly to be leaving Assuan, so it was not worth the effort of moving suites.

Tallis protested the loudest against my choice. His was the only voice of dissent. Matthias cautiously agreed with my reasoning and neither Charley or Tilly said anything either way. In the end, my decision prevailed. Matthias seemed taken by the curious fact that Charley and Tilly had not contested a word, but he merely looked thoughtful and did not comment.

"Tallis," Charley said, when the place had finally been cleared of the melee of police and hotel staff, "what were you doing anyway coming along this way at this time of the morning?"

Tallis muttered something unintelligible.

"What was that?"

Tallis gave Charley a dark look. "I didn't realize you and Lucia were planning on leaving Assuan today."

"A decision made in the spur of the moment."

"Oh," said Tallis, "so it's like that, is it?"

"Until it is otherwise," said Charley, "nothing has changed."

Tallis frowned at her. Charley countered it with a steady countenance, though I was sure that nobody was fooled for a moment that the gears in her busy brain were not spinning at high speed. I looked to Tilly and then Matthias. Tilly did not seem to comprehend the exchange any more than I did. Matthias seemed...concerned. I was on the tip of questioning Matthias when Tallis sighed and said: "Fine."

"Good."

I supposed that meant that Tallis had blinked first.

"You might have given me some scant warning at least."

"What would lead you to expect that?" Charley asked. "Have you been given any special treatment so far?"

"Well, Matthias knew."

"Matthias runs around doing his own snooping."

It was mystifying.

"Should we leave you two to argue in peace?" I asked.

"Oh no, it's all right," Charley said, far too amenably. "You and Tallis can stay here and talk since he is so keen for an audience before our departure. I'll make your apologies to the Percevals. They invited everyone to their wedding anniversary celebration luncheon today."

My suspicions were overtaken by a resurgence of shame.

I instinctively shrank back at the thought of a public humiliation, feeling my face burn anew. We were leaving Assuan this evening on the sleeper train to Cairo. The Percevals—everyone—had been so kind, so concerned after my welfare. It would not be the same as confronting an audience of voracious gossips, would it? Surely I could borrow a smidgen of Charley's mental tenacity and overcome my reluctance to make an appearance and give them my felicitations?

"I'll go," I decided. "I'll attend the Percevals' anniversary luncheon."

"There's no pressing obligation for you to be there, Lucia," Charley insisted. "It would be far less awkward if you were to decline the invitation —Tallis too—and send your regrets. They'll understand."

I looked between Charley and Tallis. "So you're suggesting that Tallis and I skulk about in hiding like lepers? Last night, you were urging me to plunge off a cliff."

"Charley?" Matthias arched a brow. Tilly gave Charley a well-worn reproving shake of her head.

"Second opinion," Charley muttered. "Biding time."

I could not help a tiny smile. It was not often I got a chance to goad Charley. "Give me a good reason why I shouldn't throw myself over right now."

"The Percevals said to invite your fiancé to the luncheon, Lucia. It wasn't clear whether they are aware... Mrs. Draycott will be at the luncheon. Mrs. Draycott may not have told anyone the news she had from New York. It's unlikely the same intelligence would have spread as quickly to the others. But if we all turn up to the luncheon and they notice that Vincent isn't there, they may ask questions." Charley's expression was unamused. "Are you sure you are ready to take that plunge?"

"Oh." I lost whatever small reserve of false bravado I had cobbled together from Charley's leftover fairy dust. The storm crashed over me again. I was engulfed by mingled panic and indecision. That was the great unanswerable question that continued to torment me, wasn't it? Was I ready?

"Where's the harm in making a public appearance?" Tallis said. "Why not turn up together to the Perceval luncheon? The scoundrel's reputation hardly deserves protection from the truth. As for the patriarchs—"

"Is that what you'd be willing to offer, Lucia," Charley asked, "in answer to those questions? The full truth instead of a half-truth or a plausible lie—and all the associated repercussions thereof?"

"You're suggesting a lie?"

"No, I'm asking you to be ready before you leap," Charley said. "It's a long way down, but as long as you're prepared, you'll land on your feet either way. Are you ready?"

Swimming to break through the oppressive weight pressing down on my chest, the weight of the future, I realized that Charley was insisting on giving me a choice—holding the gates open until I could catch up—and marshaling me into a suit of armor. And I wondered, amidst my panic, at how the paradox persisted: how could anyone have ever thought her anarchic or reckless?

"We have a lot to discuss before a single person leaves this room," said Matthias.

"Do we?" said Charley. "Lucia's decision is hers to be made in her own good time and not any sooner, certainly not to satisfy others' curiosity. If something must be told to the masses, then the bare bones should suffice: fiancé number one discovered to be a fortune-hunter and turfed out, fiancé number two an old acquaintance, nice enough boy, traveled all the way from New York at daddy's bidding, but that is no reason for Miss Bernhardt to disrupt her Grand Tour and she is heading off to European shores to put this unpleasant episode behind her and resume her holiday as intended. The end. A word in Mrs. Draycott's ear should do the trick. The only thing Lucia needs to do is tell other people she would prefer not to talk about it."

Charley's contention sparked a good deal of debate but it took little more than a few minutes for Tallis and Matthias to conclude that Charley's suggestions were sensible ones. Tilly, for her part, was soundly behind Charley on this vote; not a single sniff of disapprobation came from her way.

"Do you still want to attend the Percevals' luncheon?" Charley asked.

"I have to start somewhere, don't I?" I said. "You said small steps."

"All right. Just give your left earlobe a pull if Tallis puts his foot in it and we'll march in, chop his head off, and rescue you."

Tallis did not bother silencing his snort.

Before anyone could get a further word in, Charley promptly jumped to her feet in a signal that the meeting was over, and Tilly banished everyone from the suite so that I could dress for the luncheon. As they left the room, Tallis and Matthias and Charley appeared to be readying to carry out a continuation of their earlier encounter—that is to say, Tallis and Matthias clearly thought that they had unfinished business with Charley and Charley was determinedly avoiding that discussion.

"Your mother's diamond necklace is safe," Tilly divulged in a whisper even though we were alone in the suite. "But Miss Charley is shifting it to a new hiding place just in case."

"Is that all that Charley is up to?" I whispered back.

Tilly shrugged fatalistically.

No, of course not, what a redundant question.

And then I remembered that I had again missed telling Charley about James Dorsey in Assuan. I told Tilly.

Tilly's eyes darkened. "Miss Charley is aware," she said.

"How do you know, Tilly?"

"He has been sending messages." Tilly's mouth compressed into a very thin, very disapproving line.

Tallis was waiting for us outside the suite to escort us down to the restaurant where the Percevals were holding the luncheon.

"Did you and Charley resolve your argument?" I asked him.

Tallis gave me an odd look. "Charley doesn't argue," he said. "Charley pounds others into submission to following her edicts."

"So you lost the argument?"

"We've agreed to a difference of opinion. Charley said that if I pass the luncheon gauntlet today unscathed, and you and Tilly do not object, it would be all right for me to join your merry ragtag band on your return to the Continent," Tallis told me as we made our way down to the foyer. "It would corroborate your story."

"It's very kind of you to offer, but... Wouldn't you be bored, Tallis? We're just going to finish our Grand Tour. Unless you have an interest in being a regular tourist traveling around Italy and the rest of Europe, which I imagine you've probably seen already, there really isn't a need for you to wait on us."

"As a matter of fact, I haven't. And if the rumors are to be believed, you and Charley seem to have had a riot of a time playing tourist. Most fellows don't come anywhere near that sort of fun on their continental travels... You don't seem to mind Matthias tagging along."

"You should probably ask Matthias how easy it has been for him to locate and catch us since we left London. Charley prefers to be...elusive. She generally considers everyone besides Tilly and me to be an impediment to that elusiveness."

"Evidently. But you aren't running away from the same thing that Charley is running from, are you?"

What had the Grand Tour, all the running away, been about? Prevarication, procrastination, an untimely but unavoidable summons, enforced servitude to the hunting of a suitable husband, a way station, a reprieve, an escape, a last hurrah, limbo—or something else? Tallis's question made me pause and wonder. It had begun as one or more of those things but something more had emerged or been collected along the way like the little souvenirs we had found on the sandy shores of the Cote d'Azur or in the open air markets of Cairo. Somewhere between crossing the Atlantic in obedience to my parents' wishes and tailing Charley in running from the telegrams which pursued her, I had come to view the world differently, to see the grandeur and wilderness and terror and cruelty and possibility, to wonder whether Charley was really running away or actually running towards something, whether the things that pursued her were not so dissimilar to the monsters I feared, and, although we went about it in a different fashion (I, blindfolded and hobbling behind on crutches, Charley riding at full charge with lance in hand), whether the things that Charley chased were not also the things that I longed for—hope, spacious freedom, a future beyond the familiar cage.

But would Tallis understand? His question, some quality in the tone in which he had asked it, caught my attention. "What do you think Charley is running from?" I asked.

"It struck me that Charley isn't the type to bolt from a matter of a personal or romantic nature," Tallis mused. "I wondered whether it might have something to do with Montrose."

His words felt like the first juddering tremors of an earthquake.

"I heard some talk—not your common tea salon gossip—shop talk," Tallis continued. "Well, bankers' gossip, really, whispered in confidence within certain banking circles. A possible question mark over Montrose's continuing solvency. Only a whisper, but I've never heard Montrose's name brought up before with regard to anything of that nature. It's always had a rock solid reputation."

I turned to Tilly. Tilly's paled white face looked blankly back at me.

Tallis seemed to become aware of the effect of his remarks. "Charley hasn't mentioned it?"

Piercing shards of memory came flying back to me: the financial figures on the slips of paper inside a book with a list of names on the reverse side, Charley's cryptic remarks and even more mysterious absences, Charley's secret London whirl, the reams of telegram correspondence, the obsessive consumption of newspapers, Diego de Almadén, Nicholas Masterson, the wagers with Woolf Barnato, a meeting with Sir Victor Sassoon, the deliveries from French notaries, oh God, the sale of Esperance and Runnymede... "Hypothetically, if Montrose were in such a predicament, I would not be able to do much anyway since the reins would not be in my hands yet. The best I could do, hypothetically, would be to stay informed until it legally became my problem. And—perhaps—hypothetically—by that time I will have found an aristocratic prize to rescue me. A solvent one." Oh God, oh God, twice, thrice, eternally blind I had been—I still could not believe it—it seemed impossible that anyone would be able to joke so carelessly while standing that close to the knife's edge—I could not conceive of the magnitude of what Charley had taken upon her shoulders!

As though our thoughts had summoned her, Charley appeared like a djinn from a lamp, coming across the hotel foyer. She was hatless and scarfless for once. Her pale linen dress faded away in the fire of incandescent jewels: her earlobes and hair blazed with earrings and a choker necklace that she wore as a headband studded with diamonds and fat sapphires in a recurring geometric design of such imperious austerity that it defied any beholder to bring a charge of ostentation. Charley turned heads in the foyer as she passed queenly by.

When Charley had mentioned painting a new target, I had not quite expected this. From Tallis's expression, his thoughts were of a similar vein. Tilly, in contrast, was neither surprised nor shocked by this incarnation of Charley's but she did seem torn between worry and quiet pride.

I pried my stunned eyes away from Charley's coronet of spangled stars. "I don't think that is a good idea," I told her, indicating her adornment. Charley hardly needed one more worry added to her mountain.

Charley touched an earring and made it flutter and wink and flash indigo fire even more blindingly with the movement. "You don't approve? I borrowed these from Tilly. She liked the color of the pretty Ceylon sapphires. M. Chaumet designed the set specially."

"When did—"

"You probably don't recall. Tilly ordered them from London, but she never found an occasion to take them out before we left the city."

Tilly promptly confirmed this. (Tilly was being expertly tutored in becoming a consummate liar by Charley.) But Charley was wrong: I did remember London and Chaumet. When I thought of how far back the troubles of Montrose stretched and how constant and boundless had been Charley's generosity despite them, I felt ill.

"I don't think it will work, Charley. I don't want to put you in—"

"Let's just see if the experiment works, shall we?" Charley replied. "Are you ready?"

I could not help the churning, knotted queasiness in my stomach at the thought of walking into the restaurant but somehow since Tallis had uttered his revelation, it had whined and diminished to such a degree as to be a bare ghost of its former self, slinking off in disgrace at the appearance of a bigger, scarier monster. If the troubles at Montrose could not make Charley blink, surely I could face one innocuous luncheon?

"Shouldn't we wait for Matthias? I thought he was with you."

"He was called away." Charley showed her dimples. "I was saved from a perfectly stupefying harangue from Mr. Vandermeer by a telegram."

I was not able to appreciate Charley's humor. I was beginning to form the wisdom that nothing good ever came of a telegram. I wanted desperately to fire questions at Charley, to launch into an interrogation about Montrose but the opportunity closed as quickly as it had appeared.

Our steps had already brought us to the restaurant where the Percevals and other guests were gathered. We had no choice but to exchange enthusiastic greetings and give them our good wishes for their anniversary. Everything about the luncheon gathering had been made that much more warm and festive because someone had emptied the hotel's cellars and anonymously showered upon the Percevals an endless supply of celebratory champagne. Mrs. Perceval, arm in arm with Mrs. Draycott, winked and asked us to pass on everyone's appreciation and thanks to Mr. Vandermeer. Charley smiled sweetly and promised we would. From the moment we arrived, she and Tilly had been busy. Immediately after the exchange of greetings and introductions—Tallis had been introduced as another globetrotting New Yorker—they had whisked Mrs. Draycott aside and Charley had come back bearing her polite, engaging public smile. I did not know what tale had been relayed to Mrs. Draycott or what Mrs. Draycott passed on to the others, I was not entirely certain that Charley had not gilded the lily, but nobody asked after Vincent or asked me where my fiancé was.

By that time, I could barely give a care. How easily the terrors had melted away. It had hardly seemed worth the terrible fear earlier instilled in me. My heart pounded, bursting with impatient questions, as my mind beat an anxious tattoo. Montrose, Montrose, Montrose. Why was Fate continually conspiring to delay me from speaking to Charley about urgently important things, why were circumstances continually overtaking me?

We had just finished our aperitifs and were making our way to be seated when another set of circumstances intervened.

I spotted Matthias entering the restaurant under the striped Moorish archway. He greeted the hosts and other guests amicably but something about his bearing seemed tense and strained, and when he came up to us, there was an almighty frown line dissecting his brow.

"I had a telegram from your aunt, Charley," Matthias began.

"My aunt?" Charley repeated. "Cabling you? Is Aunt Merry—"

"She apologized. She didn't know how else to reach you on matters of urgency. Diego's son, Dominic, has been arrested on charges of embezzlement and theft. Diego apparently refused to wire you about it himself and he and Dominic refused to let her or anyone else interfere or disturb you. Your aunt tried to appeal to Diego's wife, to Dominic's siblings, the entire family, but they were no more forthcoming. Your aunt seemed to think that you would know what to do to help. Charley, why would—"

Charley rose from the table and stomped out of the restaurant, a tiny, fierce whirlwind of indignation. The sudden disruption upset the conversations of the other diners and we tried to allay their concern. A while later, we apologized and excused ourselves and slipped out of the restaurant.

We looked around everywhere for Charley. By chance, as we were passing the lobby area overlooking the terrace, we caught a million scintillations of light, blue and white fire, that seemed to have been sent from somewhere outside on the grounds. Diamonds and sapphires came immediately to mind. We followed the coruscating flashes and eventually spied a silhouette of her, refracted manifold times in the window panes opening out to the terrace, a simmering flame against the background of the serene blue Nile.

Charley remained upright and motionless in all of the window panes. I thought of the howls of a wounded animal, a rendition of torment that would haunt me to the day I die, but Charley's silhouette did not move and no sound returned to us through the glass.

Anxiously, we waited. The manner of Charley's reaction held us back from going out to her.

When her temper had cooled down sufficiently for her to form coherent speech once more, Charley returned inside, every tight, earnest step clicking sharply against the ground in barely leashed anger and resolution, a silvery-cold fury burning in her eyes like twin stars, brighter than her earrings and crown of diamonds and sapphires.

"You can tell Aunt Merry not to worry, to ignore the De Almadén idiots and just telephone Samuel Bayard," said Charley, "and to tell Bayard—and Diego—'Cry havoc'. They'll understand. And to contact Samuel Bayard if she has any further concerns. I shall cable Bayard and Diego directly with my additional instructions. Lucia, I'm dreadfully sorry to abandon you without giving more advanced warning but I must return to New York post haste. Tilly and Tallis can—"

"What the devil—"

"Charley?"

"Miss Charley!"

"Charley, what's going on?"

A chorus of voices rained down on Charley.

"Diego and his son are being martyrs is what is going on. They're trying to protect and spare me and fight this on their own. I can't believe they dragged the others into this. Idiots."

"Charley, that doesn't explain anything."

"My uncle has let slip the dogs of war," said Charley. "It's only polite that I meet him halfway."

"Halfway?" I asked. A chaos of pale fear trembled and quaked inside me.

Matthias, however, seemed to be having a quiet epiphany.

"Montrose," he murmured, and something else even more softly which I thought sounded like "Pegasus".

"The jig is up, I suppose." Charley sighed. "There is such a lot to explain but I beg your indulgence to postpone it to another occasion. Forgive me, I cannot afford to dally. It really is critical that I make arrangements to get back to New York and sort out the De Almadéns' idiocy right away."

Before we could question her further or offer our assistance, Charley spun away in her furious whirlwind, to issue commands and send cables and pluck the strings of a thousand plots that would send the world twitching and vibrating in her wake.

Beside me, Matthias cursed under his breath. He recognized as well as I did what was coming next.

Cry havoc, she had said, burning in icy containment. Charley was riding once more into battle.

I turned around to Matthias who was standing impassively still as if he had been frozen into stone, brooding after the direction Charley had vanished.

"Matthias?"

I was momentarily taken aback when his gaze slid back to us. His body might have been a monolith but if his harsh expression was any indication, his mental faculties were far from quiet; they tossed and foamed and roiled, a cauldron of seething activity.

"You must know more," I said. "Tell me what you know."

"Not here," Matthias answered. He looked about us and indicated a deserted corner off the main foyer, secluded enough that our conversation could not be overheard. We trooped over towards it, a sad little procession.

Matthias glanced at Tallis. Tallis said: "Is it about Montrose? I heard my father speak of it at the bank. So it's true then?"

"I don't think that Charley would want this to be aired but since most of it is or will shortly become public knowledge..." Matthias drew a harshened breath. "Montrose has historically been privately run and has never sought financing above its existing credit facilities to cover its working capital and liabilities. The arrest of Dominic de Almadén has blown that record to pieces. The books are awash with red. Montrose's current chairman, Charley's uncle, Nicholas Masterson, claims that Dominic, who has been working as an assistant to the treasurer at Montrose, is responsible for the parlous condition of the group's finances through years of previously undiscovered mismanagement, secret dishonest dealings and widespread embezzlement."

"How could Dominic have had the authority or connections to—"

"It's a trumped up charge. Montrose has been under Nicholas Masterson's chairmanship since his brother's death. Charley's uncle needed a fall guy and a reason to bring Charley back to New York. However, since he could not attack Diego de Almadén, who he needs to continue running the businesses, Dominic got the short straw." Something dark and frightening passed through Matthias's eyes. "As everyone in New York is so keen to relay, Charley's inheritance is tied to the fortunes of the Montrose businesses. What is not general knowledge or rumor—what I managed to confirm with Aunt Merry today—is that when Charley came into her inheritance, controlling interests in the Montrose businesses previously held in trust by the joint custodians and trustees of the Masterson trust and other persons was extinguished and ceded to Charley. No new contracts, accounts, transactions, expenditure, loans, dividend payments, or any other Montrose business may be entered into, opened, revised, amended, revoked, terminated, transferred, paid out or otherwise dealt with, without Charley's signature and at her express instruction. That is why Montrose is in such a dire state. Nicholas Masterson had lost his authority since Charley's last birthday, only he didn't notice until his petty cash dried up and the creditors began knocking at his door." He exhaled. "Didn't you also wonder why Charley has been so secretive and elusive? Even though Nicholas Masterson is still chairman, nothing at Montrose can get done without Charley—nothing officially anyway—who can say what deals he has managed to make under the table. He has no formal power, and drawing Charley back to New York by threatening Dominic—which the De Almadéns tried to hide from Charley—is the only leverage he has at present to try to change that."

"Charley has been on the run from New York since..." Tallis wrinkled his brow in tallying up the months. "Why would Charley let Montrose be run to ruin, especially when her inheritance is so inextricably linked to Montrose's fortunes?"

"I don't believe that Charley, undoubtedly with Diego's help, intends for Montrose to be run to ruin," said Matthias.

No, I didn't either. "Are you scheming a coup with Diego?" "What a good idea, Lucia." Oh Charley. She had not been running from New York for merely the duration of our Grand Tour, as Tallis thought. Whatever gunpowder, treason, and plot that Charley had planned, it had been in the making for well over a year.

"Will returning to New York hurt Charley?"

"It wasn't planned. And Diego and his family went to great lengths to stop her uncle's tactics from succeeding. So yes, the gloves are off now. The casualty rate will depend on what Charley is brewing right now. And her uncle." Matthias scowled in frustration. "Nicholas Masterson is desperate. There is no telling what else a desperate man will do. And it doesn't sound like he fights clean."

"Can Godeffroy's help in relaxing Montrose's credit terms in any way?"

I asked.

Matthias looked sharply at me. "How do you know about Godeffroy's relationship with Montrose? Did Charley tell you?"

Belatedly, I remembered where I had obtained knowledge of who Montrose's bankers were. "She might've mentioned it once."

"Lucia."

"It's just a question. I don't know anything more. Charley didn't tell me anything."

"Montrose's line of credit with Godeffroy's is about the only thing keeping the operations afloat. It isn't close to default. I don't know what has been going on within Montrose's treasury but it seems like that credit facility and the servicing of its repayments has been specially protected, as if it has been quarantined from the rest of Montrose's problems. I suspect Charley and Diego de Almadén are the only two people who know how that is even possible given the group's lack of funds and negative net cash flow position. Montrose's problem debt is to other creditors. Long before Charley legally assumed control over the Montrose businesses, Nicholas Masterson had apparently gone outside the normal treasury channels at Montrose and borrowed money from various lenders, presumably because it would not have been allowed through the usual channels under Diego's watch. Those borrowings are what is crippling Montrose."

"Charley and Diego wouldn't let Montrose fall. It's her father's legacy."

"I didn't think so either at first," said Matthias. "But I didn't think Charley would ever put the houses her father built for her mother on the market either. And it does seem like it's Charley's intention to let the Montrose group fall. If it isn't, she's cutting it awfully close to the line. Diego was hamstrung under her uncle's chairmanship of Montrose, but since Charley took over the reins, the situation at Montrose has not improved. Her inaction to date makes it seem like Charley has deliberately let Montrose stall and dwindle. There are still some things that I don't fully understand, still some missing pieces without which things simply don't make sense... Charley has been liquidating properties and holdings left, right and center. Villa Mirabeau was one of them. Esperance and Runnymede were the mere tip of the iceberg. They came from the portion bequeathed to her under her parents' trust, not from Montrose's books. But instead of increasing the trust balances, Aunt Merry said that the balances are heavily diminished from what Charley should've been entitled to as her inheritance. By New York standards, she'd no longer be considered an heiress but a pauper. Where have the assets and money gone? Not into Montrose. There is something else that... Charley is plotting something but... I don't want to speculate too much before I am certain of the facts." He looked down at the palms of his unclenched fists which he had unconsciously squeezed bloodless. "I've already instructed my lawyers and New York contact to tackle this matter regarding Dominic de Almadén's arrest. It's going to be a bloodbath when Charley arrives in New York... I'd better go send those cables Charley wanted to Aunt Merry and Samuel Bayard. God, it's just as well that Charley has a Bayard on retainer!"

"Are you returning to New York, Matthias?"

Matthias nodded. "Charley doesn't really understand the meaning of impossible, does she? But even with Diego de Almadén and Samuel Bayard on her side, I'm not sure that she'll get through this alive. I need to do what I can. What will you do about the rest of the Grand Tour? Head back to London and join Ginny?"

I turned to the group of us left behind. Tallis was shaking his head, still awestruck by what had been set in motion. Tilly... I wondered if I looked as horrified as Tilly.

"Tilly, under the circumstances, you should..."

Tilly's eyes were fraught with rue and fearful concern as she shook her head. "I'm sorry, Miss Lucia. I've been instructed to stay with you."

"But that was before, Tilly. Whatever instructions Charley gave earlier, I think they must certainly be overruled now. There is no way that Charley is sailing back to New York on her own."

"Are you sure about that, Lucia?" Matthias asked. "I think Charley would raise object—"

"What Charley doesn't find out until it's too late to push me off the ship won't hurt her, will it?"

Matthias accepted this without further question, but Tallis asked, astounded: "You're heading back too?"

I would not admit the terror that seized me. I would not be infirm of purpose. "Charley's played a lone hand long enough."

"I'll see to booking the passages," Matthias said simply and headed away to match actions to his words.

"I'd better go see to booking mine too," Tallis said after some thought.

Tilly and I paused in the midst of conferring about the necessary arrangements for returning to New York without Charley's knowledge.

"Tallis?"

"I know when a party is over." The corners of Tallis's mouth turned up slightly. "And when another one is about to start. The Mastersons don't do things by halves, do they? It'd be a shame to miss out."

"There's really no need for—"

"Matthias has told us his line of attack, but it isn't clear what yours is." Tallis's face and voice were light and smiling but his eyes were not. "Tell me, Lucia, how exactly will your presence back in New York help Charley beyond the provision of moral support?"

It had been an inchoate idea at most, to which I was planning to give quiet consideration over the course of the journey back, buried alongside the dark rumbling dread and fear which still fought to rise into the light of day. Would it seem flimsy and flawed under Tallis's independent scrutiny?

Just going through the motions—I reminded myself, adding my own qualifications—finding a worthy purpose, living bravely. "Tallis, your father's bank, North American Charter Bank of New York, is one of the creditors to Montrose's bad debts, isn't it? That is how you came to hear the talk about Montrose?"

"I... Possibly. Probably. Why?"

"If I am to return to New York an obedient daughter and fiancée, there are certain conditions that I want satisfied first."

Tallis's forehead wrinkled in perplexity for several moments until his eyes suddenly widened in shock.

"You're going to try to negotiate with my father?" Tallis gaped at me.

"And mine. And my...and with Vincent. They can have their merger smooth and scandal-free or... New York loves a scandal."

Tilly clasped my arm in alarm and worry, shaking her head vigorously. "To bargain with the devil, Tilly, one has to grow horns," I told her.

Tallis, too, shook his head in disbelief. "My God, and everyone always considered Charley the hellion! Is it some sort of competition—who can plunge off a cliff first? You need to think this through, Lucia. You can't unring the bell once— Didn't we just avert a scandal regarding Faneuil? And now you're courting this calamity? I think Charley would be the first one to tell you that it's a terrible, crazy idea. You've no idea how this will go and whether this suicidal mission will even succeed. My father's bank isn't the only creditor that Montrose has to worry about. Ask Matthias, he'll tell you how—"

Tallis's words solidified my resolution. "I'm not going to be telling Matthias just yet—or Charley—and neither will you. I have two elements of advantage—surprise and a stake as a pawn in the merger between First National Bank of Manhattan and North American Charter Bank of New York. I didn't ask to be a bargaining chip but since the role has been allotted to me, I will play it. Don't prevent me from being useful to my friend, Tallis."

"Miss Lucia," Tilly pleaded.

Tallis pinched and kneaded the bridge of his nose. "I'll contact my father," he said finally.

"No, Tallis! Why would you—"

"You can't do this on your own," Tallis said in resignation. "And it will help to find out as much as possible about the factual details such as exactly what the terms of the loan are. And you said 'fiancée'. Which necessarily implies one half of a pair."

"No! This doesn't involve you. My conditions are the price for my compliance and cooperation only, not yours. You are a free agent. You are not a part of this."

"I beg to differ."

"Tallis—"

"Let this be my score settled with Charley. And as I said before, I'd hate to miss out on a good party."

"What score? Have you lost your mind? This is serious, Tallis, not a game. The repercussions for your—"

"Pot and kettle, Lucia. Look, I'm a reliable company player. You can count on me to say all my lines and laugh and cry at all the right times."

"Are you and your father even on speaking terms at present?"

"No. But I'm always game for thumbing my nose at my father. You'll see how much fun it can be. How about it?"

Tallis was mad, absolutely mad. Tilly concurred, adding that I was cut from the same cloth and that she had not been brought on to this Grand Tour to be an accomplice to such lunacy and it most certainly was not included in amongst Miss Charley's last set of instructions. But since we were both feeling so helpless and anxious to be useful—and beggars could not be choosers, Charley needed as many allies as we could find—I was able to wear Tilly down. Matthias had just given us a tour of Charley's troubles with Montrose as if we were picking apart lukewarm entrails. What was there to hold us back from divvying up between us the chances of the Masterson empire and her future against her enemies? Gradually, Tallis and Tilly and I came to an accord and we all agreed that our plan needed to be kept a secret.

We were still discussing details when a hotel attendant interrupted us and advised that a young boy had arrived at the hotel entrance and was waiting with a message that he would only deliver personally into my hands.

"I won't be long," I told Tilly and Tallis and urged them to brook no delay in getting on with our plan.

We dispersed with our allocated tasks and an agreement to congregate again in an hour's time.

I went to the front entrance of the hotel. The messenger looked like one of the countless friendly, laughing donkey boys we had seen in Luxor and Assuan. He conscientiously handed to me the missive and thanked me when I passed him bakshish in return.

It was a brief note, a scrap of paper covered in a rapid hand, but my musings over telegrams could just as easily have applied. Nothing good came of it.

37

CHARLOTTE:

"CHARLEY DEAREST WHATEVER TRANSPIRES THE MOST IMPORTANT THING IS THAT YOU COME HOME TO ME SAFE YOUR LOVING AUNT MEREDITH"

I stared at the telegram.

"More bad news, Charley?"

"No!" I crumpled the telegram into a ball.

"Charley?"

My chin snapped up and I met Matthias's keen amber brown eyes, so light that they seemed almost golden, weighted with concern and a weariness that had not been there before.

"Those are tears, Charley. What's happened?"

"Nothing." I brushed Matthias's hands away. "Nothing has happened. Nothing has changed."

"Charley."

"I'm stuck here, half a world away, and powerless—utterly useless. The thought of Dominic makes me shake with rage. I— Please, Matthias, just let me be."

Matthias's earnest regard did not leave me but he eased back a little. "You've sent your telegrams?" he asked.

"Yes."

"I've alerted my contacts in New York. They are reaching out to Samuel Bayard and Diego. My—"

"You shouldn't— I—" I couldn't speak past the lump in my throat.

"You'd better not start lecturing me on hats, Charley. Just accept this as the price for your stubbornness. You should've told me sooner and let me help. Aunt Merry—"

"I know." Each word cost effort. I pulled myself together. This was no time to disassemble. "Thank you—but no."

"Charley, no one is going to let you or Dominic step into that ring with your uncle alone," Matthias insisted. "Lucia has decided to return to New York instead of continuing on with the Grand Tour."

"No! No, no, no, no, no! Of all the— The one thing, the single thing— I'm going to strangle Tallis!"

Matthias tried to pacify and steady me but I ducked and evaded his clutches. As I marched back towards the foyer, a litany of scenarios paraded through my head. Not one of them ended happily. We should have just stepped onto a boat bound for the Far East and not looked back.

"Charley, wait!"

A large hand closed around my wrist as I rounded a corner and came upon Tallis himself approaching from the opposite direction in comparable haste. I narrowly avoided a collision with Tallis but in falling back, caught within Matthias's tight grip, we both stumbled and nearly toppled over.

"Tallis, you—"

"Have you seen Lucia?"

Tallis and I pulled up short and stared at each other in dawning realization and horror.

"You've lost Lucia?"

I was glad Matthias asked the question. I did not trust myself to be free of rising hysteria.

"One of the hotel staff came and said that a message for her had been hand delivered to the front entrance of the hotel. She was only meant to have been gone briefly to collect it. She isn't in the restaurant. Tilly has gone up to double check the suites in case Lucia returned. I didn't want to jump to conclusions, but..." Tallis looked like he was close to tearing his hair out in agitation. "It isn't too soon to start questioning people, is it?"

We began methodically to interrogate the living daylights out of the hotel staff and everyone within the near vicinity who might have seen or come across Lucia in the brief interlude between the time we had left the Percevals' luncheon and our reconvening in the foyer. The attendant who had advised Lucia of the hand delivered message said that he had seen the American lady passing through the foyer on the way to the front entrance.

We were in the middle of questioning the attendant in the foyer about the source of the message and the messenger boy when Mr. Tainstel-Tarsted came hurrying in. He hailed us from afar and asked if the Percevals' luncheon was still in progress; he was unforgivably late but hoped to still give his wishes to the couple. He had lost track of time at the tourist offices, organizing an excursion to Wadi Halfa and had then been stuck in traffic and then happened to run into the excellent dragoman from an earlier expedition on the Corniche just outside the hotel and engaged him again for Wadi Halfa. We asked him if he had seen Lucia, not really expecting anything. Mr. Tainstel-Tarsted surprised us by replying quite readily that yes, of course, as he had been coming back to the Cataract Hotel, he had spotted Lucia outside the hotel entrance, talking to the doorman, presumably waiting for a taxi.

The doorman had been next on our list of interviewees. After the conversation with Mr. Tainstel-Tarsted, methodical went out the window. We bolted to the front entrance to question the man.

The doorman said the young boy who had brought the message had delivered it personally to the American lady and that immediately after the American lady had read it, she had asked for transport to be obtained for her. The doorman had not noticed anything amiss. The American lady had not appeared distressed but had chatted to the doorman about how hot it was in Assuan, and how she hoped the traffic would not be bad and that she hoped to return in time to join her friend Lottie for a nice cool drink on the terrace, before getting into a cab. The cab had left along the Corniche, the doorman had not caught the destination she told the cab driver.

Had it been a coincidence? I did not draw the others' attention to it before I could give it proper thought although I had noticed that Tilly's expression had momentarily wavered a little before becoming remarkably quiet.

We were left in a perplexed quandary. It did not seem as if something untoward had occurred and yet all four of us were absolutely certain that Lucia would not have wandered out into the unknown alone—well, that certainty was smashed to pieces—but we were certain that she most definitely would not have done so without leaving word, more detailed word, of her whereabouts. Ought we have called in the authorities?

"Yes," Matthias said.

On that we were agreed too.

It bothered me that Lucia had talked, without exciting notice, about the heat and cool refreshments with the doorman whilst waiting for a cab to an unknown destination after receiving a mysterious note. It seemed on the surface to have been a casual, innocuous conversation but the more I turned it over in my mind, the odder it seemed, especially in connection with the name Lottie. I asked Tilly and Tallis if they had discussed anything prior to Lucia's disappearance which may have been related to or prompted the peculiar exchange with the doorman. They said that they had not.

Matthias notified the hotel management and had them call in the police again. They were initially pleasant and polite and although it was clear that they were skeptical of Lucia being missing, given the earlier episode of the intruder in her suite and the fact that she was a foreigner, and an American at that, they made perfunctory inquiries. As the hours passed and they could not locate the boy messenger or driver of the taxi cab Lucia had taken or

Lucia herself, their inquiries, after regular prompting from us, began to assume a slightly more earnest tone.

When a message arrived at the hotel very much later that night, the police had further grounds to doubt that our concern was warranted. The message was delivered by another young boy who could give no distinctive or helpful information regarding who had instructed him to the delivery, merely that he had been given the note and payment by a man who had hailed him in the street. The message consisted of a single piece of paper written in a familiar hand.

"Charley, I was invited to afternoon tea with old friends of my parents' and am staying overnight. They have asked me to stay longer with them. It is so agreeable here, I am going to accept their invitation. Please give Lottie my apologies for missing our shopping expedition this afternoon. I lost track of the time! I shall make it up to her: her favorite Peche Melba ice cream will be my treat the next time we go out for iced coffee. Lucia"

Tilly could not hold back a surprised gasp of dismay. The second mention of the name Lottie turned the blood in my veins to ice.

"Who is this Lottie?" Tallis asked.

I looked at Tilly whose eyes were assailed by a palpable dread. I looked at Matthias: emotion scourged and darkened his amber gaze. My own fears solidified. My Chaumet necklace-headband and earrings weighed like lead. Too late, too late.

"We need to contact the American Consulate. Lucia has been abducted."

"You deducted that from the name Lottie?" exclaimed Tallis.

A mere name. Lucia must have pried it from Tilly. That she had used it as a mayday call... My list of failings grew longer.

"It's too long a story to explain but the relevant thing is that Lottie does not exist. There was no afternoon shopping expedition." I thought about my uneasiness regarding Lucia's conversation with the doorman. "I don't know what drew Lucia to leave so abruptly but she must've been under some sort of duress or feared surveillance and discovery by her abductors to have to resort to a surreptitious means of communicating with us. I don't think this is the only clue Lucia has tried to leave us. Peche Melba ice cream and iced coffee. As far as I am aware, the only place that Lucia has had Peche Melba ice cream and iced coffee is at Groppi's in Cairo."

Tilly nodded mutely.

"I don't believe Lucia is in Assuan anymore."

38

LUCIA:

I became aware of sounds and movement and a darkness which would not lift before my mind could scramble to make sense. A tightness around my temples, the feel of cloth—ah, a blindfold—that explained why the blackness stayed when I opened my eyes. I tried to feel my way around in the darkness and realized that I could not move my hands or legs because they were bound. My lips felt parched around another length of rough cloth.

"She's waking up." A deep gravelly voice penetrated my woolly-headed darkness, the same one that had cursed when it became evident that my captured fiancé had been mistaken, that I was not in possession of, and in fact had no access to, my mother's diamond necklace. There was no face attached to that voice yet. He was simply the bringer of sudden darkness, he belonged to the shadows. All I knew was the timbre of his irascible temper, the strength of his bindings, and that he spoke English like a native. I was almost able to smile at the fact that I was experiencing the same difficulty that Tallis had in identifying an accent beyond it being one spoken by an Englishman.

Longer vibrations of movement approached, and then a familiar faint sweet smell enveloped my nostrils, and the sensation of falling. The darkness swirled and became giddily more absolute as I tried to remember when I had previously encountered it, tried to hold onto the memory of finding the street address, the nondescript house door, the patch of fabric stuffed in front of my face oozing the same sickly sweet odor which suddenly turned the day to night.

I drifted, dipping between darknesses and foggy dreams and memories.

39

CHARLOTTE:

"Goddamnit, Charley, you can't accept! It's got to be a trap. You'd be walking into the lion's den and there is nothing to stop them from taking you hostage too."

40

LUCIA:

A stiff, numbing ache permeating from my torso to my limbs bothered me enough to gradually bring me awake.

"Hello?"

Or maybe it was the low, urgent, ragged whisper coming from somewhere close by which guided me to find my way back to consciousness. I opened my eyes, expecting complete darkness, but found that my gaze met dim shadows instead of a uniform void. My blindfold must have shifted. I let my gaze trace the variations in the shadows as I wiggled around in the chair to which I was bound to try to move my fingers about and feel what my surroundings were like. Between the little that I could make out from my touch and limited vision, I was in a room with dusty wooden floors and plastered walls. Quite bare. Slivers of filtered light penetrated the dimness, perhaps because the windows had been boarded up. There was only my chair and nothing else around me.

"Hello?"

I turned my head, even though I could barely see a thing, following the direction of the voice. I knew that voice... My eyes observed the same dim, shadowy, bare room... Until they fell upon a shadow that moved.

"Hello? Please speak if you can hear me."

"Vincent?"

It was a little difficult to speak around the gag but it too had worked itself looser from being wetted by my saliva and movement. It must have been an afterthought after the chloroform or perhaps my abductor had forgotten to take it off. Vincent seemed to be without one. Were there alternative methods used to keep him compliantly silent? It would not help to delve too much into those thoughts.

"Lucia? Is it really you? I didn't think that you would..."

I tried to edge closer but found I could not move very far with my legs tied down to the chair which was stubbornly immobile.

"I can't move. They have tied me up. What about you?" Vincent seemed to be similarly tethered in his corner of the room. "Are you hurt? Did they... Have they done anything to you since you were captured?"

"The sooner I get out of here, the sooner I can forget this ever happened! Did you bring them what they wanted?"

"Your note sounded urgent and it didn't mention the necklace. I thought... Well, I thought if they were after me and I came to them, there wouldn't be any point in keeping both of us captive."

"We're still alive. They must think that there is still hope that you can get it."

I had not answered his note expecting any burning terms of love. It had mostly been compelled by a sense of duty, of nostalgic obligation to the past, but that did not stop his words from being a jarring reminder of why things had come to pass as they had. Vincent was not his usual suavely turned out self. There had been a hint of the panic in the note that I had received. His quailing voice now confirmed it, pained and tormented and mortally afraid, carrying an undertone of despairing frustration and maybe a little guilt mixed within the urgency. If there had been moments when I had questioned why I had let myself be caught up in this jam after what had passed and ended between us, this answered my question. Vincent had been tangled in this web by virtue of being my (sometime) fiancé. I—and my mother's diamonds—were responsible for putting him in danger.

"We have to find a way to escape, Lucia!"

How strange it was to face Vincent, even though I could not see him, and hear, almost smell, his terror, and come to the astonishing realization that he was alone. I was not afraid. The past days' slurry of acute suffering and fear of what awaited back in New York had drained the faculty out of me leaving only a tiny trickling thread of anxiety, of uncertainty regarding what else could happen, but not the intense fear that I ought to have felt in this predicament if Vincent was any benchmark. No compulsion to fear the inevitable storm breaking, to fear obliteration. How funny that the known future in New York proved to be more frightening to me than being abducted and facing the unknown and what ought to have been the terrifying likelihood of pain and death. Perhaps I had been numbed and could no longer recognize my fear because my mind had at last started to fragment? Perhaps Charley's words had sunken their teeth deeper into me than I had thought? Without hope, there was nothing to lose, nothing to be afraid of, a blessing in disguise. But I did not feel as if I had lost hope, I felt simply that the dark fog had cleared away some of my past mindless terrors and left in its place a strange clarity regarding what one did when confronted with the abyss. It was a peculiar form of sanctuary.

"Did you hear me, Lucia? We have to figure out a plan to get away. They started arguing when they brought you in here. I overheard their raised voices. They—"

"How many of them were there?"

"What?"

"You said 'they'. I have only encountered one man, the one who took me. How many have you encountered? Have you seen them? Could you identify them?"

"I don't know. Two, I should say, at least. I'd just disembarked from the train in Cairo and was getting into a cab. The next thing I knew, I woke up blindfolded and someone was barking at me about my fiancé's diamond necklace. He never let me see his face. He made me write the note to bring you here. You were supposed to bring the diamond necklace. The man said that he was going to let us go once he got the necklace!"

"We've encountered several attempted robberies since London so precautions were taken... I'm sorry. I didn't have the necklace. But, you know, since you just got unluckily caught up in this situation and can't identify him, he might just let you go."

"Or just eliminate me." I heard Vincent slump back against the wall. "They—they stopped arguing a short time ago." His voice changed, the tremble grew a little more pronounced, his words came out more rapidly. "I don't think it's a good sign. I wasn't able to make out what they had been saying but I'm sure something's gone wrong. We have to get out of here before—"

Sounds of an approach over creaking floorboards outside the room silenced us.

The door unlocked and opened. A set of footsteps entered and stopped before me.

"Sorry to break up the lovers' reunion."

Rough hands began tugging at the ropes around my ankles. I was dragged, still blindfolded, out of the room where Vincent remained a prisoner.

"Lucia!"

Vincent's frantic, distressed cries died away behind the walls. My jailer took me to another dim room where he demanded that I pen a message to my traveling companions to explain away my unexpected absence. He removed my blindfold for the brief space of time it took me to write the note, and then—just as I laid the pen down—the sweet odor of darkness descended upon me again.

Darkness and shadows, wavering and blurred, and thick, sinuous fogginess chased each other through my mind.

I was roused from the murky, suffocating haze abruptly. The same gravelly voice said with what seemed to be a sneer: "Looks like you're going to a party."

He ordered me to pen another note. When he explained what he wanted, I set down the pen.

"Oh, is the life of that young man of yours no longer enough inducement to cooperate?" The sneer deepened. "He is getting a bit tiresome. Perhaps the company of your pretty friend would liven things up? Would it be too forward of me to bring her along to join the party?"

I thought I had left fear behind me but I was wrong.

"Dear Charley, my stay has been exceedingly pleasant and sociable. I have told my hosts of our travels together and they are keen to meet you. There is a party being held tomorrow evening at La Parisiana restaurant on the ground floor of the Windsor Hotel in Cairo. My hosts have kindly arranged for the invitation to be extended to both of us. Please come along, Charley, it will be such fun. I have copied down the details of the party and the address below. Could I ask you a favor in bringing my diamond necklace with you? There is a formal dress code for the party—I will need to be suitably attired. Lucia"

The blindfold was returned to my eyes. Darkness rushed in upon me.

41

CHARLOTTE:

"Tilly, I have a favor to ask."

42

LUCIA:

When the motor-car came to a stop in the noise of the bustling street, a maelstrom of emotions rose to the surface, threatening to overflow. With an effort, I pushed it down but it left me with a harsh acid aftertaste. I could not see Alfi Bey Street where La Parisiana stood. I did not think that I could have distinguished it by its noises from any other Cairo square or public thoroughfare either but by the dread revulsion in the pit of my stomach, I knew we had arrived at our destination.

This was what the condemned heading to the scaffold must have felt. My miserable choices had brought me here. Time would determine whether this too had been another pointless waste, whether in shrinking away from having an immediate death on my conscience, I had, in fact, sentenced three of us to the same, if delayed, fate—perhaps more, probably more and far worse, for where Charley went, Tilly and Matthias were not far behind, and there were so many others who depended on Charley—Dominic and the De Almadéns and Montrose—that my choices had placed in greater jeopardy. It was a vain hope that Charley would have read my messages and decided not to show up to roguishly brazen it out. For the first time in my life, I feared Charley's unimpeachable loyalty, her courage. Charley was not the sort of person who abandoned friends or, generally, paid much heed to warnings of danger in favor of forming her own judgment. I hoped, hoped with a burning fervor, that Charley would not come to La Parisiana, that she would not forget her responsibilities in New York and lose her head, as I had done, but that she would have the presence of mind to follow the guidance of the compass and lighthouse in riding the currents, to steer clear of pirate ships and jagged rocks and hidden reefs and deadly ruin, to crest waves and glide on the wind and navigate the way safely to shore, eluding the consequences of my poor choices.

Hadn't someone—had it been Frankie or Celeste?—or perhaps it had been my father who had once told me that hope was the special province, the last resort, of the feeble-minded?

I had been blindfolded again after being locked in a small room and warned not to try anything stupid. I had been ordered to put on an evening dress that had been folded on a chair and the shoes set beside it in readiness for a party. I had touched the dress, remembering the beautiful gowns that Charley had ordered in London and Paris, the balls and parties we had attended, half of which I had floated through as if completing a chore— trivialities, trivialities, like fireflies in the dusk, the flutter of a thousand wings against the unknown, the fleeting essence of a life...

I could have refused to go to La Parisiana, but that, in light of my message to Charley, would have been futile. If I could have had my time again, I wondered, would I have chosen differently—wisely?

The dress on the chair sat in quiet judgment.

Calling myself all kinds of fool, I tugged the dress and shoes on. They fitted me adequately. I touched my unmade up face and uncoiffed hair, combed neatly with my fingers, and decided that they too would have to do. Would I not be out of place amongst the fashionable Cairenes at La Parisiana? There was no mirror to check my appearance. I was grateful for that small mercy. I did not think I could have looked my reflection in the eye. I would not have recognized myself: a girl who weighed the fate of others in the balance and made such a wretched choice, a girl who repaid a friend's kindness with betrayal in order to spare the life of a man who cared only for himself. How had I become this girl? Would Tilly and Matthias and Aunt Merry and Diego and Dominic and the De Almadéns forgive me? Would Charley? Would Charley understand that I was too weak to watch a man be killed by my choices and instead gambled on her wits and resourcefulness to find a way out that nobody else could see? Half the time, in the dark, confused, troubled recesses of my mind, I did more than hope for it. I believed that Charley would. I so believed... It was not possible to send Charley so easily to...was it?

And what if they all did forgive me? That seemed the most dreadful fate of all.

I smoothed out my dress and hair a final time. Trivialities were all that were left when such terrible things hung in the balance. What were my abductors expecting of me? What were they expecting from Charley?

For an eternity, as I waited for the time of departure to arrive, I burned and writhed in torment in the dark solitary prison of my mind.

The return of the blindfold to my eyes was a precaution my abductor had insisted on before releasing me from the room and taking me down flights of stairs, out to a deserted street and into a waiting motor-car. The cacophony of noise which besieged my ears as we traveled to La Parisiana did nothing to dispel the strained, frigid darkness within which I had no companion other than my restless thoughts. I tried to be pragmatic and seize upon the sounds that carried from the surrounding streets and neighborhoods that we passed to try and gain directional bearings and form an idea of where we were. Had we reached downtown Cairo? Were we close to Opera Square? The pleasure gardens of Ezbekiya? Shepheard's Hotel? I tried to stymie the forebodings of doom which continually tried to insinuate themselves into my efforts to force alertness and composure. I chanted to myself that the blindfold was a good sign, that, logically, if I was not expected to survive the night, there would have been no need for it— that there was a chance that I would live to one day offer my apologies to Charley for being an unworthy friend.

Shortly after the motor-car's engine was cut, the gravelly voice to the side of me gave a final warning: "I would prefer not to use extreme measures tonight. So you will not scream or attempt to escape when I take off this blindfold. You will not speak unless I tell you to. You will obey and do exactly as you are told. You know the consequences of disobeying, do you not, Miss Bernhardt?"

"Yes." Small mercies: he had left off the gag.

"Excellent." And then the mocking smile spread in his voice. "By your leave, madam?"

The restoration of sight came as a simmering shock. Every passing motor-car, every alighting passenger, each passing parade of laughing, joking, babbling party-seekers, every strolling pedestrian, every open door and tall window overlooking the street, every patron sitting at the tables and being served on the Cairo pavement jolted into view and surrounded me, emphasizing my wretched powerlessness. Charley was not one of them, I noted, still vainly hopeful, she had not come.

Yet, my cynical mind whispered.

"La Parisiana awaits, Miss Bernhardt."

I turned my gaze back inside the motor-car to the back of the driver's head in front of me, and then to the man in the passenger seat next to me where, for the first time since my abduction, I saw the man to whom the gravelly voice belonged. He was stocky and roughly hewn, dressed disconcertingly in evening clothes. He had a head of closely cropped mane of flaxen hair, a slightly aquiline nose, deep set eyes, and a face of blunt features, hard brutish lines, and sharp edges ill-concealed by trimmed stubble. "He wasn't one of the hotel staff or a native Egyptian. He was European," Tallis had said. His resting face showed no hint of gentle feeling or kindness. The evening clothes did not contain his ferocity or his seething rancor. His pale eyes looked back at me with amusement and... For one vicious instant, I thought...

A flutter of fear stirred in my chest.

I choked out the words, "You once had a beard."

"It's a pleasure to formally make your acquaintance, Miss Bernhardt," he replied. "It's been a long time since we first crossed paths in London. I'm looking forward to enjoying your company this evening."

London. The thief felled by Dr. Bommel in Covent Garden. Had he really followed us all the way from London to France to Egypt? The attempted robberies had not been random incidents?

"You escaped the Metropolitan Police? You've been after the necklace all this time?"

"My demands are very modest, Miss Bernhardt. If I'd had my way, it would have been simple and we would all have been spared a lot of trouble, but my partner had different ideas." Snarling contempt flashed across his features before it was swiftly shuttered behind his bland disdain for me.

"Your partner?" I stole a glance back at the driver.

"Doubtful you'll meet him tonight."

His admission seemed to have cost him his patience with the conversation. His voice roughened abrasively in command: "Go on. Out. And remember, you do as I say. Don't try anything stupid." To emphasize his point, he unbuttoned his dinner jacket and revealed the handle of a pistol tucked inside a shoulder holster.

It had not been necessary to show me he had a gun. I already knew: it had sometimes suited his humor to toy with me, to trace the smooth, cold metallic tip of the barrel over my blindfold, along my temple and down my cheek, pressing it against the skin of my throat when he had issued his threats against me or Vincent or Charley. But perhaps he had a theatrical streak? And it was effective in delivering his message. Seeing the gun— seeing it so close to La Parisiana across the street in dreaded anticipation of Charley's arrival—brought another layer of agony. My throat ached from the screams I held trapped inside.

He grabbed my arm. "Hurry up. We haven't got all night."

We got out of the motor-car and crossed the street to the other pavement. We weaved a path through the foot traffic and entered the restaurant. To my relief, I did not see Charley inside or recognize anybody. All the while, he had held my arm. We might have appeared to a passerby like a couple settling down for a meal. Only after we had been shown to a table by the Egyptian waiter and seated did he release my arm. He ordered two café turques and dismissed the sundry other vendors milling about offering to tell fortunes or shine shoes. When the coffees arrived with glasses of water and a small plate of sweet pastries, he made a show of offering me sugar and cream, which I declined. He raised a silent brow and smiled archly when I did not touch my drink.

"I'm not thirsty," I said.

To my surprise, he did not insist but went on to stir sugar cubes into my demitasse cup and his own.

I had no interest in food or drink. I had been too preoccupied sifting through the faces of the waiting staff and patrons, as desperately as I had searched the faces of every person we had passed outside on the street, trying to catch a sympathetic eye, trying to find a sign that I could appeal to them for help. Each time I caught a friendly flicker, I brought my gaze away, hastily looking down, remembering that my abductor was close by and had a gun, remembering that I had already endangered others by acting rashly without thinking through the consequences, that I had enough resting on my conscience without adding the blood of another innocent stranger who tried to be kind in reaching out to give succor. It was not a choice between the lady or the tiger, it was the tiger whichever door opened. But hope was a difficult thing to wholly banish. My hungry gaze roamed again and again around the restaurant from the mirrors behind the dark mahogany counter to the lively, chicly dressed patrons sitting at individual tables to the huge windows looking directly onto the street to passing traffic on the street itself, vainly hoping...

"Wishing you'd accepted the invitation to tea with the Denholm-Kirby-Gamil sisters, aren't you?"

A cold realization rolled over me, the sense of how tightly was the web woven around us, smothering the tiny hope that I might have found an opportunity to take advantage of some tiny mistake or sloppiness or carelessness in his criminal activities. How stupidly I had behaved, I had narrowly, and through no merit of my own, escaped one trap only to fall straight into the lap of another.

I looked down at the café turque before me, a liquid as black as death.

"She'll come. We're a little early," he said. "On second thought..."

He borrowed a pen from a harried waiter to scribble a message onto a napkin. When he finished, he handed the napkin to the waiter.

"Will you make sure Miss Charlotte Masterson receives this when she arrives? She'll be looking for a Miss Lucia Bernhardt." He passed the waiter a tip to join the napkin message. Then he turned back to me. He raised his demitasse cup to sip leisurely at his coffee while he watched me over the rim. "Better drink up quickly," he prompted.

I felt a pulse of alarm. "I thought—"

He leaned forward over the table, his lips curling into a pleasant smile that did not touch his eyes. "Like you, I don't enjoy being kept waiting either."

"Please, I didn't mean—"

"It's too noisy and crowded here. Better that your friend comes to us."

My blood ran cold. I grabbed my demitasse cup and choked down a mouthful of the thick, scorching hot, bittersweet liquid. My tongue received a scalding but the burn hardly registered. I knew that drinking it was a desperate and ultimately futile attempt to delay leaving La Parisiana but I was compelled to do it because leaving meant... What had I expected? That my kidnapper would be straight with me? He had let me see his face. He had practically confessed to the thievery attempts since London. Did I really believe that he would do these things and let me survive the night— that doom did not await me and all those whose friendship I had failed?

"You never intended to stay here, did you? Where are we going?"

"Perceptive girl. You've played your part and made your appearance. Now come along." When I did not obey quickly enough, he leaned over and hissed in my ear, "Come along."

I rose from my seat and followed him, again painfully clutching my arm, out of the restaurant. We moved away from La Parisiana's prominent corner location on Alfi Bey Street and walked a very short distance up the street, past the neighboring busy night spots, towards where the motor-car had parked opposite the distinctive ornate iron awning and gated entrance of the Windsor Hotel which resembled the façades of the Khan el-Khalili souk.

As we headed back to the motor-car, I tried to stem the rising tide of fear inside me. I tried to replace it with logic, with reason and practical thoughts that might help reveal an escape route that did not involve bullets firing and death. Very little resulted from the endeavor except the frantic repetition of a prayer: "Please don't let Charley be there, please don't let Charley be there, please don't let Charley be there..."

Every time my abductor's fingers dug into my arm to remind me of my captivity, every time his gaze swept back to me from surveying our surroundings as we moved along the street, without bothering to hide his cold hateful smile, the hope which had ebbed and flowed in fitful stutters died a little more.

"Get in," he ordered. His voice was pitched quiet but unmistakably menacing.

We had reached the motor-car. I forced myself to hold out for the bitter end.

He got into the motor-car beside me. "Don't worry," he crooned mockingly, "you'll get to meet your friend soon."

"Will I? What will you do to her?"

"I haven't decided yet." He seemed to turn the question over in his mind, to give it serious thought. "It will likely depend on whether she is in a cooperative mood or not. It might be—" He paused mid-sentence at a barely perceptible head movement from the driver and looked out towards the street.

I followed his gaze.

Suddenly, all the colors in the world melted and leaked away. Whatever cautious optimism I had talked myself into believing, it all went flying out the window at the sight of a cab drawing up beside the curb beside La Parisiana and spilling out one passenger: Charley, looking like the living embodiment of a Grecian muse in the exquisite folds of creamy white silk jersey that Mme. Revyl and Mlle Alix Krebs had fashioned for her at Maison Premet—a muse who had forsaken her lofty classical post to abscond to the mortal realms with a conflagration of flawless diamonds around her neck—a muse whose projection of serene divinity ended at her eyes which were spitting fire as brilliantly as the diamonds she wore.

Heads of passersby turned in her direction and patrons at the pavement tables stared as she entered the restaurant.

Moments later, Charley emerged from La Parisiana into the dusk and began to head towards...

"Are you sending her to the Windsor Hotel?" I asked. "What—who is waiting at the Windsor Hotel? Your partner?"

My abductor chuckled softly. "Your friend will get a surprise welcome."

My eyes flew back to the young woman in the Maison Premet gown and diamonds stalking imperiously, purposefully, along the pavement and entering the Windsor Hotel. A sharp trill of fear seared through my chest cavity, filling me with an excruciating, unspeakable panic.

"Let's go," my abductor told the driver, then sat back and smiled at me as the engine rumbled to life.

No. No, no, no.

I lost control of rational thought. In my fever state, I yanked open the door on my side of the motor-car and bolted-stumbled-fell out. I scrambled to my feet and ran for dear life, screaming as loudly as my lungs would oblige: "Charley—Charley, stop! It's a trap!"

I had no idea why—how—my abductor allowed me to get so far down the street. Perhaps he had been so accustomed to my perfect obedience in always doing what was asked of me, he had not expected me to suddenly lose my mind. Perhaps he did not think I would be idiotic enough to jump from a moving vehicle. I did not question my luck. I did not question repercussions or consequences. I did not think about the gun in his possession which he could have brandished at any second and aimed if he did not care about all the people in the street. I did not think about getting run over by the traffic in the street when I crossed. I did not care about decorum or propriety or politeness in pushing past crowds of people. I did not think about how my impractical shoes hurt and how my dress impeded my progress. I just kept putting one foot before the other and running. The only thoughts that raged through my mind were about where Charley had gone: Charley had not heard me—she had disappeared inside the Windsor Hotel—I had sent Charley to her death.

"Charley!"

I raced inside the tiled lobby of the Windsor Hotel, panting with my exertions, tailed by a gesticulating doorman whom I had passed in my mindless rush. When I could not see Charley anywhere, I appealed desperately to the front desk clerks to direct me to the lady in a black and white dress who had entered the hotel in barely coherent English and broken attempts at Egyptian for "please" and "help me" and "bad man" and finally "call police" in English because I did not know the word for it in Egyptian, pointing out to the street—no, she wasn't a guest of the hotel—no, I didn't know where—she had just come in only—

When I pointed to my collarbone and tried to convey the idea of jewels, of diamonds, in a ludicrous charade, smiles lit up their faces—yes, necklace, yes, yes, big diamonds! The lady had proceeded up to the barrel lounge on the first floor, madam. The elevator was this way...

I gulped in air and gaped at the perfect Egyptian-inflected English and then inundated the splendid desk clerks and doorman with thanks for taking pity and managing to decipher the idiot ravings of an incoherent lunatic.

Despite the desk clerk kindly guiding me to the manually-operated cage elevator which took guests up to the first floor lounge, I decided against using it in favor of taking the stairs. It seemed the far swifter way to reach the first floor. With another exhorted warning about the bad man with a gun outside on the street, I sprinted up the stairwell which spiraled around the elevator shaft.

Business was brisk and buoyant at the barrel lounge that evening. Nearly every inch of its deeply scored wooden floors was occupied, certainly every seat—some of which appeared to have been fashioned from beer barrels—was taken. I looked around the room, around the walls hung with hunting lodge trophies, over the din of clinking glasses and boisterous conversations of the crowd, and finally spotted the delicate Grecian folds in the crush at the bar. Charley was standing between several other patrons leaning over the bar, speaking to the bartender over the chatter surrounding her, passing him a note.

"Charley!" I called out, making my way across the lounge.

Charley turned around. Her eyes widened to the size of dinner plates. She seized my hand, examining me from head to toe. "Lucia, are you all right? What happened to y—we need to get you cleaned up, you're bleeding! How did you escape? How did you get here? Did they—"

A few concerned patrons nearby spotted my disheveled appearance and asked if I was all right, offering assistance. Charley would not have hesitated, but the notion that any of these strangers might somehow be allied to my abductor, that I could not trust them sealed my lips in accepting their offers. I interrupted Charley, murmured polite thanks and excuses to the patrons, and then pulled at Charley's forearm and whispered urgently at her.

"We have to leave now, Charley! This is a trap. We—"

"But your— How?"

"I don't know the details. But that's what he said—the man outside—the one who is behind all this—they have Vincent, Charley—"

"Vincent Faneuil is the reason that you walked into your abductor's hands? To save his worthless hide?" Charley paused in her wild frenzy of concern. "No, of course he would still be causing grief after his defection. But I don't see why you had to be burdened with his rescue. Getting kidnapped seems like a fitting end for the short time he spent playing fiancé. Didn't we recently have a conversation about divine retribution?"

"Charley! It isn't entirely Vincent's fault. The man responsible is the thief from Covent Garden who got away. He's been after us ever since—on the French Riviera, in Assuan. He's coming here—he has a gun! And he isn't working alone. He has a partner. He is the one who wrote the note at La Parisiana. He sent you here. We have to leave!"

"Well, I did notice it wasn't your handwriting. The penmanship was rather impenetrable. This is a public place with lots of people milling about. I don't think it likely—"

"Charley, you can't be certain—please—hurry!"

"All right. Shepheard's is two blocks away. We can tend to your injuries there. But—"

I pulled Charley away from the bar and began dragging her across the floor.

"Lucia, wait, there's—"

"Charley?"

We came to an abrupt stop.

James Dorsey appeared in our path, an empty glass in hand. He stared at Charley, looking quite as surprised to find her standing before him as we were to see him.

"What are you doing here?" Charley eyed him warily.

"Got tired of all the messages you returned. Didn't feel like drowning my sorrows alone," James Dorsey drawled. "Don't look at me like that, Charley. How often do you get dismissed without a fair hearing? I tried, all right?"

"Well... We wish you a good evening," said Charley, trying to keep her voice down so we would not attract additional attention (not that there was much risk of that in the hubbub of the barrel lounge) and starting to move past him.

James Dorsey put a hand out to halt her. "You're all dressed up. Is Matthias Vandermeer taking you out for a night on the town? Are you going to the Opera?"

"We have an appointment and we are going to be late if you hold us up like this," Charley replied, coolly distant yet combative. "I'm trying to remain civil, James, don't make—"

Angry shouting carried up from below stairs.

"Charley, he's here! Oh God, he's coming for us!"

Ignoring James Dorsey, Charley tugged me along with her. "Come on, Lucia—"

"Who's here?" James Dorsey demanded, refusing to budge out of our way. "Who's coming for you? What's going on?"

"Nothing. Just let us pass."

"No," James Dorsey answered. "Tell me what is going on. I'm here. I can help. Let me help."

"It will help if you just let us pa—"

"Damn it, Charley, your friend is terrified. Tell me."

"You can't do anything to help. You're not the police. There is a man downstairs with a gun who is after us. We need to get out of here. Happy? Now, if you'll just—"

"A gunman? Does he know you're up here?"

"I'd rather not put that to the test."

"Then I'll do it," James Dorsey said. He set down his glass. There was a new resoluteness to his tone and manner. "I'll go downstairs and see if I can get him to go away. Distract him, give him false directions, whatever it takes."

"You'll be shot for an interfering ass!" Charley retorted.

"Give me some credit, Charley. I'll stall him if nothing else. I'm a stranger to this man. He won't care one way or another. You need my help. Let me help, Charley."

"No! It's madness! We—"

The shouting rose in volume.

Before Charley could finish, James Dorsey turned and left the barrel lounge. Charley rushed out to stop him but was too late. In a matter of moments, he had descended the stairwell, the top of his head sinking and disappearing below the level of the floor. Several curious patrons wandered over to see what the ruckus was about but they must have figured it to be a drunken private quarrel for they soon lost interest and wandered back to their conversations and drinks in the lounge. Charley and I seized the diversion to leave the lounge quietly. We did not dare peep over the wooden railing in case the gunman was standing directly below and happened to be looking up.

Charley turned back to me on the landing. Indecision raged in her eyes.

"We're trapped here now, aren't we?" I sought from Charley some glimmer of assurance that our predicament was not quite as dire as it looked, that perhaps I had miscalculated or missed something. "Does the stairwell— Is there another way out? I didn't notice one on my way here, but I wasn't paying very close attention."

Charley shook her head unhappily. "If we stay in the barrel lounge and the gunman comes up and sees us here... I'm afraid that we will either be handed over to him to spare greater casualties or there will be indiscriminate shooting if even one of the patrons decides to tackle him and they get into a fight. But the only way out is barred. You're right: the stairwell seems to only go in two directions: down to the lobby, where gunman is, or up to the roof. I think there is a rooftop garden up there but no other exit. Unless we can leap over rooftops, we're stranded. I don't like the idea of running further down a dead end. Unless..."

The raised voices below spurred Charley to action. She moved rapidly to take the upward flight of stairs, nudging me to join her.

"I thought you—"

"Try every single door handle you pass. If one of them opens, we'll take refuge in there. We can sort out the apologies and reparations to the room's tenant later."

Two dozen locked doors later, growing ever more frustratedly conscious of time ticking by and the shouting carrying up the stairwell from below, Charley opened her purse.

"What are you doing?" I'd not seen Charley quite so rattled before and it made my own nerves and fears grow.

"I didn't want to have to resort to this," Charley muttered as she applied what looked like a long hairpin to prod and test and jiggle inside the lock.

I was too frantic to wonder where and why Charley had needed to learn how to jimmy closed doors and pick locks. The shouting downstairs had not abated. If anything, it seemed to be getting louder—more angry—closer. And then, Charley was interrupted barely before she had gotten started on the lock when that horrifying gravelly voice roared my name. We were out of time.

Fear sizzled through my being. Fear that caused my very consciousness to waver.

"Lucia?" Charley's voice pierced through my petrified daze. A light concerned touch brushing over my arm woke me up. Charley's eyes frowned at me in worry.

"He's coming up, isn't he? What do we do now?"

Charley abandoned the unpicked lock and pointed a finger up at the stairwell. "Rooftop. Run."

I got a small head start on Charley when she paused to hitch up her silken skirts so that they would not impede her progress. My head start was of little practical advantage. Charley had been wearing sturdy boots instead of dainty heels beneath her beautiful Parisian gown. They would have served her well in carrying her swiftly up the narrow winding stairwell all the way to the rooftop without the risk of perilously tripping or twisted ankles but Charley hung back to make sure I was keeping pace with her and helping me when I lagged behind. In the end, I got tired of the ludicrous way I had zig-zagged and wobbled and nearly toppled over in my impractical shoes that I took them off and ran up the last flight of stairs in my bare feet.

We skidded to a stop when we reached the upper level and pushed out into the open air. The rooftop had been laid out and decorated with plants and trellises and trestle tables and chairs like a terrace garden. We did a quick survey of the rooftop garden and the surrounding buildings in the lengthening dusk. No other exits. It was a long way down without wings. But we were high enough that the sound of shouting from the stairwell no longer reached us. I knew that it was a double-edged sword, we had placed distance between us and the gunman but we had also lost a warning bell. Still, the absence of that gravelly voice did quell my terror a little.

Charley had begun rummaging in her purse again. "Lucia. Here. Take this." She pulled out an object wrapped up in a napkin and handed it to me. When I unwrapped it, I found that I was holding a pistol.

"Charley?" I heard my voice rise several octaves.

"Yes, it's loaded," Charley continued at a forcedly clipped pace, sliding regular sidelong glances at the stairwell entrance. "I'm going to show you how to take the safety off. If the occasion rises, aim at the largest expanse of body, hold steady and press the trigger, don't think too much about it, all right? Just shoot and then run away as fast as you can. It doesn't matter whether you've hit anything. You'll probably miss. The important point is to use your advantage of surprise to run and hide."

"What are you going to use?"

Charley waved away the question as if she was swatting mosquitoes. "Oh, can't you see that I have a purse full of handy tools? You just concentrate on the service pistol."

"Where did you get this service pistol?" It was impossible to stamp out the rising panic in my voice.

"You go stand next to the entrance to the stairwell, there's a little bit of a recess there... It is far from ideal but—we'll move the table and pot plants —just a smidge to the side—so they give you a little bit of cover next to the trellis without being an obstacle. Stay out of sight. Stay hidden. Keep very quiet. It's getting darker so the shadows will favor you. I'm going to stand over here and draw his attention away from looking your way. When the man arrives, he will see me first. Your mother's diamonds and I will distract him. Even if his back is towards you, be wary and quiet. Be alert and ready to run, make sure you seize the opportunity to sneak back into the stairwell and—"

"You've got to be joking! There is no way that I am leaving you up here alone, Charley."

"There isn't any other way. It's better that you run down and reach help than both of us remain stranded here. And remember that I am not defenseless. I have—"

"No."

"It won't be for long. I left a message with the bartender to send for help. Matthias and—"

"No." Did Charley think that the armor of a Maison Premet gown could stop a bullet or deflect a knife blade or fend off any other weapon? That I would just let her test it? "I'll be lucky if I end up shooting him in the knees, but I'm staying up here if you are. I brought you into this, Charley— and there is nothing in the world that I regret more—and I'm not leaving."

"That isn't logical—"

"It's the right course of action to take. I've done so little of that lately, Charley."

"This is not a last stand, Lucia. The cavalry is coming. It's no good if either of us get shot before then. This is the best way to avoid it. Even if you don't have faith in me, you must see that we are short on time and this plan makes practical, strategic sense. Here, let me show you how this pistol works." Rather than waiting for me to argue, Charley hurried briskly around the rooftop shifting the furniture and plants and decorations about and positioning me behind them and demonstrating the use of the service pistol.

I had reason to suspect a trick—Charley was not above telling lies—but if Charley was lying, there was a compelling element of ineluctable fact to her lie. We were short on time and her plan was practical, even if I hated it, and the risks and danger were very real. It was our best chance and Charley would squeeze every last drop out of it to ensure it succeeded. Brusque, efficient, methodical—just as she had been during the motor-race from Paris to Cannes—but I knew that her heart beat in a staccato tempo of fear corresponding to my own even if there were no visible signs of it. It made me more determined not to leave her to face it alone.

While we argued in furious whispers, I nevertheless helped move things around the rooftop in accordance with Charley's instructions.

Just as we were dragging an antique urn into place, a voice from inside the stairwell—a voice within uncomfortably close range—interrupted our preparations, calling out: "Charley, are you up there?"

Charley's eyes flashed. She began to motion vigorously to me in silence as she vaulted over obstacles on the way to the far side of the rooftop garden. We scrambled to take our places and pricked up our ears to listen intently to the scuffle of approaching steps. It was not quite the way I had imagined resolving my dilemma.

A few moments of ominous quiet gave way were followed by a careful tread. Presently, James Dorsey emerged from the dim stairwell entrance onto the rooftop garden, his corporeal form coming into view and joining to his earlier disembodied voice.

"Charley?"

"God, you scared me!" Charley snapped with a nervous crossness that was only partly affectation. "I thought you were the gunman."

"No. He's been dealt with." I saw from behind the tangle of hastily put together camouflage that James Dorsey extended his hand out and beckoned to Charley. "Come on, it's all right. We can go back down now."

"Are you sure?" Charley asked, very cautious and very skeptical. "You seem all right—but were you hurt at all? What happened? Did you see Lucia on your way up?"

James Dorsey was forced to go to Charley since she remained resolutely where she had promised to stand so that no one would be looking in my direction. "Why would—? You and your friend didn't come up here together?"

"The conventional wisdom is to split up to confuse pursuers, isn't it? To give a better chance for at least one person to get away? Lucia and I decided that we had nothing to lose by putting that theory to the test. I do hope that means that she's made it to safety." Charley peered at James Dorsey. "Are you sure you didn't run into her?"

"Strange as it may be, I did not." James Dorsey sounded perplexed. "I would've seen her if she had taken the elevator. I'm not aware of any other egress..."

"Perhaps Lucia was rescued by a guest of the hotel," Charley mused.

I marveled at Charley's sangfroid. If I had been James Dorsey, I would have believed Charley's lies too.

"It's nice to know," continued Charley, "that it is still possible to find a Good Samaritan to help one escape from mad gunmen when the need arises."

Knowing that Charley was trying to deflect attention away from me and subtly reminding me to be ready to run was not quite as straightforward as seizing the chance to comply, even without my reservations about leaving Charley on her own. For one thing, James Dorsey may have been steadily lulled into Charley's purposefully disingenuous misdirections, but there seemed to be some sort of internal conflict causing him to pause, to hesitate, revealing hairline cracks in the confidence in which he had strode out of the stairwell. For another, booming echoes coming up the stairwell seemed to suggest that it was not deserted, that someone was pounding up the stairs and that whoever it was seemed rather upset, perhaps just a little angry.

"Who—" Charley began.

"Dorsey, you swindler—you'd better run, you double-crossing scoundrel, you'd better hope I don't catch you!"

"That isn't the gunman, is it?" Charley gasped. "Didn't you say—"

James Dorsey grabbed Charley and dragged her back towards the walled ledge of the rooftop, tersely facing the dark stairwell entrance as if a monster was rising from the deep or—it did not take a fanciful imagination to conjure—a ghost returning from the dead. I jerked back to hide from his sight, shrinking into the shadows of the trellised wall and the assembled jumble of furniture and plants, and hoping that his attention would be distracted by whatever enraged beast was coming up for him.

Charley did not like following the arbitrary, peremptory dictates of others on the best of days. She was having none of it on the rooftop. Charley kept drawing away from James Dorsey to approach the stairwell and being pulled back. She kept beginning questions and being hushed up. None of it dented Charley's persistence. "Who—"

"Well, well, well, Dorsey. Looks like the rat has been caught in a trap. And with the goods no less." A shadow separated from the gloom of the stairwell entrance and stepped out onto the roof. A man with pale cruel eyes. I recognized him by his gravelly voice rather than saw him; my line of vision was obstructed from where I was hiding in order to remain out of sight.

"You!" Charley hissed.

"Miss Charlotte Masterson, it's a pleasure to meet you again." His gruff veneer of manners rubbed and grated on my fear like sandpaper. Slowly, carefully, silently, I crept back, inch by inch, to look. "Will you be so kind as to come with me? I'm going to need your escort to ferry me out of here."

"She isn't going anywhere," said James Dorsey, gripping on to Charley.

"You have no say in this matter anymore." The man turned to James Dorsey. "Give up the girl unless you want to eat a bullet."

Charley spun around and pushed away from James Dorsey's hold. "You know each other?" Flames snapped and leapt in her eyes. "You're in league with this man?"

"Sweetheart," purred the gunman, "Dorsey and I are old school buddies. We go way back. I'll tell you everything you want to know about his childhood and salad days on the way downstairs."

There was an infinitesimal pause. Had Charley's lips parted in a spasm of pain?

James Dorsey glared at the gunman. "He's trying to play you, Charley," he told her. "Don't believe—"

"You lying dog," snarled the gunman. "Get out of my way. I won't be giving you another warning." He must have pulled out his gun because there the rooftop garden was suddenly silent in the twilight except for the distant murmur of traffic from the street below.

I tried to calm the skittish beat of my heart. I could not angle myself into a position to use the service pistol Charley had given me without exposing myself to James Dorsey's view—and I did not trust that he would not give me away to benefit himself before I could take aim at the gunman. Charley was trapped between the roof ledge and stairwell and the two men standing in the way.

"Come on, sweetheart, I haven't got all day," the gunman said.

"Charley, don't!" James Dorsey appealed to her.

Charley—the brave, noble idiot—shook her head, refusing to obey the gunman, but also stepping away from James Dorsey. She never once looked in my direction, but the only reason she was moving into that dead end spot of the rooftop garden was to draw their gazes away from where I was.

The gunman growled and stepped towards her. "You don't want to put me in a bad mood, sweetheart."

"You know, I think I just might risk it," said Charley in the maddeningly even-tempered way that she used to answer a dare. "It just occurred to me that if I don't get off this roof alive, neither will you. Both of you. And I don't care if you are still friends or not. You can stop pointing that thing rudely at me now. Do unto others, yes? I'm sure you wouldn't like whoever is waiting for you downstairs to be pointing such a thing at you."

Oh God, where did Charley find the cheek to—I angled the barrel of the service pistol a few centimeters higher, my finger on the trigger, but was unable to pull because my hand was shaking so badly.

"Are you sure you want to test that theory?" The gunman's growl sounded even more feral than before.

"Well, since I'm all dressed up with nowhere to go and have plenty of time on my hands—yes, why not? You're not in a hurry, are you? Oh, wait, you are, aren't you?"

James Dorsey and the gunman moved at the same time towards Charley. "Stop!"

The gunman whipped around. When his eyes alighted on me, his lips curved into a smile. "There you are, my pet. I was wondering where you'd gone. Did you miss me? Where did you get that shiny new toy?"

He stalked towards me, undiminished in the power of his intimidation and the violence he wielded in his built frame and hands.

"No! No, Lucia—no! Hey, you big lug—"

I heard Charley as if from a distance. I was concentrating so hard to hold my hand steady, to be unafraid despite the terror rampaging though me while this terrifying predator advanced. I held the service pistol directed straight at him. "Stop or I'll shoot," I told him.

He kept advancing.

I took several steps back.

"No need to sulk, my pet. You've got my undivided attention now." He came right up in front of me, wearing his knowing sneer. "Do you even know how to use that?"

I retreated another step but instead of shooting, I drew my arm out and swung the butt of the service pistol into his face. He staggered back at the impact and swore. His temple was bleeding when he raised his boiling gaze to me.

"That wasn't very nice," he growled, and reached towards me.

I ducked and dodged him, stumbling to get away, but I did not manage to go far as my back hit the assemblage of table and plants. He kept coming until I was pressed into the edge of the table and had to crane my neck back to see his eyes. He leaned forward, as though he was going to sniff at his prey before devouring me. When I tried to strike him with the service pistol this time, he caught my wrist and squeezed. The service pistol clattered to the ground. In panic, I grabbed behind me at anything my other free hand could find on the table and swung that at him. He staggered back again in surprise. More blood dripped down his face, smeared in dirt and tangles of leaves and roots from the terracotta pot that I had broken against his forehead.

Molten red flooded his eyes. With an enraged snarl, he lunged at me.

Time slowed and stopped. I was hit by flash of paralyzing terror, expecting the world to shatter and disintegrate into an explosion of stars. I was frozen, unable to do anything but wait for the end.

"Lucia!"

Suddenly, the nightmare crushing the world before me was blurred by something—or someone—else diving in and tackling him to the ground.

"Lucia!"

The shout was punctuated by a pistol shot. There was the thud of bodies hitting the ground, grunting, swearing, screams. I blinked. Charley was struggling and kicking, trying to free herself from James Dorsey's arms holding her back. Neither of them seemed to have been shot. There was movement before them—live, vigorous movement—not dead men falling. The pistol must have been knocked out of the gunman's hand and gone off. My heart seized and began beating again. In front of Charley and James Dorsey, two men were crashing violently from corner to corner of the rooftop garden in the twilight, pummeling each other, rattling metal, hammering up sprays of dust and plaster and broken pottery every time they battered or smashed into something. One of them was the gunman—the other—no, it couldn't be...oh God, was that...Tallis?

The two men unleashed their rage on one another, slamming fists into every inch of flesh and bone within reach. Their wrestling match demolished the surrounding rooftop garden. To my surprise, Tallis—mild, civilized, charming banker, Tallis Lloyd-Chase, denizen of Park Avenue club rooms and Newport Beach cottages—kept up with the gunman's relentless pace, barely recognizable as he released his own brutal blows in retaliation. It was fairly even odds until...

"James Dorsey, I swear if you don't let me go this minute, I'm going to rip your head off and pull your entrails out through your nose when— Tallis, watch out!"

Rolling violently around on the roof floor, the gunman managed to get Tallis in an armlock and tugged a jackknife out, aiming for Tallis with murderous intent. He began furiously slashing at Tallis. Tallis tried to deflect the attacks but as Charley was screaming bloody murder at James Dorsey, crimson gashes started blooming over Tallis's limbs and staining his clothes, and his defensive moves began to grow limp.

I knew that I had to do something before the gunman succeeded in sliding his blade deep into Tallis. I scrambled to find the service pistol that I had dropped but when I found it, I did not know what to do. It was too risky to use the service pistol with the two combatants moving about and Charley on the opposite side of the roof. I was just as likely to hit Tallis or Charley, but... I snatched the nearest unbroken urn I saw and at the moment that the gunman's back turned to me, I ran forward and brought the urn down on the gunman's head.

The urn dropped to the floor, bounced, and rolled away. The gunman swayed but did not go down. He shook his head, rose to his feet, evidently deeming Tallis's unmoving figure no longer a threat, and turned his countenance around towards me, followed by the pointed end of his knife. I raised the service pistol. Too slow. He grabbed me. I jerked back uselessly.

"I'm going to teach you a lesson," he snarled through his teeth, and pounced.

Someone screamed. It might have been me. I twisted and struggled to stay out of the path of the sharp point of the blade as it bore down towards me. Somewhere behind us, Charley begged him to stop, to just take the necklace...

Suddenly, when I thought I could hold off no longer, I heard a sickening crack, followed by the gunman roaring in agony. The knife dropped, the hands clamping my wrists loosened, and he tottered to the floor and curled up, clasping his arm. A giant shadow loomed over him, tore the gunman's arms back—more agonized howls followed until a fist to the jaw silenced him—and clapped both his hands into a set of shiny handcuffs.

"Are you hurt, Lucia?"

I looked up and met the anxious brown eyes of the giant. It was Matthias.

"No." My voice came out in a croak of wonder and disbelief. "No. I'm — Don't worry about me. Did you just break the man's arm? Tallis..."

Matthias picked up the dropped service pistol and the gunman's knife. I hurried to poor Tallis's battered and abused body lying on the floor. He was groaning faintly. Still alive. Matthias was glowering across Tallis's body at James Dorsey's arms wrapped around Charley, holding her fast in his grip, shielding her—or caging her, given how fiercely Charley was still struggling against him. Matthias stepped towards them.

"Release her," Matthias said firmly.

"Well done," James Dorsey returned. "Good show. I was wondering when you'd show up."

"Release her," Matthias repeated, his hand on the service pistol.

"I'm afraid Charley and I need to clear up a misunderstanding now that this trying ordeal is over. Charley is under the mistaken impression, planted by the lies of that dangerous man you just apprehended—"

"I don't think we will," said Charley. "Guns to one's back and lies make for such disagreeable company. You'll be joining your chum over there while waiting for the police to arrive."

"Sorry, Charley, I have to disagree," said James Dorsey. His hold tightened around Charley and he brought a pistol that he had been holding out of sight—was that his own gun or the one that had been knocked out of the gunman's hand earlier by Tallis?—and pressed it to Charley's temple.

My blood chilled. Had Charley been insane, struggling and fighting against that loaded gun the entire time—all to distract him from shooting at Tallis or me?

"It would be foolish to try anything," he warned us. "I was hoping to avoid all this unpleasantness but Cartwright always did have a knack of making an unnecessary mess of things. Let me pass and no one will get hurt. Come along, Charley. The quicker we leave, the quicker you can get back to your friends and forget about all this."

Charley stared daggers at Matthias and me, commanding us not to move, to stay back. Why did she have the monopoly on insanity?

"Cartwright," said Charley, rolling the name around on her tongue, trying the syllables out for size. "I believe that the bullet waiting in the chamber of your disgruntled friend's gun, the one that you have in your hand, James, has your name on it rather than mine. I do so hate borrowing other people's—"

"Don't make the mistake of thinking I won't use this gun, Charley," said James Dorsey, pressing the barrel closer.

Beside me, a low growl escaped Matthias.

"What makes you think you're the only one who has a gun?" said Charley.

"What do you—"

A sudden pistol shot rang out. It made us all jump. James Dorsey's head snapped around towards the direction of the stairwell entrance from where the shot had originated. A woman in colorful traditional Egyptian garb stood at the entranceway, one arm raised with a gun pointed to the sky.

In the next instant, James Dorsey let out a pained groan.

I pried my gaze from the woman in Egyptian garb and found that

Charley had moved. James Dorsey's gun was no longer pointed at her head. She was now standing behind James Dorsey, twisting his arm into a backward wrench with one hand and pressing something to his back with her other hand. James Dorsey seemed to be in pain. Had Charley stomped on his toes—given him a swift kick in the shin—punched him in the—

"I have a slightly itchy trigger finger," Charley said, nudging him from behind. "It would be so helpful if you would drop your gun."

James Dorsey winced and reluctantly dropped his pistol. In a flash, Matthias launched at James Dorsey and knocked him out cold. I jumped to my feet and dashed over to collect the gun to prevent it from causing more havoc. Matthias bound James Dorsey's arms up with Dorsey's own necktie and, for good measure, the tie I helped to strip from the gunman, under the watchful eye—and gunpoint—of the woman in traditional Egyptian garb. A woman whose appearance started to stir some recollection... Had she been in La Parisiana earlier?

After James Dorsey and his friend Cartwright were safely secured, we looked around the rooftop for Charley. I was awash in a roiling mess of shock and relief and worry instead of excoriating, helpless terror. Matthias's eyes found Charley kneeling by Tallis in the deepening shadows, checking his injuries, quite undisturbed by the stunt she had pulled. Matthias's face darkened. It was not clear if he was going to hug her or strangle her.

"God almighty, Charley!" I breathed.

Charley cocked a brow inquiringly at me, as if she was unaware of why there was such a fuss. She turned to the woman in Egyptian garb and said: "Thank you, Tilly."

"Tilly?" I turned in awe to the woman covered from head to toe in colorful robes and veils.

"Miss Charley," came Tilly's long-suffering, most deeply reproving tones from behind the face veil. She lowered the pistol and handed it over gingerly to Charley to put away.

Matthias was glowering darkly at Charley too, promising that there would be words, and more, later.

"How bad is Tallis?" I asked.

Charley's apprehensive gaze flickered over me and, ever so briefly, lightened to a relieved grimace.

"We need to get Tallis inside the elevator and down to see a medic," said Charley. She turned to Matthias. "We need two people and a stretcher to carry the idiot. He shouldn't be moved unnecessarily. And Lucia needs medical attention, a bath, fresh clothes, a solid meal, and lots of sleep. I suppose a little effort might also be spared to find out where they are hiding Mr. Faneuil—unless you'd rather not—and I would have no objections whatsoever in that regard."

"I need to guard these two criminals until Aldersley arrives with the police," said Matthias. "There are formalities that I have to— Are you able to run downstairs and find—"

"Of course," Charley said. "Consider it done."

Matthias stretched out his palm towards her. "I'll need to return the service pistols to Aldersley. He's been very anxious about them since you coerced his officers into lending you the use of their firearms."

"Charley?" I cried.

Charley handed over to Matthias the pistol that Tilly had given her. She also removed the diamond necklace from her neck and gave it to me.

"And the third?" prompted Matthias.

"I only borrowed two," said Charley.

"The gun you were holding to Dors—" Matthias's face paled. A faint tremor passed through his outstretched hand. "Show me," he said hoarsely.

Charley rolled her eyes.

"Charley."

From the ruched décolletage of her silk gown, Charley drew out a silver spoon and handed it to Matthias. Matthias closed his eyes. I could almost hear him mentally count to ten. When his eyes reopened, the irises were almost black. Strangle. Unequivocally strangle.

I was in sympathy with Matthias. Tilly and I were staring at the silver spoon, the shape of its pointed cylindrical handle so very closely resembling the muzzle of a pistol that if one was not paying close attention and distracted by... Thoughts rushed like a spring torrent through my mind.

"Charley." Horror and hysteria made my voice high and reedy. "What if —what if he—"

Charley glared at Matthias as if it was all his fault, as if she had not been the one who had pulled on Death's whiskers. "I don't know. Kicked him and stabbed him in the eye with it? Luckily, we'll never have to find out. The probability was low anyway, he wanted the diamonds and he needed me to get out of here without being arrested. Oh, don't all of you look at me like that. I'll give the spoon back. Wasn't planning to keep it anyway. I'm not entirely a kleptomaniac."

"From where did you take it?"

"The barrel lounge downstairs. I already had a gun taking up room in my purse. It wasn't as though I had additional readily accessible pockets all over my gown to conceal things. If I'd known I'd need more than one weapon, I would've prepared differently and found myself a leg holster— ankle straps—worn longer boots. As it was, there were two of us and one pistol and I had to make do with what was available at the bar. Not a vast selection to serve as an impromptu weapon. No knives or forks. Plenty of hooch and matches, yes, but I wanted something easy to hide and pull out without having to undo a layer of clothing or reach down to my shoes. (Yes, I did have other equipment in there which did not come in handy, and no, I'm not going to tell you more.) In any case, I didn't want to accidentally burn the building down with us in it. So I had to resort to a spoon." She glared mutinously over at Matthias again, daring him to contradict her reasoning.

Matthias unlocked his jaws. "We deal with Tallis, Lucia, and the official formalities first," he said, caging a low growl of frustration in his throat. "But we will return to this, Charley," he promised darkly.

"If you insist." Charley shrugged, as cool as you please.

Pounding footsteps and urgent voices in the stairwell signaling the arrival of the authorities saved Charley from the rest of the inquisition. Their arrival and the night's falling veil of darkness saved me, too, from admitting the tears which threatened to well up though I fought them back, clutching to my heart my mother's diamond necklace amongst the handful of things which had been vouchsafed to me that day.

43

CHARLOTTE:

"RHYS HADDEN ARRESTED PROCEED WITH CAUTION UPDATE FORTHCOMING D"

"PLEASE ADVISE ARRIVAL NY BAYARD"

Fatigue washed over me like a tidal wave. Uncle Nick had me over a barrel this time. Had I any arrows left in my quiver?

I slumped against the back of the bathroom door. Tomb-like. Yes, Shepheard's bathrooms were vast echoing chambers fit for entombment.

"Miss Charley! Mr. Vandermeer is here. He's brought some more people who would like to take speak to you about the case if you are free."

Oh, that I had wings like a dove!

44

LUCIA:

The post mortem of the affair proved to be of more than passing interest and illuminating in many ways. To me, at least—and to Tilly, and to Tallis, who had been diagnosed for a steady recovery from his wounds, bored and eager for distraction.

After she and Matthias personally ensured that reparations had been made to the Windsor Hotel for the disturbance and damage suffered (including returning the spoon to the barrel lounge), Charley washed her hands of the matter entirely, wanted nothing to do with it, hackles up, crisp and practical, impatiently dismissive, incurious, treating each new revelation as though she was trying to ward off the evil eye. This might have just been Charley brushing off matters that she considered to be bygones and of lesser importance compared to getting back to New York as expeditiously as possible to rain hell down on the cohorts attacking Dominic and Montrose, but I doubted that was all that it was. Charley never once brought up James Dorsey's name after the encounter on the rooftop garden.

Matthias kept his own counsel, his gaze darkening often, and I wondered if there were more secrets that he, or Charley, held back and fought over in private—or would have fought over if he ever managed to catch Charley for longer than a few moments.

The American consul and the police and Captain Aldersley played their parts in trying to resolve the matter, showing great solicitude and eagerness to be helpful in their turn. Gerald Cartwright (I had been told) had given up his partner, James Dorsey, very quickly and not at all reluctantly after they had been apprehended at the Windsor Hotel. Eyewitness testimony had been provided by a Miss Matilda Fairchild, who had been present inside La

Parisiana and identified the movements of Miss Lucia Bernhardt being held prisoner by Gerald Cartwright. Additional testimony had been provided by Mr. Matthias Vandermeer, Mr. Tallis Lloyd-Chase, Captain Aldersley and an off-duty party of his fellow officers, who had been waiting at various locations and neighboring popular nights spots on Alfi Bey Street, keeping a surveillance on La Parisiana.

"We weren't allowed to show our faces too near La Parisiana in case we were recognized," Tallis explained. "Charley wasn't wholly happy with the arrangement. She wanted someone closer on the ground in case something happened to you—and not just anyone. She and Matthias and Captain Aldersley shouted at each other for about half an hour, and Tilly ended up being installed incognito inside La Parisiana."

Tilly huffed.

"How did Captain Aldersley get involved?"

"Matthias. The consul and police had been obliging but distrustful at first of the claims that you'd been abducted. To them, the evidence seemed to point to you having left of your own accord, and they hadn't moved as quickly as we'd liked, and nowhere near as quickly as Charley wanted. Matthias called in a favor. I don't think the captain realized what he'd gotten himself into when he agreed to help out."

"You mean the service pistols?"

"More than that. Charley was very worried. She was ready to seek out the black market variety if the captain and his officers had not—I don't know that 'capitulated' is the right word. You'll have to ask Charley about her exact methods. Matthias found out about them when we were waiting inside the Kursaal restaurant. Not a happy chap. But then Tilly ran in with her report that you'd left La Parisiana, and then all hell broke loose when you jumped out of the motor-car as it was about to drive off so there was no time to worry about safety and bureaucratic breaches or reading Charley the riot act."

Jumping out of a moving motor-car had not been one of my brightest ideas. It had apparently caused rather a lot of chaos on the street and, while it had delayed Gerald Cartwright from coming after me, it had also delayed Matthias and Tallis and Captain Aldersley and the others in getting to the motor-car and the Windsor Hotel. Gerald Cartwright had made hay of the ruction in arriving at the Windsor Hotel, firearm hidden away and pretending to be drunk, raising a racket about losing his girlfriend who had probably slipped into the hotel. James Dorsey had originally been planted at the Windsor to intercept Charley and surreptitiously drug her drink. A quiet abduction would have ensued. When it became obvious that Charley and I were not cooperative and the original plan would no longer work, James Dorsey had improvised and gone downstairs to the hotel lobby. We had thought he had gone to play knight errant and hold off the mad gunman.

All that terrifying shouting had been intended to keep us away and scare us up to the roof and strand us there. His partner, Gerald Cartwright, had expected James Dorsey to speak to the hotel clerks and allay their anxiety about the warnings I had given them. James Dorsey did intercept the message Charley had left with the bartender but he had also played his partner false. Instead of playing along with the staged drunken performance, he snitched on Cartwright, and while the hotel clerks and doorman tried to hold off Cartwright, James Dorsey slipped up to the roof. Cartwright's shouting had started out as a pretense but had turned into true rage. He had broken free from the clerks and stalked up to the roof after Dorsey's blood. If there had not been such bedlam in the street, Tallis and Matthias and Captain Aldersley's officers would have gotten to the Windsor Hotel sooner and prevented the encounter on the rooftop garden. Tallis had eventually found his way up to the roof because the doorman and several of the patrons in the barrel lounge had noted the angry shouting man who had gone charging up the stairwell. Tallis said that Matthias was detained even longer sorting out the mayhem since Matthias had better connections and more sway in Cairo than anyone else, but then he got waylaid by the confusion in the lobby of the Windsor Hotel, and it was the faint but distinct echo of Charley screaming abuse and threats, directed at someone who was later found to be James Dorsey, her voice percolating about halfway down the stairwell which had confirmed the situation beyond doubt.

Tallis had bruises all over his face, healing in varying multi-color shades, and a notch on the bridge of his nose which did not really behove a respectable banker's son to display. I wondered if the mark would ever vanish. I would never be able to repay this debt, amongst so many, of gratitude.

"You earned your battle scars," I told Tallis.

"I'm crushed that I missed so much of the blood and thunder action. Your rampage through the garden pottery. Vandermeer being a show-off. Tilly being Calamity Jane and saving the day." Tallis grinned at Tilly. "Is it true about Charley and the spoon?"

"You'll have to ask Charley about her exact methods. I'm surprised you haven't done so already. If you knew about the guns..."

"Haven't seen a ghost of Charley since the doctor discharged me. She sends Tilly to monitor my progress and make sure I'm eating properly and following medical instructions. What's the likelihood she is trying to hide from Vandermeer?"

Charley had been as invisible as Matthias had been busy. Tilly and I suspected that Charley had found herself other telegraph offices around Cairo besides the one at Shepheard's and haunted those on a rotating basis to avoid Matthias, amongst others. "I think Charley has a lot on her mind."

Tallis looked to Tilly but Tilly was not a turncoat and remained silent. "Are we still going ahead with the plan as originally agreed?"

"Yes." I looked at Tilly. Tilly nodded in agreement.

"I hear Faneuil's passage has been booked. When do you sail for New York?"

"As soon as Charley does. She's been held back in relation to the proceedings regarding James Dorsey and Gerald Cartwright."

Matthias had reported that Captain Aldersley's officers had surrounded the motor-car where the driver had been arrested shortly afterwards when the police arrived on the scene. He had given up the location where Vincent and I had been held captive. Several other petty criminals hired by Cartwright had also been arrested. Vincent, I was led to understand, was recovering steadily and would soon be headed back to America. Vincent had not asked to see me. I sent him my wishes for his recovery via Matthias.

The hold-up with Charley was a little bit more complicated.

Matthias had made it a point to check on me each day. It was kind of him given how hard-pressed he was for time. So much had been left to him to mop up after the events that had concluded at the Windsor Hotel. However, I could not quite understand why the arrest of James Dorsey and Gerald Cartwright in an ostensibly straightforward criminal case kept Matthias running about so frantically and distractedly pre-occupied, harried all hours of the day dealing with the police and lawyers and bureaucracy and meetings with the American and British consular mandarins and officers and agents and Captain Aldersley and telegrams and telephone calls with Godeffroy's head office and discussions about extradition treaties... It had to be about more than just smoothing things over with Captain Aldersley's superiors regarding the unauthorized possession and use of the service pistols which Charley had already claimed she had purloined from the unsuspecting officers and therefore her sole responsibility. It had to be about something else. Something out of the normal course of an arrest was happening in relation to James Dorsey and Gerald Cartwright and their attempts on my mother's diamond necklace and the abductions in relation to it. Something that was quite important. Something that also related to Charley.

When we had descended from the rooftop garden of the Windsor Hotel, I had handed the diamond necklace into Matthias's keeping for the ease of all of the police and bureaucratic procedures involved in the case investigations that he had taken it upon himself to oversee. It had been the first time that the necklace had left our side since embarking on the tour. Matthias had brought it back the following evening with a heavy frown.

I had not noticed his expression at first. Tilly had brought me back to Shepheard's after our interviews with the police and American consul and lawyer and medic had concluded. (Charley had said that she would be holed up there for a lot longer and Tallis was still undergoing medical examinations.) After a refreshing bath and dressing in the suite, Tilly and I had wandered downstairs to the terrace and were led to two chairs before an unoccupied wicker table. We sat down in amongst the diversely gossiping crowd, ordered tea. I sat with Tilly, breathing in puffs of freedom, listening to the band playing, and watching the multi-colored population drift past as I debated whether or not to send a telegram home to advise of recent events.

I saw Matthias's head first in black shadow, a vague silhouette bobbing above the multitudes flowing in from the dusk of Ibrahim Pasha Street. He separated from the pavement throng and reemerged at the head of the terrace. He came to a standing stop next to a waiter, paused, as if hovering in mid-air, as if uncertain—had he been searching the terrace's wicker tables for us or reconsidering his decision to seek us out?—and then his familiar firm gait brought him before us. He carried an attaché case in one hand, a box of chocolates from Groppi's in the other, and a furrow in his brow.

Matthias handed us the box of chocolates. "Good evening," he said. "Please accept my apologies for interrupting your tea. May I trouble you for a word in private?"

We went upstairs to the suite. Matthias opened up his attaché case and took out a velvet jewel case containing my mother's diamond necklace. Matthias asked Tilly and me where the necklace had been hidden all this time. We took him to Charley's suite and showed him.

"The necklace was moved about. More often than not, it was wrapped inside a sock and shoved into the toe of one of Charley's ankle boots, left carelessly lying around—intentionally so—in the midst of a messy hotel room in plain view. Sometimes it was placed on the brim of a hat, tucked into and obscured behind the swathes of colorful silk scarves and flowers and other ornamental and decorative millinery trimmings—which, you'll recall, Charley always wore or handed to Tilly. Sometimes it was tucked into a secret pocket sewn into one of Tilly's dresses. Sometimes it was folded into a soft velvet pouch and placed inside a full jar or box of candy, surrounded by crystallized violets or peppermints. Charley kept the jewelry she liked in the other jars—there were so many to fill—and left the unimportant pieces in her jewelry case." One could never accuse Charley of being dragon-hearted, sleeping jealously on a hoard of treasure. Tilly was constantly scolding Charley over her carelessness regarding her own jewelry. "Sometimes the necklace was placed inside the hollowed out centers of the souvenirs we'd bought. Sometimes it stayed in the false bottom or secret pockets of Charley's steamer trunk, on the interior as well as the exterior. Charley also has a pair of boots whose heels, which contain a hollow cavity, can be conveniently screwed off... All of these Charley had had custom-made before she ever left New York. Sometimes Tilly wrapped it up in a scarf or handkerchief and carried it around with her in her pocket... Those are the places I'm aware of. The one rule we abided by was that unless I was was wearing it for an occasion, it never stayed in my possession."

Matthias showed no signs of being awestruck by Charley's many and varied flashes of inspiration. The furrow in his brow deepened. "So you were the only three persons who had handled the necklace from the time your mother gave it to you?" he asked.

"Yes, that's right. Why?"

"During the procedural processing, the necklace was examined by a jeweler. Apparently he found a slight...irregularity. With your permission, Lucia, I would like to have it re-examined by Godeffroy's experts independently. I will try to get it back to you as soon as possible but it is unlikely to be before you return to New York. I will, of course, personally assure its—"

"Oh, for goodness sake, Matthias, there is no need for that. I trust you. And Godeffroy's is the insurer, isn't it? But what is this all about?"

"I'm not certain yet," Matthias answered, his voice taut and strained. "That's why I want an independent assessment done. I'll report back when I know more."

Matthias did not volunteer any more information. He fell into stretches of silent brooding in between informing us about the investigation's progress. Before he left, he assured us that he had managed to secure the non-disclosure of our names and many details in relation to the reporting of the affair in the local papers. (In spite of Matthias's maneuverings, news and gossip spread. There had been witnesses to the traffic jam I had caused outside La Parisiana and a full barrel lounge audience of patrons had been present that evening at the Windsor Hotel. A day after the incident, the number of eyewitnesses and stories about what had happened and who said and did what rose into the hundreds. Two days later, the eyewitnesses and stories multiplied and grew in flamboyance and spread across continents. Three days later... I received telegrams from Ginny and Celeste and Frankie and Belle, repeating the wildest permutations of what had taken place and been originally reported. There was no stemming of the flow or fertility of gossip, apparently. Such was the nature of the beast.)

Tilly and I walked together with Matthias downstairs to the lobby. Captain Aldersley had invited us to the Gezira Sporting Club and we were hoping that Charley's interviews might be finishing soon enough for her to join us. Matthias thanked us for including him in the invitation too, but he had to decline on account of the many responsibilities he had yet to discharge. Matthias hailed two cabs, one for himself, to return to his duties, and one for our destination. On the front steps of Shepheard's, he turned and said: "If Charley mentions Rhys Hadden, will you let me know? He was a foreman in one of Montrose's factories in Chicago, promoted to factory manager after the previous manager was dismissed. He's just been arrested in New York."

With a nod of goodbye, Matthias strode off down the steps and into the night, the darkness swallowing him whole.

"The poor man!" Tilly whispered.

Had Tilly been referring to Matthias or to Rhys Hadden? The epithet could have been applied to all of Charley's suitors whether or not they had brought her lovely posies of violets.

A day later, Charley paced around the sitting room of her suite like a frustrated bull inside the bullring who had disposed of one matador and was pawing the ground, impatient to impale another.

It was not simply the news that the London Stock Exchange had crashed following British investor Clarence Hatry and several of his associates being taken into custody for fraud and forgery, and the suspension of shares in the Hatry group from trading. Charley had refused the latest in a string of summons to the district police station. She had been recalcitrant and uncooperative and dodged all previous requests, and it had surprised me that Matthias had finally managed to run her to ground to rile her up with another petition.

"What is going on, Matthias? Why is Charley not yet cleared for departure?"

"Her uncle. And James Dorsey is refusing to cooperate. He has set a condition."

"I don't understand. Why does that affect whether Charley can sail or not? And how is James Dorsey or Charley's uncle in a position to demand anything?"

What Matthias told me was far worse than I, at my most pessimistic, could have ever foreseen. The shadows were closing in on Charley.

When Matthias had finished explaining, he asked: "Do you know where Charley really was and what she was doing while she was away from New York?"

Matthias looked tired, drained, and wary, unnaturally composed, holding his skin together and battling to stay upright through sheer force of will. Haggard would not have been an understatement. It seemed like ten years had been shaved off his life. I felt sympathy for Matthias—he had the bears mauling the London Stock Exchange to contend with along with everything else—but I could not stray from the path.

"Charley was on holiday," I said.

It would not have helped to tell him—even truthfully—"gunpowder, treason and plot".

But when Matthias simply nodded as if he had expected my answer, seeming almost relieved, I began to understand what Charley had meant about the first fall being the worst, and I wondered when she and Matthias had stopped registering the blows of the bludgeon.

45

CHARLOTTE:

"We have nothing to say to each other."

"I think Dorsey begs to differ," Matthias said, walking alongside me.

"When did he make you his mouthpiece?"

Matthias did not answer.

"Why do I have to see him?"

"You don't."

"But he won't talk unless I see him?"

"You don't have to meet with him," said Matthias. "You can turn around now and walk out of here and return to your hotel."

"That wouldn't be very civic minded or abiding by—"

"You know, for someone who's continually denied the merit of rules and convention and respectability, you're sailing dangerously close to the wind."

"And you are so often a pompous jackass."

"I delivered the message to you. I've done my part. Now I can apologize for wasting your time and escort you out and help you find a cab and then go back to doing my proper job? Why are you even here? Aren't you in hiding? Did Lucia send you?"

"Why do you think I'm here? Because I didn't ignore enough heartrending messages left at Shepheard's by your colleagues asking me to come down to the station, I thought I'd pop by in person to bask in the attention?"

"Your complaint has been duly noted. I'll pass on your message. I'm sorry for your wasted trip."

"Is Cartwright's confession not enough?"

"For the crimes carried out here, yes."

"You want them both for the East Coast heists? You want the case to be iron-clad?" Matthias nodded. "There were gaps in Cartwright's testimony but I didn't think Cartwright was the only one it incriminated. I didn't think he kept this hands entirely clean. I thought Cartwright gave sufficient detail for your corroborating evidence to be made complete and the dots to be joined and—"

"We'll get them, don't you worry."

"Matthias."

"Cartwright apparently was the brawn rather than the brains of the operation until you and Lucia came onto the scene and broke up the partnership and left Cartwright blundering along on this side of the Atlantic alone." Matthias stopped in the middle of the corridor of the police station, barricading the way. I refused to let the weight of his gaze fluster me. "You don't have to meet with him," he repeated. "I'll let the detectives know."

"But it will make your life easier, won't it? If he confesses, it will help the investigators find the rest of the stolen property and restore it to the rightful owners? And he'll do his time for his involvement here and on the East Coast? Lucia said—"

"You don't have to meet with him," Matthias said again. "And why don't you have a lawyer here with you?"

"How can you be certain that he will keep his side of the bargain if I do see him?"

"We can't. Another reason why you don't have to—"

"I'll make you a deal. I'll give him five minutes, then you can storm in and thrash him for the punishably wicked life he has led. In exchange, you'll stop poking and ferreting around Montrose and grilling me about how the London crash affected it, and I'll stop asking you how you fared."

"No."

"What? Why? You can't just reject out of hand—"

"Because you don't have to see Dorsey if you don't want to. You can't even say his name anymore, Charley!"

"Which hat ar—"

"Charley."

"I've a berth on the next liner out of Alexandria," I said.

"That's impossible!"

"Are you doubting Tilly's supreme capabilities? Everything has been taken care of. I've all the necessary stamps and authorizations."

"How? If your uncle's people have been whispering in local ears and padding pockets, trying to restrict your movements so that they can wrest you back in their custody, you can't have—"

"Oh yes, it's been a delight ever since news of the incident at the Windsor reached New York."

"I'm sorry I wasn't able to—"

"Don't be ridiculous! Even the mighty Matthias Vandermeer cannot stop that tide. I'm grateful for all the interference you've been running between the local authorities and his henchmen." Obscure, prosaic, apologetic bureaucratic delays were far more effectively obstructive than raising all sorts of outlandish accusations and petty objections and getting people arrested. I could not prove or trace it back to my uncle but I thought I recognized his hand in the coincidence of my ignoring certain imperiously demanding telegrams followed shortly thereafter by such special treatment. I had been singled out while Lucia and Tilly had been spared.

"Your uncle is understandably growing more and more worried about being deposed. He is determined not to lose track of you this time."

"One would think it quite obvious that I don't like being detained at another's pleasure."

"Charley, how?"

"Best that you don't know the details."

"But you'll tell me later—when we aren't in a public place?"

"You'll find out when you read about me in the New York papers. Or via the scuttlebutt express."

"Charley."

"Matthias."

"Cunard, White Star or other?"

"I don't know. It will be a surprise."

"When?"

"That will be a surprise too."

"Will it be a surprise to Lucia?"

"Yes."

"Truthfully?"

"Yes."

"Fine," Matthias gritted out. "Then you should make sure that you don't miss your connections."

"I can spare five minutes."

"I'm sure Rhys Hadden will be relieved to know you're heading back. Or will it be a surprise for him too?"

"You're an idiot. Five minutes—and then the door had better be open for me to walk out. And you keep your nose away from Montrose's business. Why would I need a lawyer present if he is the one doing the talking? Shouldn't he have his lawyer or a consular representative present?"

"Dorsey was offered one. He declined. He said he wanted this interview with you to be private."

"That's awfully presumptuous."

"You—"

A detective burst out of a door and hurried up to us, taking my hand and effusing greetings and thanks for agreeing assistance. "Miss Masterson,

Miss Masterson, it is so good of you to come!" The detective bubbled with fervid protestations of appreciation, for Matthias in being so effective in persuading me, for my cooperation in this case, holding onto me as if he feared I would vanish again at the slightest impulse.

Matthias glowered at the intrusion.

"Oh, let's just hurry up and get it over with. I have better things with which to idle away my time."

The detective ushered me down another corridor. I was expecting to be led to a jail cell of some sort. Instead, we stopped before a plain door with a guard standing outside. Apparently the accused was waiting inside the room. At the detective's authorization, the door was unlocked.

Matthias's voice came from behind me: "Charley, you——"

I stepped through the doorway.

James Dorsey sat inside a drab, airless cell of an interview room at an equally sad and dreary wooden table that, like the room and the other trappings of his imprisonment, was in well-preserved condition for its age and daily trials (dry mummification instead of humid antebellum decay and decline in the Deep South) but had clearly seen better days. His hands and feet were restrained by metallic cuffs. He had held up surprisingly well, slightly rumpled and frayed, looking neither sweaty or hollow-eyed and sullen, only a little worse for wear than when I had last seen him, no more worse, really, than someone who had suffered the dead heat of an Cairo summer without the relief of a fan or breeze and freshly laundered linen and the freedom of a cool drink at anytime he chose. He did not slump or seem at all defeated by his detention or interrogations. His eyes, when he raised his gaze to me as I entered the room, were as invitingly green and unfathomable as when I had first seen them. He arched a brow when the detective and Matthias followed me into the interview room and gave a brief introduction to the proceedings, advising him of my stipulations.

There were two chairs on the opposite side of the table from where he sat. The detective politely held out one of those chairs for me. I took the seat and he sat down in the other. Matthias went to stand in a corner of the room as a spectator.

James Dorsey watched all of this in silence.

I waited for him to speak first. I had decided when I entered the interview room that I would see if I could get through this without uttering a single word. If he wished to engage in a staring contest and squander his five minutes, I would not raise an objection. I was not the one who had sought this interview.

"I wasn't expecting additional company," James Dorsey finally observed to the detective.

"You demanded an interview with Miss Masterson. She's kindly agreed to grant you an audience. Five minutes. You can take it or leave it,"

Matthias cut in, poised on the edge of a growl.

James Dorsey raised his gaze to Matthias. Then he turned back to me and gave a short laugh.

"This is not how I imagined—how I wanted it to be," he said.

I looked back into his green gaze and held my tongue.

"Well, Charley? No cutting remarks? No stings of wrath and recrimination?"

I hated being turned into the subject of observation by the three men in the room when by rights I should have been part of the audience observing. Matthias's regard I was used to; with him, I could punch back. The detective's bounced back and forth, soaking up detail like a remorseless recording, devoid of nuance and understanding. James Dorsey sought to hide in the diversion. He was trying to incite me to speak, to allow self-revulsion and anger to betray me and give him direction, an advantage. Of course I was disgusted with myself. How much more degrading would it have been to have seen it reflected in others' eyes as well as my own? I choked down my wallow in those fine feelings. The savage edge of my anger gave me stronger resolve to see through my silence. It made me hold steady when I wanted to avert my eyes. I was determined not to dissolve. I had disgraced myself quite enough on his account.

I gave him his stare back.

Small details began to replace my first impressions. I had thought him untouched by the turn of circumstances, unbeaten in spirit, but perhaps it was pridefulness which kept his tone clear and smooth, held his spine straight and prevented him from caving, or desperation driving him to master a final performance rather than give way to truculence. He did not give way to the indulgences of third rate villains, no cheap petulance, no resentfulness marring a weak mouth, no evasive belligerence. Nothing I could point to and say, aha, there, there in that line, that contour, that expression, there lay treachery and rottenness and vile humiliation, there lay a warning that any simpleton would have heeded if she had not been willfully blind. No such cold comfort for Charley Masterson, played for the fool that she was. He appeared the same, unchanged in essentials from our first encounter. There was no sign of regret or anger in the cast of his face —but he was not Matthias Vandermeer after all, who would have been sweating apologies, whether or not they were merited, and indignantly challenging the basis of his being wrongfully judged, and had he been Matthias Vandermeer, he would not have landed himself in this situation— his motivations were more obscure and incalculable. It seemed strange to me that he had not tried to negotiate a deal for something more than an interview with me. He had always seemed to me a pragmatic man. He could not have failed to recognize the weight of evidence compiling against him and Cartwright, even without Matthias's thoroughness and tenacity hammering home the point. Or perhaps he had. What was he after? Surely at this late hour, after all that had transpired, he did not expect candor? Sympathy? Aid? He watched me closely, waiting, studying, assessing, searching for something. Had I always been given this sort of scrutiny and mistaken it for warmer interest? Something changed in his expression, as if he had read something in my face that he did not like. He must not have found what he was searching for because the striking golden-ringed green of his eyes flickered in a sort of frown.

"You're testing me again, aren't you, Charley?"

He did not appear to like my silence.

"No," James Dorsey said, shaking his head and sighing, "you've delivered judgment already." He dropped his voice and leaned closer over the table towards me. "Tell me one thing, Charley. I was right, wasn't I? It was in Cannes that Matthias Vandermeer first turned you against me? If he hadn't, we might have—" He reached out his hand but the detective, and movement from the corner, intervened and he withdrew it.

He rubbed his shadowed, unshaven jaw, rattling his handcuffs. It must still have been very sore from when Matthias had slugged him on the Windsor rooftop. He took another tack. "I'm incarcerated here completely at his mercy and yet your protector is still pursuing his obsession, trying to assign the guilt for all these wild plots to me. You've taken his word over mine, but ask yourself this, Charley: does he deserve to be trusted so incontestably? Why is he so obsessed with getting rid of me?"

I let him speak without interruption or encouragement. Enough rope, I told myself. It was easier to keep silent in the dread of suffering the mortification of blurting out a stream of real thoughts or emotions, especially with Matthias as an audience. I did not enjoy the sense of déjà vu. No one looked kindly upon a deceiver and a thief except the stupid fool who still had stars in her eyes.

"Do you know what the funny thing is? He didn't notice me in the slightest when we first crossed paths. I'd met him on the other side of the Atlantic. We'd even spoken." He paused to look at me while he let this revelation sink in. "It was at a masquerade ball at The Sagamore Hotel in Bolton Landing. I was there as a guest of the Fabens on their annual holiday to the Adirondacks. The talk of the evening had not been about the Rockefellers or Vanderbilts or Whitings or Phippses who had been invited and were expected to make a grand appearance at the masquerade ball but of the young Montrose heiress. I was as curious as the next man to see what the fabled heiress looked like. She remained elusive, well-guarded by her friend, whisked away before anybody could get too close, but I got her name and a place on her dance card. Then this big, lumbering chap turned up at the masquerade asking around for a Miss Charlotte Masterson who was meant to have been in attendance that evening with her friend, Miss

Olivia Routledge. He didn't recognize me at the Ritz Bar in Paris. He didn't remember asking me for directions at the masquerade because he'd only eyes for one thing. But I remembered and recognized him. He might've been wearing a mask that night but he was unmistakable He was the same big brute from the masquerade."

The dismal walls of the interview room, the worn and scratched table and chairs, the keenly attentive detective seated beside me, the faint restive movements that Matthias was making in the corner, all the unsettled, baffling, shameful things inside me, the ones I had pushed, down, down, down, but kept bobbing back up and rolling about and throwing me off balance, they all narrowed to one point, fading into his voice and the wash of the recent past.

"One thing became clear. Hearing that you were on board the Mauretania, I had thought that lightning had struck twice. It didn't fully begin to dawn upon me until the night I saw you again at the Ritz Bar that the young woman I'd met briefly at the masquerade ball—the one who'd promised me a dance and then vanished before I could claim it—she was not the same Miss Masterson that I had met on board the Mauretania and who had danced with me at the Savoy, the bold Miss Masterson who'd accepted a dare to race across France. I realized that you—unlike Matthias Vandermeer—hadn't simply forgotten about a chance meeting at a masquerade ball. You were never at the masquerade ball in the first place. And Matthias Vandermeer must have known that when I directed him towards the young woman I thought was the Montrose heiress. Yet he keeps asking about my movements. He seems to be particularly interested in my recreational activities in the United States and in connection with you. He keeps trying to pin me down on what I was doing at the ball and other social events. Frankly, I was there for the party and to have a good time like everybody else, but what was he doing there so far away from Lond—"

I had pushed my chair back and stood up with finality before James Dorsey finished the sentence. I walked over to the door. In the nearby corner, Matthias was leaning against the wall. His eyes were blazing. Neither of us spoke. I turned the doorknob. James Dorsey called out after me, his voice sharpening into a taunting growl: "Before you consign me to the Devil and ride off with him, you might want to take a closer look at—"

My feet carried me out into the corridor. I marched past the guard. Footsteps came hurrying up behind me.

"Charley, wait!"

Matthias grabbed my arm. I jerked away. "Don't follow me," I bit out. He let go. I turned on him. "There was not a witness at the Holyoke Masquerade. You were the witness!"

Matthias's silence condemned him. He stood there in the corridor, unmoving, utterly silent. James Dorsey's insinuations snaked around and surrounded him like a huge, dark wraith.

"On how many other occasions did you spy on me?"

"Charley—"

"How many?"

"Two—maybe three. I was not free to leave London at will. Even when I was able to get away, it was not easy to travel back and forth confidentially. I was there on personal business, Charley, not for the investigation. It was a coincidence that Dorsey happened to—"

"But the knowledge later became relevant and useful to the investigation."

"It was never used against you. I was the only one who knew. Nobody else."

"Then you weren't acting in a detached and impartial capacity, were you? Isn't that compromis—"

"What I was doing was not jumping to conclusions," Matthias snapped back at me, rigidly defensive, bracing for a fight, his amber eyes terrible and glowing, and yet the rest of him oddly contained in stillness as if he was struggling not to drown in a hell of fury and dismay and desperation. "Coincidence and correlation do not equal causation. I knew that you were hiding, lying, yes, but it had nothing to do with the jewelry robberies. I was certain that, for you, it was about something else entirely unrelated, and I was gathering evidence to prove it. I know now that the dance you've been doing across the States and all over London and the Continent has been for one thing—that it has always been about Montrose. I just—I didn't have— at the time, what I knew and what I could prove was not enough." Matthias leaned forward to look at my face. His gaze bored into me. "Has he succeeded, Charley? Are you beginning to doubt?"

What was the objective truth? James Dorsey was lying through his teeth, playing the maligned, injured soul? Brazening it out in a last ditch effort to escape from detention? One could not help but admire the gall of it, for him to dare, while still sitting in cuffs, to accuse the implacably conscientious Matthias Vandermeer of not merely being derelict but malfeasant in his duty, attempting to manipulate the investigation and plant false evidence to frame—I shook myself, clearing the cobwebs from my mind. What was wrong with me? Had all rational thought fled from my head? Would I let my unremitting foolishness and desire to hit out at someone in my misery overwhelm all sense? His guilt had been writ large across time. I had been shown the evidence. I had heard his associate Cartwright's confession. I had had a gun pointed at my head by him and another pointed at Lucia by Cartwright. I had been the last in a long line of quarry he had hunted for gain and wooed with ruthless devotion. I was stung by his smooth, smiling calculation, his repeated betrayals. Oh, and how I had felt the serpent's kisses. How fallible had been my judgment.

How easily he had made a patsy of me. I raged against every single one of his deceptions, and my own complicit shame and stupidity in permitting myself to be deceived, and the offensive temerity of his continuing on as if it could all be brushed away with a disarming ironical smile, as if his actions and lies had not taken place at all, as if he had not harmed or wronged anyone. And yet I was still here, still listening to him wiggle and lie. A good man—a truly good, decent, unassuming, selfless, kind man—languished unjustly in jail across an ocean while I dallied here, allowing James Dorsey to wheedle and twist me around to his ends. What was wrong with me?

I turned around and pushed into the interview room, feeling Matthias's gaze burning my back as I walked away from him. James Dorsey and the detective both looked up in surprise at my entrance.

I strode up to the table to face James. My anger focused and burned with a bright, steady flame. I broke my silence. "You should have heeded me in Assuan and walked away when you still could have."

He studied me. After a long stretched out moment, acceptance seemed to settle into his gaze. He answered: "I know. I made a hash of things. If I've ever had a regret..." His eyes softened, a slight twinkle lighting up the green. "It was fun while it lasted, wasn't it, Charley?"

I allowed myself a second to pretend he had meant his words, that this exchange at least was made in sincerity. Then I left the interview room for the final time. His five minutes were up.

VOYAGE HOME

Late September 1929, Cairo–Boulogne-sur-Mer–New York

46

LUCIA:

Tilly and I sailed from Egypt alone.

I should have known that something was not right when Charley agreed to come to Groppi's with us for ice cream. She had returned grim-faced and unforthcoming from the interview with James Dorsey at the district police station. She was again actively avoiding Matthias and, I suspected, not on speaking terms with him. It had not been unexpected. I was certain that on the rooftop of the Windsor Hotel, I had not mistaken the momentary expression of devastation which had ignited into rage. It was no coincidence that she had yet to name James Dorsey in our presence. But what had happened at the police station and what had Matthias done now?

We tried to tread softly, sympathetically, around Charley. Tallis had previously made us promise to take him to Groppi's as reward for his compliance with medical orders and swift recovery; he extended the invitation to Charley despite her being, clearly, in no mood for conversation or music or crowds. To our surprise, Charley had accepted. She had been quiet during the visit to the coffee shop, attentive enough to her Sfogliatella ice cream and our conversation, but contributing so little that it was evident she was not really with us. We were in Groppi's, cosmopolitan watering hole of Cairo society, but it might as well have been a wasteland. She had not only been silent and withdrawn, she had been, I thought, very angry; that glacial, remote, almost vacant, expression betraying a simmering fury. What else was stirring in that cauldron besides the swift passage through unforeseen grief, loss, and anger caused by the sudden dispossession of an illusion?

It was natural to want to intercede but Tilly and I knew better than to bother Charley when she chose quite adamantly not to share her distress.

329

Even Tallis grudgingly agreed that prodding Charley, however well-intentioned, was not going to work.

When we retired for the evening and exchanged good nights, Charley had responded composedly, perhaps a little somber, and had gone to stand at the open window.

"Charley?"

Charley glanced up.

"Are you all right?"

"Just peachy," Charley said. "Sleep well, Lucia." She had given me a brief, weightless wisp of a smile and turned back to the Cairene night.

I had thought that the returned calm was a favorable sign, as if in the weighted silence, her anger had been lanced and the poison drained away. I had been wrong. It had not been a dissolution. The fixed expression on Charley's face may have been frozen at mournful, but that was only the shedding of a redundant layer of skin. The core, the true self, would more accurately have been calibrated to resolute. Vengeance is mine; I will repay, saith the Lord. I should have known that the cogs in her brain never stopped turning.

The following morning, everything in the suite was exactly as it had been on the previous morning, except that Charley never came to breakfast.

Tilly announced Matthias's arrival as I stared at the steamer trunk that belonged to Charley. It lay silently on the carpet, packed full of her clothes, shoes, books, all carefully folded and tucked inside, untouched. Charley's dresses hung in the wardrobe. Toiletries and candy jars sat on the dresser. Nothing was missing, according to Tilly, except for the two plain dresses that Charley had purchased from Galeries Lafayette and Printemps and the volume by Colette that she had bought from Sylvia Beach's bookshop.

I rushed into the sitting room where Matthias was waiting. I stared at the low table before the couch, at the Chippendale side cabinet, at the walnut canterbury, at all of the flat surfaces around the room. Nothing stirred. Charley's infallible morning delivery of newspapers and telegrams had not come. A chilliness stole through my bones.

Charley had stolen off in the night!

My sluggish mind tried to catch up and make sense of it. Charley had vanished—jumped ship—had simply left everything behind in her suite and walked out of Shepheard's and into the night without a word. I ran through all the occurrences of the previous days, sifting back and forth through them trying to pinpoint what had caused Charley to bolt. James Dorsey was an obvious contender. The arrest of Rhys Hadden was another. Dominic de Almadén. The vultures circling Montrose. The London Stock Exchange crash and contagion flowing to the American markets. There were too many to count. No, I was going about it the wrong way. Those incognito uniforms of hers were the key...

"Lucia?" Matthias said, observing my behavior with a growing frown.

I looked around the suite, haunted by Charley's presence of the previous evening. Charley had stood at the window, enigmatic and distant, yet feverish with secret plottings. So many miles to go before she slept.

I turned to Matthias. "She's gone."

Matthias struggled to understand. His tired eyes searched my face with numb consternation. When the realization finally sunk into him, the light seemed to dim in them, like something hollowed out.

"She did give me fair warning," Matthias said. He held up something in his hand. "I came to deliver these."

They were travel documents. Charley's travel documents. Charley had been endlessly fuming over the enforced delays over the last few days. Matthias must have called in quite a few favors if he had managed to finally sidestep and overcome the obstacles that Nicholas Masterson's people had placed in Charley's path. That thought brought me to my senses.

"If you're delivering these now, what on earth is Charley traveling with? How would she clear all the customs and immigration formalities without her passport?"

Matthias pivoted around to Tilly. "Charley said you'd taken care of her travel arrangements, Tilly."

Of course! Of the three people standing in the suite, only one of us was not stunned and wrestling with Charley's sudden departure.

"I cannot divulge those confidences, Mr. Vandermeer," Tilly replied, apologetically but firmly.

"Is she—will she be—safe, Tilly?"

Tilly paused to consider whether answering would constitute betraying a confidence.

In those few seconds that it had taken Tilly to deliberate on an answer, Matthias and I had independently reached the same conclusion.

"You don't have to respond, Tilly," Matthias said. Matthias's had face lost the worst of its hollowed look: Tilly's circumspection pointed clearly to complicity; her lack of grave disapproval and fretful dread suggested Charley's plot was at least within the realms of sanity according to Tilly's benchmarks of the notion which were more than acceptable to the reasonable person. Matthias's voice returned, steady, quiet, and strengthened, if not exactly with renewed hope, certainly with receding bleakness. Perhaps he was remembering that quality of Charley's that resembled an indestructible rubber ball. He handed the travel documents over to Tilly along with a box of Groppi's candy. "I think I can guess."

"Matthias," I said, "what happened at the police station?"

A groove of harsh anger appeared between Matthias's dark brows. "I shouldn't have let Charley be exposed to Dorsey after what happened at the Windsor," he said. "She hadn't wanted to see him. She was stubborn about

331

doing what she thought was her duty but she was still—I should have known that Dorsey would continue to play the long game. I failed to protect her as I should have. That was my blunder. She is justifiably livid with me for that—and for the rest."

"By 'long game', you mean—"

"It's Cartwright's contention that Dorsey broke off a mutually profitable partnership because Dorsey thought he'd found a more lucrative quarry in the Montrose heiress."

"He didn't—doesn't—know about the troubles at Montrose?"

"Never crossed his mind—and if it did, I don't think he believed it—even after Charley warned him."

"Charley—"

"Obliquely. She was so insistent on a fair game." There were pale lines of emotion etched around his mouth. "Dorsey never played fair."

"You think Charley... Oh." Oh. "Do you really believe that Charley would have? She was so skeptical, so vigilant and chary. It can't have gone so deep that—"

"Then he was a fortune-hunter!" Tilly exhaled with feeling.

"Regardless, his racket worked." Disgust flitted across Matthias's face.

Had it? Had it really? "It wouldn't have mattered if..." I realized belatedly that I had voiced my thoughts aloud.

"If what, Lucia?" Matthias asked.

"It doesn't matter." I hastened to amend my slip. It was only my supposition and I could not in good conscience add anything more to what was already on Matthias's shoulders, not this fragile, delicate, barely acknowledged thing which felt as weighty as any of the secrets that Charley had entrusted to me. If Charley stood by her decision in Oxford and held to her silence, it was not my place to meddle.

"It doesn't matter," he agreed. "Dorsey took advantage of her. I won't let that go unanswered." Matthias turned away. "Next time you run into Lottie Fairchild," Matthias said, "tell her I said hey."

Matthias took his leave before I could ask what he had meant by "and the rest".

"I'm sure it isn't quite as bad as it seems," I told Tilly. "Charley always has things in hand."

Tilly tsked and clicked her tongue and shook her head at the imbroglio, clearly taking a dissenting view.

Later that morning, when Tilly and I were finishing our packing, a telegram arrived. It was addressed to me.

"LUCIA SORRY COULD NOT WAIT ANY LONGER NEXT LUNCHEON MY TREAT"

It had been sent from a telegraph office in Port Said.

A weight rolled off me. Tilly's brief smile when I showed her the telegram confirmed my relief. Charley—or rather, Lottie—had made it through the lines. She had made her crossing.

Our departure from Cairo had been a lonely one.

It had been previously arranged that Tallis would embark on the voyage home via the same route as ours. We had intended to continue on board the White Star liner, the SS Adriatic, scheming and refining our offensive on the journey back to New York. I was still downstairs at Shepheard's telegraph office, sending off my final telegram and pasting the last of my stamps onto the screeds of closely written pages to be posted back to New York and London, when the first missile arrived to wreck destruction on those carefully laid plans.

Tallis had sent a last minute messenger to deliver his apologies. An unexpected delay had come up and he was unable to accompany us to Alexandria. It was not certain whether he would be able to catch up in time to join us on the voyage back to New York when our ship set sail.

Tallis's message coincided with one from an attaché from Matthias's office who was even more apologetic in delivering the deep regrets of Mr. Vandermeer who was unable to attend upon us in person due to the escape of one man from the Cairene guard convoy during the handover of two prisoners to a second police delegation tasked with escorting the pair to another jurisdiction to face justice. A diamond necklace that had been entered in as evidence for the case, which was being transported from the safe, at the same time as the prisoners' handover, back to Mr. Vandermeer's custody, had also vanished.

Tilly and I did not know what to think as we departed from Shepheard's.

Charley. Tallis. Matthias. One after another, like dominoes, they toppled over and fell and left a void where they had once stood. I had not realized how deeply I had burrowed into the strength and comfort of their friendship until their sudden absence left me bereft. I was so grateful for Tilly, the one remaining member of our band.

Tilly and I left behind the bustling terrace on Ibrahim Pasha Street and the Ezbekiya gardens and the traffic and chaos of downtown Cairo and, as the train moved slowly out of the station, tried not to be downcast about the sink of memories draining, not to think of all of the sights and sounds and smells and heat and palm trees and domes and minarets and pyramids fading away, not to mourn the loss of the cosmopolitan city, cradle of ancient civilization, portal to such enchanting mirages and vast beautiful wilderness, as we made our way to Alexandria.

That James Dorsey had escaped, that he and my mother's diamond necklace had disappeared so swiftly following on from Charley's disappearance was a coincidence that we did not like to dwell upon, but it stuck to us like a burr, maintaining a malign presence over us as we joined the parade of pedestrians moving with unaccustomed haste along the quay.

I boarded the ship first. Tilly followed later onto the SS Adriatic, shepherding the luggage. There were no sightings of James Dorsey. We sailed out of Alexandria without incident—out of golden Egypt where so much had happened—without a single whimper.

It was hard at times not to feel abandoned, our comfort and refuge from the sharp-toothed, bruising world outside torn away. When my resolve and spirits flagged, I reminded myself that whether I was traveling alone or with a merry band or under Tilly's aegis, all those roads led back to New York where we were bound to meet again.

The SS Adriatic was due to call in at Syracuse, Naples, Monaco, and Gibraltar before crossing the Atlantic to New York. I had been expecting a long voyage home. When we entered the cabin, this erroneous assumption was put to rights when Tilly drew my attention to the details of our travel papers. We were not to be staying on board the White Star liner until it docked in New York Harbor but disembarking at the third port in Monaco. From there, we were to make our way north by rail across France to Boulogne-sur-Mer to board the Hamburg-American Line steamer SS Cleveland to New York. The reasons why we had to undertake such an unnecessarily complicated route when we could have simply stayed on board the SS Adriatic were not ones that Tilly could, or would, divulge. The bookings and arrangements had been made. It was not ours to question why.

That sounded to me very much like Charley reasoning.

People were expecting me to arrive in New York on the SS Adriatic. The last batch of telegrams that I had sent home from Cairo had been to that effect. I had no knowledge of Charley's post-disappearance arrangements and communications. Charley was probably, by extension, also assumed to be sailing on the SS Adriatic. That, I realized later, was precisely the point.

I checked the ship's first class passengers list. There, sure enough, underneath "PASSENGERS EMBARKING AT ALEXANDRIA: Disembarking at Port indicated by Letter, viz (S) Syracuse (N) Naples (M) Monaco (G) Gibraltar (Y) New York" was printed: "116. Y Masterson, Miss C.".

I looked up to find Tilly observing me.

"I guess we will give everyone a surprise when we sail into New York Harbor."

Tilly nodded in agreement. I felt my suspicions vindicated.

"There are going to be some disappointed passengers waiting to catch sight of Charley."

When Tilly did not respond, did not even blink, the wheels in my head began turning.

It had been said that the journey home was always the shortest. That had not proven to be true for Ulysses. However, our cruise from Alexandria, sailing across the Mediterranean into the port at Monaco where we disembarked, certainly felt shorter than the voyage which had taken us to Egypt. So did our return journey along the jewel-like French Riviera and the overland crossing towards the English Channel. Perhaps that was partly because Tilly and I slept through half of it in the luxury wagon-lit of the Calais-Méditerranée Express from Monte Carlo to Calais and enjoyed breakfast and luncheon the next day as northern France flew past our window. From Calais, we took a connecting service to Boulogne-sur-Mer, a former Roman port and staging area for Napoleon's troops in 1805 during his planned invasion of England, situated on the Côte d'Opale, the stretch of French coast between Calais and Normandy which had inspired artists from Turner to Victor Hugo and Charles Dickens. And hadn't the Scarlet Pimpernel and Chauvelin locked horns here, too, in Boulogne?

But now I only hear
Its melancholy, long, withdrawing roar,
Retreating, to the breath
Of the night-wind, down the vast edges drear
And naked shingles of the world.

Tilly and I gazed out at the waves of a dapple gray-blue sea crashing onto the beach with cold aggression. Boulogne was sunnier than its artistic incarnations, its skies like a field of periwinkles and hung with far less portentous clouds, the coastal breezes bracingly crisper than suggested by Eugène Boudin's landscapes. As a way station, suspended between the past and future, between uncertainty and longing and hopelessness, between the sighs of a fading dusk and the lusty cries of a new dawn, it was pleasant enough, no more or less wintry than any other would have been.

Not for the first time, or last, I thought of turning back.

Like the race from Paris to Cannes, Tilly and I had made good time. But there was no golden thread of excitement and promise running through this journey. It felt like all we were doing was eating up the miles between our starting point and our destination. Our outward journey had been more than that, darting and shining with the plumage of halcyon days and wide horizons and anticipated adventure. It had been unexpectedly bright, not marred and riddled with regrets and memories and beautiful ghosts of time past. What brightness were we heading home to? Our Grand Tour was behind us, the London market had collapsed, the New York Stock Exchange was twitchy, there was the Bernhardt-Lloyd-Chase merger to scupper, and the grave troubles at Montrose and a war with her uncle waiting for Charley.

The memory of the stone bridge suddenly came to me. The smell of autumn, the railway tracks stretching into the vanishing horizon, the dream of paradise ending, the waiting dark of winter. Charley had always feared that it was an augury of our futures. Had she foreseen that we would someday be searching for our lost selves, divining for the extinct treasure of unlived lives? Pondering the gelid, bleak waves of the Côte d'Opale that would soon sweep us back into the great void, the Mare Tenebrosum, the Sea of Darkness, where the sun would be overpowered by black tempests and plucked from the sky, I began, as I had not done so before, to agree with Charley.

Tilly and I boarded the SS Cleveland as we had done the SS Adriatic with few delays. I paid more attention this time, filled with a nauseous anticipation, surveying the embarking passengers on the gangplank and decks that I passed. Would I see someone in a familiar Galeries Lafayette or Printemps dress? I dismissed this as too obvious, risky, and unlikely. Nothing of note occurred on the way. With some disappointment, I trailed despondently back to our cabin and waited for Tilly to arrive with the luggage and wondered about the SS Cleveland. What was so special about this ocean liner? This route?

It was during these musings that I happened to flick through the passports for which Tilly had handed me responsibility for the customs and immigration formalities while she saw to the luggage. It became apparent that I had paid attention to the wrong things. I had assumed that the passports were mine and Tilly's. The passports I actually held in my hands —which I had told the officers were for me and my accompanying traveling companion who was attending to the luggage and would be coming through very shortly—were for Lucia Bernhardt and Charlotte Masterson. Charlotte. Masterson. Common enough names, I supposed, to be believable. Not necessarily the Montrose heiress. My head spun. This manner of boarding had been a repetition of what had occurred at Alexandria and on disembarkation at Monaco. This had been why, on each of these three occasions when I had asked to help with the luggage, Tilly had insisted that it would be more efficient if I went on ahead first and arranged for both passports to be stamped and let the officials know that my maid would be shortly bringing up the rear with the luggage...

The cabin door opened.

"Tilly!"

Tilly looked at my face and the two passports I held in my hand. "Yes, Miss Lucia," she answered, smiled, and resumed bustling inside our suite of apartments with the porter and the steamer trunks.

What had I been expecting? Of course, Tilly had been suborned to the cause.

Tilly told me later, after the porter had left, that it would be best left to

Miss Charley to explain. When that would be, Tilly could not say. However, it was not too difficult to surmise the purpose of this subterfuge. Charley must have carried this out at each step of our Grand Tour so that her official papers were in order. Like everything else, what had on the surface seemed casual and impromptu was revealed to hide a good deal of consideration and planning.

I thought of Charley's long absence away from New York and wondered at the vast web of plotting that she must have woven in that time.

After the SS Cleveland set sail from Boulogne, I decided to take a leaf out of Charley's book. Tilly and I behaved like exemplary recluses. We sent for cabin service whenever a need arose for food or drink, declined invitations and all social intercourse, and avoided leaving the cabin, particularly during the peak periods on the decks. We got our hands on as many newspapers as we could bribe the purser to obtain for us (notwithstanding that they might have been ordered by, and earmarked for, some other person of consequence) to keep an eye on the market situation back home. The Hatry collapse and London crash had greatly weakened the optimism of American investors. The New York Stock Exchange was unstable: intensified selling and high volumes were interspersed with brief periods of rising prices and recovery. And yet, despite threats from the Federal Reserve to put a stop to the easy credit flowing to investors and prick the "exaggerated balloon of American stock values", including the summer interest rate hike in August, the party continued, and the optimistic market bulls remained at their pulpits. If I felt nervous merely reading about it from afar, I wondered how the investors back home felt. I wondered, and dreaded, how Montrose and Godeffroy's had faired.

No wonder Charley had played endless rounds of solitaire. It did not quite settle one's nerves but it did solve the quandary of what one did with one's hands when one was not rabidly pacing up and down, tearing one's hair out to the hornet's nest buzzing about inside one's head.

Tilly helpfully fished out Charley's packs of playing cards from her steamer trunk. We played in one sitting all the games that Charley had taught us on board the Mauretania and, as night fell, tried to grind uncertainty and anxiety into dust.

Very early on the morning of the third day, I slipped out of our suite for a brief outing onto the deck for some fresh air. I had chosen the early hour in the expectation that there would be few, if any, other passengers about. Sensible people were surely still tucked up in their warm berths. I wrapped my coat and scarf tightly around me as I walked along the promenade deck. The Atlantic was a sullen, restless expanse of black and milky gray, touched by a distant speck of tangerine-gold, reflecting the hovering, and rather glum, half-light of the dawn. A few of the officers, their collars turned up against the wind, greeted me as I passed but there was otherwise nobody else that I felt the need to avoid. This did not mean, however, that I was the only one about roaming the deck, braving the cold. As I was strolling amidships, swaying with the slight rise and fall of the ship, I saw a figure ahead of me, leaning on the rail of a lower deck, head tipped up to the sky. She—for it was clear that she was a female—was swathed in a long coat and hat against the bracing ocean breezes. I only saw the back of her and hazily at that. I was curious to see more to confirm a burgeoning speculation. I hastened my steps towards the place where she had stood but as I approached nearer, encumbered by the deck partitions, stairs, railings and minor obstacles in my line of vision, I lost sight of her. When I finally arrived at the place near the bow where I thought that I had seen the figure, I found nobody there. Deserted, nobody else to ask, no echoing footfalls, no swinging doors to indicate that there had ever been a corporeal presence on the deck. She had been so indistinct in the poor light, I could not be certain if I had conjured her into existence on that dark horizon, at the quiet limit of the world, much less identify whether she had been Charley. The only thing I could argue for this sighting being real was that, well, we were on the SS Cleveland and not the SS Adriatic by someone's design other than Fate's, and who else but Charley would drag herself out at such an uncivilized hour into the whipping cold and doom-laden primordial darkness of Erebus to gaze up at the hope of a fledgling dawn—perhaps to escape the walls of a cramped cabin and the desolation of a harsh, uncertain future, closing in, to breathe more easily outside on an open, untamed, infinite ocean?

Something had slipped through my fingers with the vanishing of the mirage and the world seemed darker without it.

Returning disappointed and a little dispirited to the cabin, I told Tilly, who had arisen, about the figure who had appeared on deck in the middle of the Atlantic.

"I don't think I imagined it, Tilly," I said.

Tilly's answer was interrupted by a knock.

I flew to open the cabin door, but it was only the steward bringing in the breakfast that Tilly had ordered.

"Miss Lucia," Tilly said consolingly, like a hostler calming down a horse, "do you want to play cards again after breakfast?"

I considered trudging disconsolately back to bed. I changed into my dressing gown instead and sat down at the table with Tilly. Tilly and I resumed our card games until the sky lightened outside. There were no more dawn walks out on deck to chase down mirages on a dark churning ocean.

Several days passed.

On the fifth day, a short while after the steward had cleared away the remains of our midday meal, a knock sounded on the cabin door. I was no longer quite as excitable as I had been on the first days of the voyage and I walked leisurely to answer the door.

"I hope I haven't caught you at an inconvenient time?" a polite, cheery voice rang out from the corridor.

I gaped at the young woman standing in the doorway. Demure hat, plain shawl, long dove-gray cotton coat over a threadbare gingham house frock, sensible, worn leather shoes, all of a shabby, brindle mix of indifferent oatmeal, dark fawn, and navy, forgettable in an instant—a platonic ideal of modesty and thrift—unless one's gaze happened to stray to her eyes which held its own vivid world in their depths and were flashing with an irrepressible intelligence and humor.

"Perhaps it would be better if I came back later?" A slight smile curled up the corners of those eyes.

My jaws worked but no sound came out. I tried again. A strangled gasp and then: "Tilly!"

Tilly rushed into the sitting room. When she saw who I was gawking at in the doorway, she rushed over, dragged her inside, shut the cabin door behind her, and swiftly began fussing and berating.

"I think you'd be better advised to attend to Lucia first, Tilly. Smelling salts? She looks about to swoon." She searched around the room for a decanter, poured a glass of water and handed it to me.

I recovered my wits with an effort. I felt winded, breathing shallowly as if I had broken or cracked a rib. It took a little longer to accept that Charley was truly here, in her dun and depressing vagabond clothes, removing her shawl and taking off her ghastly hat to shake out the flattened curls of her shingled hair, standing quite comfortably inside our suite as if she had been here the whole time.

"Where have you been?" I demanded. "Have you been well? Is it safe? How did you get here? Were you followed? How have you man—"

"Yes, sorry about all this," Charley said ruefully, while Tilly continued fussing about her. "You got my telegram, I presume? I took a Mediterranean ferry to Marseilles, crossed France, and hopped on at Boulogne."

"Tilly and I embarked at Boulogne! I didn't see you at all and I was looking!"

"Well, that was the point. I didn't want to be recognized and found just yet. It would have made for a very awkward explanation."

"Are you all right, Charley?"

"Oh, you know. As well as can be expected."

"Where have you been hiding?"

"A cosy little cabin in third class."

"Under...? I saw the names on the passports. It took me long enough but..."

"Oh that." Charley waved away the triviality. "Ladies are always losing their maids to one errand or another, aren't they? Seeing to the luggage, fetching a shawl or running off to purchase a vital bottle of lavender water, those insupportably stifling crowds... The officers were terribly accommodating when I handed them the travel documents for two to officiate, so considerate in wishing to spare me the tiresome inconvenience of having to wait for my maid to rejoin me... It surprised us how often it worked. But, after all, what evil could there possibly be in acceding to such an inconsequential request from a respectable lady? Tilly would come through at a distance ahead of me, or behind, and would have her own documentation stamped separately and we would meet up again later in the cabin. Nobody remembered or connected the two occurrences. Sometimes, Tilly would go through as the harried lady's maid whose mistress had run into a friend on the pier and was too occupied chatting but, of course, would expect everything to be in order from the unpacking of the trunks to the travel documents being stamped by the time madame had come on board. I would follow on later, incognito, with my papers and change on board. Same racket, same players, different roles."

Charley suffered no qualms or blushes while she pragmatically relayed her unembellished tales of playing fast and loose with customs and immigration formalities. She was as hard-nosed as the legendary "Witch of Wall Street": "I'm not Hetty if I do look green," were words that might have easily rolled off her tongue. Standing at Charley's shoulder, her reluctant accomplice, Tilly, however, was ruefully shaking her head at all the things she would have to face on Judgment Day, if not earlier.

"So when you came from steerage that time on board the Mauretania...?"

"Oh, I was probably hiding from someone. But I always had an additional ticket booked for steerage. It was a bit of a scramble every time Matthias tried to be helpful in looking after our travel bookings and I had to discreetly get another berth and ensure that it was for the same ship."

"And what if the ship had gone down like the Titanic? Someone would've had lots of explaining to do."

"Perhaps it would've been written down as an unexplained fatality at sea?"

"They'd still be looking for a missing—"

"Well, no," said Charley. "Not for long at least. There's actually a sealed letter of instructions left with Samuel Bayard for that eventuality. No point hiding when the game is clearly up."

"Matthias managed to get your travel authorizations, Charley. He came to the hotel to deliver your passport—your proper passport—the day after you disappeared. He guessed. About Lottie Fairchild."

"Oh," said Charley. "Well, it was only a matter of time."

"Why do you even have two passports, Charley? How—and where—did you get them in time for the sailing of the Mauretania?"

Unexpectedly, a sheepish smile crossed Charley's face. "It came about as a joke between the De Almadéns. Dominic—"

"Dominic de Almadén?" Tilly echoed.

"Oh, don't be judging Dom just yet, Tilly, listen first before you pass sentence! I didn't want to go off to college and meet new people and still be tagged as the Masterson heiress. Dominic said to pick a name and then, a few days later, he came back with a fake license—Dominic said he knew someone—and he told me that I could flash it around whenever I needed it and it would lend me a degree of anonymity. I carried it around with me but never used it. Later, after—well—some time later, I remembered it. I persuaded Diego of the idea. Diego and Dominic managed to get me a much more official set of documents than Dominic's original. There, Tilly, Dominic's moral character remains intact, don't you think?"

Tilly harrumphed and muttered that Mr. Dominic, who ought to have known better, should have been setting a good example, as his younger brother Mr. Lincoln did, and not leading his friends astray.

"Aw, Tilly, be fair, Dominic was only—"

"Mr. Dominic is your senior, Miss Charley, and accordingly should know to behave appropriately."

"Pfft. Tilly, if you apply that rule—"

"Charley, what happened to your dresses from Paris?"

"Were you looking for those? They were a little too well cut. I was obliged to find a more...anonymous outfit. This seemed a nice compromise between tatterdemalion and—"

"Are you throwing off your incognito now?"

"Not yet. I thought I'd wait until all the commotion and socializing of the first few days died down before paying a call. It seemed a bit quieter after the last stop at Queenstown. Oh, Tilly, please, you're making me dizzy! Do come and sit down. There is no need to order tea, I've eaten already. I promise I've been disciplined and moderate in all things—"

A scoffing noise escaped from Tilly. "Unicorns and flying pigs," Tilly muttered.

"Charley, we've almost reached the other side of the Atlantic. We'll be sailing into Boston next."

"Yes," Charley said with a hint of apology. "I've been laying low. I should have liked to have gotten in touch sooner."

"It can't have been easy slipping up here unseen. If I'd known, I would have come to vis—"

Charley shook her head.

"No, I suppose not. It would've risked giving you away?"

"Yes."

"And today?"

"I've come to collect this." Charley held up the passport, in her own name, that had been in Tilly's safekeeping all this time.

"It still isn't safe for you to disembark in New York? You're leaving at the next stop? Boston?"

"I'm reluctant to risk showing up where there might be a not-so-welcoming party waiting for me."

"When shall we see you again?"

"Soon," Charley promised vaguely.

"Have you enough money? Clothes? Do you need help with—"

"Thank you. No, it's all been arranged." Charley smiled. "Tell me how you've been. I mean, besides being in Tilly's safe hands."

"As well as can be expected. Tilly and I have been hermits."

"Really?" Charley looked around to Tilly for confirmation. "Dearth of amusing company on board? Exhausted all of the organized leisure and recreational activities and cocktails?"

"We've been playing cards. Not much else to do." Apart from worry, plan, pace, worry.

"I'm glad they've been put to good use."

"Charley, what do you mean to do? Is there some way that I may reach you?"

Charley shook her head.

"Will you send word, at least, when you can? If you need help, send word?"

"There's no need to worry. But I'll send word through Tilly." Tilly nodded assent. "And you can always contact Diego or Samuel Bayard."

"And you'll... What will you... Will Montrose be all right?"

Charley regarded me. "Matthias?"

I nodded.

"How much has he told you?"

"Enough to wonder why you aren't petrified with terror."

Charley shrugged her shoulders. "Have you kept up to date with the papers?"

"As much as it has been possible."

"Then you'll be aware that the New York Stock Exchange is teetering— at least it looks that way from where I stand. There has not been a string of virtuous events so far—and I cannot foresee any coming in the near future —to rescue the Exchange from its current predicament. Rather, the converse seems to be on the horizon. Money troubles appear to be the plat du jour. Montrose is in illustrious company."

"Oh, Charley!"

"Bears make for such a snarly, curmudgeonly crowd. They put everyone in a bad humor. But the markets are not the only— Other contingent arrangements were made for Montrose which weren't entirely dependent on the markets."

"Is it as precarious as Matthias fears?"

"I'm going to shoot Matthias the next time I see him! Don't let Matthias scare you, Lucia. It's uncertain, that is all anybody can accurately say about the situation."

"I hope... Will Dominic and Mr. Hadden be all right?"

"Bayard is working on it. And—well, I don't know if Matthias retained Paul Drennan Cravath himself but he seems to have sent Cravath, de Gersdorff, Swaine & Wood into the fray."

"Oh, that is hopeful. And...you'll give your uncle hell?"

"We shall sit down and have a frank conversation. Our respective positions will become quite clear—if there had ever been any doubt."

"Your uncle has drawn the battle lines. He is arming himself. He will be expecting you. I think he would like to salt the earth if he could."

"Yes."

"Montrose—"

"No need to fret just yet, Lucia. My uncle may be angry but he may also be a little scared. I'm the Masterson hellion, remember? And he has—we both have—a lot to lose."

"But—"

"I can't promise pretty fireworks, even if you manage to get good seats."

In response to my long questioning silence, Charley said: "Do you remember the dinosaur skeletons we saw at the Natural History Museum in South Kensington? The replica of the great diplodocus in the entrance hall? Imagine one of those magnificent beasts in the flesh. Imagine one stumbling about, covered in gouges and welts and open wounds, ulcers, oozing abscesses, parasites, diseased, ailing, flailing in agony, crashing to the ground before you. How do you revive such a creature? How do you nurse it and bring it back to health? How do you keep it safe?"

Charley looked at me. I had no answer.

"I will not be taunted or frightened into something that will make me feel ashamed, small, lesser than. I shall give what is due."

"You're going to be Nemesis."

"I?" Charley snorted. "Hardly."

And yet giving what was due was precisely the sort of stock in trade in which the Greek goddess dealt. Divine, inescapable justice.

"What about forgiveness?"

"That, I'm given to understand, is not considered good form in the midst of war. I believe the established custom is to eat the hearts of one's enemies—or at least threaten to do so."

"I meant regarding Matthias. About what happened at the police station.

The bad feeling which followed. He's very sorry. Are you ever going to speak to him again?"

Charley's face tightened at the memory. "Matthias oughtn't to be so foolish. One person behaving so is quite enough."

"What do you mean? How so?"

"I could believe that Matthias might be willing to bend the rules, but he would never do so out of self-interest. He— Dorsey overplayed his hand."

"Charley?"

"Oh, it's a question of...moral asymmetry. It took me... I was a little befuddled."

"James Dorsey escaped."

Charley looked thoughtful at the conclusion of my recitation of the news that Matthias's attaché had relayed to me. "Did he?" she said.

Charley's skepticism made me pause. "You didn't know anything about it?"

Charley shook her head.

"You think Matthias lied to me about it?"

"Everybody lies—for different reasons," said Charley. "I don't think Matthias would have lied to you had he come in person but you did say that some young attaché or aide-de-camp had been sent to apprise you of the news because Matthias was unavoidably detained. It's unlikely that the young man was briefed on the true state of affairs. Why exactly had Matthias been suddenly detained if he has, to date, gone out of his way to report daily in person? He's quite a conscientious soul. Quite able to be relied upon for turning up according to schedule unless perhaps he was personally on the trail of the prisoner he'd released? And your necklace being taken again under such questionable circumstances... You also forget Tallis."

"Tallis?"

"A neat coincidence, don't you think?"

"It vaguely crossed my mind but so many things made me think it improbable. Why would Tal—anyway, I was more afraid that you'd be suspected of being an accessory to James Dorsey's escape, given the far more vexing coincidence of the timing of your disappearance and his. The attaché hinted at some unknown benefactor agitating for leniency and for transferring James Dorsey to another jurisdiction where— That was a lie too?"

"The attaché was probably briefed as such and relayed it faithfully to you. Matthias—and rightfully so—doesn't trust coincidences. He has—"

"Did you two plot this when you went to see James Dorsey at the police station?"

"You oscillate between wild extremes, Lucia. Need for forgiveness one minute, collusion the next." Charley shook her head. "Mr. Vandermeer is his own free agent. As am I. Quite independent of one another. If this is a plot, then he plotted this one on his own. He had been very insistent that there was no need to give in to...Dorsey's demands. This would explain why. Matthias had other irons in the fire. I'm not sure I agree with his methods, it seems to have become personal, but I suppose whatever personal motivations drive him, he has never yet failed to properly discharge his duty. Although I am a little concerned that Matthias may have underestimated... Dorsey isn't a fool. He won't be easily captured again."

That sounded to my ears rather like forgiveness.

"So you no longer blame Matthias?"

"He is so keen to assume the blame! It was never his fault. I was the one who strayed off the path."

"Charley, have you taken any walks on deck before first light?"

"Once or twice, yes."

I glanced to Tilly with triumph. "I saw you," I told Charley.

"Really? How remiss of me. What were you doing up on deck before first light?"

"Getting some fresh air. I thought you were a ghost or a figment of my imagination. What were you doing?"

"Looking for land, some spark of life or civilization," said Charley. "I feel like we're escaping Pompeii, bobbing about on the ocean, watching the eruption of Vesuvius behind us."

"Or rowing towards it," I said.

Charley stayed silent.

"Charley—"

"You shouldn't be afraid of what will happen when you return home to New York. It doesn't matter whether in the dead of the night, in the deepest chambers of your heart, you believe yourself unworthy, don't you dare let anyone else treat you as such. There's nothing that your parents or New York can do to you that you won't be able to survive." Charley looked to Tilly. "Do you know, a few days in third class rather makes one miss the taste of champagne. May I, Tilly, before I return? The food you've ordered is crying out for an accompaniment."

Tilly eyed Charley doubtfully as she gave her grudging approval. Her suspicions were justified when Charley made it clear that she was not going to be toasting alone.

The champagne came in two bottles, a bucket of ice, and three glittering glasses. Charley came back out of the sleeping apartment where, as a cautionary measure, she had hidden whilst the order was delivered, and examined the twin magnums of Louis Roederer vintage with satisfaction.

"Excellent palate, Tilly," Charley chortled. "Glass or bottle?"

Tilly sent up a petition heavenward for patience.

I blurted out: "If only..."

Charley had intended a brief visit when she had come to call, meaning to return swiftly to her cabin upon retrieving her passport. Her intentions fell by the wayside when the first magnum of Roederer was decanted into the glasses. Not even Tilly could curtail the ensuing consequences.

"If you can keep your head when all about you
    Are losing theirs and blaming it on you,
If you can trust yourself when all men doubt you,
    But make allowance for their doubting too;
If you can wait and not be tired by waiting,
    Or being lied about, don't deal in lies,
Or being hated, don't give way to hating,
    And yet don't look too good, nor talk too wise:
If you can dream—and not make dreams your master;
    If you can think—and not make thoughts your aim;
If you can meet with Triumph and Disaster
    And treat those two impostors just the same;
If you can bear to hear the truth you've spoken
    Twisted by knaves to make a trap for fools,
Or watch the things you gave your life to, broken,
    And stoop and build 'em up with worn-out tools:
If you can make one heap of all your winnings
    And risk it on one turn of pitch-and-toss,
And lose, and start again at your beginnings
    And never breathe a word about your loss;
If you can force your heart and nerve and sinew
    To serve your turn long after they are gone,
And so hold on when there is nothing in you
    Except the Will which says to them: 'Hold on!'
If you can talk with crowds and keep your virtue,
    Or walk with Kings—nor lose the common touch,
If neither foes nor loving friends can hurt you,
    If all men count with you, but none too much;
If you can fill the unforgiving minute
    With sixty seconds' worth of distance run,
Yours is the Earth and everything that's in it,
    And—which is more—you'll be a Man, my son!"

Charley blamed her tipsy babblings of Kipling on me and the Roederer. Tilly and I knew better but we did not dispute her claim.

"Will we ever fulfill the promise of our youth?"

"Not a chance." Charley raised her champagne flute in a toast and downed it in one gulp.

"I think you might exceed it, Charley."

"Are you mocking me, Lucia?" Charley tried to look stern and serious but then hiccuped.

"Oh, dear God, you're sozzled!"

"Hardly. I've only had—"

"Tilly!"

"Tilly, I've only—"

"Go on, I dare you."

"What?"

"I dare you, Charley."

"I—" Charley narrowed her eyes at me. "I'll accept your dare if you do the same."

"Me?"

"I'll jump if you jump."

"You're insane. We'll need lots more Roederer at this rate."

"Here's to... Being cast out from good society?"

"Miss Lucia! Miss Charley!"

"You're an independent woman, Tilly, you've already crossed the Rubicon and come into the promised land. You ought to be cheering us on, not begrudging us."

Tilly huffed. "In what manner—"

"Because you have the liberty of saying no, Tilly, the liberty of walking away, the liberty of being able to choose."

"But so does Miss Lucia."

Charley peered at me over the rim of her champagne glass. "And so she does," Charley said softly.

"Charley, I..." I did not know how to finish that sentence.

"After her own fashion," Charley added. "At a time of her own choosing. After weighing the costs."

I pondered my own champagne glass. "Freedom and independence?"

"They have long been steadfast friends," said Charley.

"Is there room for more in their friendship?"

"I don't think they are miserly but we shall soon find out... Here's to independence and freedom and being cast out from good society."

"And taking the plunge."

"And taking a leaf out of Tilly's book and taking the plunge. I hope to God we survive the fall."

"'No race can prosper till it learns that there is as much dignity in tilling a field as in writing a poem.'"

"I don't think that's quite apt." Charley smiled. "But I do appreciate the sentiment."

"Well, you said—"

"In a different context altogether you might recall."

"Maybe my recollection is a little hazy at present..."

"Not Washington T. Booker but perhaps... 'La nature ne m'a point dit: ne sois point pauvre; encore moins: sois riche; mais elle me crie: sois indépendant.'" For Tilly's benefit, she translated: "'Nature has not said to me: Be not poor; still less: Be rich. But she cries out to me: Be independent.'"

"Who said that?"

"Sebastien-Roch Nicolas de Chamfort. Very free with his bon mots. Friend of Honoré Mirabeau. Got caught up in the French Revolution and came to a very sad end."

"Oh."

"It'll be worse for you," Charley said, sympathetically.

"How so?"

"Your bloodlines run bluer than mine. Bigger manacles. More expectations. Much further to fall. The Masterson fortunes need a few more hundred years to lose the parvenu taint. I don't think there is anything new that I can be called or accused of, except perhaps more often and on a slightly grander scale."

"That's utter baloney. Is this a competition? I don't want to fling this at you, Charley, but if we are comparing falls, taking on your shoulders the fortunes of the entire Montrose empire is on quite a different plane altogether."

"Disagree. The stakes of each and every battle are of supreme importance. Anyway, Tilly can adjudicate."

Tilly sat next to us on the couch, holding her champagne glass as regally as a Tsarina, with a very Victorian look of resigned disapprobation.

"Well... Here's to surviving the fall."

"To surviving the fall," Charley echoed. "Money for jam."

"There's...still a magnum of Roederer standing. Shall we crack that open too?"

"I don't think I can stand and walk steadily as is. Will you and Tilly be able to polish it off on your own?"

"I suppose we could try." One glance at Tilly set us straight. "Tilly's right. I probably shouldn't if I want to still respect myself tomorrow morning."

"Let's save it. We may want it for another occasion."

Of course, there would be plenty of occasions ahead of us where the need for alcoholic solace to accompany philosophical brooding and commiseration would arise.

To taking the plunge.

And if we did survive the fall? What then?

Charley's response, the moribund turn it had taken, was one to which I had continually returned to ponder long after she had left the cabin, long after the day had waned and the moon climbed the darkness and the deep Atlantic sounded with mournful voices, potent with the shades of the past and imminent future.

Charley had thought about it for a long moment before answering. "I shall fold it and put it away in a drawer and then return to a quiet life and my interrupted studies."

"How dull it is to pause, to make an end,
To rust unburnish'd, not to shine in use!"

College had long been considered a prevarication, a faddish distraction of an excuse while one continued dilettantishly fumbling about supposedly trying to find life's purpose besides the expected destination of a socially desirable marriage alliance and motherhood. That view had waylaid many of our friends but not Charley. Her dilemma had been one of defending choice: if one did not know what one wanted, what one's aim was, how was obtaining a higher education, in possibly a completely unrelated field, a justifiable application of time?

"Sometimes," Charley had once argued, frowning, "a person needs to look about and see what is out there beyond the immediate horizon before they can make a choice. Sometimes a person needs to study to learn what questions to ask before qualifying as informed enough to make that choice. One doesn't necessarily need a college degree to achieve that, but I think I should like to try it. Men do it as a matter of course before they move on to their careers. There must be something worthwhile in the endeavor."

But Fate had disrupted Charley's endeavor and blown her off course.

My father had been one of those who had scoffed at the indulgence of Meredith Elyot continuing the Elyot tradition and sending her niece—the heiress to the Montrose fortune who would never need lift a finger—off to college. It was almost a comfort to know that despite the shoals and tempests, there was something anchoring Charley to home. She had found something—a purpose—worth returning to, a place beyond the plots and schemes and wars, a hithe safe from the storm.

"I'm glad you've thought about the aftermath, Charley. I'm glad there's something good to look forward to."

"You could come with me," Charley had said. "I'm not really sure I would be able to return to my studies peaceably—return without feeling restless. I don't know that I would feel the same. But I should like to finish what I began."

It had not been the first time my illusions had crumbled but this felt a lot worse. Charley's strength of conviction, her clarity of purpose, her forthright dreams had been a touchstone, a pillar which held up the sky. When Charley doubted, when she no longer built enchanted castles in the air, I trembled to my core.

"But—Charley? You always— What happened?"

"A person wastes an awful lot of her life when she doesn't know what she wants—when she thinks she knows what she wants, and then realizes that it isn't it at all... She doesn't fare much better than the person who does know what she wants but isn't in a position to pursue it. All this, I've realized, it's all been one long, elaborate excuse for prevarication really. And afterwards, I shall drift into... I shall go through the motions. Nothing terribly exciting about that."

"But what about— Whatever happened to aut inveniam viam aut faciam?"

"Not everyone has the stomach or the will to be a Hannibal. And our lives are far more prosaic and circumscribed and—"

"'To live, to throw oneself into life, one can't help but be exposed to risks and curiosities. Why not take the chance?' you once said."

"When I didn't know any better. Now that I know a little better, I'm more circumspect. I don't want to make a self-indulgent decision, to find later that it's been more time wasted when I—"

"Or you might find it glorious."

"Yes—or that." Charley had looked away at the distant clouds through the thick glass pane. "But it isn't just that. Responsibilities have a vicious habit of catching a person unawares when they forget themselves in...distraction."

"Charley, what happened in the months that you went away to Philadelphia, after you turned down the proposal from the wealthy German brewer's son from St. Louis, and didn't return until Aunt Merry summoned you back to New York?"

Charley had kept quiet for a long stretch of time. "I wasn't in Philadelphia," she had said at last.

"I think I guessed that long ago. Where were you?"

"Oh, all over the place."

"Charley? What happened?"

"I...I climbed over the castle walls to take a peak at the world outside."

From the shards and glimmers that Matthias had pierced together and relayed to me, I could only imagine the great vast world that Charley had seen. "And was it...scary or glorious?"

"Yes. No. It was like seeing Medusa. Mrs. Wharton was right. One expects to be blinded and turned to stone but in fact the Gorgon only opens one's eyes." Charley had inhaled unsteadily. "I can't unsee what I've seen, Lucia. I tried to, I thought it would be easy, even restful, to slip back into the familiar things, to return to ease and frivolities, but it didn't take. I can't just go back to New York, to my old—and what now seems narrow— life, however lovely and peaceful it was, and forget everything. That would be... Very few people set out to do harm with deliberate intent. It is done in the quotidian course of life, in offhand selfishness, in callous or apathetic disregard for others, in putting one's own ease, peace, comfort, profit, and well-being first."

"But, Charley, why would you heap this guilt upon yourself for something you've never—"

"No? I'm afraid I would not stand up to a close examination."

"Is this—is this sentiment on account of Mr. Rhys Hadden?"

"Rhys? No. Not specifically. He... It's a true sentiment, though, isn't it? More important, the same holds for Good: small gestures, good or evil, can make a difference, if only to one's own conscience. I owe Rhys Hadden for reminding me of that."

"It isn't— You aren't Atlas. The world doesn't just rest on your shoulders, Charley. Your own life is—"

"That's a very seductive argument for self-indulgence but it means I would have to disregard the fact that I'm not just a chess-piece in this. No, not the world, just Montrose, just this little patch that has fallen to me. It is mine to water or neglect. If I turn away, I— My choices will affect the outcome. I can't abdicate from being the heir to Montrose. I can't play dumb or ignorant. Oh, I won't try to make it into some form of salvation or absolution. I want to do it for the right reasons, but good intentions are... Sometimes thinking about the choices fills me with fear so incapacitating it makes me physically ill. My mistakes, my failures, will not be mine alone to suffer and grieve. I can't... Oh, I'm so ashamed. I've wasted so much time already. I don't want to be diminished—I don't want my life or anyone else's to be diminished—because I made the wrong, the lazy choice. 'And if I should drink oblivion of a day, so shorten the stature of my soul.' I'm vain enough to believe that what I decide matters."

"Miss Charley..."

"I don't think vanity has anything to do with it, Charley."

Were Tilly's and mine the first human ears penetrated by Charley's confessions? Were these the secret sorrows that Charley had entrusted to her playing cards, to the garden at Villa Mirabeau, to the sunrise at Abu Simbel and the Cairene night? Had the swollen black waves of the Atlantic received the rest?

"Come, my friends,
'Tis not too late to seek a newer world."

As the SS Cleveland sailed into Boston Harbor the following morning and Tilly and I stood on deck, watching the disembarkation, watching one particular disembarking passenger stepping into the harsh whiteness of the day, vanishing into the crowded pier like a pale spirit. With the dying fall of her last words in my ears, I remembered watching Charley's hands slowly unclench and the thought that had followed, as it had so often crossed my mind during our long friendship, of how Charley seemed more than anyone else I had ever known like a knight in the nursery stories we were told about honor and chivalry and valor, unable to turn away, wanting to set things right. I remembered Charley's appalling scapegrace reputation for a girl, Matthias dragging Charley out of (or being conscripted into) a multitude of fights which were not her own, Charley burning with an archangel's cold righteous wrath, preoccupied with upholding the fusty notions of fairness, probity, charity, standing tall and magnificent and fearless. "He's a small man," Charley had said after sending Nate Knowle away with boxed ears in front of the clubhouse gathering at the Piping Rock Club before which he had broken the treaty his parents had made with mine and attempted to deliver a stinging public belittlement for daring to humiliate him by breaking off our engagement, "else he wouldn't have felt the need to control and cut you down to size, time and time again." Charley had learnt subtlety and guile and circumspection in the intervening years, but she had not really changed her spots, had she? Charley had as little patience or respect for obstacles and vicissitudes as she had for bullies. No need for crossing swords or effusion of blood. Charley just...carried on, walking alongside despair and doubt and fear as if they were passing noise, inconsequential to the realization of her plans, merely random pedestrians who just happened to be sharing the section of the pavement with her until they went their separate ways. Who had taught Charley to meet those pernicious tormentors with such polite disdain, trailing it behind her like a Hollywood starlet on the red carpet trailed precious mink boas? Those ageless foes could snap and snarl and rage and threaten and claw at her all they liked but, as with obstreperous infants, they would be ignored until they learnt some civility. As stratagems went, it had a piquant flavor: even monsters, one supposed, cowered and perished under the blade of a lethal snub impeccably delivered by a daughter of Old New York.

"Are you never... Charley, when you found out about what your uncle— about Montrose... For a year—longer... You don't cry, Charley, and you've said a good deal about hopelessness, but... Does it ever... Are you ever afraid?"

"Montrose was in the same state on the day before I was told as on the day after. What difference did my awareness and quaking terror make? None. It didn't change a thing. That realization was an unexpected mercy. Fear can be such a bully, it pushes everything else out of the way. I reminded myself that I could cry and be afraid later. There was far too much yet to be done."

"But that only wins a temporary reprieve."

"Scheherazade only had a temporary reprieve—every night, for one thousand and one nights."

"Will tomorrow ever arrive?"

When the SS Cleveland sailed into New York Harbor a day later, gliding serenely past the green patina of the Statue of Liberty towards Ellis Island, Manhattan morosely looming into view, another conversation swam out from the deep wells of memory, disgorged from the same magnum of Roederer.

"I wish I could be invisible."

"Invisible?"

"Not literally. I mean, I've always wanted to not be too noticeable in any way out of the ordinary—too tall or too short, too pretty or too plain, too loud or too silent, too smart, simple, poor, wealthy, young, old, loud, meek, fashionable, dowdy, too—too different—too prominent in ways that cause people to prejudge me on the things which may be me, or related to me, but they were not of my design or of my choosing, and they obscure who and what I really am."

"And who and what are you, Lucia?"

"Myself."

"Is this invisible armor impenetrable? Will it protect you from the hordes and harridans of New York society threatening to descend?"

"Yes. I'm not brave, Charley, I'm so easy to scare. It takes such effort to not be shaking in dread of—of consequences, of other's opinions. But if I had such armor, I could go about my business without anyone noticing and bothering me until I'm ready to be seen."

"I see."

"You're probably one of the few who do, Charley. You have your own suit of armor. An entire closet of armor, in fact, not invisible but in so many bright and garish colors that they distract others from seeing what you do not wish them to see of you—which achieves the same purpose. I wish I was invisible."

"You don't need a suit of invisible armor, Lucia. You have such quiet, unassuming vices and you have the same quiet endurance and intelligence and courage to see things through. They will serve you well."

After the liner docked at the Hudson River piers, Tilly and I passed quickly through the gauntlet of first class passengers whom we had snubbed during the voyage, down the gangplank, past all the hawsers secured to the pilings, and out through Customs.

In my mind, I had been expecting the equivalent of a lynch mob convulsing with outrage, spleen, and violent denunciation, dragging behind them manacles fit to my size. We were met instead by the unexpected and gladdening sight of Charley's Aunt Merry hastening towards us through the crowds with an entourage of the Montrose household in tow like the head of a small army.

"Tilly! Lucia! Welcome home!"

Warmth curled around us in a comforting, gentle embrace. It seemed so natural to be met by this surety of care and affection and safety, I felt a pang for Charley who had been forced to forgo a homecoming that was her due, exiling herself instead to a cold, lonely reception in the Port of Boston.

"Lucia," Aunt Merry murmured. "My dear child."

There was nothing fluttery about Charley's aunt that day. Aunt Merry's gaze had flickered momentarily over the pier and, evincing astonishingly little surprise at not finding her niece in the crowds pouring out of the pier, she promptly collected Tilly and me and began marshaling us at a brisk pace along the esplanade to several awaiting motor-cars, leaving the luggage to catch up with us as best as it could. I glanced about, searching for my parents. It struck me as odd that Aunt Merry was here and yet the Bernhardts, my mother at the very least, were nowhere nearby.

"Aunt Merry—"

"We must hurry, dear, before the others arrive. Your mother can only delay them for so long."

"My mother?"

"Your mother and I agreed that it would be best that you come stay at Montrose until things settle down. Come, dear."

"Aunt Merry?"

Aunt Merry patted my arm. There were bright wells of kindness in her eyes and voice. "Charley cabled. She asked that you be given sanctuary. It will be all right, Lucia. We can talk further at Montrose."

The door of the Packard sedan opened. In my surprise, I did not protest and obediently stepped inside.

The cocoon of Aunt Merry's protection struck me even more forcibly as our motor-car edged along the streets and I spotted through the window my parents' burnished maroon Rolls-Royce Silver Ghost passing by, in the opposite lane, and, not long afterwards, turning into an adjacent street, Nicholas Masterson sitting in a chauffeured gray Isotta Fraschini, heading towards the pier. When I looked around, all I could see was kindness and understanding in Aunt Merry's eyes, and the banked fires behind Tilly's militant frown, staring after the gray Isotta Fraschini.

When we arrived at Montrose, Aunt Merry took me into the rose garden. Tilly came outside a few moments later with a tray laden with tea and cake. Aunt Merry thanked Tilly and bade Tilly to sit down with us, then made sure that we were all comfortable and supplied with sufficient sustenance from Mrs. Stone's kitchen.

"Now," said Aunt Merry. "I propose an exchange. I will answer as many questions as you like. All I ask in return is that you will also put my mind at ease with regard to what my niece has been up to."

"Miss Meredith..."

"Aunt Merry, Charley..."

Aunt Merry sighed. "I know those tones. The De Almadéns are very practiced at them. Very well. I will tell you what I know. There is a great deal, Lucia, my dear, as I am sure you must have guessed, quite apart from the predicament in which my niece has become embroiled. Then you will both divulge whatever you feel will not compromise or harm Charley. And between us, we might be able to piece together a plan to navigate a course out of this tight spot and help protect our foolhardy loved ones against themselves."

At the end, Aunt Merry pressed her hands together. Her eyes drifted shut. She said nothing for a long, thoughtful time. Aunt Merry's deep contemplation and Tilly's anxious, tightly frowning silence served only to increase my dread of the doom that awaited Charley. And I felt wretched and sick to the bone and useless. We had passed beyond the betrayals by her uncle. We were all feverishly wondering what could be done to give Charley a chance of surviving this intact, of preventing Charley from being torn up and whittled down into dust by the force of the tornado bearing down on her, of saving her light and her laughter and her magnificence from becoming a mere memory. It was not a metaphysical life or death struggle. A hardened tycoon with funds and connections and influence would have been hard-pressed to navigate and fight his way out of such a dark pit. Matthias had said that Charley had been liquidating assets, had burned through her inheritance, but the vast sums that she needed—oh, Charley might well have managed to find someone willing to lend her the money to save her dying diplodocus, to stop it from being picked apart by vultures, but on what terms, at what price? It was foolish to ignore reality, to—how had Charley put it?—to look away from the merciless eyes of the Gorgon. There were cruel, dangerous, unscrupulous, opportunistic men out there in the harsh world, there were insurmountable mountains and unbridgeable gulfs and unrevenged wrongs, and Charley, for all her friends and her indefatigable will and cunning and bravery, was still only one human girl, with brittle bones and a mortal nature, trying to assume the burden of a titan and hold up the heavens.

Foliis tantum ne carmina manda, ne turbata volent rapidis ludibria ventis; ipsa canas oro.

The sky had dimmed whilst we were talking in the garden. The chill dusk brought Titus to usher us back inside for tea. The glow of the electric lights cast from Montrose's porch windows looked so warm and rosy, an island in a wash of inky darkness, a haven of comfort and safety to which a hostile Fate laid siege. I could draw no comfort from it. The night air felt as icy and wintry as the whipping winds had been on the deck of the SS

Cleveland. I could not stop tear my gaze away from the blind, swimming blackness that whispered mockingly of disappointment and failure and defeat. I longed to do so much more than rage hopelessly at the keening dusk. I mourned hope for Charley and for myself. How could a girl pitted unfairly against a treacherous fate ever prevail? When had the will of one girl ever been enough?

"Come," Aunt Merry said at length, shaking me from my despair. "We will take tea and think on this. A solution will present itself. Or we shall fashion one. Oh, but before we have our tea, there is something I want to show you in the garage."

What else was there to do? With the thickening shadows of night on my heels, I dragged my bruised spirit behind Aunt Merry and Tilly into the house. It was cowardly and in any event too late, I reminded myself, to renege on our dare.

To be continued in...

PART THREE: THE STROKE OF MIDNIGHT

THANK YOU

Thank you for reading.

If you enjoyed this book, please consider leaving a review at the online store where you purchased the book, at Goodreads or any other reader site or blog you frequent, and recommend it to your reader friends.

Goodreads:
https://www.goodreads.com/mireillepavane
https://www.goodreads.com/book/

ABOUT THE AUTHOR

Mireille Pavane cannot recall exactly when she began messing about with books and literature but since then (brainwashed at a young age by the French and Russian writers and E.M. Forster), it has remained an abiding love. Mireille continues to scribble away in secret when not otherwise distracted by a professional career or gardening duties in her alternate life. She also has an unhealthy curiosity and fondness for footnotes which she attempts to curtail from time to time. Mireille is a member of the international and local chapters of the Village Idiots' Guild.